Lara Adrian lives with her husband in coastal New England, surrounded by centuries-old graveyards, hip urban comforts, and the endless inspiration of the broody Atlantic Ocean.

'Vibrant writing heightens the suspense, and hidden secrets provide many twists. This is a dark, steamy tale filled with intricate plotlines; it stands easily on its own . . . *Kiss of Crimson* is a winner and will have readers eager for the next Midnight Breed story.'

Romance Reviews Today

'*Kiss of Crimson* is an intensely erotic, exciting paranormal read that will keep readers engrossed. Adrian keeps the plot fresh and new and the characters engaging . . . Lara Adrian is a great storyteller and paranormal readers don't want to miss out on this book.'

Fallen Angels (5 Angels)

'I can't wait to recommend *Kiss of Crimson* to my friends and fellow book lovers . . . a delightful series.'

Romance Junkies (5 stars)

The Midnight Breed series

KISS
OF
CRIMSON

LARA ADRIAN

ROBINSON

Constable & Robinson Ltd
55-56 Russell Square
London WC1B 4HP
www.constablerobinson.com

First published in the US by Bantam Dell,
1745 Broadway, New York, NY 10019

This paperback edition published by Robinson,
an imprint of Constable & Robinson Ltd, 2011

ISBN 978-1-78033-296-3

Printed and bound in the EU

1 3 5 7 9 10 8 6 4 2

⪪ CHAPTER ONE ⪫

Dante smoothed his thumb over sweet female flesh, lingering at the carotid, where the human's pulse throbbed the strongest. His own pulse quickened too, responding to the rush of blood flowing beneath the surface of delicate white skin. Dante leaned his dark head in and kissed that tender spot, letting his tongue play over the fluttering race of the female's heartbeat.

'Tell me,' he murmured against the warm skin, his voice a low growl amid the heaving beat of the club's music, 'are you a good witch or a bad witch?'

The female squirmed in his lap, her fishnet-clad legs straddling him, black lace-up bustier pushing her breasts up under his chin like a buffet. She twirled her finger in her bright fuchsia wig, then let it trail down suggestively, past a Celtic cross tattoo and into her swelling cleavage. 'Oh, I'm a very, very bad witch.'

Dante grunted. 'My favorite.'

He smiled into her drunken gaze, not bothering to hide his fangs. He was one of many vampires in the Boston dance club that Halloween night, although most of them were pretenders. Humans sporting plastic teeth, fake blood, and various ridiculous costumery. A few others – himself and a handful of males from one of the vampire nation's Darkhaven sanctuaries, hanging out near the dance floor – were the genuine article.

Dante and the others were Breed, a far cry from the pale,

gothic vampires of human folklore. Neither undead nor devil-spawned, Dante's kind were a hot-blooded hybrid mix of *Homo sapiens* and deadly other-worlder. The Breeds' forebears, a band of alien conquerors who crash-landed on Earth millennia past and who were now long-since extinct, had bred with human females and given their offspring the thirst – the primal need – for blood.

Those alien genes had given the Breed great strengths and shattering weaknesses too. Only the human side of the Breed, those qualities passed down by their mortal mothers, kept the race civilized and adhering to any kind of Order. Even then, a few of the Breed would succumb to their savage side and turn Rogue, a one-way street paved in blood and madness.

Dante despised that element of his kind, and as one of the warrior class, it was his duty to eradicate his Rogue brethren wherever he found them. As a male who enjoyed his pleasures, Dante wasn't sure what he preferred more: a warm, juicy female vein under his mouth, or the feel of titanium-edged steel in his hand as he sliced into his enemies and dispatched them to dust in the street.

'Can I touch them?' The pink-haired witch on his lap was staring at Dante's mouth with rapt fascination. 'Dang, but those fangs look wicked real! I just have to feel them.'

'Be careful,' he warned as she brought her fingers to his lips. 'I bite.'

'Yeah?' She giggled, gaze widening. 'I'll bet you do, sugar.'

Dante sucked her finger into his mouth, contemplating the fastest way he could get the female horizontal. He needed to feed, but he was never opposed to a little sex in the process – prelude or chaser, didn't matter. It was all good as far as he was concerned.

Chaser, he decided on impulse, letting his fangs puncture the fleshy tip of her finger as she started to withdraw it. She gasped as he suckled from the small wound, refusing to let her leave him just yet. The small taste of blood inflamed him, sharpening his pupils to vertical slits in the middle of his gold-hued eyes. Hot need rushed through him, settling into the swelling bulge of his cock, which strained beneath the black leather of his pants.

The female moaned, closing her eyes as she arched catlike on his lap. Dante let go of her finger as he wrapped his hand around the back of her head and pulled her neck closer to him. Taking a Host in a public place wasn't exactly his style, but he was bored out of his skull and needed the diversion. Besides, he doubted anyone would notice tonight, when the club was rife with faux danger and open sensuality. As for the female on his lap, she would feel only pleasure as he took what he needed from her. Afterward, she'd remember none of it, her memory scrubbed of all recollection of him.

Dante came forward, tipping the female's head aside, mouth watering in hunger. He glanced past her and saw two Darkhaven vampires, part of the general Breed population, observing him from a few yards away. They looked like kids-current generation, no doubt. They whispered among themselves, clearly recognizing him as one of the warrior class and trying to decide whether or not to approach him.

Bugger off, Dante thought in their direction as he parted his lips and prepared to open his Host's vein.

But the vampire youths ignored his dark glare. The taller of the two, a blond male in desert camo pants, biker boots, and a black tee-shirt led the way. His companion, tricked out in baggy jeans, high-tops, and an oversize Lakers jersey, strutted along behind him.

'Shit.' Dante didn't mind a small bit of indiscretion, but he sure as hell didn't need an up-close audience gawking at him while he fed.

'What's wrong?' his would-be Host whined when Dante pulled away from her.

'Nothing, sweetheart.' He placed his palm against her forehead, wiping the past half hour from her mind. 'Go on now and join your friends.'

She obediently got up from his lap and walked away, fading into the press of bodies on the dance floor. The two Darkhaven vampires gave her only a passing look as they approached Dante's table.

'What's up, fellas.' Dante tossed the greeting out with zero interest in chitchat.

'Hey.' Blondie in fatigues nodded, *striking* a pose with his muscled arms crossed over his chest. Not a single visible *dermaglyph* on that young skin. Definitely current-generation Breed. Probably not even out of his twenties yet. 'Sony to interrupt, but we had to tell you, man – that was some kick-ass business you guys dealt the Rogues a few months ago. Everyone's still talking about the way the Order took out an entire colony of suck-heads in one night. Blew that mofo sky-high. Freakin' awesome, man.'

'Yeah,' added his homeboy companion. 'So, we was wonderin' . . . I mean, we heard the Order is looking for new recruits.'

'Did you, now?'

Dante leaned back in his seat and exhaled a bored sigh. This was hardly the first time he'd been approached by Darkhaven vampires hoping to join up with the warriors. Since the raid on the Rogue lair housed in the old asylum that past summer, the once secretive cadre of Breed warriors had gained a lot of unwanted notoriety. Celebrity, even.

Frankly, it was annoying as hell.

Dante kicked his chair back from the table and stood.

'I'm not the guy to talk to about that,' he told the hopefuls. 'And anyway, recruitment into the Order is by invite only. Sorry.'

He strode away from them, relieved to feel the vibration of his cell phone going off in his jacked pocket. He dug out the device and clicked on to the incoming call from the Breed compound.

'Yeah.'

'How's it going?' It was Gideon, resident genius of the warrior class. 'Any topside activity to report?'

'Not much. Things are pretty dead out here right now.' Dante scanned the crowded club, noting that the two vampires had decided to move on. They were heading for the exit, taking a couple of costumed human females with them. 'No Rogues in the vicinity at all so far. And doesn't that just suck ass? I'm itching for some action here, Gid.'

'Well, try to cheer up,' Gideon said, a grin in his voice. 'The night's still young.'

Dante chuckled. 'Tell Lucan I spared him from another couple of wannabes looking to sign on. You know, I liked things a hell of a lot better when we were feared more than revered. Is he making any progress on the recruiting, or is our boy too caught up with that gorgeous Breedmate of his?'

'Yes to both,' Gideon replied. 'As to the recruiting, we've got a candidate coming in soon from New York, and Nikolai's got feelers out to some of his contacts in Detroit. We'll have to arrange some trial runs for the newbies – you know, take them through the paces before we commit.'

'You mean, hand them their asses on a platter and see which ones come back looking for more?'

'Is there any other way?'

'Count me in,' Dante drawled as he moved through the club toward the door.

He strolled out into the night, avoiding a group of human clubbers dressed like zombies in tattered clothes and death-warmed-over face paint. His acute hearing picked up hundreds of sounds – from general traffic noise to the shrieks and laughter of drunken Halloween partygoers clogging the streets and sidewalks.

He heard something else too.

Something that raised the hackles on his warrior senses to high alert.

'Gotta go,' he told Gideon on the other end of the line. 'I'm homing in on a suckhead. Guess the night's not a total waste, after all.'

'Check back in after you smoke him.'

'Right. Later.' Dante clicked off the call and pocketed the cell phone.

He stole down a side alley, following the low grunt and stale, wafting stench of a prowling Rogue vampire as it stalked its prey. Like the other warriors of the Order, Dante had a deep contempt for members of the Breed who'd gone Rogue. Every vampire thirsted, every vampire had to feed – sometimes kill – in order to survive. But each and every one of them also knew that the line between necessity and gluttony was thin, just a few meager ounces of blood. If a vampire consumed too much, or fed his need too frequently, he ran die risk of addiction, of entering a permanent state of hunger known as Bloodlust. Lost to the disease, he would turn Rogue, becoming a violent junkie who would do anything for his next fix.

The savagery and indiscretion of the Rogues jeopardized all of the Breed to exposure to the human race, a threat that Dante and the rest of the Order would not abide. And there was a larger threat blooming as well: As of a few months ago, it had become apparent that the Rogues were organizing, their numbers increasing, tactics becoming orchestrated toward a goal that seemed nothing short of war. If they weren't stopped, and stopped soon, both humankind and Breed alike could find themselves at the center of a hellish, blood-soaked battle to rival even the worst Armageddon scenario.

For now, while the Order focused on locating the Rogues' new command post, the warriors' mission was simple. Hunt down and eliminate every Rogue possible. Exterminate them like the diseased vermin they were. It was a charge Dante relished, never more at home than when he was on the move, prowling the streets with weapons in hand, looking for a fight. It kept him alive, he was certain; even more, it kept the darkest of his demons at bay.

Dante rounded a corner, then crept into another narrow lane between a couple of old brick buildings. He heard a female scream somewhere ahead of him in the dark. Kicking it into high gear, he sped toward the sound.

And got there hardly a second too soon.

The Rogue had been stalking the two Darkhaven vampires and their female companions. It looked young, tricked out in basic goth garb beneath a long black trench coat. But young or not, it was big and it was strong, fierce with hunger. One of the women was held in a death grip, the Bloodlusting vampire already latched on to her throat while the would-be warriors stood by, shell-shocked and frozen.

Dante pulled a dagger from a sheath on his hip and let it fly. The blade struck hard, embedding between the Rogue's shoulders. The weapon was specially crafted of steel and titanium, the latter metal being extremely poisonous to the corrupted blood systems and organs of the Rogues. One kiss of that deadly blade and a Rogue vampire would start cooking from the inside out at record speed.

Except this one didn't.

It flung a savage look at Dante, its eyes glowing amber, fangs bloody as it hissed a vicious warning. But the Rogue weathered the dagger's assault, holding fast to its prey and swinging its head around to drink with even greater urgency.

What the hell?

Dante ran up on the feeding vampire with another blade in hand. He didn't waste a second, going for the neck this time, intending to cut it clean through. The blade sank in, slicing deep. But the suckhead spun out of the attack before Dante could finish it off! With a pained roar, it dropped the female and focused all of its fury on Dante.

'Get the humans out of here!' Dante shouted to the Darkhaven vampires as he yanked the woman out of the fray and shoved her toward the others. 'Move it, now! Glean them up, scrub both their memories, and get them the fuck out of here!'

The two young males jolted into action. They grabbed the shrieking women and pulled them away from the scene while Dante considered the strangeness of what he'd just witnessed.

The vampire didn't disintegrate as it should have from the double dose of titanium Dante had delivered. It wasn't a Rogue, even though it had been hunting prey and feeding like the worst blood addict.

Dante stared into the transformed face, the extruded fangs and elliptical pupils swimming in irises awash in fiery color. A foul-smelling pink spittle crusted around the vampire's mouth, turning Dante's stomach with its stench.

Offended, he backed off, guessing the vampire to be about the same age as the two Darkhaven youths. A frigging kid. Ignoring the pulsing gash in its neck, the vampire reached back and removed Dante's dagger from its shoulder. It growled, nostrils flaring as though it would spring at any moment.

But then it ran.

The suckhead bolted away at a fast clip, the hem of its trench coat flapping behind like a sail as it headed deeper into the city on a zigzagging path. Dante didn't let up for a second. He followed it down one street after another, through alleyways and neighborhoods, then farther out, into the dockyards outside Boston proper, where empty factories and old industrial parks stood like bleak sentinels along the riverfront. The low throb of music pounded from one of the buildings, the heavy bass and intermittent flashes of strobe lights no doubt coming from a rave taking place somewhere nearby.

Ahead of him a few hundred feet, the vampire sped down a

dock toward a rickety boathouse. Dead end. Spitting fury through its open jaws, the suckhead swung around and went on the offensive, roaring up on Dante like a lunatic. Fresh blood soaked the front of its clothing from the brutal assault on the human female. The vampire snapped and clawed at him, its large fangs dripping saliva, the gaping maw oozing more of the foul-smelling pinkish foam. Its amber eyes glowed with pure malice.

Dante felt the change come over him as well, battle rage coursing through him, transforming him into a creature not so different from the one he fought. With a snarl, he threw the suckhead down onto the wood planks of the dock. One knee planted in the barrel chest of his opponent, Dante drew his twin *malebranche* blades. The arced weapons gleamed in the moonlight, lethally beautiful. Even if the titanium proved useless, there was more than one way to kill a vampire, Rogue or not. Dante brought the blades down, first one, then the other, slashing deep into the fleshy throat of the crazed vampire and cleanly severing its head.

Dante kicked the remains off the dock and into the water. The dark river would conceal the corpse until morning, then the UV rays of daylight would take care of the rest.

A wind kicked up off the water, carrying the stench of industrial pollution and something . . . else. Dante heard movement nearby, but it wasn't until he felt the burn of tearing flesh in his leg that he realized he was under a further attack. He took another piercing hit, this one in his torso.

Jesus Christ.

From somewhere behind him, up near the old factory, someone was firing on him. The gun's report was silenced but unmistakably that of an automatic rifle.

His dull night was suddenly getting more interesting than he liked.

Dante dropped to the ground as another shot whizzed past him and into the river. He rolled, going for the cover of the boathouse as the sniper let another few rounds fly. One shot bit into the corner of the shingled structure, shattering the old wood like confetti. Dante had a handgun on him, a hefty 9mm backup for the blades he preferred to take into combat. He drew the piece now but knew it would be all but useless against the sniper at this range.

More rounds peppered the boathouse, one of them grazing Dante's cheek as he peered around to get a sight on his attacker.

Oh, not good.

Four dark shapes were moving down the sloping embankment from the area of the factory, all of them carrying serious hardware. While Breed vampires could live for hundreds of years and withstand severe physical injuries, they were still essentially flesh and bone. Pump enough lead into them, sever major arteries – or worse, their head – and they died, same as any other living being.

But not without one hell of a fight.

Dante kept low and waited for the newcomers to come into range. When they did, he opened fire on them, taking out a knee of one and planting a slug into the head of another. He was oddly relieved to see that they were Rogues, the titanium in the custom-crafted rounds dropping them instantly and sending them into swift cellular meltdown.

The remaining Rogues fired back, and Dante narrowly avoided the spray, moving farther back along the side of the boathouse. Damn. Taking cover meant sacrificing the position of offense. Not to mention the fact that it impeded his ability to track his enemies' approach. He heard them coming closer as he reloaded a new clip into the pistol.

Then, silence.

He waited for a second, gauging his surroundings.

Something bigger than a bullet flew through the air toward the boathouse. It clattered heavily onto the planks of the dock and rolled to a stop.

Holy Christ.

They'd lobbed a frigging grenade at him.

Dante sucked in a breath and flung himself into the river a mere instant before the thing blew, tossing the boathouse and half the dock into the air with a giant explosion of smoke, flame, and shrapnel. The percussion was like a sonic boom under the murky water. Dante felt his head snap back, his entire body racked with unbearable pressure. Above him, debris rained down onto the surface of the river, backlit by a blinding spray of orange fire.

His vision clouded as the concussion dragged him under. He started sinking, drifting with the strong pull of the current.

Unable to move as the river swept him, unconscious and bleeding, downstream.

⊰ CHAPTER TWO ⊱

'Special delivery for Doctor Tess Culver.'

Tess glanced up from a patient's file and smiled, despite the late hour and her general fatigue. 'One of these days, I'm going to learn to say no to you.'

'You think you need more practice? How about if I ask you to marry me again?'

She sighed, shaking her head at the bright blue eyes and dazzling all-American grin that were suddenly turned on her. 'I'm not talking about us, Ben. And what happened to eight o'clock? It's fifteen minutes to midnight, for Pete's sake.'

'You got plans to turn into a pumpkin or something?' He pushed off the doorjamb and sauntered into her office. Leaning down, he kissed her cheek. 'Sorry I'm so late. These things don't tend to adhere to the clock.'

'Uh-huh. So, where is it?'

'Around back, in the van.'

Tess stood, pulling an elastic hair band from her wrist and fastening it around her unbound hair. The mass of blondish-brown curls was unruly, even freshly styled. Sixteen hours into her shift at the clinic left it in a state of total anarchy. She blew a wisp of hair from her eyes and strode past her ex-boyfriend to the hallway outside.

'Nora, will you prep a syringe of ketamine-xylazine, please? And ready the exam room for me too – the big one.'

'You bet,' chirped her assistant. 'Hi, Ben. Happy Halloween.'

He shot her a wink and a crooked smile that would have melted the knees of any red-blooded woman. 'Nice costume, Nora. The Swiss Miss braids and *lederhosen* are a great look for you.'

'*Danke schön*,' she replied, beaming at his attention as she skirted the reception station and headed for the clinic pharmacy.

'Where's your costume, Tess?'

'I'm wearing it.' Walking ahead of him through the kennel area, past half a dozen sleepy dogs and nervous cats peering at them through their cage bars, Tess rolled her eyes. 'It's called the Super Vet Who's Probably Going to Get Arrested for This One Day costume.'

'I won't let you get into any trouble. I haven't yet, have I?'

'What about you?' She pushed open the door to the back storage room of the small clinic and walked through with him. 'This is a dangerous business you're in, Ben. You take too many risks.'

'You worried about me, Doc?'

'Of course I worry. I love you. You know that.'

'Yeah,' he said, a bit sulkily. 'Like a brother.'

The rear door of the place opened out onto a narrow alley that was seldom occupied, except by the occasional homeless person using the wall of her low-rent animal clinic near the riverfront as a backrest. Tonight Ben's black VW van was parked there. Low growls and snuffles sounded from within the vehicle, and there was a gentle rocking of its shocks, as if something big was pacing back and forth inside.

Which, of course, was exactly what was happening.

'It's contained inside there, right?'

'Yeah. Don't worry. Besides, it's as docile as a kitten, I promise you.'

Tess slid him a look of doubt as she stepped off the concrete stoop and walked around to the back doors of the van. 'Do I want to know where you got this one?'

'Probably not.'

For the past five years or so, Ben Sullivan had been acting as a personal crusader for the well-being and protection of abused exotic animals. He researched his rescue missions case by case, as cleverly as the most covert government spy. Then, like a one-man SWAT team, he moved in, liberating mistreated, malnourished, or endangered and illegal animals from their abusive caretakers and turning them over to legitimate sanctuaries that were equipped to properly care for the creatures. Sometimes, he made an emergency pit stop at Tess's clinic to get treatment for various animal wounds and injuries that needed immediate care.

It was actually how they'd met two years ago. Ben had brought in an abused serval with an intestinal blockage. The small exotic cat was recovered from a drug dealer's house, where it had chewed up and swallowed a rubber dog toy, and it needed to have the blockage surgically removed. It was a painstaking, lengthy procedure, but Ben had stayed the entire time. The next thing Tess knew, they were dating exclusively.

She wasn't sure how they'd gone from fooling around to falling in love, but somewhere along the way it had happened. For Ben, at any rate. Tess loved him back – adored him, really – but she just didn't see them going past the stage of good friends who happened to sleep together from time to time. Even that had cooled off lately, by her own initiative.

'Would you like to do the honors?' she asked him.

He reached out and grabbed the handle of the double doors, carefully swinging them wide.

'My God,' Tess breathed, utterly awed.

The Bengal tiger was emaciated and mangy, with an open sore oozing on its front leg from an apparent shackle burn, but even haggard as it was, it was the most majestic thing she'd ever seen. It stared back at them, its mouth slack, tongue out and panting, fear dilating its pupils until they were nearly full black. The tiger grunted, knocking its head against the bars of Ben's containment cage.

Tess cautiously moved closer. 'I know, poor baby. You've seen better days, haven't you?'

She frowned, noting the odd shape of its front paws, the lack of definition near the toes. 'Declawed?' she asked Ben, unable to mask the scorn in her voice.

'Yep. Defanged too.'

'Jesus. If they thought they needed to own a beautiful animal like this, why'd they mutilate it so badly?'

'Can't have your advertising mascot shredding your customers or their little brats, now, can you?'

Tess glanced at him. 'Advertising mascot? You don't mean the gun shop out on—' She broke off, shaking her head. 'Never mind. I really don't want to know. Let's get this big kitty inside so I can have a look.'

Ben pulled down a custom-fitted ramp from the back of the van. 'Hop in and take the back of the cage. I'll hold the front, since it will be heaviest on the way down.'

Tess did as instructed, helping him unload the wheeled container from the van down onto the pavement. When they reached the clinic door, Nora was there waiting. She gasped and cooed at the big cat, then gazed adoringly at Ben.

'Omigod. That's Shiva, isn't it? For years, I've been hoping he'd break out and run away from that place. You totally stole Shiva!'

Ben grinned. 'I don't know what you're talking about, *liebchen*. This cat is just a stray who showed up on my doorstep tonight. I thought Wonder Doc could patch him up a bit before I find him a good home.'

'Oh, you are bad, Ben Sullivan! And so totally my hero right now.'

Tess gestured to her enamored assistant. 'Nora, could you take this end with me, please? We need to lift it up over the stoop.'

Nora came around to Tess's side, and the three of them hefted the cage up and into the clinic's back room. They wheeled the tiger into the prepped exam room, which had recently been outfitted with an oversize hydraulic lift table, courtesy of Ben. It was a luxury Tess couldn't have afforded on her own. Although she had a small, devoted clientele, she wasn't exactly operating in the wealthy end of town. She'd priced her services well below their value, even for the area, feeling it was more important to make a difference than make a profit.

Unfortunately, her landlord and suppliers didn't agree. Her desk was weighted down with a pile of past-due notices that she wasn't going to be able to put off for much longer. She'd have to hit her meager personal savings to cover them, and after that was gone . . .?

'Tranquilizer's on the counter,' Nora said, breaking into her thoughts.

'Thanks.' Tess slipped the capped syringe into her lab-coat pocket, guessing that she probably wasn't going to need it after all, based on the docility and general lethargy of her patient. Besides, she wasn't going to do anything but a visual exam tonight, take a few notes on the animal's overall condition, and get a feel for what needed to be done in order to facilitate safe transportation to its new home.

'Think we can get Shiva – or whatever this stray's name is – to hop up on the table on his own, or should we use the lift?' Tess asked, watching as Ben worked the locks on the cage.

'Worth a shot. Come on, big guy.'

The tiger hesitated for a moment, head low as it glanced around the brightly lit exam room. Then, with Ben's encouragement, it stepped out of the cage and leaped fluidly onto the metal table. While Tess spoke softly to it and stroked its large head, the animal sat down, sphinxlike, more patient than the most well-behaved house cat.

'So,' Nora said, 'do you need anything else right now, or can I take off?'

Tess shook her head. 'Sure, you can go. Thank you for staying so late tonight. I really appreciate it.'

'No prob. The party I'm going to won't even get started until after midnight, anyway.' She flipped her long blond braids over her shoulders. 'Okay, so, I'm off, then. I'll lock up on my way out. 'Night, you guys.'

'Good night,' they answered in unison.

'She's a great kid,' Ben said after Nora had left.

'Nora's the best,' Tess agreed, petting Shiva and feeling for skin lesions, lumps, or other problems beneath its thick fur. 'And she's not a kid, Ben. She's twenty-one, about to start her degree in veterinary medicine after she finishes up her last semester at the university. She's going to make a great doctor.'

'No one's as good as you. Got a magic touch, Doc.'

Tess shrugged off the compliment, but there was a bit of truth in it. Just how much, she doubted Ben really knew. Tess hardly understood it herself, and what she did understand, she wished she could blot out completely. Self-consciously, she crossed her arms, concealing her hands from view.

'You don't have to stay either, Ben. I'd like to keep Shi—' She cleared her throat, arching a brow at him. 'My patient, that is, for observation tonight. I won't start any procedures until tomorrow, and I'll call you with my findings before I do any work.'

'Dismissing me already? Here I thought I might be able to talk you into dinner.'

'I ate dinner hours ago.'

'Breakfast, then. My place or yours, you can call it.'

'Ben,' she said, hedging as he came over and stroked her cheek. His touch was warm and tender, comfortably familiar.

'We've been through this already, more than once. I just don't think it's a good idea. . . .'

He groaned, and it was an entirely too sexual sound, low and throaty. There was a time when that sound turned her self-control into butter, but not tonight. Not ever again, if she had any hope of maintaining her personal integrity. It just seemed wrong to go to bed with Ben, knowing he wanted something from her that she couldn't give him.

'I could stay until you wrap up,' he suggested, backing off now. 'I don't like the idea of you being here all by yourself. This area of town isn't exactly the safest.'

'I'll be fine. I'm just going to finish my examination here, then do a bit of paperwork and close up shop. No big deal.'

Ben scowled, on the verge of arguing until Tess blew out a sigh and gave him *the look*. She knew he read it clearly, since he'd seen it more than once during their two years of couplehood. 'All right,' he agreed finally. 'But don't stay too much longer. And you call me first thing in the morning, promise?'

'I promise.'

'You sure you're comfortable handling Shiva by yourself?'

Tess glanced down at the haggard beast, which immediately began licking her hand again as soon as she put it near him. 'I think I'll be safe with him.'

'What'd I tell ya, Doc? Magic touch. Looks like he's already in love with you too.' Ben ran his fingers through his golden-blond hair, giving her a defeated look. 'I guess if I want to win your heart, I'll need to grow some fur and fangs, is that it?'

Tess smiled and rolled her eyes. 'Go home, Ben. I'll call you tomorrow.'

≒ CHAPTER THREE ⋟

Tess came awake with a start.

Shit. How long had she been dozing? She was in her office, Shiva's case file open beneath her cheek on the desk. Last she recalled, she'd fed the malnourished tiger and put it back in its containment so she could begin writing up her findings. That was – she glanced at her watch – two and a half hours ago? It was now a few minutes before three A.M. She was due back in the clinic at seven o'clock.

Tess groaned around a big yawn and a stretch of her cramped arms.

Good thing she woke up before Nora reported back to work, or she'd never hear the end of—

A loud bump sounded from somewhere in the back of the clinic.

What the hell?

Had she been jolted out of her sleep by a similar noise a minute ago?

Oh, jeez. Of course. Ben must have driven past and seen the lights on in the clinic. It wouldn't be the first time he'd come around on a late-night drive-by to check in on her. She really didn't feel like getting a lecture on her crazy hours or her stubborn streak of independence.

The noise came again, another clumsy bump, followed by an abrupt clatter of metal as something got knocked off a shelf.

Which meant someone was in the back storage room.

Tess rose from her desk and took a few tentative steps toward her office door, ears tuned to any disturbance at all. In the kennels off the reception area, the handful of post-op cats and dogs were restless. Some of them were whining; others were issuing low warning growls.

'Hello?' Tess called into the empty space. 'Is someone here? Ben, is that you? Nora?'

Nobody answered. And now the noises she'd heard before had gone still as well.

Great. She'd just announced her presence to an intruder. *Brilliant, Culver. Absolutely frigging brilliant.*

She tried to console herself with some fast logic. Maybe it was just a homeless person looking for shelter who'd found his or her way into the clinic from the back alley. Not an intruder. Nothing dangerous at all.

Yeah? So why were the hairs on the back of her neck tingling with dread?

Tess shoved her hands into the pockets of her lab coat, feeling suddenly very vulnerable. She felt her ball-point pen knock against her fingers. Something else was in there as well.

Oh, that's right. The tranq syringe, full of enough anesthetic to knock a four-hundred-pound animal out cold.

'Is someone back there?' she asked, trying to keep her voice firm and steady. She paused at the reception station and reached for the phone. The damn thing wasn't cordless – she'd gotten it cheap on closeout – and the receiver barely reached to her ear from over the counter. Tess went around the big U-shaped desk, glancing nervously over her shoulder as she started punching 911 on the keypad. 'You'd better get out of here right now, because I'm calling the cops.'

'*No . . . please . . . don't be afraid. . . .*'

The deep voice was so quiet, it shouldn't have reached her ears, but it did. She heard it as surely as if the words had been whispered right up next to her head. *Inside her head*, strange as that seemed.

There was a dry croak and a violent, racking cough, definitely coming from the storage room. And whomever the voice belonged to sounded like he was in a world of hurt. Life and death kind of hurt.

'Damn it.'

Tess held her breath and hung up the phone before her call connected. She walked slowly toward the back of the clinic, uncertain what she was going to find and really wishing she didn't have to look at all.

'Hello? What are you doing in here? Are you hurt?'

She spoke to the intruder as she pushed open the door and stepped inside. She heard labored breathing, smelled smoke and the briny stench of the river. She smelled blood too. Lots of it. Tess flicked the light on.

Harsh fluorescent tubes buzzed to life overhead, illuminating the incredible bulk of a drenched, badly injured man slumped on the floor near one of the supply shelves. He was dressed all in black, like some kind of goth nightmare – black leather jacket, tee-shirt, fatigues, and lace-up combat boots. Even his hair was black, the wet strands plastered to his head, shielding his down-turned face from view. An ugly smudge of blood and river water traveled from the back door, partially opened onto the alley, to where the man lay in Tess's storeroom. He had evidently dragged himself inside, maybe unable to walk.

If she hadn't been so accustomed to seeing the grisly aftermath of car accidents, beatings, and other bodily trauma in her animal patients, the sight of this man's injuries might have turned Tess's stomach inside out.

Instead, her mind switched from alarm and the instinctual fight-or-flight mode she'd been feeling out in the reception area to that of the physician she was trained to be. Clinical, calm, and concerned.

'What happened to you?'

The man grunted, gave a vague shake of his dark head like he wasn't going to tell her anything about it. Perhaps he couldn't.

'You're covered in burns and wounds. My God, there must be hundreds of them. Were you in some kind of accident?' She glanced down to where one of his hands was resting on his abdomen. Blood was seeping through his fingers from a fresh, deep puncture. 'Your gut is bleeding – and your leg too. Jesus, have you been shot?'

'Need . . . blood.'

He was probably right about that. The floor beneath him was slick, and dark from what he'd lost just since his arrival at the clinic. He'd likely lost a good deal more before he got there. Nearly every patch of his exposed skin bore multiple lacerations – his face and neck, his hands, everywhere Tess looked, she saw bleeding cuts and contusions. His cheeks and mouth were pale white, ghostly.

'You need an ambulance,' she told him, not wanting to upset him, but, damn, the guy was in bad shape. 'Just relax now. I'm going to go call 911 for you.'

'No!' He lurched from his slump on the floor, thrusting his hand out to her in alarm. 'No hospitals! Can't . . . can't go there. . . . They won't . . . can't help me.'

Despite his protest, Tess started to run for the phone in the other room. But then she remembered the stolen tiger hanging out in one of her exam rooms. Hard to explain that to the EMTs or, God forbid, the police. The gun shop had probably already called in the theft of the animal, or would by the time the store opened that morning, just a few short hours away.

'Please,' gasped the huge man bleeding all over her clinic. 'No doctors.'

Tess paused, regarding him in silence. He needed help in a big way, and he needed it now. Unfortunately, she looked like his best chance at the moment. She wasn't sure what she could do for him here, but maybe she could patch him up temporarily, get him on his feet, and get him the hell out of there.

'Okay,' she said. 'No ambulances for now. Listen, I'm, uh – I'm actually a doctor. Well, more or less. This is my veterinary clinic. Would it be all right if I come a little closer and have a look at you?'

She took the quirk of his mouth and ragged exhaled sigh as a yes.

Tess inched down beside him on the floor. He had seemed big from across the room, but crouched next to him, she realized that he was immense, easily six and a half feet and two hundred fifty-plus pounds of heavy bone and solid muscle. Was he some kind of bodybuilder? One of those macho meatheads who spent his life in the gym? Something about him didn't quite fit that mold. With the grim cut of his face, he looked like the kind of guy who could tear a gym rat to pieces with his teeth.

She moved her hands lightly over his face, feeling for trauma. His skull was intact, but her touch told her that he'd suffered a mild concussion in some fashion. Probably was still in a state of shock.

'I'm just going to check your eyes,' she informed him gently, then lifted one of his lids.

Holy shit.

The slitted pupil cutting through the center of a large, bright amber iris took her aback. She recoiled, freaked out by the unexpected presentation.

'What the—'

Then the explanation hit her, and she instantly felt like an idiot for losing her cool.

Costume contacts.

Chill out, she told herself. She was getting jumpy for no good reason. The guy must have been at a Halloween party that got out of hand or something. Not much she could tell from his eyes so long as he was wearing those ridiculous lenses.

Maybe he'd been partying with a rough crowd; he certainly looked big and dangerous enough to be part of some kind of gang. If he'd been rolling with gang-bangers tonight, she didn't detect any evidence of drugs on him. She didn't smell alcohol on him either. Just some heavy-duty smoke, and not from cigarettes.

He smelled like he'd walked through fire. Just before he took a dive into the Mystic River.

'Can you move your arms or legs?' she asked him, moving on to inspect his limbs. 'Do you think you have any broken bones?'

She skimmed her hands over his thick arms, feeling no obvious fractures. His legs were solid too, no real damage beyond the bullet wound in his left calf. From the look of it, the round appeared to have passed clean through. Same with the one that hit him in the torso. Luckily for him.

'I'd like to move you to one of my exam rooms. Do you think you can walk if I help hold you up?'

'Blood,' he gasped, his voice thready. 'Need it . . . now.'

'Well, I'm sorry, but I can't help you there. You'll need a hospital for that. Right now, we have to get you off this floor and out of those ruined clothes. God knows what kind of bacteria you picked up in that water out there.'

She put her hands under his armpits and started to lift, encouraging him to stand. He growled, something deep and animalistic. As the sound left his mouth, Tess caught a glimpse of his teeth behind his curled upper lip.

Whoa. That's weird.

Were those monstrous canines actually . . . *fangs?*

His eyes came open as if he had sensed her awareness. Her unease. Tess was instantly blasted by piercing bright amber light, the glowing irises sending a bolt of panic straight into her chest. Those sure as hell weren't contacts.

Good Lord. Something wasn't right with this guy at all.

He grabbed her upper arms. Tess cried out in alarm. She tried to pull out of his grasp, but he was too strong. Hands as unyielding as iron bands clamped tighter around her and brought her closer. Tess shrieked, wide-eyed, frozen in fear as he drew her right up against him.

'Oh, God. No!'

He turned his bloodied, battered face toward her throat. Sucked in a sharp breath as he neared her, his lips brushing her skin.

'Shhh.' Warm air skated across her neck as he spoke in a low, pained rasp. 'I won't . . . not going to . . . hurt you. I promise. . . .'

Tess heard the words.

She almost believed them.

Until that split second of terror, when he parted his lips and sank his teeth deep into her flesh.

～❧ CHAPTER FOUR ❧～

Blood surged into Dante's mouth from the twin punctures in the female's neck. He drew from her with deep, urgent pulls, unable to curb the feral part of him that knew only need and desperation. It was life pulsing over his tongue and down his parched throat, silky, cinnamon-sweet, and so very warm.

Maybe it was the severity of his need that made her taste so incredible, so indescribably perfect to him. Whatever it was, he didn't care. He drank more of her, needing her heat when he was chilled to his marrow.

'Oh, God. No!' The woman's voice was thready with shock. 'Please! Let me go!'

She clutched at his shoulders reflexively, fingers digging into his muscles. But the rest of her body was slowly going still in his arms, lulled to a boneless sort of trance by the hypnotic power of Dante's bite. She sighed a long gasp of breath, sagging limply as he eased her down onto the floor beneath him and took the nourishment he so badly needed.

There was no pain for her now, not since the initial penetration of his fangs, which would have been sharp but fleeting. The only pain here was Dante's own. His body shuddered from the depth of its trauma, his head splitting from a concussion, his torso and limbs laced open in too many places to count.

It's okay. Don't be afraid.
You are safe. I promise.

He sent the reassurances into her mind, even as he held her

tighter, brought her more firmly into the cage of his arms, his mouth still drawing hard from the wound at her throat.

Despite the ferocity of his thirst, a need amplified by the severity of his injuries, Dante's word was good. Beyond the bite that startled her, he would not harm the female.

I'll take only what I need. Then I'll be gone, and you will forget all about me.

Already his strength was returning. Torn flesh was mending from the inside out. Bullet and shrapnel wounds were healing over.

Burns cooling.

Pain fading.

He eased up on the female, willing himself to slow, even though the taste of her was beyond enticing. He'd registered the exotic note of her blood scent on his first draw, but now that his body was rejuvenating, his senses coming back online-fully, Dante couldn't help but savor the sweetness of his unwilling Host.

And her body.

Beneath the shapeless white lab coat, she was strong, lean muscle and long, graceful limbs. Curvy in all the right places. Dante felt the mash of her breasts pressing against his chest where he pinned her on the storeroom floor, her legs tangled with his. Her hands were still gripped hard on his shoulders, no longer pushing against him but simply holding on to him as he took a final sip of her life-giving blood.

God, she was so exquisite he could drink from her all night.

He could do a hell of a lot more than that, he thought, suddenly aware of the erection that was wedged hard and demanding at her pelvis. She felt too good beneath him. His blessed angel of mercy, even if she'd come into the role by force.

Dante breathed in her spicy-sweet scent, gently dropping a kiss on the wound that had fed him a second chance at life.

'Thank you,' he whispered against her warm, velvet-soft skin. 'I think you saved my life tonight.'

He smoothed his tongue over the small punctures, sealing them closed and erasing all traces of his bite. The female moaned, stirring from her temporary thrall. She moved under him, the subtle shifting of her body only heightening Dante's desire to be inside her.

But he'd already taken enough from her tonight. In spite of the fact that she would remember none of what had occurred, it seemed less than sporting to seduce her in a puddle of stale river water and spilled blood. Particularly after going at her neck like an animal.

He moved slightly off her and brought his right hand up near her face. She flinched, understandably wary. Her eyes were open now – mesmerizing eyes, the color of flawless aquamarine.

'My God, you are beautiful,' he murmured, words he'd casually tossed out to numerous females in the past but surprisingly never meant more than he did now.

'Please,' she whispered. 'Please, don't hurt me.'

'No,' Dante said gently. 'I'm not going to hurt you. Just close your eyes now, angel. It's almost over.'

A brief press of his palm against her brow, and she would forget all about him.

'Everything's all right,' he told her as she shrank back from him on the floor, her eyes locked on to his as if she waited for him to strike her. Dared him to. Dante smoothed her hair off her cheek with the tenderness of a lover. Her felt her tension ratchet a little tighter. 'Relax now. You can trust—'

Something sharp stuck him in the thigh.

With a vicious snarl, Dante rolled away, flipping onto his back. 'What the hell?'

Heat spread from that stabbing point of contact, burning through him like acid. A bitter taste gathered at the back of his throat, just before his vision began to swim crazily. Dante tried to heave himself upright from the floor but fell back again, his body as uncooperative as a lead slab.

Panting rapidly, those bright blue-green eyes wide with panic, Dante's angel of mercy peered over him. Her pretty face warped in and out of his vision. One slender hand was pressed to her neck, where he'd bitten her. The other was raised up at shoulder level, holding an empty syringe in a white-knuckled grip.

Holy Christ.

She'd drugged him.

But as bad as that news was, Dante registered something even worse as his blurring gaze struggled to hold on to the small hand that had managed to fell him with one blow. Between her thumb and forefinger, in that fleshy juncture of soft skin, the female bore a small birthmark.

Deep scarlet, smaller than a dime, the image of a teardrop falling into the bowl of a crescent moon seared into Dante's brain.

It was a rare mark, a genetic stamp that proclaimed the female sacred to those of Dante's kind.

She was a Breedmate.

And with her blood now pulsing within him, Dante had just completed one half of a solemn bond.

By vampire law, she was his.

Irrevocably.

Eternally.

The very last thing he wanted or needed.

In his mind, Dante roared, but all he heard was a low, wordless growl. He blinked dully, reaching out for the woman, missing her by an easy foot. His arm dropped like it was weighted down with irons. His eyelids were too heavy to lift more than a fraction. He moaned, watching his erstwhile savioress's features blur before his eyes.

She glared down at him, her voice edged with defiant fury.

'Sleep tight, you psychotic son of a bitch!'

Tess leaped back from her attacker, breath heaving out of her in a raw, rapid pant. She could hardly believe what had just happened to her. Or that she had managed to escape the crazed intruder at all.

Thank God for the tranquilizer, she thought, relieved that she'd had the presence of mind to remember the syringe in her pocket. Not to mention the opportunity to use it. She glanced at the spent needle, still clutched tightly in her hand, and winced.

Shit. She'd plugged him with the entire dose.

No wonder he dropped like a ton of bricks. He wasn't going to be waking up anytime soon either. Eighteen hundred milligrams of animal tranq was one long kiss good night, even for a massive guy like him.

A sudden pang of worry stabbed her. What if she'd killed him?

Unsure why she should be concerned about someone who seemed bent on tearing her throat out with his teeth just a few minutes ago, Tess inched her way back to where the man lay.

He wasn't moving.

But he was breathing, she was relieved to note.

He was sprawled flat on his back, his muscular arms flung out on the floor where they'd fallen. His hands – those large mitts of brutal strength that had held her in a vise grip as he'd attacked her – were slack and still now. His face, which had been concealed by the fall of his dark hair, was almost handsome at rest.

No, not handsome, because even unconscious, his features held their stark angles and knife-edge planes. Straight black brows cut dark slashes over his closed eyes. His cheekbones were razor sharp, giving the slope of his face a lean, feral quality. His nose might have been perfect at one time, but the strong line of its bridge had a faint jag in it from an old break. Maybe more than one.

There was something strangely compelling about him, although she was certain she didn't know him. He wasn't exactly the kind of guy she'd associate with, and trying to picture him coming into the clinic for pet care seemed absurd.

No, she had never seen him before tonight. She could only pray that once she called the cops to come and collect him, she'd never see him again either.

Tess glanced down, and her gaze caught on the glint of metal concealed beneath his sodden jacket. She moved the leather aside and drew in her breath to see a curved blade of steel sheathed under his arm. An empty holster on the other side seemed to be missing a gun. Other hand-to-hand implements studded a wide black belt that wrapped around his slim hips.

This man was a menace, no doubt about that. Some kind of thug, who made the hard-asses down here on the riverfront look like rank poseurs. This man was hard and deadly, everything about him throwing off an air of violence.

His mouth was the only bit of softness on him. Wide and sensual, lips parted slightly in his drugged state, his mouth was profanely beautiful. The kind of mouth that could wreak havoc on a woman from about a hundred different angles.

Not that Tess was counting.

And she hadn't forgotten about those wicked canines either.

Moving cautiously around him despite the heavy dosage of tranquilizer that was swimming through his system, Tess reached out and lifted his upper lip to get a better look at him.

No fangs.

Just a row of perfect pearly whites. If he'd been sporting costume teeth when he attacked her, they'd been pretty damn convincing. Now those huge fangs seemed to have vanished into thin air.

A fact that made no sense at all.

A quick visual scan of the area around her came up empty.

He hadn't spat them out somewhere. And she sure as hell hadn't been imagining them.

How else would he have been able to pop her throat open like a soda can? Tess brought her hand up to the bite wound in her neck. The skin felt smooth beneath her fingertips. No blood or stickiness, no trace of the holes he'd chewed into her jugular. She probed the whole side of her neck with her fingers. The area wasn't even tender.

'That's impossible.'

Tess got up and hurried into the nearest exam room, flipping on all the lights. Smoothing her hair away from her neck, she walked up to a mounted paper-towel dispenser and peered at her reflection in the polished stainless steel. The skin on her neck was clear, intact.

Like the terrifying attack had never happened.

'No way,' she told her stricken expression. 'How can that be?'

Tess stepped back from the makeshift mirror, astonished.

Thoroughly confused.

Not more than a half hour ago, she was fearing for her life, feeling her blood being drained from her neck by the heavily armed, black-clad stranger she'd found lying unconscious near the clinic's back door.

It *had* happened.

So how on earth could her skin show zero trace of the assault?

Tess's feet felt detached from her body as she walked back out of the examination room and toward the storeroom. Whatever he'd done to her, no matter how he managed to disguise the wounds he'd inflicted on her, Tess intended to see him arrested and charged.

She came around the open doorway of the back room and drew up short.

The puddle of river water and spilled blood her attacker had brought in with him swamped a large area of the linoleum floor. Tess's stomach gave a little turn at the sight of it, but there was something else that put a knot of ice-cold terror in her gut.

The storeroom was empty.

Her attacker was gone.

A gorilla-size dose of anesthetic, yet he was somehow up and gone.

'Looking for me, angel?'

Tess spun around and screamed.

⤳ CHAPTER FIVE ⤝

Adrenaline poured through her, putting her feet into motion. Tess dodged past him and tore up the hallway, her thoughts racing a thousand miles an hour.

She had to get out of there.

She had to get her purse and her money and her cell phone and get the hell out.

'We need to talk.'

There he was again – standing right in front of her, blocking her path into her office.

As though he'd simply vanished from where he'd been standing before and materialized in the doorway she needed to get through now.

With a yelp of alarm, Tess made a quick pivot and launched herself into the reception area. She grabbed the desk phone and punched one of the speed-dial numbers.

'This is not happening. This is *not* happening,' she whispered under her breath, repeating the mantra as if she could make it all go away if she hoped for it hard enough.

The call began to ring on the other end.

Come on, come on, answer.

'Put the phone down, female.'

Tess whirled around, shaking with fear. Her attacker moved slowly, with the deliberate grace of a skilled predator. He came closer. Bared his teeth in a harsh smile.

'Please. Put it down. Now.'

Tess shook her head. 'Go to hell!'

The receiver flew out of her grasp of its own free will. As it clattered onto the desk beside her, Tess heard Ben's voice come on the line. 'Tess? Hello . . . that you, babe? Jesus, it's after three o'clock in the morning. What are you still doing at the—'

There was a loud snap behind her, like the telephone wire had been yanked from the wall jack by invisible hands. Tess jumped at the noise, fear coiling in her stomach in the silence that followed.

'We have a serious problem. *Tess.*'

Oh, God.

Now he was pissed off, *and* he knew her name.

In the back of her mind, Tess registered the fact that aside from her attacker's impossible state of consciousness, he had also experienced a miraculous recovery of his injuries. Beneath the grime and smudged ash that marred his skin, all of his sundry scrapes and lacerations were healed. His black fatigues were still torn and bloodstained from the wound in his leg, but he wasn't bleeding anymore. Not from the likely gunshot wound in his abdomen either. Through the shredded fabric of his black shirt, Tess saw only smooth, bunching muscle and flawless olive skin.

Was this whole thing some kind of sick Halloween joke?

She didn't think so, and she knew better than to let her guard down with this guy for so much as a second.

'My boyfriend knows I'm here. He's probably already on his way. He might even have called the cops—'

'You have a mark on your hand.'

'W-what?'

His voice had sounded accusatory, and now he pointed to her, indicating her right hand, which was trembling up near her throat.

'You're a Breedmate. As of tonight, you are mine.'

His lip curled at the corner as he said it, like he found the words not at all to his taste. Tess didn't particularly like the sound of them either. She backed up several paces, feeling the blood rush out of her head as he tracked her every move.

'Look, I don't know what's going on here. I don't know what happened to you tonight, or how you ended up in my clinic. I sure don't know how it is that you could be standing in front of me right now, after I gave you enough tranq to knock ten men cold—'

'I am not a man, Tess. I am something . . . else.'

She might have scoffed at that if he hadn't sounded so deadly serious. So deadly calm.

He was crazy.

Right. Of course he was.

Off the chain, raving lunatic, psycho crazy.

That was the only explanation she could come up with, staring in wide-eyed dread as he closed the space between them, the sheer power and size of him forcing her toward the wall at her back.

'You saved me, Tess. I didn't give you a choice, but your blood healed me.'

Tess shook her head. 'I didn't heal you. I'm not even sure your wounds were real. Maybe you thought they were, but—'

'They were real,' he said, a faint, rolling accent in his deep voice. 'Without your blood, they might have killed me. But in drinking from you, I've done something to you. Something that I can't take back.'

'*Oh, my God.*' Tess felt sick, swamped with a sudden wave of nausea. 'Are you talking about HIV? Please don't tell me you have AIDS. . . .'

'Those are human diseases,' he said dismissively. 'I am immune to them. And so are you, Tess.'

Somehow, that wacko declaration didn't give her a lot of hope. 'Stop using my name. Stop acting like you know anything about me—'

'I don't expect this is easy for you to understand. I'm trying to explain as gently as I can. I owe you that much now. You see, you are a Breedmate, Tess. That's something very special to my kind.'

'Your kind?' she asked, growing weary of his game. 'Okay, I give up. Just what is your kind?'

'I am a warrior. One of the Breed.'

'Right, a warrior. And breed, as in . . . what kind of breed?'

For a long moment, he just looked at her, like he was weighing his answer. 'As in vampire, Tess.'

Holy Moses on a pogo stick. He was *beyond* crazy.

Sane people did not go around pretending to be bloodsucking fiends – or worse, actually acting out their perverted fantasies, like this guy had with her.

Except there remained the fact that Tess's neck bore no trace of injury, even though she was certain – really, bone-chillingly sure – that he had chomped into her throat with razor-sharp fangs and swallowed quite a bit of her blood.

And then there was the incredible fact that he was standing here, walking and talking with no effect whatsoever of the tranquilizer that should have laid him low well into next week.

What could possibly explain any of that?

Distant police sirens wailed from someplace outside, the steady whine seeming on the approach to the clinic's section of the city. Tess heard them, and so did the psycho-ward escapee holding her hostage. He cocked his head slightly, his whiskey-colored eyes never leaving her for a second. He smiled wryly, just the barest curve of his broad mouth, then cursed low under his breath.

'Sounds like your boyfriend phoned in some backup.'

Tess was too anxious to answer, uncertain what might provoke him now that he knew the authorities were on the way.

'Brilliant way to fuck up an evening,' he growled, seemingly to himself. 'This isn't the right way to leave things between us, but right now it doesn't appear I have much choice.'

His hand came up near Tess's face. She flinched to evade his touch, expecting the crush of a hard fist or some other brutality. But she felt only the warm press of his large open palm against her forehead. He leaned in to her, and she felt the feather-soft brush of his lips against her cheek.

'Close your eyes,' he murmured.

And Tess's world went dark.

'No signs of any suspicious activity, folks. We checked all points of entry around the building, and everything looks tight and in order.'

'Thank you, Officer,' Tess said, feeling like an idiot for creating all the fuss at such a late – or, rather, early – hour.

Ben stood next to her in her office, his arm slung lightly around her shoulders in a protective, if a bit territorial, stance. He'd arrived a short while ago, not long after police sirens woke her out of an unusually deep sleep. She'd been working too late, evidently, and had dozed off at her desk. Somehow, she had knocked the phone and activated the speed dial for Ben's cell. He'd seen the clinic number come up on caller ID and worried that she was in some kind of trouble.

His subsequent three A.M. call to 911 sent two officers out to the clinic on a drive-by.

While they had not found any cause for alarm as far as break-ins or late-night intruders, they did find Shiva. One of the cops had questioned them on where the tiger had come from, and when Ben insisted that he'd found the animal, not stolen it, the officer was quietly skeptical. He allowed that with it being Halloween night, advertising mascots were unusually high targets for adolescent mischief, a fact that Ben was quick to assure him must have been the case with Shiva.

Ben was lucky he hadn't ended up in handcuffs. As it stood,

he'd gotten off with a warning and a stern suggestion that he return Shiva to the gun shop first thing in the morning, just so nobody got the wrong idea and wanted to press charges.

Tess slid from under the weight of Ben's arm and held her hand out to the officer. 'Thanks again for coming by here. Can I get you some coffee or hot tea? I've got both, and it will only take a few minutes to make it.'

'No, thank you, ma'am.' The policeman's comm device gave a short burst of static, followed by a coded string of new orders from Dispatch. He spoke into a mic clipped to his lapel, giving the all-clear on the veterinary clinic. 'Looks like we're all set here, then. You folks take care now. And, Mr. Sullivan, I trust that you'll get that tiger back where it belongs.'

'Yes, sir,' Ben agreed, his smile tight as he accepted the officer's hand and gave it a brief shake.

They walked the police to the door and watched as the squad car eased out onto the quiet city street.

When they were gone, Ben closed the clinic door and turned to face Tess. 'You sure you're okay?'

She nodded, gave a long sigh. 'Yes, I'm perfectly fine. I'm sorry I worried you, Ben. I must have fallen asleep at my desk and bumped the phone.'

'Well, I still say no good can come from you working such late hours. This isn't exactly the best part of town, you know.'

'I've never had any problems here.'

'There's always a first time,' Ben said, his expression grim. 'Come on, I'll take you home.'

'All the way to the North End? You don't have to do that. I'll just call a cab.'

'Not tonight, you won't.' Ben picked up her purse and held it out to her. 'I'm wide awake, and my van is right outside. Let's go, Sleeping Beauty.'

≒ CHAPTER SIX ⋟

Dante came off the elevator at the Breed warriors' compound, looking and smelling as foul as he felt. He'd been seething – mostly at himself – the entire ride down, some three hundred feet below one of Boston's most affluent addresses and the high-security gated mansion on street level that belonged to the Order. He'd made it inside with only a few minutes to spare before dawn crested over the city to put a nice toast on his UV-allergic skin.

Which would have been the perfect topper to a night that had FUBAR written all over it.

Dante headed down the stark white corridor that twisted and turned through the heart of the labyrinthine compound. He needed a hot shower and some shut-eye and looked forward to sleeping off the daylight hours alone in his private quarters. Maybe he'd sleep off the next twenty years, long enough to avoid dealing with the glorious mess he'd made topside tonight.

'Yo, D.'

Dante muttered a curse under his breath when he heard the voice calling him from the other end of the corridor. It was Gideon, resident computer genius and right-hand man to Lucan, the Order's venerable leader. Gideon had the compound wired tight inside and out; he'd probably been on to Dante's arrival from the second he stepped onto the property.

'Where you been, man? You were supposed to call in your status hours ago.'

Dante turned around slowly in the long hallway. 'I guess you could say my status got a bit fucked up.'

'No shit,' the other vampire replied, taking him in with a shrewd glance over the top of square-cut pale blue shades. He chuckled, shaking his spiky crown of blond hair. 'Gad, you look like hell. And you smell like toxic waste. What the devil happened to you?'

'Long story.' Dante gestured to his shredded, bloodied, sodden clothing, which was rank with brine, sludge, and God knew what else from his trip down the Mystic River. 'I'll fill everyone in later. Right now I need a shower.'

'Industrial strength,' Gideon agreed. 'But cleanup is gonna have to wait awhile. We've got company in the lab.'

Annoyance sparked in Dante. 'What kind of company?'

'Oh, you're gonna love this.' Gideon gestured with his head. 'Come on. Lucan wants you present for input.'

Exhaling a long breath, Dante fell in step alongside Gideon. They walked up another twisting length of the corridor, heading for the tech lab, the surveillance and intel hub where the warriors held most of their meetings. As the glass wall of the lab came into view, Dante saw the three other vampire warriors who were like kin to him: Lucan, the Order's dark leader; Nikolai, the brash gearhead of the group; and Tegan, the eldest next to Lucan, and the deadliest individual Dante had ever known.

The Order was missing two other members of late. Rio, who had been severely injured by a Rogue ambush a few months ago and remained in the infirmary at the compound, and Conlan, who was killed by Rogues around the same time, in an explosion that took place on one of the city's train lines.

As Dante scanned the assembly of warriors, his gaze lit on one unfamiliar face. Evidently, this was the company Gideon had mentioned. The vampire male had the clean-cut looks of an accountant – right down to the dark suit and white shirt, crisp gray tie, and glossy black oxford shoes. His golden-brown hair was short, impeccably styled, not a strand out of place. Although the male was sizable beneath all that spit and polish, he brought to mind one of those chiseled pretty boys that you see in human magazine ads, hawking designer clothing or expensive cologne.

Scowling, Dante shook his head. 'Tell me that's not one of the new warrior candidates.'

'That,' said Gideon, 'is Agent Sterling Chase, of the Boston Darkhaven.'

A Darkhaven law-enforcement agent. Well, that made some sense. Certainly explained the vampire's buttoned-up, useless-bureaucrat appearance. 'What's he want with us?'

'Information. Some kind of alliance, from what I gather. The Darkhaven has sent him here in the hopes of obtaining the Order's help.'

'Our help.' Dante scoffed, skeptical. 'You gotta be kidding me. It wasn't so long ago that the general population of the Darkhavens were condemning us as lawless vigilantes.'

Walking beside him, Gideon glanced over with a smirk. 'Dinosaurs who'd outlived their time and ought to be forced into extinction was, I believe, one of the more polite suggestions.'

Ironic, considering the populations of those sanctuaries existed directly because of the warriors' continued efforts in fighting the Rogues. In the dark ages of man, long before Dante's eighteenth-century birth in Italy, the Order had acted as sole protector of the vampire race. Then, they were revered as heroes. In the time since, as the warriors hunted down and executed Rogues all over the globe, putting down even the smallest uprisings before they had a chance to take root, the Darkhavens had relaxed into a state of arrogant confidence. Rogue numbers had been few in modern times but were growing again. Meanwhile, the Darkhavens had adopted laws and procedures for dealing with Rogues as mere criminals, foolishly believing that incarceration and rehabilitation were viable solutions to the problem.

Those of the warrior class knew better. They saw the carnage up close and personal, while the rest of the population hid in their sanctuaries, pretending they were safe. Dante and the rest of the Order were the Breed's only true defense, and they chose to act independently – some might argue in defiance of – impotent Darkhaven law.

'Now they're asking for our help?' Dante fisted his hands at his side, in no mood to deal with Darkhaven politics or the fools who peddled them. 'I hope Lucan's called this meeting so we can prove we're savages and kill their friggin' messenger.'

Gideon chuckled as the glass doors of the lab whisked open in front of them. 'Try not to scare Agent Chase away before he's had a sporting chance to explain why he's here, will you, D?'

Gideon strode inside. Dante followed, giving a nod of respect to Lucan and his brethren as he entered the spacious control room. He turned his gaze on the Darkhaven agent, holding it steady as the civilian vampire rose from his chair at the conference table and looked upon Dante's bloodied, battered condition in barely concealed disgust.

Now he was damn glad he hadn't paused to tidy up before coming in. Hoping to offend further, Dante strolled up to the agent and held out his grimy hand in offered greeting.

'You must be the warrior called Dante,' said the low, cultured voice of the Darkhaven representative. He accepted Dante's outstretched hand and clasped it briefly. The agent sniffed almost imperceptibly, fine nostrils flaring as they picked up on Dante's certain stench. 'A privilege to meet you. I am Special Investigative Agent Sterling Chase, of the Boston Darkhaven. *Senior* Special Investigative Agent,' he added, smiling. 'But I've no wish to stand on ceremony, so please, all of you, feel free to address me as you will.'

Dante merely grunted, biting back the choice form of address that leaped to his tongue. Instead, he dropped into the seat next to the agent, holding him in a cool, unwavering stare.

Lucan cleared his throat, all it took for the eldest of the Breed to resume command of the gathering. 'Now that we're all here, let's get down to business. Agent Chase has brought some disturbing news from the Boston Darkhaven. There's been a rash of young vampires going missing lately. He'd like the Order's help in recovering them. I've told him we will.'

'Search and rescue's not exactly our thing,' Dante said, his eyes on the civilian as a rumble of agreement kicked up from around the table of warriors.

'That's true,' Nikolai put in. The Russian-born vampire grinned from under a long hank of sandy-colored hair that didn't quite conceal the wintry chill of his ice-blue gaze. 'We're more of a bag-and-tag operation.'

'There's more to this than just a few stray vampires out past curfew and in need of collars,' Lucan said. His grim tone dialed down the attitude in the room at once. 'I'll let Agent Chase explain what's going on.'

'Last month, a group of three Darkhaven youths left for a rave somewhere in the city and never returned. A week later, another two went missing. More disappearances have been happening from Boston area Darkhavens every night in the time since.' Agent Chase reached into a briefcase on the floor beside him and pulled out a thick file. He tossed it to the center of the conference table. From within the manila jacket, about a dozen snapshots spilled out – faces of smiling, youthful vampire males. 'These are just the reported disappearances so far. We've probably lost another couple of individuals in the time I've been here meeting with you.'

Dante sifted through the pile of photographs and passed the folder around the table, figuring they couldn't all be runaways. Life in the Darkhavens could be a bore to young males with something to prove to the world, but nothing was so bad it would drive groups of them away at a time. 'Have there been any recoveries at all? Any sightings? This many missing individuals in such a short period of time – seems like someone ought to know something about it.'

'There have been only a handful of recoveries.'

Chase brought out another file from his case, this one considerably thinner than the first. He withdrew a few photographs and fanned them out before him on the table. They were morgue shots. Three civilian vampires, current generation, and probably not one of them older than thirty-five years. In each photo, a pair of sightless eyes stared up at the camera lens, pupils elongated to hungered slits, the natural color of the irises saturated in the amber-yellow glow of Bloodlust.

'Rogues,' Niko said, practically hissing the word.

'No,' Agent Chase replied. 'They died in the throes of Bloodlust, but they hadn't yet turned. They were not Rogues.'

Dante got out of his chair and leaned over the table to have a closer look at the pictures. His gaze was drawn immediately to the crust of dried pinkish foam that circled the subjects' slack mouths. The same kind of saliva residue he'd spotted on his attacker outside the club earlier tonight. 'Any idea what killed them?'

Chase nodded. 'Narcotic overdose.'

'Any of you hear chatter around town about a new club drug called Crimson?' Lucan asked the group of warriors. None had. 'From what Agent Chase has told me, it's a particularly nasty bit of chemistry that's been showing up lately among the Breed's younger crowds. It's a stimulant and mild hallucinogenic that also produces a burst of enormous strength and endurance. But that's just the appetizer. The real fun starts about fifteen minutes into ingestion.'

'That's right,' Agent Chase added. 'Users who eat or inhale

this red powder soon experience extreme thirst and feverlike chills. They convulse into a mindless, animal state, exhibiting all the traits of Bloodlust, from the fixed, elliptical pupils and permanently extruded fangs to the insatiable need for blood. If the individual is left to quench that need, he is almost certain to turn Rogue. If he continues to use Crimson, this,' Chase said, pointing to the morgue photos, 'is the other outcome.'

Dante cursed, half in frustration for the epidemic hysteria just waiting to erupt among the Darkhaven populations, but also for the realization that the young Bloodlusting vampire he'd killed tonight was a Breed youth, like these, hopped up on the shit Chase had just described. He had a hard time feeling bad about taking the kid out when he'd been coming at Dante like a ton of bricks.

'This drug, Crimson,' Dante said. 'Any thought on where it's coming from, who might be manufacturing it or distributing it?'

'We have nothing more to go on than what I've presented here.'

Dante saw Lucan's grave expression and understood where this was heading. 'Ah, and so this is where we come in, is that it?'

'The Darkhavens have asked for our assistance in identifying and, if practical or even possible, bringing back any missing civilians we might run across in our nightly patrols. Obviously, as a part of that, it is in our shared interest to put a stop to Crimson and those who deal in it. I think we can all agree that the last thing the Breed needs is more vampires turning Rogue.'

Dante nodded along with the others.

'The Order's willingness to assist with this problem is greatly appreciated. My thanks to all of you,' Chase said, letting his gaze settle on each of the Breed warriors in turn. 'But there is one more thing, if I may?'

Lucan gave a slight incline of his head, gesturing for the agent to continue.

Chase cleared his throat. 'I would like to have an active part in the operation.'

A long, heavy silence stretched out as Lucan scowled, leaning back in his chair at the head of the table. 'Active in what way?'

'I want to ride along with one or more members of the Order, to personally monitor the operation and to assist in the retrieval of these missing individuals.'

Seated on the other side of Dante, Nikolai burst out laughing.

Gideon raked his fingers through his cropped hair, then threw his pale blue shades onto the table. 'We don't take civilians along on our operations. Never have, never will.'

Even Tegan, the stoic one, who hadn't uttered a single word one way or the other throughout the entire meeting, was finally moved to voice his disagreement. 'You won't live to the end of your first night, Agent,' he said without inflection, only cold truth.

Dante held his disbelief inside, certain that Lucan would shut the agent down with the power of his level glare alone. But Lucan didn't reject the idea outright. He stood up, his fists braced on the edge of the conference table.

'Leave us,' he told Chase. 'My brethren and I will discuss your request privately. Our business here is finished for now, Agent Chase. You may return to the Darkhaven to await our decision. I will be in contact with you.'

Dante and the rest of the warriors stood too; then, after a long moment, so did the Darkhaven agent, retrieving his polished leather case from the floor beside him. Dante took a step out from the table. When Chase tried to move past him, he got the edge of Dante's thick shoulder blocking his path. Given no choice, he paused.

'Folks like you call us savages,' Dante said harshly, 'yet here you are, all posh and shiny in your suit and tie, asking for our help. Lucan speaks for the Order, and if he says we're going to bail your ass out on this little problem, then that's good enough for me. But it doesn't mean I have to like it. Doesn't mean I have to like you either.'

'I'm not hoping to win any popularity contests. And if you have misgivings about my proposed role in this investigation, by all means, state them.'

Dante chuckled, surprised by the challenge. He didn't think the guy had it in him. 'Well, now, I don't mean to stand on ceremony, Special Investigative Agent Chase – 'scuse me, *Senior* Special Investigative Agent – but what I do, what all of us in this room do, each and every night, is some dirty fucking work. We fight. We kill. We sure as shit don't run some kind of tourist program for Darkhaven agents looking to build their political careers on our blood and sweat.'

'Nor is that my intention, I assure you. All that matters to me is my charge to locate and recover the individuals who've gone missing from my community. If the Order can stop the proliferation of Crimson in the process, so much the better. For all of the Breed.'

'And how is it you feel you're even remotely qualified to go out on patrols with us?'

Agent Chase glanced around the room, possibly looking for support from any one of the warriors standing around the table. The room was quiet. Not even Lucan spoke on his behalf. Dante narrowed his gaze and smiled, half-hoping the silence would drive the agent away. Send him running back to his quiet little sanctuary with his tail between his legs.

Then Dante and the rest of the Order could get back to the business of dealing death to the Rogues – preferably without an audience and a goddamn scorecard.

'I hold a BA in Political Science from Columbia University,' Chase finally said. 'And, like my brother and my father before me, I have a law degree from Harvard, where I graduated at the top of my class. In addition, I am trained in three schools of martial arts and have an expert-marksman rating in a shooting range of eleven hundred feet. That measure being without the aid of a scope.'

'Is that right?' The résumé was impressive, but Dante hardly flinched in reaction. 'So, tell me, Harvard, how many times have you used your training – martial arts or weapons – outside of a classroom? How much of your blood have you spilled? How much have you taken from your enemies in the heat of battle?'

The agent held Dante's flat stare, the clean-shaven, square chin climbing up a notch. 'I'm not afraid to be tested on the street.'

'That's good,' Dante drawled. 'That's real good, because if you're thinking about going to the dance with any of us, you sure as hell will be put to the test.'

Chase bared his teeth in a tight smile. 'Thanks for the warning.'

He brushed past Dante, murmured his good-byes to Lucan and the others, then strolled out of the lab with his briefcase clutched hard in his hand.

When the glass doors slid closed behind the agent, Niko ground out a curse in his native Siberian tongue. 'That's some messed-up shit, Darkhaven pencil-pusher thinking he's got balls enough to ride with us.'

Dante shook his head, sharing the same opinion, but his thoughts were churning on something else equally troubling. Maybe more so.

'I got jumped downtown tonight,' he said, meeting the tense faces of his brethren. 'I thought it was a Rogue stalking prey outside a club. I fought with the son of a bitch, but he wasn't going down easy. Ended up pursuing him down to the riverfront, where I ran into a whole new mess of trouble. A group of heavily armed suckheads came at me hard.'

Gideon slanted a narrowed gaze on him. 'Damn, D. Why didn't you call in for support?'

'There wasn't time to do anything but try to save my own ass,' Dante said, recalling the viciousness of the attack. 'The thing is, that suckhead I chased down there fought like a demon. Virtually unstoppable, like a Gen One Rogue – maybe worse. And titanium didn't affect him.'

'If he was Rogue,' Lucan said, 'the titanium should have smoked him on the spot.'

'Right,' Dante agreed. 'He showed all the signs of advanced Bloodlust, but he hadn't actually turned Rogue. And there's more. That dried pink foam you can see in Chase's morgue shots? That suckhead had it too.'

'Shit,' Gideon said, picking up the photographs and showing them to the other warriors. 'So, in addition to dealing with the continuing problem of the Rogues, now we're coming up against Breed vampires hopped up on Crimson too. In the heat of the fight, how're we going to know what we've got in our crosshairs?'

'We won't,' Dante said.

Gideon shrugged. 'Suddenly things don't seem so black and white.'

Tegan, his expression placid and cool, exhaled a wry laugh. 'As of a few months ago, our problem with the Rogues became a war. Not a lot of room for gray in that picture.'

Niko nodded his head in agreement. 'If a suckhead wants to get in my shit – Crimson eater or Rogue – he's got one thing to look forward to: death. Let the Darkhavens sort through the rubble once it's all over.'

Lucan turned his attention to Dante. 'What about you, D? Care to weigh in on this?'

Dante crossed his arms over his chest, more than ready for that shower now and an end to a night that had only proceeded to go downhill since he got out of bed. 'From what little we know of Crimson, it doesn't sound good. All these missing civilians, with more all the time, is bound to start a panic in the Darkhaven populations in general. Bad enough we've got this new complication of Crimson users to deal with, but can any of you imagine the clusterfuck situation of having the streets overrun with a bunch of Darkhaven agents trying to ID missing persons and apprehend them on their own?'

Lucan nodded. 'Which brings us back to Agent Chase and his request to participate in this operation. He's come to us with the same concerns, not wanting to cause widespread panic yet needing to recover the missing and find a swift solution to the problem Crimson seems to be causing among the Breed. I think he could be a benefit to us, not only in the operation itself but down the road as well. It might be good for the Order to have an ally in the Darkhavens.'

Dante could not contain his scoff of incredulity. 'We've never needed them. We've been pulling their nancy assess out of fires for centuries, Lucan. Don't tell me we're going to start kissing up to them now. Fuck that, man! If we let them into our business, next thing you know, we'll have to ask their permission to take a piss.'

He'd gone too far. Lucan said nothing, but a glance to the other warriors and then the door sent all but Dante out of the room. Dante stared at the white marble floor beneath his sodden boots, getting the sense that he'd just stepped into a pit of misery.

No one lost control in front of Lucan.

He was the leader of the Order, had been since the initial formation of the elite cadre of warriors nearly seven hundred years ago, long before Dante or most of the other current members had been born. Lucan was first-generation Breed, his blood flowing with the genes of the Ancients, those vicious otherworlders who came to this planet millennia past, bred with human females, and started the first line of the vampire race. Gen Ones like Lucan were few now and remained the most powerful – and most volatile – of all the Breed.

He was Dante's mentor, a true friend, if Dante could be so bold as to claim the formidable warrior as such.

But that didn't mean Lucan wouldn't tear a hole in him if he felt Dante needed it.

'I could give a shit for Darkhaven PR, same as you,' Lucan said, the cadence of his deep voice measured and cool. 'But the news of this drug disturbs me. We need to find out who's sourcing it and sever that chain. It's too important to leave it to Darkhaven involvement. If keeping a lid on this operation for the time being so that we can get the situation under control, *on our terms*, means letting Agent Chase play warrior for a few nights, then that's the price we have to pay.'

When Dante opened his mouth to voice a further argument against the idea, Lucan arched a black brow and cut him off before he could get the first word out.

'I've decided that you will be the one to pair up with Agent Chase on patrol.'

Dante bit his tongue, knowing Lucan would abide no argument in this now.

'I choose you because you're the best one for the job, Dante. Tegan would probably kill the agent outright, just because he annoyed him. And Niko, while a capable warrior, does not have your years of experience on the street. Keep the Darkhaven agent out of trouble, but don't lose sight of the true goal: exterminating our enemies. I know you won't let me down. You never have. I'll contact Chase and let him know that his tour begins tomorrow night.'

Dante gave a low nod of acceptance, not trusting himself to speak when outrage was pouring through his veins. Lucan clapped him on the shoulder as if to say he understood Dante's simmering anger, then headed out of the lab. Dante could only stand there for a moment, his jaw clamped so tight his molars burned with the pressure.

Had he really walked into the compound thinking that this night couldn't get any worse?

Holy hell, had he been wrong about that.

After everything he'd been through the past twelve hours, culminating with this unwanted babysitting assignment, he was going to have to seriously recalibrate his idea of Fucked Up Beyond All Recognition.

CHAPTER SEVEN

'Here you go, Mrs. Corelli.' Tess lifted a plastic cat carrier over the reception counter, passing the growling, hissing white Persian back to its owner. 'Angel's not too happy right now, but he should be feeling back up to snuff in a couple of days. I wouldn't let him outside until the sutures have dissolved, though. Not that he's going to be feeling like much of a Romeo anymore.'

The elderly woman clucked her tongue. 'For months now, all up and down my street, what do I see? Little Angels running around. I tell you, I had no idea! And my poor smoochie-puss, coming home every night looking like a prizefighter, that pretty face of his torn up and bloody.'

'Well, he won't have a lot of interest in fighting anymore. Or in his other apparent pastime. You've done the right thing by having him neutered, Mrs. Corelli.'

'My husband would like to know if you'd do the same for our granddaughter's current boyfriend. *Ay*, but that boy is a wild one. Nothing but trouble and he's only fifteen!'

Tess laughed. 'My practice is limited to animals, I'm afraid.'

'More's the pity. Now, what do I owe you, dear?' Tess watched the elderly woman dig out her checkbook with chapped, arthritic hands. Even though she was well past retirement age, Mrs. Corelli cleaned houses five days a week, Tess knew. It was hard work, and the wages were meager, but since her husband's disability pay had dried up a few years ago, Mrs. Corelli had become the sole provider for her household. Whenever Tess felt tempted to sulk because she was strapped and struggling, she thought about this woman and how she soldiered on with dignity and grace.

'We're actually running a special on services right now, Mrs. Corelli. So your grand total for today is twenty dollars.'

'Are you sure, dear?' At Tess's insistent nod, the woman paid the clinic fee, then tucked the pet carrier under her arm and headed for the exit. 'Thank you, Doctor Tess.'

'You're very welcome.'

As the door closed behind her client, Tess glanced to the clock on the waiting-room wall. Just after four. The day had seemed to drag on endlessly, no doubt due to the strange night she'd had. She had considered canceling her appointments and staying home, but she'd marshaled herself and worked the full day. One more appointment, and then she could get out of here.

Although why she was so eager to race home to her empty apartment, she had no idea. She felt edgy and exhausted at the same time, her entire system buzzing with an odd kind of disquiet.

'You have a message from Ben,' Nora announced as she came out of one of the dog-grooming rooms. 'It's on a sticky note by the phone. Something about a fancy art thing tomorrow night? He said you mentioned you'd go with him a few weeks ago, but he wanted to make sure you hadn't forgotten.'

'Oh, shit. The MFA dinner exhibit is tomorrow night?'

Nora gave her a wry look. 'Guess you forgot. Well, it sounds like fun anyway. Oh, and your four-twenty vaccination called to cancel. One of the girls called in sick at the diner, so now she's working a double shift. She wanted to reschedule for next week.'

Tess gathered her long hair off her neck and rubbed the tight muscles at her nape. 'That's fine. Will you call her back and rebook the appointment for me?'

'Already did. You feeling okay?'

'Yeah. It was a long night, that's all.'

'So I heard. Ben told me what happened. Fell asleep at your desk again, eh?' Nora laughed, shaking her head. 'And Ben getting worried, calling the cops to look in on you? I'm glad he didn't get into hot water with them about that *stray cat* he picked up.'

'Me too.'

Ben had promised when he dropped her off at home that he'd turn right around and pick up Shiva from the clinic so he could take the animal back to its owners, like the police had instructed him to do. He wouldn't promise that another rescue attempt was out of the question, however. For what wasn't the first time, Tess wondered if his tenacious zeal, as well-intentioned as it was, might one day be his downfall.

'You know,' she said to her assistant, 'I still don't understand how I could have accidentally speed-dialed his number in my sleep. . . .'

'Huh. Maybe subconsciously you wanted to call him. Hey, maybe I should try that one night. Think he'd ride out to my rescue too?' At Tess's eye roll, Nora held up her hands in surrender. 'I'm just saying! He seems like a really great guy. Good-looking, smart, charming – and let's not forget totally into you. I don't know why you won't give him a fighting chance.'

Tess had given him a chance. More than one, in fact. And even though the problems she'd had with him seemed to be a thing of the past – he'd vowed time and again that they were – she was wary of becoming involved again beyond anything but friendship. Actually, she was beginning to think she might not be cut out for the whole relationship thing with anyone.

'Ben is a nice guy,' she said finally, picking up his message and stuffing it into the pocket of her khakis under her long white lab coat. 'But not everyone is all that they seem.'

With Mrs. Corelli's check topping off the day's receipts, Tess stamped it for the bank and started preparing a deposit slip.

'You want me to run that out for you on my way home?' Nora asked.

'No. I'll do it. Since we're clear of appointments now, I think I'm going to call it a day.' Tess zipped the deposit slip into the leather receipts envelope. When she looked up, Nora was gaping at her. 'What? What's wrong?'

'I don't know. Who the hell are you, and what have you done with my workaholic boss?'

Tess hesitated, sudden guilt about several days' worth of filing yet to be done making her second-guess the idea of quitting early – or rather, as it actually happened to be, on time.

'I'm kidding!' Nora said, already racing around the desk to herd Tess out into the small lobby. 'Go home. Relax. Do something fun, for crissake.'

Tess nodded, so grateful to have someone like Nora in her corner. 'Thanks. I don't know what I'd do without you.'

'Just remember that at my next pay review.'

It took only a couple of minutes for Tess to ditch her lab coat, grab her purse, and shut down the computer in her office. She left the clinic and walked out into the afternoon sunshine, unable to recall the last time she'd been able to quit work and stroll to the T station before dark. Enjoying the sudden freedom – her every sense seeming more alive and attuned than ever before – Tess took her sweet time, making it to the bank just before they were closing and then catching the subway home to the North End.

Her apartment was a tidy but unimpressive one-bedroom, one-bath unit, close enough to the expressway that she'd learned to consider the steady hiss of flowing, high-speed traffic to be her own brand of white noise. Not even the frequent horn blasts of impatient drivers or the squeal of vehicle brakes on the streets below her place ever really bothered her.

Until now.

Tess jogged up the two flights of stairs to her apartment, her head ringing with the din of street noise. She shut herself inside and sagged against the door, dropping her purse and keys onto an antique sewing machine table that she'd bought cheap and reincarnated into a vestibule sideboard. Kicking off her brown leather loafers, Tess padded into the living room to check her voice mail and think about dinner.

She had another message here from Ben. He was going to be in the North End that evening and hoped she wouldn't mind if he dropped by to check in on her, maybe head out to one of the neighborhood's pubs for a beer together.

He sounded so hopeful, so harmlessly friendly, that Tess's finger hovered over the call-back button for a long moment. She didn't want to encourage him, and it was bad enough she'd promised to be his date for the Boston MFA's modern-art exhibit.

Which was tomorrow night, she reminded herself again, wondering if there was any way for her to wiggle out of it. She wanted to, but she wouldn't. Ben had bought the tickets specifically because he knew she loved sculpture, and the works of some of her favorite artists would be on display in limited engagement.

It was a very thoughtful gift, and backing out now would only hurt Ben. She would attend the exhibit with him, but this would be the last time they did the couple thing, even just as friends.

With that matter as good as resolved in her mind, Tess flipped on her television, found an old rerun of *Friends*, then wandered into her galley kitchen in search of food. She went straight for the freezer, her usual source of sustenance.

Which orange box of frozen boredom would it be tonight?

Tess absently grabbed the nearest one and tore it open. As the cellophane-covered tray clattered onto her counter, she frowned. God, she was pathetic. Was this really how she intended to spend her rare evening out of the office?

Do something fun, Nora had said.

Tess was pretty sure nothing she had on her personal schedule right now would constitute fun. Not to Nora, anyway, and not to Tess herself either.

At nearly twenty-six years old, was this what she'd let her life become?

While her bitter feelings didn't stem merely from the prospect of bland rice and rubbery chicken, Tess eyed the frozen brick of food with contempt. When was the last time she'd actually cooked a nice meal from scratch, with her own two hands?

When was the last time she'd done something good just for herself?

Too damn long, she decided, and swept the stuff off the counter and into the trash.

Senior Special Investigative Agent Sterling Chase had reported to the warriors' compound promptly at dusk. To his credit he'd lost the suit and tie, opting for a graphite-colored knit shirt, black denim jeans, and lug-soled black leather boots. He'd even covered his light hair with a dark skullcap. Dressed like he was now, Dante could almost forget the guy was civilian.

Too bad no amount of camo could hide the fact that Harvard was, as of this very hour, Dante's official pain in the ass.

'If we ever need to knock over a bank, at least I know who to go to for wardrobe tips,' he said to the Darkhaven agent as he pulled on a leather trench coat loaded down with all manner of hand-to-hand weapons, and the two of them made their way to one of the Order's fleet vehicles in the compound's garage.

'I won't hold my breath waiting for your call,' Chase shot back drolly, taking in the prime collection of machinery. 'Looks like you folks do all right without resorting to grand larceny.'

The hangar-style garage held dozens of choice cars, SUVs, and cycles, some vintage, some current makes, every one of them a high-performance thing of beauty. Dante led him to a brand-new basalt-black Porsche Cayman S and clicked the remote locks open. The two of them climbed into the coupe, Chase looking around the sleek interior with clear appreciation as Dante fired up the engine, hit the code to open the hangar door, then let the sweet black beast begin its stealth prowl out into the night.

'The Order lives very well,' Chase remarked from next to Dante in the Porsche's dimly lit cockpit. He exhaled an amused chuckle. 'You know, a lot of the Darkhaven population believes that you are crude mercenaries, still living like lawless animals in underground caves.'

'That so,' Dante murmured, glaring out at the twilit stretch of road ahead of him. With his right hand, he flipped open the center console and pulled out a leather satchel containing a small cache of weapons. He dropped the lot of them – sheathed knives, a length of thick chain, and a holstered semiautomatic pistol – into the agent's lap. 'Suit up, Harvard. I assume you can figure out which end of that tricked-out Beretta 92FS is the one you're gonna need to point at the bad guys. You know, seeing how you're from the rarefied halls of the Darkhavens and all.'

Chase shook his head, muttered an expletive. 'Look, that wasn't what I meant—'

'I don't give a shit what you meant,' Dante replied, taking a hard left around a city warehouse and peeling down an empty back street. 'I don't give a shit what you think about me or my brethren. Let's get that straight right up front, *capisce?* You're riding along only because Lucan says you're riding along. The best thing you can do through all of this is sit tight, shut up, and stay the hell out of my way.'

Anger spiked in the agent's eyes, the heat of it rolling off him in waves. Although Dante could tell Chase was not accustomed to taking orders – especially from someone he might consider a few steps beneath him in the social order of things – the Darkhaven male kept his irritation to himself. He rigged up in the hardware Dante had given him, checking the safety on the pistol and then shrugging into the leather chest holster.

Dante drove into Boston's North End, following a tip Gideon had gotten about a possible rave to take place in one of the area's old buildings. At seven-thirty in the evening, they still had about five hours to kill before any activity around the location would prove out the tip one way or the other. But Dante had never been one to abide that kind of patience. He didn't do sit-and-wait, being more of the mind that death had a harder time catching up to a moving target.

He cut the lights and parked the Porsche down the street from the building they'd be staking out. A breeze kicked up, sending a smatter of leaves and city dust skating across the hood of the vehicle. When it had passed, Dante slid the window down and let the coolness come inside. He took a deep breath, dragging in a lungful of the crisp, late-autumn air.

Something spicy-sweet tickled his nostrils, sending every cell in his body into instant alert. The scent was distant and elusive, nothing manufactured by man, Breed, or any of their collective sciences. It was dusky warm, like cinnamon and vanilla, although to call it such only captured the smallest fraction of its mystique. The scent was something exquisite and singular.

Dante knew it at once. It belonged to the female he'd fed from – the Breedmate he'd so carelessly claimed as his less than twenty-four hours ago.

Tess.

Dante opened the car door and got out. 'What are we doing?'

'You're staying here,' he instructed Chase, drawn inexorably toward her, his feet already moving on the pavement.

'What is it?' The agent drew his gun and started to get out

of the Porsche like he meant to tail Dante on foot. 'Tell me what's happening, damn it. Do you see something out there?'

'Stay in the fucking car, Harvard. And keep your eyes and ears on that building. I've got to check something out.'

Dante didn't think anything was going to go down at their posted location in the next few minutes, but if it did, at that moment he didn't really care. All he knew was the scent of that perfume on the night wind and the realization that the female was near.

His female, came the dark reminder from somewhere inside him.

Dante tracked her like a predator. Like all of the Breed, he was gifted with heightened senses, super speed, and animal agility. When they wanted, vampires could move among humans undetected, nothing more than a cool breeze on the back of their necks as they passed them by. Dante used that preternatural skill now, navigating the clogged streets and back alleys, his senses trained on his quarry.

He rounded a corner onto the busy main street, and there she was, across the width of the pavement, on the other side.

Dante went still where he stood, watching as Tess shopped in a lighted open-air market, carefully selecting fresh greens and vegetables. She dropped a yellow squash into her canvas shopping bag, then perused a bin of fruit, stopping to lift a pale cantaloupe to her nose and test its ripeness.

Thinking back on the moment he first saw her in her clinic, even through the haze of his injuries, Dante had recognized that she was beautiful. But tonight, under the strand of small white lights illuminating the produce bins, she looked radiant. Her cheeks were flushed pink, her blue-green eyes sparkling as she smiled over at the old proprietess and complimented her on the quality of the stand's offerings.

Dante moved up his side of the street, keeping to the shadows, unable to take his eyes off her. This close, the scent of her was inebriating and lush. He breathed in through his mouth, letting the spicy sweetness of her sift through his teeth, relishing the way it played across his tongue.

God, but he wanted to taste her again.

He wanted to drink of her.

He wanted to take her.

Before he knew what he was doing, Dante stepped down off the curb and into the street. He could have been at her side in half a second, but something strange caught his eye.

He wasn't the only male watching Tess with evident interest.

A human stood in the shelter of a building entrance just a few doors down, peering around the casement at the market in an attempt to not be seen as he observed Tess finishing up her shopping. He didn't fit the stalker mold, with his tall, lean frame and college-boy good looks. Then again, neither had Ted Bundy.

Tess paid for her groceries and wished the old woman a good night. The instant she started to step away from the lighted awnings of the produce stand, the human carefully came out of his hiding place.

Dante seethed at the idea that Tess might meet with harm. He crossed the street in a blink, coming up on the human from behind and stalking within a few yards, ready to tear the man's arms off if he so much as breathed on her.

'Hey, Doc,' the man called out, familiarity in his voice. 'What's up?'

Tess spun around, gave him a surprised little smile. 'Ben, hi! What are you doing here?'

She knew him. Dante pulled back at once, easing off into the flow of pedestrians milling about the shops and restaurants.

'Didn't you get my message at your place? I had business up here, and I thought maybe we could have dinner or something.'

Dante watched as the human went up and hugged her, then

leaned down to give her a fond kiss on the cheek. The man's adoration was obvious. More than adoration; Dante detected the sharp tang of possessiveness radiating off the human male.

'Are we still on for the dinner exhibit at the museum tomorrow night?' the man asked her.

'Yeah, sure.' Tess nodded, surrendering her tote when he reached to take the burden from her. 'So, what should I wear to this thing, anyway?'

'Whatever you want. I know you'll be gorgeous, Doc.'

Of course. Dante understood it now. This was the boyfriend Tess had called at the clinic last night. The one she had turned to out of terror for what Dante had done to her.

Jealousy curdled in his gut – jealousy he had no true right to feel.

But his blood said different. His veins were alive and burning. The part of him that was not human at all urged him to plow through the crowd and tell the female that she was his, and his alone. Whether she knew it or not. Whether or not either of them willed it.

But a saner part of him lashed a collar around that beast and dragged it back.

Forced it to heel.

He didn't want a Breedmate. Never had, never would.

Dante watched Tess and her boyfriend stroll off ahead of him, their casual chatter all but lost amid other conversations and the general buzz of street noise swirling all around him. He hung back for a minute, blood pounding in his temples as well as other, lower regions of his anatomy.

Turning around, he loped off into the shadows, back to the building where he'd left Harvard on watch. He hoped like hell Gideon's tip about Rogue activity there was going to prove solid – the sooner, the better – because right about now he was itching for a good, bloody fight.

≈ CHAPTER EIGHT ≈

The North End stakeout was a bust. There had indeed been a rave at the old, empty building, but the partygoers were just a lot of humans. Not a Rogue in sight, and no sign of any Darkhaven vampires, let alone any misguided Breed youths jacked up on Crimson. Maybe it should have come as a relief that the city was quiet for a few hours, but after a patrol that had netted zero action all night, Dante was a good long way from relieved. He was frustrated, tense, and in severe need of some chill.

The cure for that was simple enough. He knew of about a dozen places topside where he could find a willing female with juicy veins and a warm, welcoming pair of thighs, and after dropping Chase off at his Darkhaven residence, Dante drove to an after-hours nightclub and parked the Porsche at the curb. He dialed the compound on his cell phone and gave a quick recap of the night's nonevents to Gideon.

'Look at the bright side, D. You went seven full hours without killing the Darkhaven agent,' Gideon remarked slyly. 'That's an impressive benchmark in itself. We've got a pool going over here about how long the guy's going to last. For what it's worth, my money's on nineteen hours, tops.'

'Yeah?' Dante chuckled. 'Put me down for seven and a half.'

'That bad, eh?'

'I suppose it could have been worse. At least Harvard knows how to follow orders, even if he seems the type to prefer being in charge.'

Dante glanced in his side mirror, distracted by a wedge of pale female belly and half-exposed, leather miniskirt-clad hips that were currently snaking around the left taillight of the vehicle. Perched on steep platform heels, she rolled toward the closed window with a practiced strut that suggested she was a pro. When she leaned down and shot him a glimpse of fleshy tits, a street-hardened smile, and heroin-vacant eyes, she removed all doubt.

'Lookin' for some company, handsome?' she mouthed at the darkened glass, unable to see who she was propositioning and evidently not caring, based on the quality of his ride.

Dante ignored her. Even a live-for-the-moment libertine like himself had certain standards. He hardly noticed as the prostitute shrugged, dejected, and moved on up the street. 'I need you to run a search on something for me, Gid.'

'You got it,' he said, the clack of a keyboard being drafted into action sounding in the background. 'What do you need?'

'Can you find anything on some kind of museum event taking place tomorrow night? A dinner or something like that?'

It took only a second for Gideon to come back with a reply. 'I've got a social-pages listing for a chichi patrons' dinner exhibit at the Museum of Fine Arts. Tomorrow night, seven-thirty.'

That had to be the event Tess and her boyfriend were talking about at the produce stand. *Their date.*

Not that he should care what the female was doing, or with whom. It shouldn't put his blood on a hard boil to think of another man touching her, kissing her. Burying himself inside her body.

It shouldn't register on his fury meter at all, but damn if it didn't.

'What's going down at the MFA?' Gideon asked, breaking into his thoughts. 'You got a lead on something over there?'

'No. Nothing like that. Just curious, that's all.'

'What, you're suddenly into the arts?' The warrior chuckled.

'Jesus, maybe a few hours with Harvard is having an adverse effect on you. Never figured you for the highbrow shit.'

Dante wasn't a total cultureless heathen, but he wasn't in any frame of mind to explain himself right now.

'Forget it,' he all but snapped into the cell phone.

His irritation was only slightly improved when he noticed he was being sized up again. This time it was two pretty females who looked like they'd come in from the suburbs for a good time. College girls, he was guessing, based on the fresh faces, perky twenty-something bods, and torn, faux-vintage designer jeans. They were giggling and trying to act unimpressed as they approached the car on their way into the club.

'So, where are we, D? You on your way back to base now?'

'No,' he said, voice low as he cut the engine and let his gaze trail the women as they passed. 'Night's still young. I think I'll stop off for a quick bite first. Maybe two.'

Sterling Chase prowled his Darkhaven residence like a caged animal, edgy and anxious. Although the night hadn't exactly been a success by any measure, he had to admit a certain exhilaration his first time out on his mission. He didn't care much for the arrogant, antagonistic warrior he'd been partnered with, but he reminded himself that his purpose in seeking the Order's help far outweighed any of the bullshit he would likely be subjected to by Dante or his brethren these next few weeks.

He'd been home for a couple of hours now. A couple more and it would be daybreak, not that he would feel much like sleeping.

At the moment, he felt like talking to someone.

Of course, the first to come to mind was Elise.

But at this hour she would be retired to her quarters, preparing for bed. It didn't take much for him to picture her seated at her delicate little vanity, probably nude beneath yards of gauzy white silk and brushing out her long blond hair. Her lavender eyes were likely closed as she hummed absently to herself – a habit she'd had since he'd first met her, and one that only endeared her to him all the more.

She was fragile and sweet, a widow going on five years now. Elise would never pair with another; in his heart of hearts, he knew that. And part of him was glad for her refusal to love again – the right of every Breedmate who lost her beloved – because while it meant he would live in the misery of wanting her, he would not have to accept the even more crushing blow of seeing her bonded to another male.

But without a male of the Breed to nourish her with the time-altering gift of his blood, Elise, born human like every other Breedmate, would one day grow old and die. This was the thing that saddened him the most. He might never truly have her, but it was a certainty that one day, probably no more than a scant sixty or seventy years from now – a blink of time, to those of his kind – he would lose her completely.

Perhaps it was that idea that made him want so badly to spare her every hurt that he could.

He loved her now, as always.

It shamed him, how much she affected him. Just thinking of her, his skin felt tight and too warm. She made him burn inside, and she could never know the truth of that. She would despise him for it, he was sure.

But that didn't stop the clawing itch to be near her.

To be naked with her, even just once.

Chase stopped his pacing and dropped down onto the large sofa in his den. He sat back, thighs spread, head back on his shoulders, staring up at the tall white ceiling some ten feet above him.

She was there, in that bedroom over this very space.

If he breathed deeply enough, he could catch the faint rose and heather scent of her. Chase sucked in a long draft of air. Hunger coiled in him, stretching his fangs from his gums. He licked his lips, almost able to imagine the taste of her.

Sweet torture, that.

He imagined her padding barefoot across the carpeted floor of her room, unlacing the ties of her flimsy nightgown. Letting the silk fall near the bed as she climbed onto cool sheets and lay there, uncovered, uninhibited, her nipples like rosebuds against the paleness of her skin.

Chase's throat was desert dry. His pulse kicked into a hard drum, blood flowing hot through his veins. His cock was stiff within the confinement of his black jeans. He reached for the ache of his sex, palming his erection over the thick fabric and straining buttoned fly. Stroking himself the way Elise never would.

He rubbed more urgently, but it only made the need worse.

He would never stop wanting . . .

'Jesus Christ,' he muttered, disgusted with himself for his weakness.

He yanked his hand away and got up with a hiss of anger, denying himself even so much as the fantasy of bedding his perfect, unattainable Elise.

Heat licked along the length of Dante's bare legs. It climbed higher, over his hips and torso, snaking up his spine and around his shoulders. Relentless, consuming, the heat pressed deeper, like an unstoppable wave crashing over him in slow-motion torment. It burned ever stronger, growing ever hotter, all but engulfing him.

He couldn't move, no longer in control of his limbs or even his own thoughts.

All he knew was the fire.

And the fact that it was killing him.

Flames were twisting all around him now, smoke churning black, searing his eyes and scorching his throat with every futile, gasping breath he tried to take.

No use.

He was trapped.

He felt his skin blistering. Heard the sickening crackle of his clothing – his hair too – catching fire while he registered it all in stark, debilitating horror.

There was no way out.

Death was coming.

He felt the dark hand descend on him, pushing him down, toward a vortex of seething, endless nothing –

'No!'

Dante came awake with a jolt, every muscle tensed to fight. He tried to move, but something held him down. A slight weight draped across his thighs. Another lying limply across his chest. Both females stirred on the bed, one of them making a purring noise as she nestled against him and stroked his clammy skin.

'What'sa matter, baby?'

'Get off me,' he muttered, his voice raw and thready in his parched throat.

Dante extricated himself from the tangle of naked limbs and put his bare feet on the floor of the unfamiliar apartment. He could hardly catch his breath yet, his heart still hammering hard. He felt fingers running up the small of his back. Irritated by the unwanted touch, he got up off the sagging mattress and began searching for his clothes in the dark.

'Don't go,' one of them complained. 'Mia and I aren't finished with you yet.'

He didn't answer. All he wanted right now was to be moving. He'd been still for too long. Long enough for death to come looking for him.

'You okay?' asked the other girl. 'You have a bad dream or something?'

Bad dream, he thought wryly.

Far from it.

He'd been seeing the same vision – living it in vivid detail – for as long as he could remember.

It was a glimpse of the future.

His own death.

He knew every agonizing second of his final few moments of life; all that remained unanswered was the why, the where, and the when of it. He even knew who to credit for the curse of his vision.

The human woman who bore him in Italy some 229 years ago had seen not only her own death but that of her beloved mate, the Darkhaven vampire who had been Dante's scholarly, aristocratic father. Just as she'd envisioned it, that gentle female met a tragic demise, drowning in an ocean riptide after she'd swum out to pull a child from the same disaster. Dante's father, she had predicted, would be slain by a jealous political rival. Some eighty years after her death, outside a crowded meeting hall in the Rome Darkhaven, Dante had lost his father just as his mother had described.

His mother's unique Breedmate gift had passed down to her sole offspring, as was often the case among the Breed, and now Dante was the one damned with death visions.

'Come back to bed,' one of the young women pleaded from behind him. 'Come on, don't be such a drag.'

Yanking on his clothes and boots, Dante strolled back over to the bed. The females pawed at him as he came near, their movements drowsy and fumbling, their minds still sluggish from the thrall of his earlier bite. He had sealed their wounds right after he'd fed, but there remained one thing to do before he could make his escape. Dante reached out and put his palm against the brow of one girl, then the other, scrubbing all recollection of this night from their thoughts.

If only he could do the same for himself, he thought, his throat still dry with the taste of smoke and ash and death.

❧ CHAPTER NINE ❧

'Relax, Tess.' Ben's hand came to rest at the small of her back, his head bent low near her ear. 'In case you hadn't noticed, this is a cocktail reception, not a funeral.'

Which was a good thing, Tess thought, glancing down at her garnet-colored dress. Although the simple, resale-shop halter was a favorite, she was the only one wearing color amid the general sea of black. She felt out of place, conspicuous.

Not that she was used to fitting in among other people. She never had, not from the time she was a little girl. She was always . . . different. Always apart from the rest of the world in ways she didn't fully understand and had learned it better not to explore. Instead, she tried to fit in – pretended she did – like now, standing in a crowded room of strangers. The urge to bolt from the crush of it all was strong.

Actually, more and more, Tess was feeling like she was standing at the front of a rising storm. As if unseen forces were gathering all around her, shoving her out onto a bare ledge. She thought if she looked down at her feet, she might find nothing but chasm beneath her. A steep fall with no end in sight.

She rubbed her neck, feeling a dull sort of ache in the tendons below her ear.

'You okay?' Ben asked. 'You've been quiet all night.'

'Have I? I'm sorry. I don't mean to be.'

'Are you having a good time?'

She nodded, forcing a smile. 'This is an amazing exhibit,

Ben. The program says it's a private patrons' event, so how did you manage to get tickets?'

'Ah, I've got a few connections around town.' He shrugged, then downed the last of his champagne. 'Someone owed me a favor. And it's not what you're thinking,' he said, his tone chiding as he took her empty soda glass from her hand. 'I know the bartender, and he knows one of the girls who works in events here at the museum. Knowing how much you enjoy sculpture, a few months ago I put a bug in his ear about scoring me a couple of extra tickets for this reception.'

'And the favor?' Tess prompted, suspicious. She knew that Ben often mingled with some questionable people. 'What did you have to do for this guy?'

'His car was in the shop and I loaned him my van one night for a wedding he had to work. That's it, all on the up and up. Nothing shady.' Ben gave her one of his melting grins. 'Hey, I made you a promise, didn't I?'

Tess nodded vaguely.

'Speaking of the bar, how about I refresh our drinks – another mineral water with lime for the lady?'

'Yes, thank you.'

As Ben wended through the crowd, Tess resumed her perusal of the art collection on special display around the grand ballroom. There were hundreds of pieces of sculpture, representing thousands of years of history, all encased in tall Plexiglas kiosks.

Tess came up behind a group of blond, bronzed, be-jeweled society women who were blocking a case of Italian terra-cotta figurines and chattering about so-and-so's botched brow lift and Mrs. Somebody-or-other's recent affair with a country-club tennis pro less than half her age. Tess hovered in back of them, sincerely trying not to listen as she attempted to get a closer look at the elegant sculpture of Cornacchini's *Sleeping Endymion*.

She felt like an impostor, both as Ben's date tonight and

among these people at the museum patrons' event. This was more his crowd than hers. Born and reared in Boston, Ben had grown up around art museums and theater, while her cultural background had been limited to county fairs and the local cinema. What she knew about art was modest at best, but her love of sculpture had always been something of an escape for her, particularly in those troubled days back home in rural Illinois.

Back then, she'd been a different person, and Teresa Dawn Culver knew a few things about impostors. Her stepfather had made sure of that. From all appearances, he'd seemed a model citizen: successful, kind, moral. He was none of those things. But he was dead almost a decade now, her estranged mother recently dead as well. As for Tess, she had left that painful past nine years and half a country behind her.

If only she could leave the memories there too.

The awful knowledge of what she'd done . . .

Tess refocused her attention on the handsome lines of Endymion. As she studied the eighteenth-century terracotta sculpture, the fine hairs at the back of her neck began to tickle. A flush of heat washed over her – just the briefest skate of warmth, but enough to make her look around for the source. She found nothing. The pack of gossiping women moved on, and then it was only Tess at the display.

She peered into the glass case once more, letting the beauty of the artist's work transport her away from her private anxieties to a place of peace and comfort.

'*Exquisite.*'

A deep voice tinged with a faint, elegant accent drew her head up with a start. There, on the other side of the clear kiosk, stood a man. Tess found herself looking into whiskey-colored eyes fringed with thick, inky-black lashes. If she thought she stuck out like a sore thumb at this ritzy event, she had nothing on this guy.

Six and a half feet of darkness stared at her with hawkish

eyes and a stern, almost menacing air of confidence. He was a study in black, from the glossy waves of his hair, to the broad lines of his leather coat and body-hugging knit shirt, to his long legs, which appeared to be outfitted in black fatigues.

Despite his inappropriately casual attire, he held himself with a confidence that made him seem like he owned the place, projecting an air of power even in his stillness. People stared at him from all corners of the room, not with scorn or disapproval but with a deference – a respectful wariness – that Tess couldn't help feeling herself. She was gaping, she realized, and quickly glanced back into the case to avoid the heat of his unwavering gaze.

'It's – it's beautiful, yes,' she stammered, hoping like hell she didn't look as flustered as she felt.

Her heart was racing inexplicably, and that strange tingly ache was back in the side of her neck. She touched the place below her ear where her pulse now throbbed, trying to rub it away. The sensation only got worse, like a buzzing in her blood. She felt twitchy and nervous, in need of air. When she started to move on to another case of sculpture, the man came around the display, subtly stepping into her path.

'Cornacchini is a master,' he said, that silky growl rolling over the name like the purr of a big cat. 'I don't know all of his works, but my parents were great patrons of the arts back home in Italy.'

Italian. So that explained his gorgeous accent. Since she couldn't manage a smooth escape now, Tess nodded politely. 'Have you been in the States long?'

'Yes.' A smile pulled at the corner of his sensual mouth. 'I've been here for a very long time. I am called Dante,' he added, extending his large hand to her.

'Tess.' She accepted his greeting, nearly gasping as his fingers wrapped around hers in a moment of contact that was nothing short of electric.

Good Lord, the guy was gorgeous. Not model pretty but rugged and masculine, with a square-cut jaw and lean cheekbones. His full lips were enough to make any one of the collagen-plumped socialites at the reception weep with envy. In fact, his was the kind of profanely masculine face that artists had been trying to capture in clay and marble for centuries. His only visible flaw was a jag in the otherwise straight bridge of his nose.

A fighter? Tess wondered, some of her interest fading already. She had no use for violent men, even if they looked and sounded like fallen angels.

She offered him a pleasant smile and started to walk away. 'Enjoy the exhibit.'

'Wait. Why are you running away?' his hand came to rest on her forearm, only the slightest brush of contact, but it stilled her. 'Are you afraid of me, Tess?'

'No.' *What a strange question for him to ask.* 'Should I be?'

Something flickered in his eyes, then disappeared. 'No, I don't want that. I want you to stay, Tess.'

He kept saying her name, and every time it rolled off his tongue, she felt some of her anxiety melt away. 'Look, I'm, uh . . . I came here with someone,' she blurted out, reaching for the easiest excuse that came to her.

'Your boyfriend?' he asked, then turned his shrewd gaze unerringly toward the crowded bar where Ben had gone. 'You don't want him to come back and see us talking?'

It sounded ridiculous and she knew it. Ben had no claim over her, and even if they were still dating, she wouldn't let herself be dominated so much that she couldn't even talk with another man. That was all she was doing here with Dante, yet it felt intensely intimate. It felt illicit.

It felt dangerous, because despite everything she'd learned about protecting herself, about keeping her guard up, she was intrigued by this man, this stranger. She was attracted to him.

More than attracted, she felt connected to him in some inexplicable way.

He smiled at her, then began a slow prowl around the Cornacchini display. '*Sleeping Endymion*,' he said, reading the placard for the sculpture of the mythical shepherd boy. 'What do you think he dreams about, Tess?'

'You don't know the story?' At the subtle shake of his head, Tess drifted toward him, almost unaware that she was moving. Unable to stop herself until she was standing right beside Dante, their arms brushing against each other as she looked into the Plexiglas with him. 'Endymion dreams of Selene.'

'The Greek moon goddess,' Dante murmured next to her, his deep voice vibrating in her bones. 'And are they lovers, Tess?'

Lovers.

Warmth stirred somewhere deep inside her just to hear him speak the word. He'd said it casually enough, yet Tess heard the question as if he'd meant it for her ears alone. The low, ticklish hum in the side of her neck intensified again, pulsing in time to the sudden rise of her heartbeat. She cleared her throat, feeling strange and unsettled, all her senses sharpening.

'Endymion was a handsome shepherd boy,' she said finally, drawing on recollections of what she'd learned in a college mythology course. 'Selene, as you said, was the goddess of the moon.'

'A human and an immortal,' Dante remarked. She could feel his eyes on her now, that whiskey-colored gaze watching her. 'Not the ideal combination, is it? Someone usually ends up dead.'

Tess glanced at him. 'This is one of the few times things worked out.' She stared hard at the sculpture in order to avoid looking Dante's way again and confirming that he was still watching her, so close she could feel the heat of his body. She started talking again, needing to fill the space with something other than the awareness that was crackling around her. 'Selene could only be with Endymion at night. She wanted to be with him forever, so she begged Zeus to grant her lover eternal life. The god agreed and put the shepherd into an endless sleep, where he waits each night for his beloved Selene to visit him.'

'Happily ever after,' Dante drawled, a note of cynicism in his voice. 'Only in myths and fairy tales.'

'You don't believe in love?'

'Do you, Tess?'

She glanced up at him, into a penetrating, probing gaze that felt as intimate as a caress. 'I'd like to believe in it,' she said, not sure why she was admitting this now, to him. The fact that she had said so to him confused her. Anxious suddenly, she strolled over to a neighboring case of Rodin pieces. 'So, what's your interest in sculpture, Dante? Are you an artist or an enthusiast?'

'Neither.'

'Oh.' Dante kept pace with her, pausing beside her at the kiosk. Tess had dismissed him as out of place when she first saw him, but hearing him speak, seeing him up close, she had to admit that despite the fact that he looked like something out of a Wachowski brothers' action movie, there was an unmistakable level of sophistication about him. Beneath the leather and muscle, he had a worldly wiseness that intrigued her. Probably more than it should. 'What then? Are you a patron of the museum?'

He gave a mild shake of his dark head.

'Working security for the exhibit?' she guessed.

It would certainly explain his lack of formal wear and the laser-sharp intensity that radiated around him. Maybe he was from one of those high-end insurance units that museums often hired to protect their collections while on public display.

'There was something here I wanted to see,' he replied, his

mesmerizing eyes unflinching on her. 'That's the only reason I came.'

Something about the way he looked at her as he said it – the way he seemed to look right through her – gave her pulse a little jolt of electricity. She'd been hit on enough in the past to know when a guy was working some kind of angle, but this was different.

This man held her gaze with an intimacy that said she was already his. Not bravado or threat, but fact.

It didn't take much to imagine his large hands on her body, stroking her bare shoulders and arms. His sensual lips pressing against her mouth, his teeth gently grazing her neck.

Exquisite.

Tess stared up at him, at the slight curve of his lips, which hadn't moved despite the fact that she just heard him speak. He moved toward her regardless of the milling crowd – none of whom seemed to notice them at all – and tenderly traced the line of her cheek with his thumb. Tess could find no will to move as he leaned down and brushed his mouth along the curve of her jaw.

Heat ignited in her core, a slow burn that melted even more of her reason.

I came here tonight for you.

She couldn't have heard correctly – if for nothing else, the very fact that he hadn't said a word. Yet Dante's voice was in her head, soothing her when she should be alarmed. Making her believe, when everything reasonable told her she was experiencing the impossible.

Close your eyes, Tess.

Her eyelids fell shut and then his mouth moved over hers in a soft, mesmerizing kiss. It wasn't happening, Tess thought desperately. She wasn't really letting this man kiss her, was she? In the middle of a crowded room?

But his lips were warm on hers, his teeth roughly grazing as he sucked her lower lip between them before drawing back. Just like that, the sudden, surprising kiss was over. And Tess wanted more.

God, how she wanted.

She couldn't open her eyes for the way her blood was thrumming, every part of her hot with need and an impossible yearning. Tess weaved a little on her feet, panting and breathless, astonished at what she'd just experienced. She felt a cool breeze skim her body, raising goose bumps in its wake.

'Sorry I took so long.' Ben's voice jolted her eyes open as he strode up with drinks in hand. 'This place is a zoo. The line at the bar took forever.'

Startled, she glanced around for Dante. But he was gone. No sign of him at all – not anywhere near her or in the circulating crowd.

Ben handed her a glass of mineral water. Tess drank it quickly, half tempted to take his champagne and down that too.

'Oh, shit,' Ben said, frowning as he looked at her. 'There must be a chip in that glass, Tess. You've cut your lip.'

She brought her hand up to her mouth as Ben scrambled to give her a small white napkin. Her fingertips came away wet, vivid scarlet.

'Jesus, I'm sorry about that. I should have looked—'

'I'm okay, really.' She didn't quite know if that was true, but none of what she was feeling was Ben's fault. And she didn't have to check the glass to know there was no rough edge that might have caught on her lip. She must have bitten it herself when she and Dante . . . Well, she didn't even want to think about the strange encounter she'd had with him. 'You know, I'm feeling a little tired, Ben. Would you mind if we called it a night?'

He shook his head. 'No, that's fine. Whatever you want. Let's go get our coats.'

'Thank you.'

As they headed out, Tess cast one last glance at the clear display case where Endymion slept on, waiting for darkness and his otherworldly lover to come for him.

⇥ CHAPTER TEN ⇤

What the hell was he thinking?

Dante paced the shadows outside the museum, strung out in a bad way. Mistake number one had been coming here in the first place, thinking he'd just take another look at the female who, by Breed law, belonged to him. Mistake number two? Seeing her on the arm of her human boyfriend, looking like a vivid jewel in her dark red dress and strappy little sandals, and thinking he wouldn't have the need to look closer.

To touch.

To taste.

From there, things had pretty much sped out of the poor-judgment category and straight into disaster. His sex was raging for release, his vision sharpened by the narrowing of his pupils, still contracted to slits by his desire for the woman. His pulse was throbbing, his fangs stretched long in carnal hunger, all of which did nothing to curb his frustration over nearly losing control of the situation in there with Tess.

Dante could only imagine how far he would have been tempted to take things with Tess if her boyfriend hadn't returned when he did, with the crowd watching or not. There had been a moment, as the human male approached them from the bar, that Dante had entertained some rather primitive thoughts. Murderous thoughts, brought on by his want for Tess.

Jesus Christ.

He should never have come here tonight.

What had he been trying to prove? That he was stronger than the blood bond that linked her to him now?

All he'd proven was his own arrogance. His raging body would be reminding him of that fact for the rest of the night. The way he was knotted up right now, he might be strung out for the rest of the week.

Although he was finding it damn hard to regret feeling Tess melt for him so sweetly. The taste of her blood on his tongue when he'd nicked her lip with his fangs stayed with him, making the rest of his torment seem like child's play.

What he felt right now surpassed base need, carnal or otherwise. It had only been sixteen hours since he'd last fed, yet he thirsted for Tess like he'd gone sixteen days without nourishment. Sixteen hours since he'd last gotten off, and yet he could think of nothing he craved more than to bury himself inside her.

Seriously bad news, that's what he was dealing with here.

He needed to get his head on straight, and quick.

He hadn't forgotten that he still had a mission to contend with tonight. He was more than ready to focus on something other than the furious pound of his libido.

Digging into the pocket of his dark coat, Dante pulled out his cell and dialed the compound. 'Chase report in for patrol yet?' he barked into the device when Gideon picked up the call.

'Not yet. He's not due 'til ten-thirty.'

'What time is it now?'

'Uh, it's quarter to nine. Where are you, anyway?'

Dante exhaled a dry chuckle, every cell in his body still hardwired for want of Tess. 'Somewhere I never thought I would be, brother.'

And far too much time to kill before his second night of show-and-tell with Harvard began. Dante didn't have that much patience normally, let alone now. 'Call the Darkhaven for me,' he told Gideon. 'Tell Harvard that class begins early tonight. I'm on my way there to pick him up.'

Ben insisted on escorting her up to her apartment after the taxi dropped them off. His van was parked on the street below her place, and while Tess had hoped for quick a good-bye at the curb, Ben was intent on playing the gentleman and seeing her to her door on the second floor. His footsteps echoed hollowly behind her as the two of them climbed the old wooden stairs, then paused outside Apartment 2-F. Tess opened her evening bag and felt around inside for her key.

'I don't know if I told you,' Ben said softly at her back, 'but you look really beautiful tonight, Tess.'

She winced, feeling guilty for going with him to the exhibit, especially in light of what had so unexpectedly happened with the man she'd met there.

With Dante, she thought, his name sliding through her mind like dark, soft velvet.

'Thank you,' she murmured, and stuck her key into the lock. 'And thank you for taking me tonight, Ben. It was very sweet of you.'

As the door creaked open, she felt his fingers toy with a strand of her loose hair. 'Tess—'

She pivoted to tell him good night, to tell him that this would be the last time that she would go out with him as a couple, but as soon as she was facing him, Ben's mouth came down on hers in an impulsive kiss.

Tess drew back just as abruptly, too startled to couch her reaction. She didn't miss the wounded look in his eyes. The flash of bitter understanding reflected there as she lifted her hand to her lips and shook her head.

'Ben, I'm sorry, but I can't . . .'

He exhaled sharply, running a hand through his golden hair. 'Nah, forget it. My mistake.'

'I just . . .' Tess struggled for the right words. 'We can't keep doing this, you know. I want to be your friend, but—'

'I said forget it.' His voice was curt, stinging. 'You've told me how you feel, Doc. I guess I'm just a little slow on the uptake.'

'This is my fault, Ben. I shouldn't have gone with you tonight. I didn't mean for you to think that—'

He gave her a tight smile. 'I don't think anything. Anyway, I've got to go. Things to do, places to be.'

He started moving back toward the stairs. Tess came out into the hallway, feeling terrible for the way things were going. 'Ben, don't leave like this. Why don't you come in for a while? Let's talk.'

He didn't even answer, just looked at her for a long moment, then pivoted around and jogged down the steps. A few seconds later, the door of her apartment building banged shut. Tess went back inside, locked her door behind her, then drifted over to watch from her front window as Ben climbed into his van and sped away into the dark.

Behind the cover of dark sunglasses and the flickering light of strobes in the dance club, Dante scanned the crowd of flailing, gyrating humans. Since picking Chase up from his Darkhaven residence a couple of hours earlier, they'd run across only one Rogue, a rangy-looking male who'd been sniffing out prey among the homeless. Dante had given Harvard a quick lesson in the miracle of titanium when it meets a Rogue's corrupted blood system, smoking the suckhead on the spot.

More's the pity, because Dante was still itching for some up-close-and-personal combat. Before the night's patrol was through, he wanted to get bruised and bloody. Call it attitude adjustment, after the clusterfuck way he'd kicked things off tonight.

Harvard, on the other hand, looked like he'd kill for a long shower. Maybe a cold one, Dante thought, following the vampire's gaze across the club, to where a petite female with a long mane of cascading pale blond hair was standing with some other humans. Every time she tossed some of that flaxen silk over her shoulder, the Darkhaven agent seemed to crank tighter. He watched her hungrily, tracking her slightest movements and looking like he was ready to pounce.

Maybe she sensed the heat of the vampire's stare; human nervous systems tended to respond instinctively to the feeling of being stalked by otherworldly eyes. The blonde twirled a length of hair around her finger and cast a sidelong look over her shoulder, zeroing in on the Darkhaven agent with dark, inviting eyes.

'You're in luck, Harvard. Looks like she digs you too.'

Chase scowled, ignoring Blondie as she broke away from her pack for an obvious flyby. 'She is nothing that I want.'

'Could have fooled me.' Dante chuckled. 'What, you Darkhaven types don't do hot and interested?'

'Unlike others of our kind, I find it personally degrading to give in to my every urge, like some kind of animal who can't be brought to heel. I try to maintain some level of self-control.'

There was certainly something to be said for that, Dante thought irritably. 'Where the hell were you with that advice a few hours ago, Dr. Phil?'

Chase shot him a questioning look. 'Excuse me?'

'Never mind.'

Dante gestured to a knot of clubbers near the other end of the place. Among the humans was a small group of Darkhaven vampires, young civilian males who seemed less interested in the females throwing off fuck-me vibes than they were in whatever one of the human males appeared to be peddling in the center of the rowdy crowd.

'Some shit going down in the far corner,' he told Chase. 'Looks like they're busting out party favors. Come on, let's go crash—'

He'd barely gotten the words out before Dante realized what he was seeing. By then, all hell had broken loose.

One of the vampires took a hit of something, snorting it hard. His head snapped back on his shoulders and he let out a deep howl.

'Crimson,' Chase snarled, but Dante had already gathered that.

When the Darkhaven youth's chin came down again, he roared, baring long fangs and feral, glowing yellow eyes. The humans screamed. Chaos sent the small group scattering, but it was a clumsy break, and one of the females wasn't quite fast enough to escape. The vampire lunged for her, leaping on top of her, knocking her to the floor beneath him. The kid was lost to sudden, swift Bloodlust, his sharp teeth stretching longer in anticipation of his kill.

Two hundred people were about to witness a very bloody, very violent – and very public – vampire feeding.

Moving too fast for human eyes to see, Dante and Chase sliced through the crowded dance floor. They were closing in on the catastrophe taking place in the corner when Dante caught a glimpse of the human who was standing there holding a spilled vial of Crimson powder, his jaw slack with horror in the split second before he bolted out the club's back door.

Holy hell.

Dante knew the son of a bitch.

Not by name, but by face. He'd seen him just a few hours ago – with Tess, at the art museum.

The Crimson dealer was her boyfriend.

❧ CHAPTER ELEVEN ❧

'Go after him!' Dante called to Chase.

Although his gut impulse was to leap on the fleeing human and shred the bastard before his feet got their first taste of pavement, Dante had a bigger problem to deal with right here in the club. He catapulted onto the back of the raving Darkhaven youth and peeled him off his shrieking human prey. Dante threw the vampire into the nearest wall and crouched low to spring on him again.

'Get out of here!' he ordered the stricken female when she lay there at his feet, immobile in her shock. Everything would be happening too fast for her human mind to sort out, Dante's voice no doubt coming to her ears as a growled, disembodied command. 'Move, damn it. Now!'

Dante didn't wait to see if she obeyed.

The Crimson eater came up off the floor, snarling and hissing, his fingers curled into claws. His gaping mouth dripped pink foam, globs of it stretching from the ends of his huge fangs. His pupils were narrowed to thin vertical slits, nothing but a blast of yellow fire surrounding them. The vampire's Bloodlusting focus was twitchy, head cocking from side to side as if he couldn't decide what he wanted more: an open human carotid or a piece of the one who'd interrupted his meal.

The vampire grunted, then made a lunge for the nearest human.

Dante flew at him like a hurricane.

Hurtling bodily down the back corridor of the club, the both of them smashed through the exit and rolled out onto the alley behind the place. There was no one out there – no sign of Chase or Tess's dealer boyfriend. There was only darkness and damp pavement and a Dumpster that reeked of week-old garbage.

With the Crimson eater snapping and clawing at him in a feral chaos of movement, Dante flicked a sharp mental command on the club's back door, slamming the thing shut and jamming the lock to keep the curious from wandering out into the fray.

The young Darkhaven vampire fought like he was crazed, bucking and kicking, thrashing and fighting like he was amped up on a shot of pure adrenaline. Dante felt something hot clamp down on his forearm and realized with not a little fury that the kid had sunk his fangs into his arm.

Dante roared, what little patience he had for the situation evaporating as he gripped his attacker's skull and launched the kid off him. The Darkhaven youth crashed against the side of the steel Dumpster, then slid to the pavement in a heap of gangly arms and legs.

Dante stalked over to him, his own eyes sharp with anger, throwing off the amber glow of fury. He could feel his fangs extruding, a physical reaction to the heat of battle. 'Get up,' he told the younger male. 'Get up, before I lift you up by your balls, asshole.'

The kid was growling low under his breath, muscles bunching as he collected himself. He stood up and pulled a knife out of the back pocket of his jeans. As weapons went it was pitiful, just a stubby blade with a fake horn handle. The utilitarian knife looked like something the kid had pilfered out of his father's toolbox.

'Now, what the fuck do you think you're gonna do with that?' Dante asked, coolly sliding his *malebranche* blade out of its sheath. The arc of polished steel with its sleek titanium edge gleamed like molten silver, even in the dark.

The Darkhaven youth eyed the custom-made dagger, then snarled and took a careless swipe at Dante.

'Don't be stupid, kid. That hard-on you're feeling is just the Crimson talking. Drop your blade, and let's take this shit down a notch, get you the help you need to come off your high.'

If the youth even heard Dante talking, it might as well have been coming at him in a foreign language. Nothing seemed to register. The vampire's glowing yellow eyes remained fixed and unresponsive, his breath sawing in and out of him from between his bared teeth. Thick pink spittle gathered at the corners of his mouth. He looked rabid, completely out of his mind.

He snarled. Took another swipe at Dante with the knife. As the edge of the blade came toward him, Dante moved his own weapon into the path to deflect it. The titanium-edged steel made contact, slicing across the back of the other male's hand.

The Darkhaven youth hissed in pain, but the sound stretched long, like a slow, wet sizzle.

'Ah, fuck,' Dante muttered, having come to know that sound well enough in his many years of hunting Rogues.

The Crimson eater was beyond saving. The drug had induced Bloodlust, strong enough in this young vampire that he had turned Rogue. The truth of that irreversible transformation was in the acid burn of his flesh where the titanium of Dante's blade had cut him.

The metal alloy worked fast; already the skin of the vampire's hand was corroding, dissolving, falling away. Red trails running up the Rogue's arm showed the poison racing through his bloodstream. Another few minutes and there would be nothing left of him but a percolating mass of melting flesh and bone. Hell of a way to go.

'Sorry, kid,' Dante told the wild-eyed Rogue before him.

In an act of mercy, he flipped the arced blade around in his hand and sliced it cleanly across the other vampire's neck.

'Jesus Christ – no!' Chase's shout preceded the hard pound of his footsteps on the asphalt of the alleyway. 'No! What the fuck are you doing?'

He drew up short next to Dante, just as the Rogue's body dropped lifelessly to the ground, its severed head rolling to rest nearby. Decomposition was swift but grisly. Chase recoiled, watching the process in abject horror.

'That was a—' Dante heard a thick catch in the agent's voice, like he was choking back bile. 'Son of a bitch! That was a Darkheaven civilian you just killed! He was a goddamn kid—'

'No,' Dante answered calmly as he cleaned his blade and resheathed it on his hip. 'What I killed was a Rogue, no longer a civilian or an innocent kid. The Crimson turned him, Chase. See for yourself.'

On the street in front of them, all that was left of the Rogue was a scattered pile of ash. The fine dust caught in the slight breeze, tracing across the pavement. Chase bent down to recover the crude knife from the scattering remains of its owner.

'Where's the dealer?' Dante asked, hoping like hell to get his hands on him next.

Chase shook his head. 'He got away from me. I lost track of him a few blocks from here. I thought I had him, but then he ran into a restaurant and I just . . . I lost him.'

'Forget it.' Dante wasn't worried about finding the guy; he only had to look for Tess, and sooner or later her boyfriend was bound to make an appearance. And he had to admit that taking the human out personally was something he looked forward to.

The Darkhaven agent swore under his breath as he stared down at the knife in his hands. 'That kid you killed – that Rogue,' he corrected, 'was from my community. He was a good kid from a good family, goddamn it. How am I going to tell them what happened to their son?'

Dante didn't know what to say. He couldn't apologize for the killing. This was war, no matter what the Darkhavens' official position might be on the situation. Once a Breed vampire turned Rogue – whether he turned from Crimson or the weakness present in all of the Breed – there was no coming back, no hope of rehabilitation. No second chances. If Harvard was going to run with the Order for any length of time, he'd better get a grip on that fact ASAP.

'Come on,' Dante said, clapping the grim-faced agent on the shoulder. 'We're finished here. You won't be able to save them all.'

Ben Sullivan didn't ease up on the gas until Boston's city lights were a distant glow in the rearview mirror. He turned off Route I just inside Revere, flooring the vehicle onto one of the industrial drives down near the river. His hands were shaking on the wheel, palms slick with sweat. His heart was beating like a jackhammer behind his rib cage. He couldn't catch his breath.

Holy shit.

What the *fuck* just happened back there at that club?

Some kind of overdose – it had to be. The guy who'd taken the hit of Crimson and lapsed into convulsions was a regular customer. Ben had sold to him at least half a dozen times in the past couple of weeks alone. He'd been manufacturing and dealing the mild stimulant on the club and rave circuit for months now – since the summer – and to his knowledge, nothing like this had ever happened before.

A goddamn overdose.

Ben pulled the van into a gravel yard outside an old warehouse, cut the lights, and sat there with the engine running.

He'd been tailed by someone on foot when he fled the club – one of the two big dudes who'd been somewhere inside the place and evidently had seen him dealing. They might have been undercover cops, maybe even DEA, but both the dark-haired one in sunglasses and his equally intimidating companion who came at Ben like a freight train looked to be the shoot-first, ask-questions-later types.

Ben wasn't about to wait around and find out. He'd run out of the club and made a frantic, helter-skelter dash in and out of the surrounding streets and alleyways, finally ditching his pursuer long enough to circle back, reach his van, and get the hell out of Dodge.

The situation at the club was still playing through his head in a haze of confusion. Everything had happened so fast. The kid taking the jumbo hit of Crimson. The first sign of trouble, when his body began to spasm as the drug entered his system. The freakish roar that came out of his mouth an instant later. The answering screams of the people around him.

The sheer chaos that ensued.

Most of those intense several minutes were still spinning through Ben's mind in strobe-light flashes of memory, some images clear, others lost to the dark fog of his panic. But there was one thing he was absolutely sure of. . . .

The kid had sprouted fucking fangs.

Sharp-ass canines that would have been damn hard to hide, not that the kid had been trying to conceal anything when he'd let out that bloodcurdling howl and made a grab for one of the club girls standing next to him.

Like he meant to rip her throat out with his teeth.

And his eyes. For crissake, they had been glowing bright amber, like they were on fire in his skull. Like they belonged on some kind of alien creature.

Ben knew what he saw, but it made zero sense. Not in this world, not by any brand of science he knew, and not in this reality, which cast things like that firmly into the realm of fiction.

Frankly, by everything he knew to be logical and true, what he had witnessed just wasn't possible.

But logic had little to do with the fear pounding through him right now or the chilling sense that his harmless little 'pharming' endeavor had suddenly veered way off the track. An overdose was bad enough, even worse that it had happened in a very public place, with him still on the premises to be identified. But the incredible effect the Crimson seemed to have on that kid – the monstrous transformation – was something off-the-charts unreal.

Ben turned the key in the ignition, sitting numbly as the van's engine rattled to a rest. He had to check his formula for the drug. Maybe the current batch was bad; he might have accidentally altered it somehow. Maybe the kid simply had an allergic reaction.

Yeah. An allergic reaction that just so happened to turn an otherwise normal-looking twentysomething into a bloodthirsting vampire.

'Jesus Christ,' Ben hissed as he climbed out of the van and hit the gravel below at an anxious jog.

He reached the old building and fumbled for the key to the big padlock on the door. With a metallic snick and a creak of the door's hinges, he entered his private lab. The place looked like shit outside, but inside, once you got past all the dilapidation and ghostly manufacturing remnants of the paper mill's previous occupation, the setup was actually pretty sweet – all of it provided by a wealthy, anonymous patron who'd commissioned Ben to focus his pharming efforts solely on the red powder known as Crimson.

Ben's office was located behind a spacious cell of ten-foot-high steel-link fencing. Inside, there was a gleaming stainless table weighted down by a collection of beakers, burners, a mortar and pestle, and a state-of-the-art digital scale. A wall of combination-locked cabinets housed canisters of assorted pharmaceutical drugs – serotonin accelerators, muscle relaxants, and other ingredients – none of it too hard to come by for an ex-chemist with business contacts in debt to him for numerous and varied favors.

He hadn't set out to be a drug dealer. In the beginning, after he was released from the cosmetics company where he'd been working as a chemical engineer and research-development manager, Ben would never have considered operating on the other side of the law. But his staunch opposition to animal abuse – the very thing that got him fired in the first place, after witnessing years of torture in the makeup company's testing labs – put a fire in Ben's belly to take a stand.

He started rescuing abandoned and neglected animals. Then he started stealing them when regular, legal channels proved too sluggish to be effective. From there, it was a short fall into other questionable activities, club drugs being an easy, relatively low-risk venture. After all, what was the crime in dealing fairly harmless recreational drugs to consenting adults? The way Ben saw it, his rescue operation needed funding and he had something of value to offer to the clubbers and candykids of the rave crowds – something they were going to get anyway from someone, somewhere, so why not him?

Unfortunately, Tess hadn't seen things from his perspective at all. Once she learned what he was doing, she broke it off with him. Ben had sworn up and down he would quit dealing – just for her – and he truly had, until his current patron came knocking last summer with a fat wad of cash in hand.

At the time, Ben hadn't understood the focused interest in Crimson. If he'd been paid to step up production and distribution of Ecstasy or GHB, maybe it would have made more sense, but Crimson – Ben's own private recipe – had been one of the milder products he had produced. In Ben's trials, conducted primarily on himself, he found that the drug generated a slightly more intense buzz than a caffeinated energy drink, with an increase in appetite and a lessening of inhibitions.

Crimson was a fast-hitting high, but fast-fading too. Its effects vanished after about an hour. In fact, the narcotic had seemed so innocuous, Ben could hardly justify the generous payment he'd been collecting for its manufacture and sale.

After what had happened tonight, he imagined those generous payments were about to come to an abrupt – and understandable – end.

He had to get in contact with his benefactor and report the terrible incident he'd witnessed at the nightclub. His patron needed to know about the apparent problems with the drug. Certainly he would have to agree that Crimson had to be taken out of circulation immediately.

⊸ CHAPTER TWELVE ⊷

D ante followed the soft rumble of conversation coming
from the formal dining room of the compound's mansion
at street level. He and Chase had arrived at the Order's
headquarters a few minutes before, after securing the scene at
the nightclub and doing a further comb of the area for signs
of trouble. Now Chase was in the tech lab below, logged on to
the Darkhaven computers, making his report of the night's
events.

Dante had his own report to make as well, one that definitely
wasn't going to win him any attaboys with the formidable
leader of the warriors.

He found Lucan seated at the head of the long, elegantly
set table in the candlelit dining room. The warrior was dressed
for combat, as though he had only recently returned from
patrol himself. From beneath his black leather jacket, an array
of weapons glinted, giving the impressive Gen One male an
even greater aura of danger and command than what normally
shrouded him.

His Breedmate didn't seem to mind his hard edges. Gabrielle
sat across Lucan's lap, her head resting lovingly on his shoulder
while she spoke across the table to Gideon and his mate, Savannah.
Whatever she'd said made the others laugh, including Lucan,
whose humor had been rare to nonexistent before the arrival of
the beautiful human female at the compound. The warrior smiled,
stroking her ginger-hued hair as gently as he might a kitten, a

gesture that seemed to have become automatic in the short few months since the pair had been blood-bonded and mated.

Lucan had it bad for his woman, and he didn't seem to give a damn for trying to pretend otherwise.

Even Gideon and Savannah, the other couple in the dining room, looked to be head over heels in love with each other. It was a fact that Dante hadn't ever questioned in the thirty-plus years they'd been together but hadn't really taken pointed notice of until this moment either. Seated together at the table, Gideon and his mate held hands, his thumb idly stroking the buttery brown skin of her long, tapered fingers. Savannah's dark cocoa eyes were soft when she gazed at her man, filled with a quiet joy that said there was nowhere else she'd rather be than at his side.

Was this what it meant to be blood-bonded to someone? Dante wondered.

Was this what he'd been denying himself all these long years?

The feeling struck him hard, from out of nowhere. He had forgotten what true love looked like, it had been so long since he'd paused to notice it. His parents had known a deep bond with each other. They had set an example for him that seemed untouchable, more than he could ever hope for. More than he had ever dared to imagine. Why should he, when death could take it all away in an instant? Death hadn't spared either one of them. He didn't want to feel that kind of pain, or bring it onto another.

Dante watched the two couples in the dining room, struck by the sense of intimacy – the deep and easy sense of family. It was so overpowering that he had the sudden, strong urge to back away and forget he'd been there at all. Screw his report of what went down tonight. It could wait until the other warriors came in from patrol too.

'You plan on standing in the hallway all night, or are you coming in?'

Shit.

So much for getting the hell out of there unnoticed. Lucan, among the most powerful of the Breed, had probably sensed Dante's presence in the mansion before he'd even come off the elevator from the compound below.

'What's going on?' Lucan asked as Dante reluctantly strode inside. 'We got trouble out there?'

'It's not good news, unfortunately.' Dante shoved his hands into his coat pockets and leaned a shoulder against the wainscoted wall of the dining room.

'Harvard and I had front-row seats tonight for a Crimson deal gone bad. A kid out of the local Darkhaven had a little more than he could handle, evidently. He went into Bloodlust at a dance club downtown, attacked a human, and nearly tore her throat open in front of a couple hundred witnesses.'

'Jesus,' Lucan hissed, his jaw clamped tight. Gabrielle slid off his lap, giving her mate the freedom to stand up and begin a hard pace. 'Tell me you were able to avert that disaster.'

Dante nodded. 'I peeled him off the woman before he could hurt her, but the kid was in bad shape. He'd turned, Lucan, just like that. By the time I hauled him out of the place, he was full-on Rogue. I took him behind the club and smoked him.'

'How awful,' Gabrielle said, her fine brows pinched.

Gideon's mate gestured to the bite wound on Dante's arm, which had nearly stopped bleeding. 'Are you all right?' Savannah asked. 'Looks like you and your coat could both use a few stitches.'

Dante shrugged, feeling awkward for all the feminine concern. 'It's nothing; I'm fine. Harvard's a little shook up, though. I'd sent him after the dealer, and he came back around just as I was finishing the job in the alley. I thought he was going to lose it seeing the Rogue go into cellular meltdown, but he managed to hold his shit together.'

'And the dealer?' Lucan prompted grimly.

'Got away from us. But I got a good look at him, and I think I know how to find him.'

'Good. That's your new priority one.'

A digital trill punctuated Lucan's order, the sound coming from the cell phone on the table near Gideon. The vampire reached for the device and flipped it open. 'It's Niko,' he said as he clicked on to the call. 'Yeah, buddy.'

The conversation was short and concise. 'He's on his way down to the compound,' Gideon told the others. 'He took out a Crimson eater who'd gone Rogue tonight too. He says Tegan's tally was at three the last time they touched base a couple of hours ago.'

'Son of a bitch,' Dante growled.

'What's going on out there, baby?' Savannah asked Gideon, her look of concern echoed in Gabrielle's eyes as well. 'Is it some kind of accident that this drug is turning vampires into Rogues, or is it something worse than that?'

'We don't know yet,' Gideon answered, his tone grave but honest.

Lucan halted his pacing, crossing his arms over his chest. 'But we need to find out quick, and I mean quick as in yesterday. We need to find that dealer. Find out where the shit is coming from and cut the supply off at the knees.'

Gideon scraped his fingers through his cropped blond hair. 'You want to hear an ugly scenario? Let's say you're a megalomaniac vampire on a quest for world domination. You start growing your army of Rogues, only to be thwarted when your headquarters is blown into the next century by your enemies. You run away with your tail between your legs, but you're still alive. You're pissed off. And let's not forget, you're still a dangerous lunatic.'

On the other side of the dining room, Lucan exhaled a vicious curse. As they all knew, Gideon was talking about Lucan's own kin, a Gen One vampire who was at one time a warrior himself and long presumed dead. It wasn't until the past summer, when the Order routed a growing faction of Rogues, that they'd discovered Lucan's brother was still alive.

Alive and well, and fashioning himself as the self-appointed leader of what had been shaping up to be a massive Rogue uprising. What could still be, considering that Marek had managed to elude the assault that took out his fledgling army and their base of operations.

'My brother is many things,' Lucan said thoughtfully, 'but I assure you, he is utterly sane. Marek has a plan. Wherever he escaped to, we can be sure that he is working on that plan. Whatever he's up to, he means to see it through.'

'Which means he needs to rebuild his numbers and build them fast,' Gideon said. 'Since it takes time and a lot of bad luck for a Breed vampire to go Rogue on his own, perhaps Marek has started looking for a way to give his recruiting efforts a little boost—'

'Crimson would make a hell of a draft card,' Dante interjected.

Gideon shot him a sober look. 'I shudder to think what Marek could do with the drug if it went global. We wouldn't be able to contain an epidemic of Breed civilians suddenly turning Rogue on Crimson. It would be complete anarchy all over the world.'

While Dante hated to consider that Gideon's speculations might be right, he had to admit he'd been having similar thoughts himself. And the idea that Tess's boyfriend was involved – that Tess herself might have anything at all to do with the problem Crimson was posing for the Breed – made his blood run cold in his veins.

Could Tess know anything about this? Could she be involved in some way, maybe aiding her boyfriend with pharming supplies from her clinic? Did either one of them realize what Crimson was capable of? Worse still, would either of them care, once they learned the truth: that vampires were walking among humankind and had been for thousands of years? Maybe the idea of a few dead bloodsuckers – or the entire race – wouldn't seem like such a bad thing from a human's perspective.

Dante needed to know what Tess's role in this situation was, if any, but he wasn't about to put her in the crosshairs of a Breed war until he found out that truth for himself. And there was a mercenary part of him that wasn't at all opposed to getting close to Tess in order to get close to her scumbag boyfriend. Close enough to kill the bastard, if need be.

Until then, he just hoped the Order could clamp a lid on the Crimson problem before things escalated any further out of control.

'Hi, Ben. It's me.' Tess closed her eyes, sank her forehead into her hand, and let out a sigh. 'Look, I know it's late to be calling, but I wanted you to know that I really hate the way we left things earlier tonight. I wish you had stayed and let me explain. You're my friend, Ben, and I've never wanted to hurt—'

A piercing *beeeeep* sliced into Tess's ear as Ben's answering machine cut her off. She hung up the phone and settled back on her sofa.

Maybe it was just as well that she didn't get a chance to finish. She was rambling anyway, too wired to sleep, even though it was almost midnight and her shift at the clinic would be starting in roughly six hours. She was awake, unnerved by the entire evening, and worrying over Ben, whom, she reminded herself again now, was a grown adult and not her responsibility.

She shouldn't worry, but she did.

Aside from Nora, who never met a stranger, Ben was Tess's closest friend. Her only friends, in fact. Without them, she had no one, although she had to admit her solitary way of living was by her own design. She wasn't like other people, not really, and that awareness had always kept her separate. It kept her alone.

Tess looked down at her hands, idly tracing the little birthmark between her right thumb and forefinger. Her hands were her trade, her source of creative outlet as well. When she was younger, back home in Illinois, she used to sculpt when sleep eluded her. She loved the feel of cool clay warming under her fingertips, the smooth stroke of her knife, the slowly emerging beauty that could be coaxed out of a shapeless mound of plaster or resin.

Tonight she had brought out some of her old supplies from the closet in the hallway; the box of tools and half-rendered pieces sat in a cardboard file box on the floor beside her. How often had she retreated into her sculpting to distance herself from her own life? How many times had the clay and knives and awls been her confidante, her best friend, always there for her when she could count on nothing else?

Tess's hands had given her purpose in life, but they were also her curse and the reason she couldn't trust anyone to truly know her.

No one could know what she'd done.

Memories battered the edges of her consciousness – the angry shouts, the tears, the stench of liquor and heated, panting breath blasting across her face. The frantic pumping of her arms and legs as she tried to escape hard, grasping hands. The weight that crushed down upon her in those last few moments before her life tumbled into a chasm of fear and regret.

Tess shoved all of that out of her mind, just as she'd been doing for the past nine years since she'd left her hometown to start her life over again. To try to be normal. To fit in somehow, even if that meant denying who she really was.

Is he breathing? Oh, my God, he's turning blue! What have you done to him, you little bitch?

The words came back so easily, the furious accusations as

cutting now as they had been then. This time of year always brought the memories back. Tomorrow – or rather, today, now that it was past midnight – marked the anniversary of when it all went to hell back home. Tess didn't like to remember it, but it was hard not to mark the day, since it was also her birthday. Twenty-six years old, but she still felt like that terrified girl of seventeen.

You're a killer, Teresa Dawn!

Getting up from the sofa, she padded over to the window in her pajamas and lifted the glass, letting the cold night air rush over her. Traffic hummed from the expressway and on the street below, horns honking intermittently, a lone siren wailing in the distance. The chill November wind sawed through the screen, riffling the sheers and drapes.

Look what you've done! You fix this right now, goddamn you!

Tess threw the window wider and stared out into the darkness, letting the night noises cocoon her as they muted the ghosts of her past.

⇥ CHAPTER THIRTEEN ⇤

'Jonas Redmond has gone missing.'

At the sound of Elise's voice, Chase turned off his computer monitor and looked up. Discreetly, without letting her see his movements, he slid the utility knife he'd recovered several hours ago while on patrol with Dante into one of his desk drawers.

'He went out last night with a couple of friends, but he didn't return with them.'

Elise stood in the open doorway of his study, a vision of beauty, even in the shapeless white mourning clothes that had been a constant about her for the past five years. The bell-sleeved tunic and long skirt fluttered around her petite figure, the only color being the red silk widow's sash that was tied loosely at her hips.

Never assuming, always rigidly proper, she wouldn't enter Chase's domain until he invited her in. He rose from his desk chair and held his hand out to her in welcome. 'Please,' he said, unable to take his eyes off her as she glided over the threshold and stood against the far wall.

'They say he took some kind of drug while they were at a nightclub, and he became crazed,' she said softly. 'He tried to attack someone. His friends got frightened and ran off. They lost him in the panic, and they don't know what happened to him. The whole day has passed without any word from him at all.'

Chase didn't reply. Elise wouldn't want to know the truth of it, and he would be the last person to subject her to the ugly details of his own firsthand knowledge of the young vampire's agonizing final moments of life.

'Jonas is one of Camden's best friends, you know.'

'Yes,' Chase said quietly. 'I know.'

Elise's smooth brow pinched, then she glanced away from him, fidgeting with her wedding band. 'Do you think it's possible that they might have found each other out there? Maybe Cam and Jonas are hiding together somewhere. They must be so scared, needing to find shelter from the sun. At least it will be dark again soon, just a few more hours. Maybe tonight there will be good news.'

Chase didn't realize he was moving until he saw that he was on the other side of his desk, only a few paces away from the spot where Elise stood. 'I will find Camden. I promised you I would. You have my vow, Elise: I won't rest until he is safe at home with you again.'

Her head bobbed weakly. 'I know you're doing all that you can. But you are sacrificing so much to search for Cam. I know how much you enjoyed your work with the Agency. Now you're getting involved with those dangerous thugs of the Order. . . .'

'You don't worry about any of that,' he told her gently. 'My decisions are my own to make. I know what I'm doing – and why.'

When she looked up at him now, she smiled, a rare gift that he devoured greedily and held close. 'Sterling, I understand that you and my husband had your differences. Quentin could be . . . inflexible at times. I know that he pushed you a great deal at the Agency. But he respected you more than he did anyone else. He always said you were the best, the one with the most potential to be something great. He cared for you, even if he often had trouble expressing that to you.' She drew in a breath, then exhaled it on a rushing sigh. 'He would be so grateful for what you are doing for us, Sterling. As I am.'

Looking into her warm lavender eyes, Chase pictured himself bringing Elise's son home like a prize he'd won just for her pleasure. There would be joyful tears and emotional embraces. He could almost feel her arms thrown around him in cathartic relief, her moist eyes anointing him as her personal champion. Her savior.

He lived for that chance now.

He craved it with a ferocity that startled him.

'I just want you to be happy,' he said, daring to move closer to her.

In a shameful instant, he imagined an alternate reality, where Elise belonged to him, her widow's garb flung away along with her memory of the strong, honorable mate she had loved so deeply and lost. In Chase's private dream, Elise's small body would be grown full and ripe with his child. He would give her a son to love and hold close. He would give her the world.

'You deserve to be happy, Elise.'

She made a small noise in the back of her throat, as though he had embarrassed her. 'It's very sweet of you to care. I don't know what I would do without you, especially now.'

She stepped toward him and put her hands on his shoulders, just the lightest touch, but enough to send a flood of heat racing through him. He braced himself, hardly breathing as she rose up on her toes and pressed her lips to the corner of his mouth. The kiss was brief, heartbreakingly chaste.

'Thank you, Sterling. I couldn't have asked for a more devoted brother-in-law.'

Tess perused the pastry case of a North End coffee shop, finally deciding on a decadent seven-layer brownie drizzled in caramel sauce. She normally didn't indulge and probably had no right to now, given her tight finances, but after a long day at work – a day that came on the heels of a long, nearly sleepless night – she was going to enjoy her brownie and cappuccino without a moment of guilt. Well, maybe just a small moment of guilt, which would be forgotten the instant all that sticky sweet goodness touched her tongue.

'I'll pay for that,' said a deep male voice from beside her.

Tess drew up sharply. She knew that low, beautifully accented voice, even though she'd heard it only once before.

'Dante,' she said, turning around to face him. 'Hi.'

'Hi.' He smiled, and Tess's heart did a crazy flutter in her chest. 'I'd like to pay for your, er . . . God, don't tell me that's your dinner?'

She laughed and shook her head. 'I had a late lunch at work. And you don't have to pay—'

'I insist.' He handed the barista a twenty and didn't accept the change. He didn't seem to notice the pretty cashier's coy look either, all of his focus rooted on Tess. The intensity of his gorgeous eyes, his entire presence, seemed to suck some of the air out of the too-warm room.

'Thank you,' she said, taking her bagged brownie and the paper cup away from the counter. 'Aren't you having anything?'

'I don't do sugar or caffeine. They're not my thing.'

'They're not? It just so happens they're two of my favorite vices.'

Dante made a soft sound in his throat, almost a purr. 'What are your others?'

'Working, mostly,' she said quickly, feeling her face flush as she turned to grab a few napkins from the dispenser at the end of the counter. A peculiar heat also traveled along her neck, tingling like a mild electrical charge. She felt it down to her marrow, in every surging vein. She was eager to change the subject, far too aware of the heat he was putting off as he trailed her casually toward the coffee-shop door. 'This is a surprise, seeing you here, Dante. Do you live nearby?'

'Not far. And you?'

'Just a couple of blocks away,' she said, walking with him outside into the cool night air. Now that she was standing next to him again, she couldn't stop thinking about their strange, sexually charged encounter at the museum exhibit. She'd been thinking about those incredible few moments pretty much constantly ever since, wondering if he might have been just a figment of her imagination – some dark kind of fantasy. Yet here he was, flesh and bone. So real that she could touch him. It shocked her how much she wanted to do just that.

It unnerved her, made her twitchy and anxious. Made her want to get away before the urge became something even stronger.

'Well,' she said, as she tipped her steaming cappuccino cup in his direction. 'Thanks again for the sugar and caffeine buzz. Good night.'

As she turned to walk up the sidewalk, Dante reached out and touched her arm. His mouth curved into an amused, if suspicious, smile. 'You're always running away from me, Tess.'

Was she? And really, why the hell shouldn't she? She hardly knew him, and what she did know of him seemed to send all of her senses into overdrive. 'I am not trying to run away from you—'

'Then let me give you a ride home.'

He pulled a small key ring out of his coat pocket, and a black Porsche parked at the curb gave a chirp, its lights flashing once in response. Nice car, she thought, not really surprised to find him driving something sleek, fast, and expensive.

'Thanks, but . . . that's okay, really. It's such a nice night, I was actually going to walk for a while.'

'May I join you?'

If he'd insisted in that confident, dominating way of his, Tess would have turned him down flat. But he was asking politely, as if he understood just how far she could be pushed. And although Tess had been craving alone time, tonight of all nights, when she thought about making excuses to leave him, the words simply wouldn't come. 'Um, sure. I guess so. If you want to.'

'I'd like nothing more.'

They began a slow stroll up the sidewalk, just another couple on a street full of tourists and residents enjoying the quaint neighborhood of the North End. For a long time, neither one of them spoke. Tess sipped her cappuccino and Dante surveyed the area with a hawkish intensity that made her feel both anxious and protected. She didn't see danger in any of the faces they passed, but Dante had a fierce vigilance about him that said he was ready for any situation.

'You never did tell me the other night what you do for a living. Are you a cop or something?'

He glanced over at her as they walked, his expression serious. 'I'm a warrior.'

'Warrior,' she said, skeptical of the antiquated term. 'What exactly does that mean – military? Special Forces? Vigilante?'

'In a sense, I'm all of those things. But I'm one of the good guys, Tess, I promise you. My brethren and I do whatever is necessary to maintain order and make sure that the weak and innocent are not preyed upon by the strong or corrupt.'

She didn't laugh, even though she wasn't at all certain he was serious. The way he described himself called to mind ancient ideals of justice and nobility, as though he subscribed to some kind of knightly code of honor. 'Well, I can't say I've ever seen that job description on a résumé before. As for me, I'm just your basic private-practice veterinarian.'

'What about your boyfriend? What does he do for a living?'

'Ex,' she admitted quietly. 'Ben and I have been broken up for a while now.'

Dante paused to look at her, something dark flashing across his features. 'You lied to me?'

'No, I said I was at the reception with Ben. You assumed he was my boyfriend.'

'And you let me believe it. Why?'

Tess shrugged, unsure. 'Maybe I didn't trust you with the truth.'

'But you do now?'

'I don't know. I don't trust very easily.'

'Neither do I,' he said, watching her more closly than ever now. They resumed walking. 'Tell me. How did you become involved with this . . . Ben?'

'We met a couple of years ago, through my practice. He's been a good friend to me.'

Dante grunted but said nothing more. Ahead of them less than a block was the Charles River, one of Tess's favorite places to walk. She led the way across the street and onto one of the paved trails that meandered along the riverfront.

'You don't really believe that,' Dante said when they neared the dark, rippling water of the Charles. 'You say he's a good friend, but you're not being honest. Not with me, and not with yourself either.'

Tess frowned. 'How could you possibly know what I think? You don't know anything about me.'

'Tell me I'm wrong.'

She started to say as much, but his unwavering gaze stripped her bare. He *did* know. God, how was it possible that she could feel so connected to him? How could he read her so clearly? She'd felt this same awareness – this instant, peculiar bond with him – at the museum.

'Last night, at the exhibit,' she said, her voice quiet in the cool darkness, 'you kissed me.'

'Yes.'

'Then you all but vanished without a word.'

'I had to leave. If I hadn't, I might not have stopped at just kissing you.'

'In the middle of a crowded ballroom?' He didn't say anything to deny it. And the slight, inviting curve of his lips sent arrows of fire licking through her veins. Tess shook her head. 'I'm not even sure why I let you do that to me.'

'Do you wish I hadn't?'

'It doesn't matter if I wished it or not.'

She picked up her pace, moving ahead of him on the walking path.

'You're running away again, Tess.'

'I am not!' She surprised herself by the frightened tone of her voice. And she was running, her feet trying to carry her as far away from him as possible, even though everything else within her was drawn to him like a magnetic field. She forced herself to stop. To remain still as Dante came up next to her and turned her to face him.

'We're all running away from something, Tess.'

She couldn't help scoffing a little. 'Even you?'

'Yeah. Even me.' He stared out at the river, then gave a nod as his gaze came back to her. 'You want to know the God's honest truth? I've been running all my life – longer than you could know.'

She found it hard to believe. Granted, she knew very little about him, but if she'd been asked to describe him in one word, it likely would have been *fearless*. Tess couldn't imagine what could make this immensely confident man doubt himself for a second. 'From what, Dante?'

'Death.' He was quiet for a moment, reflective. 'Sometimes I think if I just keep moving, if I don't allow myself to become anchored by hope or anything else that might tempt me to miss a step . . .' He exhaled a curse into the darkness. 'I don't know. I'm not sure it's possible to cheat fate, no matter how fast or how far we run.'

Tess thought about her own life, the damning past that had been haunting her for so long. She had tried to outrun it, but it was always there. Always shadowing every decision she made, reminding her of the curse that would never permit her to truly live. Even now – more and more lately – she wondered if it might be time to move on, start over.

'What do you think, Tess? What is it you run from?' She

didn't answer, torn between the need to protect her secrets and her longing to share them with someone who might not judge her, who might understand what had brought her to this place in her life, if not forgive her for it.

'It's okay,' Dante said gently. 'You don't have to tell me now. Come on, let's find a bench so you can sit and enjoy your sugar and caffeine. Never let it be said that I'd deny a woman any of her favorite vices.'

Dante watched Tess eat the thick, caramel-laced brownie, feeling her pleasure radiate across the small space that separated them on the river-walk bench. She'd offered him a bite, and although his kind could not consume crude human food in anything more than a mouthful, he accepted a small taste of the sticky chocolate confection if only to share in Tess's unabashed enjoyment. He swallowed the heavy, pretty much revolting bit of pasty sweetness with a tight smile.

'Good, huh?' Tess licked her chocolate-coated fingers, slipping one after the other into her mouth and sucking them clean.

'Delicious,' Dante said, watching her with his own brand of hunger.

'You can have some more if you want it.'

'No.' He drew back, shaking his head. 'No, it's all yours. Please. Enjoy it.'

She finished it off, then sipped the last of her coffee. As she got up to toss the empty bag and cup into a park trash bin, she was distracted by an elderly man who was walking a pair of small brown dogs along the riverfront. Tess said something to the old man, then dropped down into a crouch and let the dogs climb all over her.

Dante watched her laugh as the pair of them rolled and danced for her attention. That rigid guard he was so unsuccessful in breaching with her was gone now. For a few brief minutes, he saw what Tess was really like, without fear or mistrust.

She was glorious, and Dante felt an insane stab of envy for the two mutts who were benefiting from her uninhibited affection.

He strolled over and gave a nod of greeting to the old man as the gentleman and his dogs began to move on. Tess rose, still beaming, as she watched the beasts trot off with their master.

'You have quite a way with animals.'

'They're my business,' she said, as if she needed to explain her delight.

'You're good at it. That's obvious.'

'I like helping animals. It makes me feel . . . useful, I guess.'

'Maybe you could show me what you do sometime.'

Tess cocked her head at him. 'Do you have a pet?'

Dante should have said no, but he was still picturing her with those two ridiculous furballs and wishing that he could bring her some of that same joy. 'I keep a dog. Like those.'

'You do? What's its name?'

Dante cleared his throat, mentally casting about for what he might call a useless creature that depended on him for survival. 'Harvard,' he drawled, his lips curving with private humor. 'I call it Harvard.'

'Well, I'd love to meet him sometime, Dante.' A chilly breeze kicked up, and Tess shivered, rubbing her arms. 'It's getting kind of late. I should probably think about heading home.'

'Yeah, sure.' Dante nodded, kicking himself for making up a pet, for God's sake, just because it might win him some favor with Tess. On the other hand, it might also be a convenient way to spend more time with her, figure out just what she knew about Crimson and her ex-boyfriend's dealing operation.

'I enjoyed our walk, Dante.'

'So did I.'

Tess glanced down at her feet, a wistful look on her face.

'What is it?'

'Nothing. I just . . . I wasn't expecting anything good to happen tonight. It's generally not one of my favorite days.'

'Why not?'

She glanced up then, gave a vague shrug of her shoulder. 'It's my birthday.'

He chuckled. 'That's a bad thing?'

'I don't usually celebrate it. Let's just say I had a rather dysfunctional upbringing. It's not a big deal, really.'

Really, it was. Dante wouldn't have needed any part of a blood bond with Tess to understand that she was still hurting from a very old wound. He wanted to know everything about her pain and its source, his protective instincts firing up at the thought of Tess suffering any kind of unhappiness. But she was already moving away from him, inching toward the path that would lead them up to the street, back to her neighborhood. He reached for her hand, delaying her retreat. He wanted to pull her into his arms and hold her there.

'You should have reason to celebrate every day, Tess. Especially this one. I'm glad you let me spend some of it with you.'

She smiled – truly smiled, her eyes glimmering in the soft glow of the park lamps, her luscious mouth spreading into a beautiful, soft arc. Dante couldn't resist his need to feel her close to him. He tightened his fingers around hers and gently brought her toward him.

He looked down into her beautiful face, half lost to desire for her. 'No birthday is complete without a kiss.'

Like a gate slamming down before him, Tess's expression fell. She froze, then stiffened, pulling away from him. 'I don't like birthday kisses,' she blurted out on a rush of breath. 'I just . . . I think we should call it a night now, Dante.'

'Tess, I'm sorry—'

'I have to go.' She was already moving onto the path. Then she pivoted around and ran off at a quick jog, leaving him standing alone in the park to wonder what the hell had just happened.

⊰ CHAPTER FOURTEEN ⊱

Chase drove away from the Order's estate, itchy with frustration. There would be no patrol for him tonight. All of the warriors were out on solo missions, leaving Chase with several hours of darkness to kill on his own.

The death last night of Camden's friend still ate at him, making him all the more aware that the clock was ticking fast if he stood any hope of bringing his nephew home in one piece. Chase drove by some of the places Dante had taken him on their patrols of the city, both the known and lesser-known locations where humans and vampires tended to mingle.

He searched the streets and dockyards for Camden, prowling for any sign of him or any of his friends. Several hours into it, he was still coming up empty.

He was parked somewhere in Chinatown, about to head back to the Darkhaven, when he saw two Breed youths and a couple of human females enter an unmarked door up ahead of him. Chase cut the Lexus's engine and stepped out of the vehicle. As he approached the place where the group had gone, loud music bumped from somewhere down below street level. He opened the door and crept inside.

Down a long, barely lit flight of stairs was another door. This one had a human bouncer stationed outside it, but Chase had no trouble getting past the goth steak-head as he pressed a hundred-dollar bill in the guy's hand.

Deep, thumping bass filled Chase's head as he entered the

crowded club. Bodies thrashed everywhere he looked, the dancing having overtaken the room in a giant, bobbing mass. He scanned the thick crowd as he waded in farther, blue and red strobe lights blasting his eyes.

He stumbled into a drunken female who'd been dancing with some friends. Chase murmured an apology that she probably couldn't hear over the din. Belatedly, he realized that his hands were on her tight, round ass as he tried to keep her from falling.

She smiled up at him invitingly, licking her lips, which were stained bright red from the lollipop she was nursing. She danced up closer to him now, blatantly sexual as she rubbed her body against his. Chase stared at her mouth, then at the slender white column of her neck.

His veins started buzzing, a fever rising in his blood.

He should go. If Camden was in here somewhere, the odds of finding him were low. Too many people, too much noise.

The female snaked her hands up around his shoulders, grinding in front of him, her thighs brushing his. The skirt she wore was ridiculously short, so short that when she turned around and pressed her bottom into his groin, Chase saw that she wore nothing beneath it.

Jesus Christ.

He really had to get out of here –

Another pair of arms came around from behind him, one of the girl's friends deciding to play too. A third moved in and took the first one in a long wet kiss, both of them looking at Chase as their tongues slithered together like serpents.

His cock went instantly stiff in his pants. The female at his back reached down, stroking the bulge ever harder with her skilled, relentless fingers. Chase closed his eyes, feeling lust twine with another hunger, one he hadn't sated in nearly as long as his sexual urge. He was starving, his body craving both fulfillment and release.

The two females brought their kiss to him now, sharing his mouth while the crowd around them kept dancing, not caring about the carnal display taking place right there in the open. They weren't alone; Chase spotted more than one couple getting busy, more than one Breed vampire finding a Host amid the open sensuality of the place.

With a growl, Chase slid his hands under the first female's short skirt. He rucked the material up harshly, exposing her to his hungry gaze as her friend licked a hot trail along his neck.

Chase's fangs stretched long in his mouth as he plumbed the wet slit straddling his thigh. Her friends worked his zipper, tugging it down and reaching in to fondle his erection. Need coiled in him, the urge to fuck and feed overwhelming him. With a rough hand, he grabbed one of the females by the shoulders and pushed her down before him. She knelt there, freeing his cock and taking it into her mouth.

As she vigorously sucked him, and the other female rode his hand toward her own climax, Chase brought the third closer to his mouth. His fangs were throbbing even more than his sex, his vision sharpening as hunger slitted his pupils and heightened all of his senses. He parted his lips as the female's neck pressed against his mouth. With a sharp thrust, he clamped down on her, opening her vein and drawing the rich, warm blood through his teeth.

Chase fed quickly, if thoroughly, finding this uncharacteristic loss of control revolting. But he couldn't stop. He drank hard, and with each pull at his Host's vein, his release spiraled tighter in his groin. He pumped his hips, fisting one hand in the female's hair as she worked him toward climax. It was coming fast now, roaring through him. . . .

With a furious thrust he exploded. His mouth was still latched tight on his Host. He smoothed his tongue over the puncture wounds, sealing them closed. She was panting from her own release, all three women pawing him as they mewled and whimpered for more.

Chase pushed away from their grasping hands, hating what he'd just done. He brought his palm up to the forehead of his Host and wiped her memory. Then he did the same to the other two. He wanted to get out of there so badly, he was practically shaking with the idea. Stuffing himself back into his pants, Chase felt a niggle of awareness travel along his spine.

There were eyes on him somewhere across the room. He searched the crowd for the intrusion ... and found himself staring at one of the Order's warriors.

Tegan.

So much for holding himself to a higher standard than the Breed males who chose to live a life of violence and almost vigilante justice.

How much of Chase's degrading lack of control had Tegan seen? Probably all of it, although the vampire's expression betrayed nothing, just held him in a cold, flat, knowing gaze.

The warrior stared for another moment, then simply turned and strolled out of the place.

A pair of bright yellow eyes with slivered pupils stared back at Dante from his flat-screen computer monitor. The beast's mouth was dropped open, lips curled back from a fairly impressive set of fangs. It was a look of hissing fury, but the caption beneath the photograph described the subject as *a sweet and cuddly diva who would love to go home with you today.*

'Jesus,' Dante murmured, repulsed. He saw enough of that spitting, feral look every night he spent topside, hunting Rogues.

Hell, sometimes he saw the same hideousness reflected in his own mirror, when blood hunger, lust, or rage brought out his primal nature. Pain from his nightmare visions often did the trick too: slitting his pupils, turning his light brown eyes to fiery amber, and stretching his fangs out from his gums.

He'd had another one of those hellish dreams just today. It woke him out of a dead sleep around noon and left him sweating and shaky for several hours afterward. The damn things were getting more frequent lately, more intense. And the splintering headaches they left in their wake were real ass-kickers.

Dante nudged the wireless mouse next to his keyboard, scrolling past the *Felines* category to the *Canines*. He clicked the button to bring up the inventory of available animals, then did a quick scan through the photos. A few looked promising for his purposes, in particular a sad-faced hound named Barney who was *in need of special care and dreaming of a nice place to spend the last of his golden years.*

That ought to work. He certainly wasn't looking for anything long term.

Dante flipped open his cell phone and dialed the shelter's number. A gum-smacking young woman with a thick Boston accent picked up on about the fifth ring.

'Eastside Small Animal Rescue, can I help you?'

'I need one of your animals,' Dante told her.

'Excuse me?'

'The dog from your website, the old one. I want it.'

There was a beat of silence, then a loud crack of the girl's gum. 'Oh! You mean Baah-ney?'

'Yes, that one.'

'Well, I'm sorry, but he's been adopted. Is he still on our front page? They must have forgotten to update the website for him. What kind of dog are you looking for? We have several others who need good homes.'

'I need an animal tonight.'

She gave an uncertain little laugh. 'Um, that's not really how we work. We'd need you to come in and fill out an application, and then meet with one of our—'

'I can pay.'

'Well, that's fine, because we do require a small donation to help cover treatment and—'

'Would a hundred dollars suffice?'

'Er . . .'

'Two?' he asked, not really caring what it cost. 'It's very important to me.'

'Yeah,' she said, 'I'm, uh . . . I'm getting that idea.'

Dante lowered his voice and focused on the pliable human mind at the other end of the telephone connection. 'Help me out here. I really need one of your animals. Now, let's give it some thought, and you tell me what it's going to take to make this happen.'

She hesitated for a long few seconds, then, 'Look, I could totally get fired for this, but we do have a dog that just came in today. He hasn't even been examined yet, but he doesn't seem like he's in the best shape. And I'll be honest with you, he's not much to look at either. We don't have space for him right now, so he's actually on the list for euthanasia in the morning.'

'I'll take him.' Dante checked the time. It was just past five o'clock, already dark topside, thanks to New England sitting on the front end of the Eastern Time Zone. Harvard wouldn't be showing up at the compound for another four hours. Plenty of time for him to complete this little transaction before he had to link up with the agent for the night's patrol. He stood up, grabbing his coat and keys. 'I'm on my way. I'll be there in twenty minutes.'

'Okay. We close at five-thirty, but I'll wait for ya. Just come around back and ask for Rose. That's me.' She cracked her gum again, her jaw working audibly in a flurry of quick snaps. 'Ah, about the money – the two hundred bucks? Can you pay cash?'

Dante smiled as he started for the door. 'Done.'

↜ CHAPTER FIFTEEN ↝

Tess double-checked the last figure on her computer monitor, making sure the amount was correct before she clicked the button to complete the funds transfer. The overdue clinic bills were paid now, but her savings account was more than a thousand dollars lighter. And next month, the bills would start all over again.

'Hey, Tess?' Nora appeared in the open doorway and gave a hesitant rap on the jamb. 'Sorry to interrupt, but it's almost six o'clock and I have to take off to study for an exam tomorrow. You want me to lock up?'

'Okay,' Tess said, rubbing at her temples, where twin knots of stress had begun to settle. 'Thanks, Nora. Have a good night.'

Nora looked at her for a long moment, then down at the stack of bills on the desk. 'Everything all right?'

'Yeah.' Tess attempted a reassuring smile. 'Yes, everything is fine.'

'I saw the notice from the building landlord today. Rent's going up after the first of the year, huh?'

Tess nodded. 'Just eight percent.'

It wasn't much, actually, but she could barely cover the clinic lease as it was. The increase would likely be the final nail in the coffin, unless she started charging more for services. That would probably cost her half of her clients, which would put her right back in the hole. The only reasonable alternative was to close the clinic, pull up stakes, and move on to something else.

Tess wasn't afraid of that option; she was used to moving around. Sometimes she wondered if it wasn't easier for her to start over than to really dig in somewhere. She was still searching for that soft place to fall. Maybe she would never find it.

'Look, Tess, I've, um, been meaning to talk to you about something. My classes are getting pretty intense this last semester, and I really need to buckle down.' She hesitated, lifting her shoulder. 'You know I love working here, but I'm going to have to scale back my hours.'

Tess nodded, accepting. 'Okay.'

'It's just that between the clinic and studying, I hardly have time to breathe anymore, you know? My dad's getting remarried in a few weeks, so I also have to think about moving out of his place. Anyway, my mom really wants me to come back to California after I graduate in the spring. . . .'

'It's okay. Really, I understand,' Tess said, relieved in a small way.

She'd shared with Nora some of the business's financial struggles, and while Nora had insisted on riding it out with her, Tess still felt responsible. In fact, there were times she felt as though she was keeping the clinic afloat more for her clients and Nora than for herself. She was good at her work – she knew that – but she couldn't help feeling that this new life she had made was just another form of hiding. From her past, certainly, but also from the here and now. From something that she was afraid to examine too closely.

You're always running away, Tess.

Dante's words from last night replayed in her mind. She'd been reflecting on what he said, knowing that his observation of her was right. Like him, she often felt that if she just kept moving, kept running, she might – just might – be able to survive. She didn't fear eventual death, though. Her demon was always close by her side.

Deep down, she knew that what she was really running from was herself.

Tess straightened a stack of papers on her desk, pulling herself back to the conversation. 'When were you thinking of cutting back your hours?'

'Well, as soon as you can let me, I guess. It kills me that you've been bankrolling my paycheck from your personal funds, anyway.'

'You let me worry about that,' Tess said, her words interrupted by the jangle of bells on the clinic's front entrance.

Nora glanced over her shoulder. 'That must be UPS with our supply order. I'll run out and grab it before I go.'

She jogged away and Tess heard muffled conversation in the reception area. Then Nora was back again, a flush of pink in her cheeks.

'It's definitely not UPS in the lobby,' she said, keeping her voice low as if she didn't want to be overheard. 'It's an absolute *god.*'

Tess laughed. 'What?'

'Are you up for a walk-in? Because this amazing-looking guy is waiting out there with a pitiful little dog.'

'Is it an emergency?'

Nora shrugged. 'I don't think so. No obvious blood or trauma, but the guy is pretty insistent. He asked for you. And did I mention he's drop-dead gorgeous?'

'You did,' Tess said, standing up from her desk and coming around to put on her white lab coat. A tingle kicked up below her ear, an odd prickling sensation like the one she'd felt at the museum exhibit and again last night, when she was standing next to Dante at the coffee shop. 'Tell him I'll be right out, please.'

'No problem.' Nora hooked her hair behind her ear, smoothed her low-cut sweater, and trotted off.

It was him. Tess knew it was Dante, even before she heard his voice rumble in the lobby. She found herself smiling into her hand, weathering a wild current of excitement to think that he had sought her out after the embarrassing way she'd left things with him last night in the park.

Oh, God. This jolt of hormones was bad, bad news. She wasn't the type to go all giddy over a man, but Dante did something to her that she'd never felt before.

'Get a grip,' she whispered to herself as she headed out of her office and into the hallway that opened onto the lobby area.

Dante stood at the tall reception station, holding a small bundle in his arms. Nora was leaning across the countertop to pet the little dog, cooing adoringly and flashing Dante a nice shot of her cleavage. Tess couldn't blame Nora for flirting. Dante just had that effect on a woman; not even Tess was immune to his dark allure.

His eyes had locked on to her the instant she entered the room, and if Tess wanted to act cool and unaffected, she was probably failing miserably. Her smile wouldn't dim, and her fingers trembled a bit as she brought her hand up to the side of her neck, where the queer tingling seemed to gather the strongest.

'This must be Harvard,' she said, glancing to the rather emaciated-looking terrier mix in Dante's arms. 'When I said I wanted to meet him, I guess I didn't expect it would be so soon.'

Dante frowned. 'Is this a bad time?'

'No. No, it's fine. I'm just . . . surprised, that's all. You keep surprising me.'

'You guys know each other?' Nora was gaping at Tess like she wanted to high-five her.

'We, uh . . . we met a couple of nights ago,' Tess stammered. 'At the museum reception. Last night we ran into each other again in the North End.'

'I was out of line,' Dante said, looking at her as if they were the only people in the room. 'I didn't mean to upset you last night, Tess.'

She waved off his concern, wishing she could forget the whole thing. 'It was nothing. I wasn't upset, really. You didn't do anything wrong. I should be the one apologizing to you for running off like I did.'

Nora's gaze bounced between the two of them, as if the tension Tess felt from being near Dante was palpable to the other woman as well. 'Maybe you two would like to be alone—'

'No,' Tess answered abruptly, at the same time that Dante calmly said, 'Yes.'

Nora hesitated for a second, then turned and gathered her coat and handbag from a hook behind her desk. 'I'll just . . . um, see you in the morning, Tess.'

'Yeah, all right. Good luck with your studying.'

With her back to Dante, Nora looked at Tess and silently mouthed the words *Oh, my God!* as she started off for the back exit, where her car was parked. A few seconds later, the low rumble of an engine sounded, then faded away as Nora took off.

Until now, Tess had been so distracted by Dante's presence, she'd hardly noticed the condition of the dog. Now she couldn't help feeling a wash of pity for the animal. Its dull brown eyes were half closed, and a faint but audible respiratory wheeze sawed out of its lungs. On sight alone, Tess could tell that the dog was in need of care.

'Do you mind if I take a look at him?' she asked, glad to have something to focus on aside from Dante and the awareness that seemed to crackle between them. At his nod of agreement, Tess took a stethoscope out of her lab-coat pocket and hooked it around her neck. 'When's the last time Harvard had veterinary care?'

Dante gave a vague shrug. 'I'm not sure.'

Tess gently took the dog from Dante's arms. 'Come on. Let's have a closer look in one of the exam rooms.'

Dante followed in watchful silence, coming to stand right beside her as Tess placed the trembling animal onto the stainless steel table. She put the scope under the dog's chest and listened to the rapid beat of his heart. There was a pretty significant murmur, and his respiration was definitely off, as she suspected. She felt carefully around his pronounced rib cage and made a note of the lack of elasticity in his flea-ridden fur. 'Has Harvard been sleeping a lot lately? Lethargic?'

'I don't know.'

Although Tess hardly noticed Dante moving, their arms brushed against each other, his solid, muscled body like a warm, protective wall beside her. And he smelled incredible – something spicy and dark that probably cost a fortune. She drew in a deep breath of him, then bent to inspect the dog's mite-infested ears. 'Have you noticed a loss of appetite or a problem keeping food and water down?'

'I couldn't say.'

Tess lifted the terrier's lips and checked the color of his diseased gums. 'Can you tell me when was Harvard's last vaccination?'

'I don't know.'

'Do you know anything about this animal?' It sounded accusatory, but she couldn't bite it back.

'I haven't had it very long,' Dante said. 'I know it needs care. Do you think you can help, Tess?'

She frowned, knowing it was going to take a lot to reverse everything the dog suffered from. 'I'll do what I can, but I can't make any promises.'

Tess reached for a ballpoint that was lying on the countertop behind her and fumbled it. The pen dropped to the floor at her feet, and before she could bend down to pick it up, Dante was there. He caught the Bic in nimble fingers and held it out to her. As she took it from him, she felt his thumb skim over the back of her hand. She drew her arm against her body in an abrupt motion.

'Why do I make you so nervous?'

She shot him a look that probably broadcast that very thing. 'You don't.'

'Are you sure? You seem . . . agitated.'

She was, actually. She hated to see neglected animals such as this one, which looked like a poster child for the SPCA. And stress over everything that was going wrong in her life right now was also weighing her down.

But running undercurrent to all of that was the disquiet she felt just being in the same room with this man. God help her, but when her gaze lit on his, she was blasted with a very vivid, very real impression of the two of them naked together, limbs entwined, bodies moist and glistening, arching into each other on a bed of scarlet silk sheets.

She could feel his large hands caressing her, his mouth pressing hot and hungry against her neck. She could feel his sex sliding in and out of her, as his teeth grazed the sensitive spot below her ear, which throbbed now like the heavy beat of drums.

She was held suspended in his smoky amber eyes, seeing all of it as clearly as if it was memory. Or a future that danced just beyond her grasp . . .

With effort, Tess managed to blink, severing the strange connection.

'Excuse me,' she gasped, and hurried out of the room, awash in confusion.

She closed the door behind her and took a couple of quick paces down the hallway. Leaning back against the wall, she closed her eyes and tried to catch her breath. Her heart was racing, pounding against her sternum. Her very bones seemed to vibrate like a tuning fork.

Her skin was warm to the touch, heat blooming around her neck and in her breasts, and down, in her core. Everything in her seemed to have awakened in his presence, all that was female and elemental coming online at once, reaching out for something. Reaching out for him.

God, what was wrong with her?

She was losing it. If she was smart, she'd leave Dante and his sickly pet in the exam room and hightail it out of here right now.

Oh, sure. That would be really professional. Very adult.

So he'd kissed her once before. All he'd done now was brush fingertips with her; she was the one overreacting. Tess took a deep breath, then another, willing her hyperactive physiology to calm down. When she was finally in control again, she turned around and went back to the exam room, running through a dozen lame reasons for why she felt the need to run away.

'I'm sorry about that,' she said as she opened the door. 'I thought I heard the phone—'

The flimsy excuse cut short when she saw him. He was sitting on the floor as if he'd dropped there not a second before, his head hung low and caught between his large palms. His fingertips were white where they dug into the thick hair of his scalp. He looked to be in excruciating agony, his breath hissing through his teeth, eyes squeezed tightly shut.

'Oh, my God,' she whispered, stepping farther inside the room. 'Dante, what happened? What's the matter with you?'

He didn't answer. Maybe he was incapable.

Although it was clear that he was hurting in some major way, Dante radiated a dark, wild danger that seemed almost inhuman it was so powerful.

Seeing him there in pain on the floor, Tess felt a sharp stab of déjà vu, a niggle of foreboding that tickled her spine. She started to back away, ready to call 911 and let his problem –

whatever it was – belong to someone else. But then his big shoulders hunched over in a tight, pained ball. He let out a moan, and that low, anguished sound was more than she could bear.

Dante didn't know what hit him.

The death vision came on fast, nailing him like an explosion of blistering daylight. He was awake, at least, but suspended in a paralyzing state of awareness, all of his senses gripped in a debilitating, full-on assault. The vision had never come to him outside of sleep. It had never been so fierce, so ruthlessly strong.

One minute he'd been standing next to Tess, swamped with the erotic images of what he wanted to do with her; the next thing he knew, he was ass-planted on the linoleum of the examination room, feeling himself becoming engulfed in smoke and flame.

Fire climbed toward him from all sides, belching thick plumes of black, acrid smoke. He couldn't move. He felt shackled, helpless, afraid.

The pain was immense, as was the despair. It shamed him how deeply he felt both of those things, how hard it was for him not to yell out in torment for what he was living through in his mind.

But he held on, the only thing he could do whenever the vision struck him, and he prayed it would be over soon.

He heard his name on Tess's lips, asking him what he needed. He couldn't answer. His throat was dry, his mouth filled with ash. He sensed the honesty of her concern and the truth of her apprehension, as she drew closer to him. He wanted to tell her to go, to let him suffer it out on his own, the only way he knew how.

But then he felt cool and gentle fingers come to rest on his shoulder. He felt the white calm of sleep float down over him like a sheltering blanket as she stroked his taut spine and the sweat-dampened hair at his nape.

'You'll be all right,' she told him softly. 'Let me help you, Dante. You're safe.'

And for the first time he could ever recall, he believed that he was.

✎ CHAPTER SIXTEEN ✐

Dante lifted his eyelids, waiting for the splintering headache to blind him. Nothing happened. No staggering aftershocks, no cold sweat, no bone-numbing fear.

He blinked once, twice, staring up at a white acoustic-tile ceiling and an extinguished fluorescent-light panel above his head. Strange surroundings – the muted-taupe walls, the small upholstered sofa underneath him, the tidy wooden desk across from him, its orderly surface illuminated by a ginger-jar lamp next to the computer workstation.

He breathed in, smelling none of the familiar smoke or other burning stench that had filled his nostrils in the hellish reality of his death vision. All he smelled was a spicy-sweet warmth that seemed to cocoon him in peace. He brought his hands up from his sides, smoothing them over the fleece throw that only partially covered his big body. The plush cream-colored blanket smelled like her.

Tess.

He turned his head just as she was coming into the room from the hallway outside. The white lab coat was gone; she looked incredibly soft and feminine in an unbuttoned pale green cardigan over her beige knit top. Her jeans rode her hips, baring a thin wedge of smooth creamy flesh where the hem of her shirt didn't quite meet the top of her pants. She'd let her hair down from the plastic claw that held it before. Now the honeyed brown waves fell down around her shoulders in loose glossy curls.

'Hi,' she said, watching him sit up and swivel around to put his feet on the carpeted floor. 'Are you feeling better?'

'Yeah.'

His voice was a dry croak, but he felt surprisingly well. Rested. Cooled out, when he should have been jacked up tense and hurting – the usual hangover that came in the wake of his death vision. On impulse, he ran his tongue along the line of his teeth, feeling for fangs, but the fearsome canines were receded. His eyesight felt normal, not the sharp, otherworldly twin laser beams that marked him as one of the Breed.

The storm of his transformation, if it had come at all, was past.

He moved the fluffy throw off him and realized he was missing his coat and boots. 'Where's my stuff?'

'Right here,' she said, pointing to the black leather coat and the lug-soled Doc Martens that had been placed neatly on a guest chair near the door. 'Your cell phone is on my desk. I turned it off a couple of hours ago. I hope you don't mind. It was ringing pretty continuously and I didn't want it to wake you.'

A couple of hours ago? 'What time is it now?'

'Um, it's quarter to one.'

Shit. Those calls were probably the compound, wondering where the hell he was. Lucy was gonna have some 'splaining to do.

'Harvard's resting, by the way. He's got a few problems that could be very serious. I fed him and gave him fluids and some IV antibiotics, which should help him sleep. He's in the kennels down the hall.'

For a few seconds, Dante was confused, wondering how she could possibly know the Darkhaven agent and why the hell he'd be medicated and sleeping in the kennels of her clinic. Then his brain kicked into gear and he remembered the mangy little animal he'd used as a means of ingratiating himself further with Tess.

'I'd like to keep him overnight, if you don't mind,' Tess said. 'Maybe a couple of days, so I can run a few more tests and make sure he's getting everything he needs.'

Dante nodded. 'Yeah. Okay.'

He looked around at the small, comfortable little office setup, with its minifridge in the corner and the electric hot plate that sat next to a coffeemaker. Obviously, Tess spent a lot of time in the place. 'This isn't the room I was in before. How did I get here?'

'You had some kind of seizure in the examination room. I got you on your feet and helped you walk back here to my office. I thought it would be more comfortable for you. You seemed pretty out of it.'

'Yeah,' he said, rubbing his hand over his face.

'Is that what it was, a seizure?'

'Something like that.'

'Does it happen frequently?'

He shrugged, seeing no cause to deny it. 'Yeah, I guess so.'

Tess came toward him then, taking a seat on the arm of the sofa. 'Do you have medication for it? I wanted to check, but I didn't feel right going through your pockets. If there's something you need—'

'I'm good,' he said, still marveling at the absence of pain or nausea following what had been the worst assault he'd experienced to date. The only one that had ever come on while he was awake. Now, aside from being a bit groggy from a hard sleep, he could barely tell he'd had the damn vision at all. 'Did you . . . give me something, or maybe . . . do something to me? I felt your hands on my back at one point and moving around my head. . . .'

A strange expression came over her face, almost a look of momentary panic. Then she blinked and glanced away from him. 'If you think it will help, I have Tylenol in my desk. I'll get you some and a glass of water.'

She started to get up.

'Tess.' Dante reached out and took her wrist in a loose grasp. 'You stayed with me the whole time – all these hours?'

'Of course. I couldn't very well leave you here by yourself.'

He got a sudden, clear mental picture of what she must have seen if she was anywhere near him while he fought the onslaught of his death vision. But she hadn't run away shrieking, and she wasn't looking at him in terror now either. In fact, he had to wonder if being with her hadn't somehow eased the worst of his nightmare before it had even begun.

Her touch had been so soothing, so cool and tender. 'You stayed with me,' he said, awed by her compassion. 'You helped me, Tess. Thank you.'

She could have drawn her hand out of his easy hold at any moment, but she hesitated there, a question in her blue-green gaze. 'I think ... Since you seem to be all right now, I think it's time to call it a night. It's late, and I should go home.'

Dante resisted the urge to point out that she was trying to run again. He didn't want to scare her off, so he slowly got up from the sofa and stood near her. He looked at their fingers, still touching at the tips, neither one of them willing to break the unexpected contact.

'I have to ... go,' she said quietly. 'I don't think this – whatever this is that's happening between us – is a good idea. I'm not looking to get involved with you.'

'And yet you've been sitting here taking care of me for the past four-plus hours.'

She frowned. 'I couldn't have left you alone. You needed help.'

'What do you need, Tess?'

He curled his fingers, capturing hers in a firmer hold now. The air in the small office seemed to constrict and throb with awareness. Dante could feel Tess's pulse kick-start into a faster beat, a vibration he picked up through her fingertips. He could read her interest, the desire that had been there when he'd kissed her at the art exhibit and been sorely tempted to seduce her in front of a few hundred witnesses. She had wanted him then, maybe even last night too. The delectable, trace scent coming off her skin as she held his meaningful stare told him plainly enough that she wanted him now.

Dante smiled, desire flaring in him for the woman whose blood was a part of him.

The woman who just might be in league with his enemies, if Tess had any hand at all in her onetime boyfriend's pharmaceutical ventures.

She wasn't thinking of the human now, that was for sure. Tess's eyes darkened, and her breathing picked up speed, rushing shallowly from between her parted lips. Dante flexed his biceps, just the slightest pull of his arm to bring her closer. She came toward him without resistance.

'I want to kiss you again, Tess.'

'Why?'

He chuckled, low under his breath. 'Why? Because you're beautiful, and because I want you. And I think you want me too.'

Dante brought his free hand up to her face and gently stroked the line of her jaw. She felt like silk against his fingertips, as delicate as glass. He brushed his thumb across the dusky swell of her lips.

'God, Tess. I'm dying to taste you right now.'

She closed her eyes, exhaling a sigh. 'This is crazy,' she whispered. 'I don't . . . this isn't . . . something that I normally—'

Dante lifted her chin and bent to press his lips to hers. He'd meant only to sample the feel of her mouth on his, an urge he'd been harboring since those few heated moments they'd shared at the museum reception. Then he'd been something of a ghost to her, stealing a taste of her passion, then slipping away before she could know if he was real or imagined. Now, for a reason he could hardly comprehend, he wanted her to know he was flesh and bone.

He was, evidently, a goddamn idiot.

Because right now he wanted her to feel him – all of him – and understand that she was his.

He'd meant only to taste, but she was too sweet on his tongue. She was so responsive, her hands coming up around his neck to hold him closer as their mouths crushed together in a deep, prolonged joining. Seconds melted into a minute, then minutes more. A mad, timeless oblivion.

As he kissed her, Dante buried his hands in the luxurious mass of her hair, reveling in the softness of her, the heat of her. He wanted her undressed. He wanted her naked beneath him, screaming his name as he pushed inside her.

God, how he wanted.

His blood was pounding, hot and furious, through his body. His sex was stiff with need, the hard length of him fully aroused, and he was only just getting started with Tess.

The way he felt now, he hoped this was only the start.

Before Dante could stop himself, he was guiding her around to the sofa, easing her down onto the cushions.

She fell back, looking up at him from under those thick-fringed lashes, the aqua color of her eyes gone dark like stormy azure. Her mouth was glistening and swollen from his kiss, her lips blushing a deep, dark rose. The front of her neck was pink with the flush of her desire, color that fanned down into the V of her clingy shirt. Her nipples were hard little buds, straining against the fabric with each rise of her breath. She was ripe with want, and he had never seen anything more exquisite.

'You're mine, Tess.' Dante moved over her, kissing a path from her lips to her chin, then along her throat, to the soft skin below her ear. She smelled so good. Felt so good against him.

Dante groaned, his nostrils picking up the sweet perfume of

her arousal. Lust made his gums ache with the stretching of his fangs. He could feel the sharp points coming down, throbbing with the steady beat of his pulse. 'You are mine. And you know that, don't you?'

Although her voice was small, little more than a breath of air rushing out of her lungs, Dante heard her plainly, and the word went through him like fire.

She said *yes*.

God, what was she saying?

What was she doing, letting herself be kissed and touched – seduced – like this?

It was reckless and so unlike her at all. Probably dangerous too, for a dozen reasons she couldn't quite bring herself to care about right now.

She'd never been easy – far from it, given her general distrust of the male gender – but something about this man made fear and inhibition fly right out the window. She felt linked to him somehow, a connection that went deeper than anything she knew, into uncharted territory that made her think of fairy-tale concepts like fate and destiny. Those things weren't part of her normal lexicon, but she couldn't deny that despite all she should be feeling about this moment, it just felt . . . right.

It felt too good to doubt, even if her body was inclined to listen to reason. Which it wasn't, not when Dante was kissing her, touching her, making all that was female in her awaken as though it had been asleep for a hundred years.

She didn't resist as he carefully pulled off her sweater, then lifted the hem of her shirt up over her breasts. He drew in a sharp breath as he bent down and kissed her bare stomach, teasing her with gentle nips as he moved up her belly to the front closure of her bra. He snapped it open and slowly peeled the satin away from her breasts.

'Christ, you are lovely.'

His voice was rough, his breath hot on her skin. Her nipples ached to be touched, to be drawn into his mouth and suckled hard. As though he knew the direction of her thoughts, Dante flicked his tongue over one of the tight buds. He pulled with teeth and tongue, while he took the other in his palm, caressing her, driving her crazy with need.

Tess felt him reaching down for the button of her jeans. He worked it free, then tugged the zipper open. Cool air hit her abdomen, then her hips, as Dante nudged her pants down around her thighs. With a long pull of her nipple, he lifted his head and looked at her partial nakedness.

'Exquisite,' he said, the same word he'd spoken the other night.

He reached up tenderly, smoothing his palm down the length of her throat, then along the center of her. Her body arched up for him as though attached to an invisible string that he was pulling. When he reached the core of her, he slid his fingers underneath her panties, not stopping until he found her moist cleft. Tess closed her eyes in tormented bliss as he cupped her, one long finger cleaving between her folds.

His breath leaked out of him in a hiss. 'You feel like silk, Tess. Wet, hot silk.'

He penetrated her as he spoke, just the tip of his finger, the smallest invasion. She wanted more. She lifted her hips, a quiet moan in her throat as he drew back, teasing, sliding her moisture up around her clit with the tip of his slick finger.

'What?' he asked her in a gruff whisper. 'What do you want, Tess?'

She writhed under his touch, reaching for him. Dante bent down and kissed her stomach as he put both hands on the loose waistband of her jeans and pushed them down. Her panties followed. Dante kissed her navel, then traced his tongue in a downward path, toward the small patch of curls at her groin. With one hand, he lifted her thigh, spreading her open.

'Do you want me to kiss you here?' he asked, pressing his mouth to her hipbone. His dark head moved lower, to the sensitive skin of her inner thigh. 'How about here?'

'Please,' she gasped, her spine arcing as heat roared through her.

'I think,' he said, moving off the sofa and positioning himself between her slack legs, 'that you want me to kiss you . . . here.'

The first press of his mouth to her sex took her breath away. He kissed her deeper then, using his tongue on her, driving her wild. Tess's pleasure spun higher, tighter. She didn't know it was possible to feel this kind of need, but now that she was burning with it, there was only one thing that could sate it.

'Please,' she said, her voice sounding broken and thick. 'Dante, please . . .'

'Do you want me inside you, Tess? Because that's where I want to be right now. I want to be driving into you, feeling all of your wet heat milking my cock dry.'

Oh, God. He was going to make her come just thinking about it.

'Yes,' she managed to croak. 'God, yes. That's what I want.'

He drew back and stripped off his shirt. Tess opened her eyes, watching him through heavy lids as his muscles bunched and flexed in the dim light of her office. His chest was bare, sculpted like something out of Roman myth, and decorated with an amazing pattern of tattoos that tapered down the ridge of his firm stomach and beneath the waistband of his pants.

At least, she thought they were tattoos. Through her desire-soaked eyes, the geometric designs seemed to change colors as she stared at him, the lines muting from deep wine red to purplish blue and oceanic green.

'Your skin is beautiful,' she said, as curious as she was awed. 'God, Dante . . . your tattoos . . . they're incredible.'

She glanced up at his face and thought she saw something

flash like amber in his eyes. And when his lips curved into a smile, his mouth seemed fuller somehow.

Dante unfastened his black pants and pulled them off. He wasn't wearing anything under them. His sex sprang free, huge and erect, as breathtaking as the rest of him. To her surprise, the beautiful pattern of tattoos continued all the way down here, curling around the root of his erection like adoring, multihued fingers. Thick veins ridged the length of his long shaft, which was crowned with a broad head, as supple and dark as a plum.

She could have looked at him forever, but then he reached over to her desk and doused the light. Tess mourned the darkness that hid him, but an instant later his heat was covering her and she let her hands explore everything her eyes could no longer see.

He pressed her down beneath him, parting her thighs with his pelvis as he moved into position between her legs. His sex was hard, so hot, as he wedged it between her folds, just teasing her with the length of him, making her crave him even more.

'Dante.' Her breath heaved out of her, she was so ready for him, so needful of him. It took immense focus to break from the havoc he was wreaking on her senses and think rationally for a second. 'Dante, wait. I'm . . . I'm on the pill, so I . . . but maybe we should—'

'It's okay.' He kissed her as his erection nudged the mouth of her core. His tongue swept between her lips, the taste of her own juices a musky sweetness that lingered on his tongue. 'You're safe with me, Tess. I promise you.'

Ordinarily she would be the last person to rely on trust alone, but somehow she knew that she could believe him. Incredibly, she felt safe with him. Protected.

He kissed her again, pushing his tongue deeper. Tess let him in, kissing him back as she arched her hips and seated herself on the blunt head of his penis to show him what she wanted.

He exhaled sharply, pelvis bucking as their bodies began to join.

'You are mine,' he gasped against her mouth. Tess couldn't deny it. Not now.

She clutched at him hungrily, and then, with a low growl, he thrust forward, plunging deep.

⇥ CHAPTER SEVENTEEN ⇤

In his private lab across town, Ben Sullivan had decided to make some adjustments to his Crimson formula. From the beginning he'd never stored the final recipe in the lab, figuring it to be a prudent measure of job security if he carried it with him instead of leaving it behind for his patron's cronies – or anyone else – to find. He'd been paranoid about getting cut out of his lucrative little venture; after the phone call he'd made to his benefactor earlier tonight, he was feeling like his paranoia might have been more of a spot-on hunch.

He had relayed everything that happened the other night, right down to the near miss with the guys who had chased him out of the club and the incredible notion that Crimson had had some kind of dangerous – vampiric, he'd been inclined to call it – effect on one of Ben's recent best customers.

The news had been accepted with his patron's usual nonreactionary calm. Ben had been advised to divulge none of the details to anyone, and a meeting had been set up for him with his employer for the following evening at nightfall. After all the months of secrecy and anonymity, he was finally getting a face-to-face with the guy.

With a little less than fifteen hours before that rendezvous was to occur, Ben thought it wise to cover his bases as best he could, in the event he might need some leverage when he went to meet with the boss. He didn't know precisely who he was dealing with, after all, and he wasn't foolish enough to discount the fact that it might be someone with some pretty serious underworld connections. Wouldn't be the first time a kid from Southie thought he could play ball with real thugs and ended up a floater in the Mystic.

Downloading both formulas – the original and the new, altered one that he considered his own job security – Ben popped the flash drive from his computer. He erased all traces of the files from his hard drive, then headed out of the lab. He took side roads back into the city, just in case he was being followed, and ended up in the North End, not too far from Tess's apartment.

She would be surprised to know how often he cruised past her place, just to see if she was there. She'd be more than surprised, he admitted to himself. She'd be a little skeeved out if she had any idea how obsessed he truly was with her. He hated that he couldn't let go of her, but the fact that she had always insisted on holding him at arm's length, particularly since their breakup, only made him want her more. He kept waiting for her to come around and let him back in, but after the other night, when he'd felt her cringe as he kissed her, some of that hope had slipped away.

Ben wheeled his van around a corner and headed up Tess's street. Maybe this would be the last time he drove by her place. The last time he'd humiliate himself like some pathetic Peeping Tom.

Yeah, he thought, putting his foot on the brake for a red light, maybe it was time to cut loose, move on. Get a fucking life.

As his van idled, Ben watched a sleek black Porsche roll up to the traffic light from a side road and hang a right in front of him, cruising down the nearly empty street toward Tess's apartment building. His stomach squeezed as he got a look at the driver. It was the guy from the club – not the one who ran after him, but the other dude, the big one with the dark hair and the lethal vibe about him.

And damn if he didn't recognize the female passenger sitting next to the guy.

Tess.

Jesus Christ. What was she doing with him? Had he been questioning her about Ben's activities or something, maybe checking up with his friends and acquaintances?

Panic swam like acid up the back of his throat, but then Ben realized that at almost three in the morning, it was a little goddamn late for a police or DEA interview. No, whatever the guy was selling Tess, it wasn't on any sort of official basis.

Ben tapped his steering wheel impatiently as the traffic light kept blaring red in front of him. Not that he was afraid of losing the Porsche. He knew where it was heading. But he wanted to see for himself. Needed to see for himself that it really was Tess.

Finally the light changed, and Ben gunned the gas. The van lurched up the street just as the car rolled to a stop outside Tess's building. Ben pulled over to the curb a few yards back and cut his lights. He waited, watching in slow simmering fury as the guy leaned over from the driver's side and pulled Tess into a long kiss.

Son of a bitch.

The embrace lasted for a long time. Too damn long, Ben thought, seething now. He threw the van into drive and turned the wheel into the street. He drove by the car at a leisurely pace, refusing to look as he passed, and then slowly continued on his way.

Dante navigated his way back to the compound in a state of distraction, so much so that he'd actually taken a wrong turn coming out of the North End and had to backtrack a few blocks just to resume course. His head was filled with the scent of Tess, the taste of her. She lingered on his skin and on his tongue, and all it took was the remembered feel of her gorgeous body clinging to him, sheathing him, to give him a massive hard-on.

Damn it.

What he'd done tonight with Tess was unplanned and straight-up stupid. Not that he could muster a lot of remorse for the way he'd spent the last few hours. He'd never been so on fire with a woman, and it wasn't as if he was lacking for comparisons. He wanted to blame the fact that Tess was a Breedmate and that her blood was alive inside him, but the truth was slightly worse than that.

The woman simply did something to him that he couldn't explain, let alone deny. And after she had eased him out of the tailspin of his death vision, all he wanted – all he needed – was to lose himself even deeper in whatever spell it was that she was casting. Except having Tess naked beneath him only cranked him up tighter. Now that he'd had her, he just wanted more.

At the least, the visit to her clinic had netted some good news.

As Dante wheeled onto the compound's property, he pulled a crumpled sticky note out of his coat pocket and smacked it down onto the smooth surface of the dashboard. In the dim glow of the gauge lights, he read the handwritten message of a couple days ago, which he'd retrieved from Tess's appointment book on her desk.

Ben called – museum dinner tomorrow night, 7 pm. Don't forget!

Ben. The name rolled through Dante's mind like battery acid. Ben, the guy Tess had been with at the fancy art reception. The human scum who was dealing Crimson, probably at the direction of the Rogues.

There was a call-back number on the message, a Southie exchange. With that bit of information in hand, Dante was betting that it would take all of two seconds to locate the human via Internet or utility records.

Dante gunned the Porsche up the gated drive toward the Order's mansion, then rolled into the large, secured fleet garage. He cut the lights and engine, grabbed the piece of paper off the dash, then pulled one of his *male-branche* blades out of the center console beside him.

The bowed length of metal felt cold and unforgiving in his hand – just like it was going to feel against good old Ben's naked throat. He could hardly wait for the sun to set again so he could go and make a formal introduction.

⊰ CHAPTER EIGHTEEN ⊱

Tess slept well for the first time in what felt like a week and in spite of the fact that her head was spinning with thoughts of Dante. He'd been in and out of her dreams all night and was the first thing on her mind when she awoke early that next morning, before the alarm clock on her nightstand had a chance to go off with its usual six A.M. blare.

Dante.

His scent still clung to her skin, even after twenty minutes under the warm spray of her shower. There was a pleasant sort of ache between her thighs, an ache she relished because it called to mind everything they'd done together last night.

She could still feel all the places where he'd touched her and kissed her.

All the places on her body that he'd mastered and claimed as his.

Tess dressed quickly, then left her apartment, stopping only to grab a cup of Starbucks on her way to make the 5:20 train at North Station.

She was the first one in at the clinic; Nora probably wouldn't arrive much before seven-thirty. Tess went in through the back door, leaving it locked behind her since the clinic didn't open for another couple of hours. As soon as she entered the kennel area and heard the labored wheeze in one of the cages, she knew she had problems.

Dumping her purse, office keys, and the half-empty paper

cup on the counter next to the washbasin, Tess hurried over to the little terrier Dante had brought in the night before. Harvard wasn't doing well. He lay on his side in the cage, chest rising and falling in a slow pace, soft brown eyes rolled back in his head. His mouth was slightly open, his tongue a sickly gray color and lolled out to the side.

His breath was a dry rattle, the kind of sound that said all the bloodwork and tests she'd run the night before didn't need to be sent out to the lab after all. Harvard would be gone before the samples made it into the mail.

'Poor baby,' Tess said as she unlatched the cage and carefully stroked the dog's fur. She could feel his weakness through her fingertips. He was holding on by the thinnest strand of life, probably too far gone even before Dante had brought him in to see her.

Sympathy for the animal curled around Tess's heart like a fist. She *could* help him. She knew the way. . . .

Tess retracted her hands and clasped them together in a knot in front of her. She'd made a decision about this a long time ago. She'd promised herself, never again.

But this was just a helpless animal, not a human being. Not the vile man from her past who hadn't deserved any pity or her help.

What would be the harm, really?

Could she actually stand there and watch the poor dog die, knowing she had the unique ability to do something?

No. She couldn't.

'It's all right,' she said softly as she reached back into the cage.

Very gently, Tess brought Harvard out, cradling his little body in her arms. She held him like she would an infant, supporting his slight weight with one hand as she placed her other hand on his gaunt belly. Tess focused on the feel of his breathing, the faint but steady beat of his heart. She could read his weakness, the combination of ailments that had been slowly sapping his life away for probably several long months.

And there was more – her fingertips tingled as she moved down to the dog's abdomen. A bitter taste began to form at the back of her throat as the cancer made itself known to her touch. The tumor wasn't very large, but it was lethal. Tess could picture it in her mind, seeing the web of fibrous strands that clung to the dog's stomach, the ugly bluish clump of disease whose sole purpose was to drain away life.

Tess let the tumor come into her mind through her fingertips as the vibration of her blood began to simmer with power. She concentrated on the cancer, seeing it illuminate from within and then break apart. Feeling it dissolve as she held her hand over it and willed it away.

It came back to her so easily, her unexplainable ability.

My curse, she thought, although it was hard to think of it that way when the small bundle nestled in the crook of her arm whimpered softly and turned to lick her hand in gratitude.

She was so caught up in what she was doing, she almost didn't hear the noise that came from one of the clinic's empty exam rooms. Then it came again: a short, metallic scrape of sound.

Tess's head came up sharply, the fine hairs at the back of her neck tingling with alarm. She heard another noise then: a heavy foot scuffing on the floor. She glanced up at the clock on the wall and knew that it was still much too early for Nora to be arriving.

She didn't think she had anything to fear, yet as she started heading out to the other area of the clinic, she was hit with a sudden blast of memory – a light flicking on in the storeroom, a beaten and bloodied intruder slumped over on the floor. She paused, her feet stopping dead as the vivid image flashed through her mind, then vanished just as quickly.

'Hello?' she called out, trying not to jostle the dog in her arms as she walked out from the vacant kennels. 'Is someone here?'

A hissed curse came out of the large examination room off the reception area.

'Ben? Is that you?'

He came out of the room holding an electric screw-driver. 'Tess – Christ, you scared the shit out of me. What are you doing here so early?'

'Well, I happen to work here,' she said, frowning as she took in his flushed face with the dark rings under his eyes. 'What about you?'

'I, uh . . .' He gestured back to the exam room with his screwdriver. 'I noticed the hydraulic lift was sticking on this table the other day. I was up, and since I still have the spare key to the place, I thought I'd come in and fix it for you.'

It was true, the table had needed some adjustment, but something about Ben's flummoxed appearance didn't sit right. Tess walked toward him, gently petting Harvard when the dog started to stir in her arms. 'It couldn't wait until we opened?'

He ran a hand over his scalp, further mussing his disheveled hair. 'Like I said, I was up. Just trying to help out where I can. Who's your friend?'

'His name's Harvard.'

'Cute mutt; kind of runty, though. A new patient?'

Tess nodded. 'Just came in last night. He wasn't doing too well, but I think he'll be feeling better soon.'

Ben smiled, but it seemed too tight for his face. 'Working late again last night, Doc?'

'No. Not really.'

He glanced away from her, and the smile turned a little sour.

'Ben, are we . . . okay? I tried to call you the other night, after the museum reception, to apologize. I left you a message, but you didn't call back.'

'Yeah, I've been kind of busy.'

'You look tired.'

He shrugged. 'Don't worry about me.'

More than tired, Tess thought now. Ben looked strung out. There was an anxious energy about him, like he hadn't slept for the past two days. 'What have you been up to lately? Are you working on another animal rescue or something?'

'Or something,' he said, sliding a shuttered look at her. 'Listen, I'd love to stay and chat, but I really have to go.'

He pocketed the screwdriver in his loose jeans and started heading for the clinic's front door. Tess trailed after him, feeling a chill as an emotional distance that hadn't been there before now began to crack open between them.

Ben was lying to her, and not just about his purpose in being at the clinic.

'Thanks for fixing the table,' she murmured to his fast-retreating back.

From within the opened door, Ben swiveled his head around to glance at her over his shoulder. His gaze raked her with its bleakness. 'Yeah, sure. You take care, Doc.'

An icy drizzle ticked against the glass of Elise's living-room window; overhead, the stone-gray afternoon sky was bleak. She parted the sheers of her second-floor private residence and stared out at the cold streets of the city below, at the clumps of people rushing to and fro in an effort to escape the weather.

Somewhere, her eighteen-year-old son was out there too.

He'd been gone for more than a week now. One of the growing number of Breed youths who'd disappeared from their Darkhaven sanctuaries around the area. She prayed Cam was underground, safe in some manner of shelter, with others like him to give him comfort and support, until he found his way home.

She hoped that would be soon.

Thank God for Sterling and all he was doing to help make

that return happen. Elise could hardly fathom the selflessness that made her brother-in-law devote himself completely to the task. She wished Quentin could see all that his younger sibling was doing for their family. He would be astonished; humbled, she was sure.

As for how Quentin would feel about her right now, Elise was loath to imagine.

His disappointment would be enormous. He might even hate her a little. Or a lot, if he knew that it was she who drove their son out into the night. If not for the argument she'd had with Camden, the ridiculous attempt to control him, maybe he wouldn't have gone. She was to blame for that, and how she wished she could call back those terrible few hours and erase them forever.

Regret was bitter in her throat as she gazed out to the world beyond her own. She felt so helpless, so useless in her warm, dry home.

Beneath her spacious living quarters in the Back Bay Darkhaven were Sterling's private apartments and underground shelter. He was Breed, so while there was even a hint of sun overhead, he was forced to remain indoors and out of the light, like all of his kind. That included Camden as well, for even though he was half hers – half human – he had his late father's vampire blood in him. His father's otherworldly strengths, and his weaknesses.

There would be no searching for Cam until dark, and to Elise, the waiting seemed an eternity.

She took up pacing in front of the window, wishing there was something she could do to help Sterling look for him and the other Darkhaven youths who'd gone missing along with Cam.

Even as a Breedmate, one of the rare females of the human species who were able to produce offspring with vampires – who were solely male – Elise was still fully *Homo sapiens.* Her skin could bear sunlight. She could walk among other humans without detection, although it had been many long years – more than a century, in fact – since she had done so.

She'd been a ward of the Darkhavens since she was a little girl, brought there for her own safety and well-being when poverty destituted her parents in one of Boston's nineteenth-century slums. When she was of age, she'd become the Breedmate of Quentin Chase, her beloved. How she missed him, gone just five short years.

Now she might have lost Camden too.

No. She refused to think it. The pain was too great to consider that for even a second.

And maybe there was something she could do. Elise drew to a halt at the rain-spattered window. Her breath steamed the glass as she peered out, desperate to know where her son might be.

With a burst of resolve, she pivoted around and went to the closet to retrieve her coat from where it had been since several winters past. The long navy wool covered her widow's whites, falling down around her ankles. Elise put on a pair of pale leather boots and left her quarters before fear could call her back.

She dashed down the stairwell to the door at street level. It took her a couple of attempts to punch in the correct security code needed to unlock the door, for she couldn't remember the last time she'd been out of the Darkhaven property. The outside world had long represented pain to her, but maybe now she could bear it.

For Camden, she could bear anything. Couldn't she?

As she pushed the door open, chilly sleet stung her cheeks, carried toward her on a rush of cool fresh air. Elise braced herself, then walked out, down the brick steps with their wrought-iron railing. On the sidewalk below, thin clusters of people passed, some huddled together, others walking alone, dark umbrellas bobbing with their hurried gaits.

For a moment – the smallest suspension of time – there was silence. But then the ability that had forever been her bane, the extraordinary skill that came in unique form to every Breedmate, pressed down upon her like a hammer.

– I should have told him about the baby –

– not like they're going to miss twenty measly bucks, after all –

– told that old woman I'd kill her fucking dog if it shit in my yard again –

– he'll never even know I was gone if I just go home and act like nothing's wrong –

Elise brought her hands up to her ears as all the ugly thoughts of the human passersby bombarded her. She couldn't blot them out. They flew at her like so many winged bats, a frenzied assault of lies, betrayals, and all manner of sin.

She couldn't take another step. She stood there getting soaked with drizzle, her body frozen on the walkway below her Darkhaven apartments, unable to will herself to move.

Camden was out there somewhere, needing her – anyone – to find him. Yet she was failing him here. She couldn't do anything but hold her head in her hands and weep.

⇥ CHAPTER NINETEEN ⇤

Dusk came early that night, ushered in on the steady spit of a cold November rain coming down from a fog of thick black clouds. The Flats section of Boston's Southie neighborhood – probably nothing special to look at during the day, with its thickly settled collection of aluminum-sided duplexes and brick three-decker tenements – was reduced to a wet, colorless slum under the monotonous deluge.

Dante and Chase had arrived on Ben Sullivan's dilapidated block about an hour ago, right after sunset, where they still waited in one of the Order's dark-windowed SUVs. The vehicle was out of place here simply on the basis of its well-tended appearance, but it put off a distinct don't-fuck-with-me vibe, which helped keep most of the gangbangers and other street thugs from coming too close. The few who had wandered near the window to have a peek decided to move on in a hurry after getting a flash of fang through the glass from Dante.

He was twitchy for all the waiting and half-hoped one of the idiot humans would be fool enough to make a move just so he could work out some of his idle energy.

'You're sure this is the dealer's address?' Chase asked from beside him in the dark front seat.

Dante nodded, drumming his fingers on the steering wheel. 'Yeah. I'm sure.'

He had considered paying this visit to Tess's Crimson-dealing ex-boyfriend by himself but thought he'd better bring along some backup just in case. Backup for Ben Sullivan, not himself. Dante wasn't at all sure the human would be breathing when he was finished with him if he'd come alone.

And not just because Sullivan was drug-dealing scum either. The fact that the guy knew Tess, and no doubt knew her intimately, flipped a trigger on Dante's rage. An unbidden sense of possession stole over him, a need to protect her from losers like this Ben Sullivan person.

Right. Like Dante himself was some kind of prize.

'How did you find it?' Chase's question cut into his thoughts, snapping him back to his mission. 'Aside from seeing the human jackrabbit out of the club ahead of us the other night, we didn't have much to go on as far as IDing him.'

Dante didn't even glance over at Chase, just lifted his shoulder in a shrug as memories of his hours with Tess swamped his senses in vivid recall. 'Doesn't matter how I got it,' he said after a long minute. 'You Darkhaven suits have your methods; we have ours.'

Just as another wave of itchy impatience flooded through him, Dante caught a glimpse of his quarry. He sat up in the driver's seat of the vehicle, glaring out into the dark. The human came around a corner, head down, face partially shielded by a gray hooded sweatshirt. His hands were thrust into the pockets of a bulky parkalike vest, and the guy was walking fast, throwing continuous looks over his shoulder as if he expected trouble on his heels. But it was him, Dante was certain.

'Here's our man now,' he said as the human jogged up the concrete steps outside his flat. 'Let's go, Harvard. Look alive.'

They left the vehicle on alarm and followed him right into the building before the door closed behind him, both Breed males moving with the speed and agility that came naturally to those of the vampire race. By the time the human stuck his key in the lock of his third-floor apartment door and pushed it open, Dante was shoving him into the dark, tossing the guy across the spartan living room.

'Motherfu—' Sullivan came up out of his crash on one knee, then froze, his face caught in a wedge of light from the bare bulb glowing in the hall outside.

Something flashed in the human's eyes, something beneath his immediate fear. Recognition, Dante thought, figuring he probably remembered them from the club the other night. But there was anger there too. Pure male animosity. Dante could smell it seeping out of the human's pores.

He slowly got to his feet. 'What the fuck's going on?'

'How about you tell us,' Dante said, willing a lamp to come on as he strode farther into the place. Behind him, Chase closed and locked the door. 'I'm pretty sure you can guess this isn't a social call.'

'What do you want?'

'We'll start with information. It'll be up to you how we go about getting it.'

'What kind of information?' His gaze swung anxiously between Dante and Chase. 'I don't know who you guys are, and I don't have any idea what you're talking abou—'

'Now, see,' Dante said, cutting him off with a chuckle, 'that kind of bullshit answer puts us off to a real bad start.' As the human's right hand slid into the deep pocket of his down-filled vest, Dante smirked. 'You wanna convince me you're an idiot, go ahead and pull that gun out. Just so we're clear, I really hope you do.'

Ben Sullivan's face blanched as white as his apartment's unpainted walls. He pulled his hand back out, nice and slow. 'How did you—'

'You expecting somebody besides us tonight?' Dante strode up to him and removed the beat-up .45-caliber pistol from his pocket without any resistance. He turned to Chase and handed him the safety-locked weapon. 'Piece-of-shit-looking hardware for a piece-of-shit drug dealer, eh?'

'I just got that for protection, and I'm not a drug deal—'

'Have a seat,' Dante said, and dropped the guy onto a fake-suede recliner, the room's sole piece of furniture aside from the computer workstation in the corner and the shelf of stereo equipment against the wall. To Chase, Dante said, 'Give the place a good sweep, see what you can find.'

'I'm not a drug dealer,' Sullivan insisted as Chase moved off to begin searching. 'I don't know what you think—'

'I'll tell you what I think.' Dante got down in his face, feeling his anger flare in the sharpening of his eyes and the slight prick of his fangs against his tongue. 'I know you're not going to sit there and deny that we saw you dealing Crimson in the back of that club three nights ago. How long have you been trafficking in that shit? Where are you getting it?'

The human glanced down, formulating his lie. Dante grabbed his chin in a bruising grip and yanked his gaze back up to him. 'You don't really want to die over this, do you, asshole?'

'What can I say? You're mistaken. I don't have any idea what you're talking about.'

'Maybe she can tell us something,' Chase put in, coming out of the bedroom just as Dante was about to coldcock the human into a little honesty. Chase carried a framed snapshot in his hand, holding it out in front of him. It was a photo of Ben and a shorter-haired, still-stunning Tess, looking very much the happy couple as they posed outside her clinic's Grand Opening sign. 'You two look cozy. I'll bet she can shed a little light on your after-hours activities.'

The human shot a narrow-eyed stare at Chase. 'Stay the hell away from her, or so help me, I'll—'

'Is she involved?' Dante asked, his voice a rough scrape in his throat.

The human scoffed. 'You gotta ask me that? You're the one who had his tongue jammed down her throat last night in front of her apartment. Yeah, I was there. I saw you, son of a bitch.'

The news flash came as a surprise to Dante, but it certainly explained the man's simmering anger. Dante could feel Chase's eyes on him in question, but he kept his attention focused on Tess's jealous ex.

'I'm about out of patience with you,' he snarled, then shook his head. 'No, screw that. I'm totally out of patience.' Drawing one of the twin curved blades out of its sheath in a split-second blur of flashing steel, he pressed the edge to Ben Sullivan's throat. He smiled thinly as the human's eyes went round with terror. 'Yeah, that feels much better to me too. Now, I'm going to give your larynx a little room to breathe, and you're going to start talking. No more bullshit or stalling. Blink once if you're with me, Benny boy.'

The human lowered his lids, then resumed his fearful study of Dante's blade.

'They told me not to say anything to anyone,' he said, words rushing out of him.

'Who's they?'

'I don't know – whoever's been paying me to manufacture the shit.'

Dante scowled. 'You make Crimson yourself?'

The human attempted a nod, his movement restricted by the cold steel still hovering near his throat. 'I'm a scientist – at least, I was. I used to work as a chemist for a cosmetics firm until I got fired a few years ago.'

'Skip the unemployment record and tell me about Crimson.'

Sullivan swallowed carefully. 'I created it for the nightclub scene, just to make some extra cash. Last summer, not too long after I started dealing it, this dude approached me about stepping up production. He said he had contacts who wanted to get in with me, and they were willing to pay big for it.'

'But you don't know who your business partners are?'

'No. Don't ask, don't tell. Never mattered to me, really. Whoever it is, they pay in cash, lots of it. They leave my payments in a safe-deposit box at the bank.'

Dante and Chase exchanged a look, both of them knowing what the human was probably ignorant of – that he was dealing with Rogues, most likely tied in with the leader of the new faction of suckheads who, as of a few months ago, had been organizing, preparing for a war their leader intended to ignite among the vampire race. Dante and the rest of the Order had put a serious kink in those plans when they blew up the asylum headquarters, but they hadn't eliminated the threat completely. So long as the Rogues could recruit and increase their numbers – particularly with the aid of a drug like Crimson – the possibility of war was more a question of when than if.

'What's the big fucking deal anyway? Crimson's not hardcore. I've even taken it myself in my own trials. It's just a mild stimulant, not much different from X or GHB.'

Standing next to Dante, Chase scoffed. 'Not much different. The hell it isn't. You saw what happened the other night.'

Dante pressed the blade a bit closer. 'You got a front-row seat to that little freak show, didn't you?'

Sullivan's jaw clamped tight, his eyes latched on to Dante in uncertainty. 'I . . . I'm not sure what I saw. I swear.'

Dante pinned him with a narrow, measuring glare. He could tell the human was anxious, but was he lying? Damn, he wished Tegan had come along. No one, human or Breed, could hide the truth from that warrior. Of course, knowing Tegan, he'd be just as liable as Dante to want to take the human out for bringing this misery to the vampire population.

'Listen.' Sullivan tried to stand up but got Dante's palm in the center of his chest, planting his ass right back down on the chair. 'Hear me out, please. I never wanted to hurt anyone. Things have gotten . . . Christ, everything's messed up now, dangerous. I'm in over my head, and I'm getting out. Tonight, in fact. I called my contact, and I'm going to meet with them to let them know I'm finished. They're coming to get me in a couple of minutes.'

At the window, Chase put a finger between the aluminum miniblinds and peered out to the street below. 'Dark sedan idling at the curb,' he advised, then glanced at the human. 'Looks like your ride's here.'

'Shit.' Ben Sullivan shrank back in the chair, his hands moving nervously on the ratty arms of the La-Z-Boy. He flicked a wary glance up at Dante. 'I have to go. Damn it, I need my gun back.'

'You're not going anywhere.' Dante sheathed his *malebranche* blade and went over to the window. He peered out at the waiting vehicle. Although it was impossible to tell much about the driver from overhead, he was willing to bet it was either a Rogue or a Minion at the wheel, and another one sat on the passenger side. He turned back to the human. 'If you get in that car, you're as good as dead. How do you get in touch with your contact – you got a number to reach him?'

'No. They gave me a disposable cell phone. It's got a single number programmed into speed dial, but they encrypted it, so I don't know where I'm actually calling.'

'Let me see it.'

Sullivan reached into his vest pocket and pulled out the device, then handed it to Dante. 'What are you going to do?'

'We'll hang on to this for you. Right now you need to come with us so we can continue this little chat someplace else.'

'What? No.' He got to his feet, looking around anxiously. 'Fuck that. I'm not sure I should trust you guys either, so thanks but no thanks. I'll take care of myself—'

Dante crossed the room and had the human's throat in his hand before the guy could blink. 'It wasn't a request.'

He released the Crimson dealer, shoving him toward Chase. 'Get him out of here. Find a back way to the SUV and drive him to the compound. I'm going to go down and deliver his regrets to the assholes waiting at the curb.'

As Chase took hold of the human's arms and started moving

him out, Dante slipped through the doorway to the hall. He was on the rainy street in no time, coming to a halt in front of the idling sedan and glaring through the windshield at the two humans seated inside.

As Dante had suspected, they were Minions, mind slaves of a Gen One vampire who'd made them by draining them of their humanity while bleeding them to within an inch of their lives. Minions were living, breathing humans, but they were devoid of conscience, existing only to carry out their Master's orders.

And they could be killed.

Dante grinned at them, more than ready to finish them off.

The bonehead in the passenger seat blinked a couple of times as if he wasn't sure what he was seeing. The one at the wheel had better reflexes; as his companion mouthed a bunch of useless curses, the driver threw the car into gear and stomped on the gas.

The engine roared to life, lurching the sedan forward, but Dante saw it coming. He planted his hands on the hood of the vehicle and held it back, sneering as the tires spun out on the wet pavement, squealing and smoking but going nowhere. When the Minion at the wheel dropped the car into reverse, Dante leaped onto the hood. He climbed up the length of it as the car made a swerving effort to leave the curb.

Balancing on the jostling ride like he was a surfer holding a wave, Dante brought the heel of his boot down and smashed in the windshield. The shattered sheet of glass caved in, breaking away from its frame. Pebbles spat in every direction as he swung himself into the car between the two Minions.

'Hello, boys. Where the fuck are we heading tonight?'

They went nuts, grabbing for him, punching him – even biting him, for crissake – but it was just a lot of annoyance. Dante threw the sedan into park, the hard change of gears sending them into a tailspin in the street.

He felt something sharp lance across his right thigh, then smelled the metallic flush of his own blood spilling. His fangs sprang out of his gums with his furious roar, his vision going sharp as laser beams as his pupils narrowed in his rage. Reaching over, he took the Minion on the passenger side by the hair at the back of his head. With one violent jerk of his arm, he plowed the human's face into the dashboard, killing him instantly.

On the other side of him, the driver was scrambling to get out of the car. He fumbled for the door handle and wrenched it open, falling out onto the wet asphalt and then bolting for one of the narrow passages between the three-decker houses.

Dante lunged after him, tackling the Minion to the ground. He fought hand to hand, knowing that he couldn't kill this one until he had a few answers about who he served and where that vampire could be found. Dante figured he didn't need the name of the one who made this Minion; after everything that had gone down a few months ago, he and the rest of the Order were well aware that the vampire they needed to eliminate was Lucan's own brother, Marek. What they didn't know was where the bastard had fled to after he escaped the warriors' attack last summer.

'Where is he?' Dante demanded, flipping the Minion over and giving him a punishing blow to the chin. 'Where can I find the one who owns your sorry ass?'

'Fuck you,' the Minion spat.

Dante threw another punch, then drew his blade and leaned it against the human's cheek.

'Go ahead and kill me, vampire. I'll tell you nothing.'

The urge to oblige the mind slave was hugely tempting, but Dante hauled him off the ground instead. He slammed the Minion into the cinder-block wall of the nearest tenement house, taking dark pleasure in the audible crack of his skull as it bounced off the hard bricks.

'How about if I just cut you up piece by piece?' he hissed,

his voice a low growl through his fangs. 'I don't care if you talk, but I'll sure as hell enjoy hearing you scream.'

The Minion grunted as Dante's blade pressed into his fleshy neck. Dante felt him squirm, heard the click of a safety coming off a handgun. Before he could wrestle it away from him, the Minion's arm came up to the side of them.

He didn't raise the weapon on Dante but on himself. In a split second, the human had the barrel up to his temple, then he fired.

'Goddamn it!'

The explosion flashed orange in the darkness, the percussion ricocheting off the tall buildings around them. The Minion dropped to the wet ground like an anvil, blood and gore spread around him in a grisly halo.

Dante looked down at his own injuries, the sundry scrapes on his hands, the deep wound cutting across his right thigh. It hadn't been that long since he'd fed, so his body was strong and it wouldn't take much time for him to heal. A couple of hours, maybe less. But he needed someplace safe to do so.

Above him, lights came on in a few of the surrounding apartments. A curtain parted in a window across the way. Somebody let out a horrified scream. It wouldn't be long before a call went out to the police, probably already had.

Shit.

He had to get out of there, pronto. Chase was already long gone in the SUV, which was good, all things considered. As for Dante, he couldn't very well drive off in the busted-out sedan and not be conspicuous. Sucking up the pain in his lacerated thigh, he pivoted around and took off on foot, leaving the dead Minions and the abandoned car behind him in the street.

⊰ CHAPTER TWENTY ⊱

Tess dried the last of the dinner dishes and put them away in the cabinet next to the sink. As she snapped the plastic lid onto the leftover chicken marsala, she felt a pair of eyes boring into the back of her skull.

'You've got to be kidding me,' she said, pivoting her head over her shoulder to look down at the whining little beast at her feet. 'Harvard, are you still hungry? You do realize you've been eating practically nonstop since you got here.'

The terrier's tufted brows quirked over his chocolate-brown eyes, his ears lifting high as he cocked his head at an adorable angle. When that didn't get her to move fast enough, he tilted his head in the other direction and raised one paw off the tile.

Tess laughed. 'All right, you shameless charmer. I'll give you some of the good stuff.'

She walked over and retrieved the small bowl that had been licked clean of its second helping of canned lams. Harvard trotted along, following her every step of the way. He'd been glued to her side all day, her new shadow since she'd made the decision to bring him home so she could keep a closer eye on him.

It wasn't something she'd ever done before with her patients, but then she'd never used her hands to heal one of them either. Harvard was special, and he seemed to be equally attached to her, as if he knew she'd brought him back from the brink today. After a round of IV fluids, some food, and a flea dip, he was a whole new dog. She didn't have the heart to leave him alone in the empty clinic kennels after everything he'd been through. Now he had decided she was his new best friend.

'Here you go,' she said, cutting up a few small pieces of cooked chicken and dropping them in his bowl. 'Try to pace yourself this time, okay?'

As Harvard went to town on the food, Tess put the rest of the leftovers in the refrigerator, then turned and poured herself another glass of chardonnay. She strode into the living room, where she'd left off with her sculpting. It had felt good to be working with her clay again, especially after the strange couple of days – and nights – she'd had.

Although she hadn't sat down with any plan for what she would make, Tess wasn't surprised when the lump of light brown Westklay began to take a familiar form. It was rough so far, only the general hint of a face beneath the tousled waves of thick hair she'd worked into the clay. Tess sipped her wine, knowing that if she went back to continue, she would only obsess and be at it all night, unable to tear herself away until the piece was finished.

Like she and Harvard had bigger plans or something?

Putting her wineglass down on the worktable, Tess pulled her wheeled stool over and took a seat. She started shaping the face, using a wire loop to gently carve the slope of the strong forehead and brow, then the nose and the lean angle of the cheekbones. In little time, her fingers were moving on automatic pilot, her mind disengaged and gone into its own flow, her subconscious directly commanding her hands into action.

She didn't know how long she'd been working, but when the hard rap sounded on her apartment door some time later, Tess nearly jumped out of her skin. Sleeping next to her feet on the rug, Harvard woke with a grunt.

'You expecting someone?' she asked quietly as she got up from her stool.

God, she must have been really zoned out while she was sculpting, because she'd seriously messed up around the mouth area of the piece. The lips were curled back in some kind of snarl, and the teeth . . .

The knock sounded again, followed by a deep voice that went through her like a bolt of electricity.

'Tess? Are you there?'

Dante.

Tess's eyes flew wide, then squeezed into a wince as she did a quick mental inventory of her appearance. Hair flung up into a careless knot on top of her head, braless in her white thermal henley and faded red sweats that had more than one dried clay smudge on them. Not exactly fit for company.

'Dante?' she asked, stalling for time and just wanting to be sure her ears weren't playing tricks on her. 'Is that you?'

'Yeah. Can I come in?'

'Um, sure. Just a sec,' she called out, trying to sound casual as she threw a dry work cloth over her sculpture and quickly checked her face in the reflection off one of her putty spatulas.

Oh, lovely. She had a slightly crazed, starving-artist look going on. Very glamorous. *That'll teach him to do the pop-in visit,* she thought, as she padded over to the door and twisted the dead bolt.

'What are you do—'

Her question cut off as she opened the door and caught a glimpse of him. He was drenched from the rain, his dark hair spiked where it clung to his forehead and cheeks, leather coat dripping onto his black combat boots and the tattered welcome mat in the hall outside her place.

But that wasn't all he was dripping. Splotches of blood mingled with the rainwater, falling at a steady clip from an unseen injury.

'Oh, my God! Are you okay?' She moved aside to let him in, then closed the door behind him. 'What happened to you?'

'I won't stay long. I probably shouldn't have come at all. You were the first person I thought of—'

'It's okay,' she said. 'Come in. I'll go get you a towel.'

She ran down the hall to her linen closet and pulled out two towels, one to dry the rain off him and another for his wound. When she came back into the living room, Dante was in the process of taking off his coat. As he reached up to unzip it, Tess saw that his knuckles were bloodstained. There were splatters of the stuff on his face too, most of it diluted by the water that was still running off his chin and wet hair.

'You're pretty banged up,' she said, concerned for him yet more than a little unsettled to see him looking like he'd been in some kind of nasty street fight. She didn't see any cuts on his hands or face, so maybe most of the blood there didn't belong to him. But that wasn't the case elsewhere.

As the heavy leather came open in the front, Tess sucked in her breath. 'Oh, Jesus . . .'

A long laceration ran across the width of his right thigh, clearly a knife wound. The injury was still fresh, soaking his pant leg with blood.

'It's not a big deal,' he said. 'Trust me, I'll live.'

He peeled off the coat and Tess's sympathy turned to ice.

Dante was armed like something out of an action-movie nightmare. A thick belt went around his hips, studded with several different kinds of blades, not the least of which were huge curved daggers sheathed on either side of him. Strapped across the chest of his black long-sleeved shirt was a gun holster sporting a deadly looking brushed-stainless monstrosity; she didn't even want to imagine the size of hole that thing could blast into someone. He had another gun secured around his left thigh.

'What the hell . . .' Tess instinctively shrank away from him, holding the towels against her like a shield.

Dante met her stricken, uncertain gaze and frowned.

'I won't hurt you, Tess. These are just tools of my trade.'

'Your *trade*?' She was still inching backward, movement she wasn't aware of until the backs of her calves came up against the coffee table in the center of the living room. 'Dante, you're dressed like an assassin.'

'Don't be afraid, Tess.'

She wasn't. She was confused, concerned for him, but not afraid. He began taking off his weapons, unfastening his leg holster and holding it like he didn't know where to put it down. Tess gestured beside her, to the squat coffee table.

'May I have one of those towels, please?'

She handed him one, watching as he carefully placed his weapon on the table like he didn't want to add another nick to the already well-worn wood. Even armed to the teeth and bleeding, he was still considerate. Polite, even. A real gentleman, if you could get past all the deadly hardware and the aura of danger that seemed to radiate in visible waves off his huge body.

He took in her apartment with a quick glance, including the little dog who was sitting near Tess in guarded silence.

Dante frowned. 'That can't be . . .?'

Tess nodded, her tension eroding as Harvard went up to Dante, shyly wagging his tail in greeting. 'I hope you don't mind that I brought him home with me. I wanted to keep a close watch on him, and I thought . . .'

Her excuse trailed off as Dante reached down to pet the animal, nothing but kindness in his touch and in his deep voice. 'Hey, little guy,' he said, chuckling as Harvard licked his hand, then dropped down on the floor for a belly rub. 'Someone sure took good care of you today. Yeah, looks like somebody gave you a whole new leash on life.'

He glanced up at Tess with a question in his eyes, but before he could ask her about the dog's sudden turnaround, she took his wet towel and nodded in the direction of her bathroom down the hall. 'Come on, let me have a look at you now.'

Idling at a red light on the other side of South Boston, Chase glanced over at his passenger in the SUV with barely concealed contempt. He personally had no use for the drug-dealing scum. Part of him enjoyed knowing that the human might have been heading for his own funeral if not for Dante and Chase showing up at his apartment tonight.

It didn't seem fair, a lowlife like Ben Sullivan getting a lucky break while innocent youths like Camden and the others who were missing ended up dead or worse, lost to Crimson-induced Bloodlust and gone Rogue by the shit this human peddled to them.

Chase weathered a sudden, sickening recollection of Dante putting a blade to Jonas Redmond's throat in the alley outside the club the other night. That good kid was dead, not because of the warrior but because of the human sitting just an arm's length away from him now. The urge to reach over and blow him away with a bullet to the head came up on Chase like a tsunami, rage he was unused to feeling in himself.

He stared ahead out the tinted windshield, willing the temptation to pass. Killing Ben Sullivan wasn't going to solve anything, and it sure wouldn't bring Camden home any sooner.

And that, after all, was his primary objective.

'He's sleeping with her, isn't he – that other guy and Tess?' The human's voice rattled Chase out of his contemplation, but he didn't acknowledge the question. Ben Sullivan cursed, his head turned to stare out the passenger-side window. 'When I saw them together outside her place last night, the son of a bitch had his hands all over her. What's that all about – is he just using her to get to me?'

Chase remained silent. He'd been wondering about that revelation since it had first come up at Sullivan's apartment. Dante had said he'd used his own methods to find the Crimson dealer, and hearing that he'd been with a woman whom Sullivan had apparently been close to, Chase had initially assumed she'd been a means to an end for Dante.

But the warrior's face had taken on an odd cast at the mention of the female, something that seemed to go beyond simple duty to his mission. Did he care for her?

'Shit. I guess it doesn't really matter,' Sullivan muttered. 'Where are you taking me, anyway?'

Chase didn't feel compelled to answer. The Order's compound was just outside the city proper, a short drive northeast from where they were now. In a few hours, after he was interrogated by Dante and the others, Ben Sullivan would be sleeping in a dry, warm bed – a prisoner for all intents and purposes, but nevertheless protected behind the secured gates of the warriors' headquarters. Meanwhile, dozens of Darkhaven youths were out in the elements topside, exposed to the dangers of the street and the terrible effects of Sullivan's corrosive, deadly drug.

It wasn't right, not just at all.

Chase flicked his eyes up at the light as it turned green, but his foot hovered over the gas. Behind him, someone laid on their horn. He tuned it out, drumming his fingers on the steering wheel for a second as he thought about Camden and Elise, about his promise to bring the boy home.

He didn't have a lot of options here. And time was running out, he could feel it.

When a second horn blast sounded from the rear, Chase brought his foot down on the accelerator and hung a left at the light. In grim silence, he put the SUV on a southbound path, heading back into the city, toward the old industrial area near the river.

CHAPTER TWENTY-ONE

'Good Lord,' Tess gasped, feeling a little queasy as she knelt down in front of Dante to inspect his wound. He was sitting on the edge of the white porcelain bathtub, wearing only his shredded black fatigues. The cut on his thigh seemed better than it had on initial glance in her living room, but in the bright lights of the bathroom, the sight of so much blood – Dante's blood – made her stomach dip sharply and her head spin. She had to reach out for the lip of the tub to keep from swaying on her heels. 'Sorry. I'm not usually affected like this. I mean, I see a lot of ugly injuries at the clinic, but—'

'You don't have to help with this, Tess. I'm used to taking care of myself.'

She gave him a dubious look. 'From the amount of blood on you, I'd say this wound is pretty deep. It's going to require stitches, a lot of them. Somehow I don't think you're up to doing that yourself, are you? And you're going to need to get out of these pants. I can't do much so long as you're wearing them.'

When he didn't move, she frowned. 'You're not going to just sit here and bleed all over my tile, are you?'

His gaze on hers, he gave a slight shrug, then stood and unfastened the button at his waistband. When he started sliding the zipper down over his tattooed skin and the dark thatch of hair at his groin, Tess's cheeks warmed. God, after last night, she should have remembered that he wasn't a boxers *or* briefs kind of guy.

'Um, here's another towel,' she said, pulling one off the bar for him to cover himself.

She turned her head as he finished undressing, although it was probably a little late for modesty considering what they'd done together the night before. Being with him again, especially when he was sitting there naked except for a piece of terry cloth, made the small bathroom seem as tight as a closet and as humid as a sauna.

'So, are you going to tell me what happened to you?' she asked without looking at him yet, busying herself with the small collection of medical supplies she'd assembled on the sink vanity. 'What were you doing tonight to end up on the business end of an obviously very large knife?'

'Just par for the course. My partner and I were in the process of apprehending a drug dealer, and I ran across a couple of obstacles. I had to remove them.'

Remove them, Tess thought, instinctively understanding what that actually meant. She set a roll of gauze bandage down on the basin, feeling an inward shudder at Dante's cold admission. She didn't like what she was hearing, but he'd sworn he was a good guy, and maybe it was crazy, but she trusted him at his word on that.

'All right,' she said, 'let me have a look at your leg.'

'Like I said, I'll live.' She heard his pants hit the floor with a soft rasp. 'I don't think it's as bad as you might have thought.'

Tess swiveled her head to regard him over her shoulder, prepared for the sight of a ghastly open wound. But he was right, it wasn't that bad after all. Beneath the edge of the towel that draped his groin and upper thigh, the laceration was a clean slice but not that deep at all. Not even half an inch down into the flesh of his thigh. The bleeding was tapering off, even as she looked at him.

'Well, that's . . . a relief,' she said, puzzled but glad that her concern had been overblown. She shrugged. 'Okay. I guess we'll just clean it up, then, and bandage it, and you should be good as new.'

Turning back to the sink, Tess wet a cloth under the faucet and squeezed a drop of antiseptic onto the thick terry weave. She was working up the lather when she heard Dante get up and come toward her. In half a stride he was at her back, taking out the clip that held her hair in its messy knot and letting the waves tumble down around her.

'That's better,' he said softly, slowly, something darkly sensual in his voice. 'Your beautiful bare neck was driving me to distraction. As it is, all I can think of is how much I want to put my mouth on you.'

Tess's breath caught in her throat, and for a second she wasn't sure if she should stay rigidly still and hope he'd simply move away or if she should turn to face whatever insanity was going to pass between them again tonight.

She inched herself around in the small space between the sink and Dante's towel-clad body. This close, the tattoos on his bare chest were mesmerizing, a flourish of geometric symbols and swirling arcs rendered in a range of hues from deep russet to gold and green to peacock blue.

'Do you like them?' he murmured, watching her gaze follow the strange, interlocking patterns and beautiful colors.

'I've never seen anything like them. I think they're stunning, Dante. Are they tribal-inspired?'

He gave a vague shrug. 'More of a family tradition. My father was similarly marked; so was his father before him, and all the other males of our line.'

Wow. If the men of Dante's family looked anything like him, they must have wreaked holy havoc on the hearts of women everywhere. Recalling just how far down the tattoos went below the hem of the towel at Dante's hips made Tess's face flush with heat.

He merely smiled, a knowing curve of his lips.

Tess closed her eyes and worked to steady her breath, then looked to him once more as she brought the warm, wet cloth between them and dabbed at the smudged stains on his cheeks and brow. He had some drying blood on his hands too, so she swabbed it away, holding his upturned palm in her own. His fingers were large and long, dwarfing hers when he curled them around her hand.

'I like feeling you touch me, Tess. I've been wanting your hands on me since the first time I saw you.'

She looked up to meet his eyes, her mind flooding with memories of the night before. The whiskey-gold color of his gaze drew her in, telling her that it was going to happen again – the two of them naked, bodies joined. She was getting the definite idea that it was always going to be hot and heavy like this with him. Her core tightened at the thought, a knot of intense hunger that bloomed out from the center of her, loosening her limbs.

'Let me just . . . see your leg now. . . .'

She reached down to where the edges of the towel split at his right hip and followed the muscular length of his thigh. The wound had stopped bleeding, so she gently cleansed the area, far too aware of the masculine beauty of his lines, the power in his firm legs, the soft, tawny skin that stretched over the slight jut of his pelvic bone. As she brought her cloth back up, she felt his sex rouse beneath the towel, the rigid shaft brushing her wrist as she withdrew.

Tess swallowed on a dry throat. 'I'll get the bandages now.'

She dropped the washcloth in the sink and pivoted to reach for the roll of white gauze, but Dante caught her hand. He held it in his warm grasp, smoothing his thumb over her skin as if he were silently asking her permission. When she didn't pull away, only turned back to face him, his eyes were glittering, the center of them seeming to glow within the bourbon-dark rim of color that surrounded his pupils.

'I should stay away from you,' he said, his voice low and thick. 'I should, but I can't.'

He captured the back of her neck in his large palm and brought her toward him, the few inches between them vanishing as their bodies pressed together. He lowered his mouth, and Tess's breath left her on a long sigh as his lips brushed hers in a slow, sweet kiss. One of his hands went around to the small of her back, sliding up under her loose knit shirt. His touch was hot, fingertips leaving trails of electricity all along her spine as he caressed her bare skin.

Dante's kiss deepened, his tongue thrusting into her mouth. Tess opened to him, moaning as the hard length of his erection prodded at her belly. Desire shot through her, wet and molten. His hand came around her rib cage, drawing slowly beneath the weight of her breast, then up over the tight nipple. A spray of goose bumps rose on her limbs, making her shiver with the need for more of his touch. For a long while there was only the sound of their combined breathing, the tender strokes of their hands on each other's bodies.

She was panting when he broke their kiss, boneless as he lifted her off the tiled floor and sat her down on the vanity's countertop. He pulled off her clingy white shirt and dropped it beside them. Her sweatpants went next. Dante eased her out, of them, leaving her sitting on the cabinet in just her panties. Her legs were parted, the wide V filled with Dante's perfect, masculine body, the terry cloth that covered his jutting arousal rasping softly against her inner thighs.

'Look what you have done to me,' he said, running his hand along her forearm as he guided her fingers beneath the towel to that enormous length of hard flesh that tented it.

Tess couldn't feign shyness as she touched him. She stroked his thick shaft and the weighted sac beneath, drawing up and down his velvety skin, taking her sweet time, her fingers hardly able to circle his width. As she palmed the smooth head of his sex, she leaned forward to kiss his ridged belly, reveling in all the softness that sheathed so much strength.

Dante groaned as she played her tongue along the intricate lines of his tattoos, the rumble of his deep voice vibrating against her lips. His arms caged her on either side, the huge muscles bulging as he gripped the edges of the vanity and let her have her way with him. His head was dropped down on his broad chest, his eyes hooded but burning with intensity when Tess ventured a glance up at him. She smiled, then leaned back in to swirl her tongue around the rim of his navel, unable to resist the urge to nip at his smooth skin.

He hissed a curse through his teeth as she grazed him. 'Ah, God – yes. Do it harder,' he growled. 'I want to feel your little bite, Tess.'

She didn't know what came over her, but she did what he asked, bringing her teeth together as she sucked some of his flesh into her mouth. She didn't break his skin, but the sharp bite seemed to travel through Dante's body like a current. He gave a sharp thrust of his hips, dislodging the towel, which had long since become an annoyance to her too. He shuddered as she smoothed her tongue over the spot she'd just abused.

'Did I hurt you?'

'No. Don't stop.' He curled himself over her and dropped a kiss on her bare shoulder. His muscles were clenched taut, his arousal surging even fuller in her hand. 'God, Tess. You are such a surprise to me. Please, don't stop.'

She didn't want to stop. It made absolutely no sense to her why she should feel such a strong connection to this man – such a fierce need – but then, when it came to Dante, there was a lot she didn't understand. She'd only just met him and yet he'd been with her for so long, as if fate had paired them up ages ago, then brought them together now.

Whatever it was, Tess had no desire to question.

She nipped her way down his belly, to his narrow hip, then

bent forward and took the head of his sex into her mouth. She sucked him deep, letting her teeth gently graze his shaft as she withdrew. He moaned sharply, braced before her as rigid as a column of steel. She felt Dante's pulse kick as she took him into her mouth again, felt the throb of his heartbeat traveling along the veined length.

She could feel the rush of his blood coursing through his body, scarlet-dark and ferocious, and for one startling, utterly insane moment, she wanted to know what all that power would taste like against her tongue.

The moonlit river was an undulating ribbon of black outside the tinted passenger window of the SUV And it was quiet, no other cars on the empty, weed-choked stretch of concrete that used to be the parking lot for an old paper mill, condemned about twenty years ago. Ben Sullivan was guessing it was a decent place for a murder, and the stony silence of the intense, heavily armed man at the wheel of the vehicle wasn't giving him a lot of reason to hope otherwise.

As the SUV rolled to a stop, Ben prepared himself for a fight, wishing to hell he'd found a way to get his hands back on that .45 he'd lost at his apartment. Not that he expected he'd have much of a chance with this guy, even if he was armed. Unlike his dark-haired partner, who broadcasted menace in his voice and his actions, this one held his cards close to his chest. He was icy calm, but Ben could read the seething rage that ran underneath the surface of that polished Mr. Cool demeanor, and it terrified him.

'What's going on? Why'd we stop here? Are we waiting for someone?' The questions poured out of him, but he was too anxious to care if he sounded like a chicken-shit. 'Your partner back there said he wanted you to take me to "the compound," didn't he?'

No reply.

'Well, wherever that is,' Ben said, looking around at the desolate lot, 'I don't suppose this is the place.'

With the vehicle idling in park, the driver blew out a long breath of air and turned a cold look on him. The guy's pale blue eyes were killer sharp, filled with barely restrained fury. 'You and I are going to have a private talk.'

'Am I going to survive it?'

He didn't answer, just stuck his hand into an inside pocket of his coat and pulled out a folded piece of paper. A photograph, Ben realized, catching the gloss in the dashboard light.

'Have you ever seen this individual?'

Ben glanced at the image of a clean-cut young man with tousled light brown hair and a broad, friendly smile. He wore a Harvard sweatshirt and was giving the photographer the thumbs-up sign with one hand, while the other held out a sheet of formal stationery emblazoned with the university's symbol on the letterhead.

'Well? Is he familiar to you?'

The question was a low snarl of sound, and while Ben was sure he'd seen the kid around, even dealt Crimson to him a few times this week alone, he didn't know whether or not that answer would be the one to save him or damn him right now. He slowly shook his head, lifting his shoulder in a noncommittal shrug.

Suddenly he was choking, his face caught in a bruising grip that crushed him so tightly he thought his jawbone would crack. God, the guy had struck like a viper – faster than that, because Ben hadn't even seen his hand move in the small space of the front seat.

'Have a closer look,' Mr. Cool demanded, pushing the photo up into Ben's face.

'O-okay,' Ben sputtered, tasting blood in his mouth as his teeth cut into the insides of his cheeks. 'Yeah, okay! Shit!'

The pressure eased and he coughed, rubbing his screaming jaw.

'Have you seen him?'

'Yeah, I've seen him. His name's Cameron or something.'

'Camden,' he corrected, voice tight and wooden. 'When did you last see him?'

Ben shook his head, trying to remember. 'Not too long ago. This week. He was hanging with some ravers at a tech-trance club in the North End. La Notte, I think it was.'

'Did you sell to him?' The words came out slowly, thick sounds that seemed obstructed by something in his mouth.

Ben flicked a wary glance across the seats. In the dim glow of the dash, the guy's eyes were throwing off a funky sheen, like his pupils were disappearing, stretching thin in the center of all that glacial blue. A chill entered Ben's bones, instinct kicking into high alert.

Something was off here, way off.

'Did you give him Crimson, you goddamn piece of shit?'

Ben swallowed hard. Gave a wobbly nod of his head. 'Yeah. The dude might have bought from me a couple of times.'

He heard a vicious growl, saw a flash of sharp white teeth in the dark in the split second before the back of his head smashed against the passenger-side window and the guy launched on top of him in an explosion of hellish fury.

❦ CHAPTER TWENTY-TWO ❧

S he was killing him.

Each swirl of Tess's tongue, every long draw of her tight mouth over his swollen flesh – *holy Christ, the teasing rasp of her teeth on him* – sent Dante further into a vortex of pleasured torment. Leaning over her as she sucked on him, he clutched the sides of the bathroom vanity in a vise grip, his face twisted, eyes squeezed shut in sweet agony.

His hips began pumping, his cock surging harder, reaching for the back of her throat. Tess took all of him in, moaning softly, the vibration buzzing against his sensitive head.

He didn't want her to see what he looked like now, lost to a lust he could hardly control. His fangs had stretched long in his mouth, nearly impossible to hide behind his tightly clenched lips. Underneath his closed eyelids, his vision burned red with hunger and need.

He could feel Tess's need too. The sweet scent of her arousal perfumed the humid air between them, filling his nostrils like the most potent aphrodisiac. And within that drenching perfume was another need, a curiosity that floored him.

Each tentative graze of her teeth on his skin tonight posed a question, each little nip and bite communicating a hunger she likely didn't understand, let alone have words to express. Would she break his skin and take his blood into her body?

God, to think she actually might . . .

It stunned him, how badly he wanted her to sink her tiny,

blunt human teeth into his flesh. When she withdrew from his sex and nipped his belly, Dante roared, the desire to urge her into drawing his blood and drinking it down nearly overpowering his far saner impulse to protect her from the Breedmate bond, which would tie her to him for as long as they both lived.

'No,' he growled, his voice rough, speech obstructed by the presence of his fangs.

With shaking hands, Dante took hold of Tess's hips. He lifted her toward him, cradling her bottom on his arms as he tore away her silk panties and filled the juncture of her thighs with his body. His cock glistened from the wetness of her mouth and his own need, engorged to the point of pain. He couldn't be gentle; with a hard thrust, he seated himself to the hilt.

Tess's breath rushed against his ear, her spine arching in his hands. Her fingers dug into his shoulders as he pistoned between her legs, his rhythm urgent, release coiling in the base of his shaft. He drove her hard, feeling her own climax building swiftly as her channel gripped him like a warm, wet fist.

'Oh, God . . . Dante.'

She broke apart an instant later, contracting around him in delicious ripples. Dante followed her over the edge, his orgasm shooting up his shaft and boiling out of him in a fierce torrent of heat. Wave after wave tore through him as he pumped into her like he never wanted to stop.

Dante peeled his eyes open as his body shook with the force of his release. In the mirror over the sink, he caught his feral reflection – the true picture of who, and what, he was.

His pupils were slivers of black in the center of glowing amber, his cheekbones stark, animalistic. His fangs were fully extended, long white points that flashed with every panting breath he hauled into his lungs.

'That was . . . incredible,' Tess murmured, hooking her arms under his shoulders to raise herself closer against him.

She kissed his damp skin, her lips trailing over his collarbone and up to the curve of his neck. Dante held her to him, his body still wedged inside hers. He waited, unmoving, willing the hungered part of him to heel. He flicked a glance back to his face in the mirror, knowing it would be a few minutes before his transformation subsided and he could look at Tess without terrifying her.

He didn't want her afraid of him. God, if she saw him now – if she knew what he had done to her that first night he'd seen her, when she had offered him kindness and he'd repaid her by taking her throat in his teeth – she would hate him. And rightly so.

Part of him wanted to sit her down and tell her all that she had forgotten about him. To lay it all out in the open. Start fresh, if they could.

Yeah, he imagined that little talk would go down about as smoothly as a glass of tacks. And it certainly wasn't a conversation he intended to strike up while she was still impaled on the resurgent length of him.

As he deliberated over the deepening complication he was making with Tess, a growl rumbled in from the open doorway. It was a small noise but unmistakably hostile.

Tess shifted, pivoting her head. 'Harvard! What's the matter with you?' She laughed a little, sounding shy now that the intensity of the moment was broken. 'Urn, I think we may have just traumatized your dog.'

She ducked out from the cage of Dante's arms and grabbed a terry bathrobe off a hook near the door. She slipped it on, then bent down to retrieve the terrier. Scooping up the animal, she got an immediate and vigorous chin-washing. Dante watched them from under a hank of his dark hair, relieved to feel his features coming back to normal.

'That dog has certainly made a quick recovery under your care.' A dramatic turnaround, Dante was guessing, and one that seemed too quick for normal medicine.

'He's a scrapper,' Tess said. 'I think he's going to be just fine.'

Although Dante had been concerned that she would detect his feral appearance, he realized he didn't need to worry. She seemed intent on avoiding looking at him directly now, as if she herself had something to hide.

'Yes, it's amazing how the animal has improved. I'd call it a miracle, if I believed in such things.' Dante watched her closely, curious and not a little bit suspicious. 'What exactly did you do to him, Tess?'

It was a simple question, one she probably could have satisfied with any number of explanations, yet she all but froze in the bathroom doorway. Dante sensed a sudden, swelling panic begin to rise in her.

'Tess,' he said. 'Is it such a difficult thing to answer?'

'No,' she replied hastily, but the word seemed to strangle in her throat. She shot him a fleeting, terrified look. 'I need to . . . I should, um . . .'

With the dog held tight in one arm, Tess brought her free hand to her mouth, then pivoted and made a fast retreat out of the bathroom without another word.

By the time she got to the living room and put the dog down on the sofa, Tess was pacing, feeling trapped and lacking air. God help her, but she actually wanted to tell him just what she'd done to save the little dog's life. She wanted to confide in Dante about her unique, damning ability – about everything – and it terrified her.

'Tess?' Dante came out right after her, a towel slung and knotted around his hips. 'What's wrong?'

'Nothing.' She gave a shake of her head, forced a smile that felt too tight for her mouth. 'There's nothing wrong, really. Do you want anything? If you're hungry, I made chicken for dinner. I could—'

'I want you to talk to me.' He caught her shoulders in his hands and held her still. 'Tell me what's going on. Tell me what this is about.'

'No.' She shook her head, thinking about how desperately she'd kept her secret and her shame. 'I'm just . . . You wouldn't understand, okay? I wouldn't expect you to understand.'

'Try me.'

Tess wanted to break away from his penetrating eyes but found she couldn't. He was reaching out to her, and a part of her needed so desperately to grab hold of something solid and strong. Something that wouldn't let her down.

'I swore I would never do it again, but I . . .'

Oh, God. She wasn't really going to crack open that ugly chapter of her life for him, was she?

It had been her secret for so long. She had protected it fiercely, had learned to fear it. The only two people who knew the truth about her ability – her stepfather and her mother – were dead. It was a part of her past, and her past was miles behind her.

Buried there, where it belonged.

'Tess.' Dante eased her down onto the sofa next to Harvard, who clambered onto her lap, tail wagging with eager joy. Dante sat beside her, his hand caressing her cheek. His touch was so tender, so warm. She nestled into it, unable to resist him. 'You can tell me anything. You are safe with me, Tess, I promise you.'

She wanted to believe that so badly, hot tears welled in her eyes. 'Dante, I . . .'

A silence stretched out to some long seconds. When the words failed her, Tess reached over to where the hem of the towel split over Dante's right thigh, exposing the gash on his leg. She lifted her gaze to him, then held her palm over the wound. She focused all her thoughts, all her energy, until she felt the healing begin.

Dante's injured skin began to fuse together, sealing as cleanly as if the damage had never occurred.

After a few moments, she drew her hand away and cradled her tingling palm against her body.

'My God,' Dante said, his voice low, dark brows knit into a deep frown.

Tess stared at him, uncertain what to say or how to explain what she'd just done. She waited in terrible silence for his reaction, uncertain what to make of his calm acceptance of what he'd just experienced.

He traced his fingers over the smooth, uninjured skin, then looked back at her. 'Is this how you do your work at the clinic, Tess?'

'No.' She denied it quickly, giving a vigorous shake of her head. The uncertainty she'd felt a second ago began sliding into fear of what Dante would think of her now. 'No, I don't – not ever. Well . . . I made an exception when I treated Harvard, but that was the only time.'

'What about humans?'

'No,' she said. 'No, I don't—'

'You've never used your touch on another person?'

Tess got to her feet, a cold panic washing over her when she thought about the last time – the final, damning time – she'd put her hands on another human being before this rash demonstration with Dante. 'My touch is a curse. I wish I didn't have this ability at all.'

'It's not a curse, Tess. It's a gift. A very extraordinary gift. Jesus, when I think of all that you could do—'

'No!' She shouted the refusal before she could bite it back, her feet carrying her a few steps away from where Dante was now getting up from the sofa. He looked at her with a mix of confusion and concern. 'I never should have done this. I never should have showed you.'

'Well, you have, and now you have to trust me to understand.

Why are you so afraid, Tess? Is it me you fear or is it your gift?'

'Stop calling it that!' She hugged herself in a tight grip, memories flooding her like a black, clutching undertow. 'You wouldn't call it a gift if you knew what it has made me into – what I have done.'

'Tell me.'

Dante came toward her then, moving slowly, his large body filling her vision and crowding her in the small living room. She thought she should want to run – to hide, as she'd been doing for the past nine years – but an even stronger impulse made her want to fly into his arms and let everything spill out of her in an ugly but cleansing rush.

She drew in a breath and was embarrassed to hear the hitch of a sob catching in the back of her throat.

'It's all right,' Dante said, his gentle voice and the tender way he took her into his embrace nearly making her break apart. 'Come here. It's okay.'

Tess clung to him, balancing on the edge of an emotional chasm she could feel but didn't dare look into yet. She knew the fall would be steep and painful, so many jagged rocks waiting to cut her open if she let go. Dante didn't push her. He just held her in the warm circle of his arms, letting her draw from his steady, solid strength.

Finally, the words found their way to her tongue. The weight of them was too much, the taste too vile, so she forced them out into the open.

'When I was fourteen, my father died in a car accident in Chicago. My mother remarried that next year, to a man she met at our church. He had a successful business in town and a big house on a lake. He was generous and friendly – everyone liked him, even me, despite the fact that I missed my real father very much.

'My mother drank, a lot, as long as I can remember. I

thought she was getting better after we moved into my stepfather's house, but it wasn't long before she fell into it again. My stepfather didn't care that she was an alcoholic. He always kept the bar stocked, even after her worst binges. I started to realize that he preferred her drunk, so much the better if she spent entire evenings passed out on the sofa and wasn't aware of what he was doing.'

Tess felt Dante's body go rigid around her. His muscles vibrated with a dangerous tension that felt like a shield of strength, cocooning her within their shelter. 'Did he . . . touch you, Tess?'

She swallowed hard, nodded against the warmth of his bare chest. 'At first, for almost a full year, he was careful. He hugged me too close and too long, looked at me in a way that made me uncomfortable. He tried to win me over with presents and parties for my friends at the lake house, but I didn't like being home, so once I turned sixteen I spent a lot of time out. I stayed over with friends, spent the summer at camp, anything to be away. But eventually I had to come home. Things escalated in the months leading up to my seventeenth birthday. He became violent toward both my mother and me, knocking us around, saying awful things to us. And then, one night . . .'

Tess's courage faltered, her head swimming with the remembered din of profanity and hysterical rantings, the clumsy racket of drunken stumbling, the splintering crash of breaking glass. And she could still hear the soft creak of her bedroom door that night her stepfather woke her from a fitful sleep, his breath stinking of liquor and cigarette smoke.

His meaty hand had been salty with sweat when he clamped it over her mouth to keep her from screaming:

'It was my birthday,' she whispered numbly. 'He came into my bedroom around midnight, telling me that he wanted to give me a birthday kiss.'

'That disgusting son of a bitch.' Dante's voice was a vicious growl, but his fingers were gentle as he stroked her hair. 'Tess . . . Christ. The other night by the river, when I tried to do the same thing—'

'No. It wasn't the same thing. It reminded me, yes, but it wasn't at all the same thing.'

'I'm so sorry. About everything. Especially what you've been through.'

'Don't,' she said, not willing to accept his sympathy when she hadn't gotten to the worst of it yet. 'After my stepfather came into my room, he got on the bed with me. I fought him, kicking him, slapping him, but he was much stronger than me and he pinned me down with his weight. Sometime during the struggle, I heard him draw in a sharp breath. He choked a little, like he was in pain. He stopped trying to hold me down, and I finally managed to roll him off me. He let go because his heart had seized up. He was turning deep red, then blue – dying right there on the floor of my bedroom.'

Dante said nothing in the long silence that followed. Maybe he knew where her confession was heading. She couldn't stop now. Tess pushed out a long breath, approaching the point of no return. 'About this time, my mother came in. Drunk as usual. She saw him and she went hysterical. She was furious – with me, I mean. She screamed at me to help him, to not let him die.'

'She knew what you could do with your touch?' Dante asked gently, easing her through it.

'She knew. She'd seen it firsthand, when I would take away her bruises and heal the broken bones. She was so mad at me – she blamed me for my stepfather's heart attack. I think she blamed me for everything.'

'Tess,' Dante murmured. 'She wasn't right to blame you for any of it. You do know that, right?'

'Now, yes. I know. But in that moment, I was so afraid. I didn't want her to be unhappy. So I helped him, just like she ordered me to do. I started his heart and cleared the blockage in his artery. He didn't know what happened to him, and we didn't tell him. It wasn't until three days later that I discovered just how bad of a mistake I'd made.'

Tess closed her eyes and she was back in time, walking out to her stepfather's toolshed to look for a putty knife for one of her sculpture projects. She was taking out the stepladder, climbing up to search the top shelves of the old shed. She didn't see the small wooden box until her elbow knocked it to the floor.

Pictures fell out, dozens of them. Polaroids of children of various ages, in various states of undress, some being touched by the photographer as he snapped the picture. She would have known those terrible hands anywhere.

Tess shuddered in Dante's arms, chilled to her marrow.

'I wasn't the only one my stepfather victimized. I found out that he'd been abusing kids in worse ways for what had to have been years, maybe decades. He was a monster, and I had given him a second chance to hurt someone else.'

'Jesus,' Dante hissed, drawing her away from him now but holding her tenderly as he looked on her with a sickened, furious look. 'It wasn't your fault. You couldn't have known, Tess.'

'But once I did,' she said, 'I had to make it right.' At Dante's frown, she let out a soft, wry laugh. 'I had to take back what I had given him.'

'Take it back?'

She nodded. 'That same night, I left my bedroom door open and I waited for him. I knew he'd come, because I asked him to. When he crept in after my mother was asleep, I invited him onto my bed – God, that was the hardest part of all, pretending that the sight of him didn't make me want to vomit. He stretched out beside me, and I told him to close his eyes, that I wanted to repay him for the birthday kiss he'd given me a few nights before. I told him not to peek, and he obeyed me, he was so damn eager.

'I straddled his waist and put my hands on his chest. All my anger rushed to my fingertips in a second, like an electrical current that ripped through me and directly into him. His eyes flew open, and he knew – the look of terror and confusion in his eyes told me that he knew exactly what I intended for him. But it was too late for him to react. His body spasmed violently, and his heart went into immediate arrest. I held on with every ounce of my resolve, feeling his life leak away. I didn't let go for twenty minutes, long after he was gone, but I had to be sure.'

Tess didn't realize she was crying until Dante reached out and wiped away her tears. She shook her head, voice strangling in her throat. 'I left home that same night. I came out here to New England and stayed with friends until I was able to finish school and get a fresh start.'

'What about your mother?'

Tess shrugged. 'I never spoke to her again, not that she cared. She never tried to find me, and I was glad for that, to tell you the truth. Anyway, she died a few years ago of liver disease, from what I understand. After that night – after what I did – I just wanted to forget everything.'

Dante gathered her close again, and she didn't fight the warmth. She burrowed into his heat, drained from reliving the nightmare of her past. Speaking the words had been hard, but now that they were out, she felt a sense of liberation, of sagging relief.

God, she was so exhausted. It seemed as though all her years of running and hiding had caught up with her at once, pulling her into a deep fatigue.

'I swore to myself that I would never use my ability again, not on any living thing. It's a curse, like I told you. Maybe now you understand.'

Tears stung her eyes and she let them fall, trusting that she was in a safe harbor, at least for now. Dante's strong arms were wrapped around her protectively. His softly murmured words were a comfort she needed more than she could ever have imagined.

'You did nothing wrong, Tess. That human scum had no right to live as he was doing. You dispensed justice on your own terms, but it was justice. Never doubt that.'

'You don't think I'm . . . some kind of monster? That I'm not much better than him to have killed him like I did, in cold blood?'

'Never.' Dante lifted her chin on the edge of his hand. 'I think you're courageous, Tess. An avenging angel, that's what I think.'

'I'm a freak.'

'No, Tess, no.' He kissed her tenderly. 'You're amazing.'

'I'm a coward. Just like you said, I always run away. It's true. I've been afraid and running for so long, I'm not sure I can ever stop.'

'Then run to me.' Dante's eyes were fierce as he held her gaze. 'I know all about fear, Tess. It lives in me too. That "seizure" I had in your clinic? It's not a medical condition, not even close.'

'What is it?'

'Death,' he said woodenly. 'For as long as I can remember, I've had these attacks – these visions – of my last moments alive. It's hellish beyond imagining, but I see it as if it's happening. I feel it, Tess. It's my fate.'

'I don't understand. How can you be sure of that?'

His smile was wry. 'I'm sure. My mother had similar visions of her own death, and my father's too. They happened precisely as she envisioned them. She couldn't change what was to happen, or turn it back. So I've been trying to outrun my own end. I've been running from it forever. I've kept myself insulated from things that might make me want to slow down and live. I've never permitted myself to truly feel.'

'There's danger in feeling,' Tess murmured. Although she could not begin to imagine what kind of pain Dante carried within him, she felt a kinship growing between them. Both alone, both adrift in their worlds. 'I don't want to feel anything for you, Dante.'

'God, Tess. I don't want to feel anything for you either.'

He held her gaze as his lips slowly descended on hers. His kiss was sweet and tender, something reverent. It broke down all of her walls, the bricks of her past and her pain tumbling away, leaving her naked to him and unable to hide. Tess kissed him back, needing more. She was cold to her bones, and she needed all the warmth he could give her.

'Take me to bed,' she whispered against his mouth. 'Please, Dante . . .'

⇥ CHAPTER TWENTY-THREE ⇤

Chase entered his Darkhaven residence from around the back, thinking it best not to alarm the whole house by coming in through the front, seething like an animal and covered in blood. Elise was up; he could hear her soft voice in the first-floor living room, where she and some of the community's other Breedmate females had gathered.

And he could smell her too. His senses were heightened from the rage still boiling through him – the violence he'd delivered – and the feminine scent of the woman he desired more than any other was like a drug shot directly into his vein.

With a feral snarl, Chase turned in the opposite direction of his sister-in-law and headed for his private quarters. He kicked the door shut as he entered, his hands working furiously at the zipper of his jacket, which was ruined with the human's spilled blood. He tore the jacket off and threw it to the floor, then pulled off his shirt and discarded it too.

He was a mess, from the bleeding scrapes and contusions on his hands after beating Ben Sullivan nearly to a pulp to the fevered, savage thirst that made him want to destroy something, even now, some time after he'd left the scene of his uncontrollable fury. It had been a stupid thing to do, attacking the Crimson dealer like he had, but the need to enact some measure of vengeance had been overwhelming.

Chase had given in to savage impulse, something he rarely did. Hell, had he ever? He always prided himself on his rigid, righteous ideals. His refusal to let emotion overrule his logic.

Now, in one careless moment, he'd fucked everything up.

Although he hadn't killed the Crimson dealer, he had leaped on him with full intent for murder. He'd bared his fangs and sunk them into the human's throat, not caring that in doing so he was exposing himself as a vampire. He had attacked savagely, but in the end he had brought his fury to heel and let the human go. Maybe he should have scrubbed his memory to protect the Breed from exposure, but Chase wanted Ben Sullivan to remember exactly what was waiting for him if he reneged on their agreement.

The entire situation was an outright betrayal of the trust he'd been granted by Dante and the rest of the warriors, but Chase couldn't see where he had much choice. He needed Ben Sullivan on the streets, not tucked away under the protective custody of the Order. Repugnant as the idea was, he needed the dealer's cooperation in helping him find Camden. It was a bargain he'd made the human scum swear upon over his own spilling blood. Sullivan was no idiot, and after the taste of vampiric fury he'd gotten tonight, he'd begged to help Chase in whatever way he could.

Chase understood that he was solo on his mission now. There would be some hell to pay with Dante and the others, but so be it. He was too far into this personal crusade to care about his own consequences. He'd already forfeited his position at the Agency, the career he'd worked so hard to make. Tonight he'd given up some of his honor. He'd give up anything to see this mission through.

Flicking on the light in his bathroom, Chase caught a sudden, stark glimpse of his own reflection. He was blood-spattered and sweating, his eyes glowing like amber coals, the pupils winnowed down to slits by residual anger and his body's thirst to feed. The *dermaglyphs* on his bare chest and shoulders pulsed in hues of pale scarlet and faded gold, indications of his general need for blood. The small taste he'd consumed when he bit Ben Sullivan's throat hadn't helped; the bitter copper tang lingering in his mouth only made him long to erase it with something sweeter.

Something delicate, like heather and roses – the blood scent he could trace coming closer to his apartments even as he stood there, glaring at the feral creature who stared back at him in the mirror.

The hesitant knock on the door outside went through his body like cannon fire.

'Sterling? Have you returned?'

He didn't answer. Couldn't, in fact. His tongue was cleaved to the roof of his mouth, his jaw ground tight behind the pained sneer of his pale, curled-back lips. He had to clamp down hard on his mind to keep himself from throwing the door open with the force of his will.

If he let her in now, unbalanced as he currently was, nothing would stop him from pulling her into his arms and slaking the twin hungers that were raging within him. He would be at her vein in a second; little more than that and he would be pushing inside her, damning himself completely.

Proving to himself just how far down he could sink in the course of one night.

Instead, he marshaled his mental strength and used it to cut the lights in the bathroom, plunging the space into a more comfortable darkness as he waited the long eternity that seemed to pass in those moments of answering silence. His eyes burned like embers. His fangs were ripping farther out of his gums, echoing the swelling ache of his arousal.

'Sterling . . . are you home?' she called again, and his ears were so attuned to her presence that he could detect her little sigh across the span of his apartments and through the solid panel of the door. He knew her well enough that he could picture the tiny frown that was certain to be creasing her forehead as she listened for him, then, finally, decided he wasn't there after all.

Chase stood stock-still, silent, waiting to hear her footsteps retreat softly down the hallway. Only when she was gone, the scent of her fading with her departure, did he release his pent-up breath. It leaked out of his lungs on a deep, miserable howl, vibrating the darkened mirror in front of him.

Chase let it go, focusing his frustration – his damnable torment – on that rattling sheet of polished glass until it shattered off the wall into a thousand razor-edged shards.

Dante stroked his fingers over the soft skin of Tess's bare shoulder as she slept. He lay in bed next to her, spooning the back of her naked body against the front of his and simply listening to her breathe. Around them, the room was quiet and dark, as peaceful as the wake of a passed storm.

The persistent calm was strange, the sense of comfort and contentment something entirely unfamiliar to him.

Unfamiliar, but . . . nice.

Dante's body stirred with interest as he held Tess in his arms, but he had no intention of disturbing her sleep. They'd made love tenderly after he brought her to bed, at a pace he'd let her set and control, letting her take whatever she needed from him. But now, even though his body was awake with arousal, all he wanted to do was comfort her. To simply be with her for as long as the night could last.

A shocking revelation for a male unaccustomed to denying himself any pleasure or desire.

But then, as far as this evening was going, shocking revelations were practically a given.

It was not unusual for a Breedmate to have at least one extraordinary or extrasensory ability – a gift that also typically passed down to her Breed offspring. Whatever the genetic anomaly was that made the rare human's womb capable of accepting a vampire's seed and her aging process halt with the regular ingestion of his blood, it also made her something more than her basic *Homo sapiens* sisters.

For Dante's mother, the talent was a terrible precognition. For Gideon's mate, Savannah, it was psychometry, the talent to read the history of an object – more specifically, she could also read the history of the object's owner. Gabrielle, the Breedmate who'd only recently come into the Order's fold as Lucan's woman, had an intuitive vision that drew her to vampire lairs and a strong mind that made her all but impervious to thought control, even by the most powerful of Dante's kind.

For Tess, it was the amazing ability to heal a living creature with her touch. And the fact that she had been able to heal Dante's leg wound meant that her restorative talents extended to those of the Breed as well. She would be such an asset to the race. God, when he thought of all the good she could bring –

Dante clipped the idea before it could take shape in his head. What happened here didn't change the fact that he was living on borrowed time or that his duty was, first and foremost, to the Breed. He wanted Tess shielded from the pain of her past, but it seemed unfair to ask her to leave the life she was building for herself. Even more unfair was what he'd done by taking her blood that very first night, linking them inextricably to each other.

Yet, as he lay there beside her, caressing her skin, breathing in the cinnamon-sweet scent of her, Dante wanted nothing more than to scoop Tess up and carry her away with him, back to the compound, where he knew she would be safe from all the evil that might touch her topside.

Evil like the stepfather who'd given her so much anguish. Tess worried that killing the bastard had made her as bad as him, but Dante had only respect for what she'd done. She'd slain a monster, sparing herself and who knew how many other children from his abuse.

To Dante, Tess had proven herself a warrior at that tender age, and the ancient part of him that still subscribed to things like honor and justice wanted to shout to the entire sleeping city below that this was *his* woman.

Mine, he thought fiercely, selfishly.

As he leaned in and pressed a kiss to her delicate shoulder blade, the phone in her kitchen began to ring. He blasted the device with a sharp mental command, silencing the ring before it could wake her completely. She roused, moaning a little as she murmured his name.

'I'm here,' he said quietly. 'Sleep, angel. I'm still here.'

As she drifted off again, nestling tighter against him, Dante wondered how long he had before dawn would drive him away. Not long enough, he thought, astonished that he could feel that way and knowing that he couldn't blame his feelings on the inconvenience of the blood bond he had unintentionally forced on them both.

No, what he was beginning to feel for Tess went a lot deeper than that. It went all the way to his heart.

'God damn it, Tess. Pick up!'

Ben Sullivan's voice was shrill, quivering, his entire body shaking uncontrollably from trauma and a fear so intense he thought he might pass out from it.

'Fuck! Come on – *answer.*'

He stood in a nasty pay phone booth in one of the worst areas of town, the chewed-up, crusted-over receiver gripped in his bloody fingers. His free hand was clamped at the side of his neck, sticky from the horrific bite wound inflicted there. His face was swollen from the savage pounding he'd taken, the back of his head screaming with pain from a goose-egg-size lump he'd gotten from the window of the SUV

He couldn't believe he wasn't dead. He had thought for sure he would be killed, based on the fury with which he'd been attacked. He'd been stunned when the guy – Jesus, was he even human? – ordered him to get out of the vehicle. He'd thrust the photograph of the kid he was looking for into Ben's hand and let him know that if this Cameron, Camden, whatever, turned up dead, Ben would be held solely responsible.

Now Ben had been enlisted to help find him, to make sure the kid got home in one piece. Ben's life depended on it, and as much as he wanted to hightail it out of town and forget he ever heard the word *Crimson*, he knew the lunatic who attacked him tonight would find him. The guy had promised he would, and Ben wasn't about to test his rage in a second round.

'Damn it,' he grumbled, as the call to Tess's apartment went into voice mail.

As bad off as he was now – as deep in the shit as he'd landed tonight – he felt a moral obligation to warn Tess about the guy she'd been messing around with lately. If his buddy was a psychotic freak of nature, Ben was betting that the other one was just as dangerous.

God, Tess.

When the voice-mail greeting left off with a beep, Ben rushed through the night's events, from the surprise ambush at his place by the two thugs to the attack on him a short while ago. He blurted out that he'd seen her with one of the guys the other night and that he worried she was risking her life if she continued to see him.

He could hear the words spilling out of him in a breathless stream, his voice pitched higher than normal, fear edging on hysteria. By the time he'd gotten it all out and slammed the phone back down onto the chipped cradle, he could hardly breathe. He leaned back against a graffiti-tagged panel of the phone booth and bent over, closing his eyes as he tried to calm his rattled system.

A barrage of feelings came at him in a giant swell: panic, guilt, helplessness, bone-deep terror. He wanted to take it all back – the past several months, everything that had happened, everything he'd done. If only he could go back and erase things, make them right. Would Tess be with him, then? He didn't know. And it didn't fucking matter, because he couldn't take any of it back.

The most he could hope to do now was survive.

Ben dragged in a deep breath and forced himself to stand. He pushed out of the phone booth and started walking down the darkened street, looking like holy hell. A homeless person recoiled from him as he cut across the road and hobbled toward the main drag. As he walked, he dug out the picture of the kid he was supposed to look for.

Glancing down at the snapshot, trying to focus on the bloodstained image, Ben didn't hear the approaching car until it was nearly on top of him. Brakes screeched and the vehicle was thrown into an abrupt stop. The doors opened in tandem, a trio of unfamiliar bouncer types pouring out.

'Going somewhere, Mr. Sullivan?'

Ben jolted into flight mode, but he didn't even get two steps on the pavement before he was seized by all of his limbs. He watched the photograph land on the wet asphalt, a large boot trampling it as the men started carrying him back to the waiting car.

'So glad we finally located you,' said a voice that sounded human but somehow wasn't. 'When you failed to show up at your meeting tonight, the Master became very concerned. He'll be pleased to hear that you are on your way now.'

Ben struggled against his captors, but it was no use. They stuffed him into the trunk and slammed the lid, plunging him into darkness.

CHAPTER TWENTY-FOUR

The early-dawn colors seemed brighter to Tess, the November air crisply invigorating outside her apartment as she finished up her short walk with Harvard. As she and the terrier jogged up the stairs of her building, she felt stronger, lighter, no longer weighed down by the awful secret she'd been carrying all these years.

She had Dante to thank for that. She had him to thank for so much, she thought, her heart throbbing, her body still humming with the sweet ache of their lovemaking.

She'd been hugely disappointed to wake up and find him gone, but the note he'd left folded on her night-stand took away most of that sting. Tess dug the piece of paper out of the pocket of her fleece track pants as she pushed open her apartment door and let Harvard off his leash.

Strolling into her kitchen in need of coffee, she read Dante's bold handwriting for about the tenth time, her broad smile seeming permanently stuck on her face: *Didn't want to wake you but had to leave. Have dinner with me tomorrow night? I want to show you where I live. I'll call you. Sleep tight, angel. Yours, D.*

Yours, he'd signed it.

Hers.

A wave of fierce possessiveness swamped her at the thought. Tess told herself that it meant nothing, that she was foolish to read anything into Dante's words or to imagine that the powerful connection she felt toward him might be mutual, but she was practically giddy as she set the note down on the counter.

She glanced at the little dog who was dancing around her feet, waiting for his breakfast. 'Well, Harvard, what do you think? Am I getting in too deep here? I'm not actually falling for him, am I?'

God, was she . . . falling in love?

A week ago she hadn't known he existed, so how could she even consider that her feelings might go that far this fast? But somehow they did. She was falling in love with Dante, maybe already had, judging by the sharp tumble her heart was taking just thinking about him now.

Harvard's eager bark snapped her out of the emotional free fall. 'Right,' she said, looking down into his furry face. 'Kibble and coffee, not necessarily in that order. I'm on it.'

She filled her Mr. Coffee machine with Starbucks grounds and cold water from the tap, hit the button to start it brewing, then went to retrieve a bowl and the dry dog food from the pantry. As she passed her kitchen phone, she saw that the message indicator was flashing.

'Here you go, baby,' she said, pouring a serving of Iams into Harvard's dish and setting it down on the floor. '*Bon appétit.*'

With more than a little hope that the message might' have been from Dante calling while she was out walking his dog, Tess pressed the play button and put the voice mail on speaker. She waited anxiously, punching in her pass code and listening as the automated greeting announced that she had one new message, time-stamped from late last night, and began playing it back to her.

'*Tess! Jesus Christ, why aren't you picking up your fucking phone?*'

It was Ben, she realized, her disappointment over that fact swiftly draining into alarm at the odd tone of his voice. She'd never heard him sound so panicked, so unglued. He was breathing hard, panting, his words spilling out of him. He wasn't merely afraid. He was terrified. Worry clutched at her with icy talons as she listened to the rest of his call.

'– *needed to warn you. The guy you're seeing, he's not what you think. They busted into my place tonight – him and some other dude. I thought they were going to kill me, Tess! But it's you I'm afraid for now. You've got to stay away from him. He's into some fucked-up shit. . . . I know this sounds crazy, but the guy he was with tonight . . . I don't think – ah, Jesus, I just have to say it – I don't think he's human. Maybe neither of them is. The other guy took me away in an SUV – I should've tried to get the number off the plates or something, but everything was happening so fucking fast. He drove me down to the river and he attacked me, Tess. The son of a bitch had these huge teeth – they were fangs, I swear to God, and his eyes were lit up like they were on fire! He wasn't human. Tess, they're not . . . human.*'

She backed away from the counter as the message played on, Ben's voice chilling her as much as the things he was telling her.

'*Asshole bit me – smashed my head into a car window, beat me nearly unconscious, and then . . . he fucking bit me! Ah, Christ, my neck is still bleeding. I gotta get to a hospital or something. . . .*'

Tess retreated into her living room, as if the distance from Ben's voice would somehow insulate her from what she was hearing. She didn't know how to make sense of any of it.

How could Dante be involved – even peripherally – in an attack on Ben like the one he described? True, after he'd arrived at her place last night loaded down with weapons and bleeding from an obvious altercation, he had said he'd been pursuing a drug dealer. It certainly could have been Ben he was talking about. Tess had to admit, albeit sadly, that it wasn't that big of a stretch to imagine Ben falling back into his old ways.

But he was talking absolute nonsense now. Men who could turn into fanged monsters? Savagery that belonged in a horror movie? Those things had no place in real life, not even in the harshest realm of reality. It just wasn't possible.

Was it?

Tess found herself standing in front of the shrouded sculpture she'd been working on last night, the one of Dante's likeness. The one she'd botched and would probably end up throwing away. She'd gotten his mouth all wrong, hadn't she? Given him some strange sort of sneer that didn't look like him at all?

Now her fingers tingled as she reached for the scrap of cloth that covered the piece. Confusion and an odd, niggling dread sat in her stomach like a stone as she grasped the edge of the fabric and drew it clear of the bust. Her breath caught in her throat when she saw what she had done – the mistake she'd made had given Dante a wild, almost animal-like appearance . . . right down to the sharp canines that turned his smile into a feral-looking sneer.

Inexplicably, she had given him fangs.

'*I'm really afraid, Tess. For both of us,*' Ben's voice said over the speaker of her answering machine. '*Just . . . whatever you do, stay the hell away from these guys.*'

Dante flipped his *malebranche* blades, one in each hand, the steel flashing in the fluorescent lights of the compound's training facility. He spun at blinding speed and struck hard at the polymer target dummy, ripping twin razor-sharp lacerations several inches into the thick plastic hide. With a roar, he pivoted around and went at it again with a further assault.

He needed to feel at least the semblance of combat, because if he sat still for more than a second, he was going to kill someone. Top on his list at the moment was Darkhaven Agent Sterling Chase. Ben Sullivan was a damn close runner-up. Hell, if he could take both of them out at once, so much the better.

He'd been fuming ever since he returned to the compound and learned that the agent had been a no-show with their Crimson dealer. Lucan and the others were giving Chase the benefit of the doubt for now, but Dante had a feeling in his gut that Chase, for whatever his reasons, had willfully defied his order to take Ben Sullivan into custody at the compound.

Dante meant to find out what had happened, but phone calls, e-mails, and pages to the agent's Darkhaven residence had gone unanswered. Unfortunately, an in-person interrogation was going to have to wait until sundown.

Which is roughly ten frigging hours away, Dante thought, delivering another savage attack on the target dummy.

The wait was made even worse by the fact that he'd been unable to reach Tess either. He called her apartment first thing in the morning, but she had apparently already left for work. He hoped she was somewhere safe. Assuming Chase hadn't killed Ben Sullivan, the human could be loose on the streets, and that meant he could get to Tess. Dante didn't think she was in danger from her ex-boyfriend, but he really wasn't willing to take that risk.

He needed to bring her inside, explain to her every-thing that was happening, including who he truly was – what he truly was – and admit how he had brought her into the middle of this war between the Breed and its enemies.

He was going to do it tonight. He'd already set the stage with the note he'd left at her bedside, but now the sense of urgency was growing. He wanted it done and over with already, hated being so far removed from her while he waited for night to fall.

With a roar, he flew at his target again, hands moving so fast even he couldn't track them. He heard the glass doors to the training facility slide open some distance behind him, but he was too lost in his own angry frustration to give a damn if he had an audience. He kept slicing, jabbing, brutalizing his target until he was panting with the exertion, a sheen of sweat breaking out on his bare chest and brow. Finally he paused, astonished at the depth of his fury. The polymer dummy was cut to pieces, most of it in shredded chunks around his feet.

'Nice work,' Lucan drawled from across the large facility. 'You got something against plastic, or is this just a warm-up for tonight?'

With an exhaled curse, Dante flipped his blades between his fingers, letting the curved metal dance before he thrust both weapons into the sheaths belted at his hips. He pivoted to face the Order's leader, who was leaning back against a weapons cabinet, a grave look on his dark features.

'We've got some news,' Lucan said, obviously expecting it wasn't going to go over well. 'Gideon just hacked into the Darkhavens' Enforcement Agency personnel database. Turns out Agent Sterling Chase doesn't work for them anymore. They released him from service last month, after a spotless twenty-five-year career.'

'He was fired?'

Lucan nodded. 'For insubordination and flagrant refusal to follow Agency directives, according to the file.'

Dante pushed out a humorless chuckle as he toweled off. 'Agent Sterling's not so sterling after all, eh? Goddamn it, I knew there was something off about the guy. He's been fucking playing us this whole time. Why? What's he after?'

Lucan shrugged idly. 'Maybe he needed us to get him close to the Crimson dealer. What's to say he didn't take the guy out last night? Some kind of personal vendetta.'

'Maybe. I don't know, but I mean to find out.' Dante cleared his throat, feeling suddenly awkward in the presence of the elder vampire, who had long been a brother-in-arms – a friend, in fact. 'Listen, Lucan. I haven't exactly been playing straight lately either. Something's happened – the night I almost got my ass handed to me down at the river by those Rogues. I, uh, I came to in the back room of an animal clinic. There was a woman there, working late. I needed blood in a bad way, and she was the only one around.'

Lucan's dark brows came down in a scowl. 'You kill her?'

'No. No, I was out of my head, but it didn't go that far. Far enough, though. I didn't realize what I had done to her until it was too late. When I saw the mark on her hand—'

'Ah, Jesus, Dante.' The large male stared at him, those gray eyes lancing into him. 'You drank from a Breedmate?'

'Yeah. Her name is Tess.'

'Does she know? What have you told her?'

Dante shook his head. 'She doesn't know anything yet. I scrubbed her memory that night, but I've been, uh . . . spending time with her. A lot of time. I have to cop to her about what I've done, Lucan. She deserves to have the truth. Even if she ends up hating me for it, which wouldn't surprise me.'

Lucan's shrewd gaze narrowed. 'You care for her.'

'God. Yeah, I do.' Dante's answering chuckle sounded sharp in his ears. 'Sure as hell didn't see this coming, let me tell you. And to be honest, I don't know what I'm going to do about it. I'm not exactly premium mate material.'

'You think I am?' Lucan asked wryly.

It was only a few months ago that Lucan was fighting a similar personal battle, having lost his heart to a female bearing the Breedmate mark. Dante didn't know the specifics of how Lucan won Gabrielle over, but part of him envied the long future the pair would share together. All Dante had to look forward to was a death he'd been dodging for a couple of centuries.

Thinking about Tess being anywhere near him on that day made his blood run cold with dread.

'I don't know how things are going to shake down, but I need to tell her everything. I'd like to bring her here tonight, maybe help it all make sense.' He ran a hand through his damp hair. 'Hell, maybe I'm just a pussy and I need to know I've got my' – he almost said *family* – 'the Order behind me on this.'

Lucan smiled, nodding slowly. 'You always will,' he said, reaching out to clap Dante on the shoulder. 'Gotta tell you,

I'm looking forward to meeting the woman who can scare the shit out of one of the fiercest warriors I've ever known.'

Dante laughed. 'She's fine, Lucan. Damn, she is just so incredibly *fine*.'

'At sundown, you take Tegan with you when you head out to question Chase. Bring him back in one piece, we clear? Then you go make things right with your Breedmate.'

'Chase I can handle,' Dante said. 'It's the other part I'm not so sure about. You got any advice for me on that, Lucan?'

'Sure.' The vampire grunted, his smile filled with dark amusement. 'Dust off your knees, brother, because you may damn well end up walking on them before the night is through.'

CHAPTER TWENTY-FIVE

Tess had a full day of appointments and walk-ins at the clinic, work she was grateful for because it helped give her something to think about besides Ben's disturbing telephone message. Yet it was impossible to put his call out of her mind completely. He was in some serious trouble – injured and bleeding besides.

Now, it seemed, he had simply vanished.

She'd tried calling his apartment several times, and his cell phone, the area hospitals . . . but there was no sign of him anywhere. If she had known how or where to contact his parents, she would have tried them too, even though the odds of Ben turning up there were slim to none. As it stood, the only other thing she could think of was to go past his place after work and see if she could find some sign of him there. She wasn't holding out a lot of hope, but what were her alternatives?

'Nora, patient in Two needs a combo test and urine sample,' Tess said, coming out of the examination room. 'Can you get those for me while I check the X-rays of our collie with the joint inflammations?'

'You got it.'

'Thanks.'

As she grabbed the films for her next patient, her cell phone went off in her lab-coat pocket, the vibration beating against her thigh like bird's wings. She dug the device out and checked the ID to see if it might be Ben. The number was blocked.

Oh, God.

She knew who it was, who it had to be. She'd been suspended in an awful state between anticipation and dread all morning, knowing that Dante was going to call. He'd called her apartment as she was leaving early that day, but she'd let the blocked call go straight to voice mail. She hadn't been ready to talk to him then; she wasn't at all sure she was ready now.

Tess walked down the hall to her office and closed the door, her spine sagging against the cool metal. The phone trembled in her hand as it rang for the fifth and probably final time. She shut her eyes and touched the talk button.

'Hello?'

'Hey, angel.'

The sound of Dante's deep, delicious voice sent a slow current through her. She didn't want to feel the warmth that spread along her limbs and pooled in the center of her being, but it was there, melting the edges of her resolve.

'Everything okay?' he asked when she fell silent, an air of protective concern in his tone. 'You still with me, or did I lose you?'

She sighed, unsure how to answer that.

'Tess? What's wrong?'

For a long few seconds, all she could do was breathe in and out. She hardly knew where to begin, and she was terrified of where it was all going to end now. A thousand questions crowded her mind, a thousand doubts that had been raised in the hours since she'd listened to Ben's bizarre message.

Part of her doubted Ben's outrageous claims – the rational part of her that knew better than to believe there could be monsters loose on the streets of Boston. Yet there was another part of her that wasn't as quick to dismiss the unexplainable, the stuff that existed with or without tidy logic or conventional science.

'Tess,' Dante said amid the quiet, 'you know you can talk to me.'

'Do I?' she said, finally pushing words out of her mouth.

'I'm not sure what I know right now, Dante. I'm not sure what to think – about anything.'

He swore, a snarled oath spoken in Italian. 'What happened? Are you . . . hurt? Jesus, if he touched you in any way—'

Tess scoffed. 'I suppose that answers one thing for me already. We're talking about Ben, aren't we? He was the drug dealer you were after last night?'

There was a slight hesitation. 'Have you seen him today, Tess? Have you seen him at any time since you and I were together last night?'

'No,' she said. 'I haven't seen him, Dante.'

'But you spoke with him. When?'

'He called last night and left a message, evidently while we were . . .' She shook her head, not wanting to remember how wonderful it had felt to lie in her bed in Dante's arms, how protected and peaceful she'd felt. Now all she felt was a pervading chill. 'Is that why you've been screwing around with me, because you needed me in order to get close to him?'

'Christ, no. It's a lot more complicated than that—'

'How complicated? Have you been playing me all this time? Or did the real game start the night you showed up here with your dog and we – Oh, my God, now even that makes more sense. Harvard isn't your dog at all, is he? What did you do, take some stray animal off the street to use as bait for reeling me into your sick game?'

'Tess, please. I wanted to explain—'

'Go ahead. I'm listening.'

'Not like this,' he growled. 'I'm not going to do this over the phone.' She felt a dark tension growing in him as he spoke, could almost see him pacing on the other end, alive with restless energy, his black brows low over his eyes in a scowl, his strong hand raking over his scalp. 'Listen, you need to stay away from Ben Sullivan. He's involved in something very dangerous. I don't want you anywhere near him, do you understand?'

'That's funny. He said the same thing about you. He said a lot of things, actually. Crazy things, like how your partner brutally assaulted him last night.'

'What?'

'He said he'd been bitten, Dante. Can you explain that to me? He said the man you were with when the two of you broke into Ben's apartment took him away in a car and then savagely attacked him. According to Ben, he was bitten in the throat.'

'Son of a bitch.'

'Can that be true?' she asked, horrified that he hadn't even attempted to deny it was possible. 'Do you know where Ben is? I haven't heard from him since that call. Have you or your friends done something to him? I have to see him.'

'No! I don't know where he is, Tess, but you have to promise me you'll stay away from him.'

Tess felt miserable, scared, and confused. 'What's happening here, Dante? What are you really involved in?'

'Tess, look. I need you to go somewhere safe. Right now. Go to a hotel, a public building, anywhere – just go right now and stay there until I can come and get you tonight.'

Tess laughed, but it was a humorless sound that grated in her ears. 'I'm working, Dante. And even if I wasn't, I don't think I'd go anywhere to wait for you. Not until I understand what's going on here.'

'I will tell you, Tess. I promise you. I had planned to tell you all of it, even if this hadn't happened.'

'Okay, fine. My schedule is booked solid today, but I can break for lunch in a couple of hours. If you want to talk to me, you'll have to come here.'

'I . . . God *damn* it. I can't do that right now, Tess. I just . . . can't. It has to be tonight. You have to trust me.'

'Trust you,' she whispered, closing her eyes and tipping her head back against the office door. 'I guess that's something *I* can't do right now, Dante. I have to go. Good-bye.'

She flipped the cell phone closed and shut the ringer off altogether. She didn't want to talk anymore, not to anyone.

As Tess walked over to put the cell on her desk, her gaze caught on something else that had been troubling her since she'd found it earlier that morning. It was a computer flash drive, a slim, portable data-storage device. She'd discovered it underneath the lip of the examination table in one of her clinic rooms – the very room where Ben had been yesterday, when she'd caught him unexpectedly and he'd made excuses that he came in to repair the table's sticky hydraulics.

Tess had suspected he wasn't being truthful with her – about a lot of things. Now she knew that was the case. But the question was, why?

In a furious mental outburst, Dante glared at his cell phone and sent the device hurtling against the opposite wall of his living quarters. It shattered with the impact, emitting a shower of sparks and smoke as it broke into a hundred tiny pieces. The destruction was satisfying, if brief. But it did nothing to assuage his anger, all of it self-directed.

Dante resumed the tight pacing he'd been doing while on the phone with Tess. He needed to be moving now. He just needed to keep his limbs in action, his mind alert.

He'd been making a brilliant mess of everything lately. While he'd never held an inkling of regret for being born of the Breed, now his vampire blood seethed with frustration over the fact that he was trapped inside. Denied the possibility of fixing things with Tess until the sun finally retreated below the horizon and freed him to move about in her world.

He thought the wait was going to drive him out of his mind.

It nearly had.

By the time he went to find Tegan in the training facility at a few minutes to sundown, his skin was hot and prickling, too tight everywhere. He was antsy and itching for combat. His ears were ringing, the incessant buzz like a swarm of bees in his blood.

'You ready to roll, T?'

The tawny-haired Gen One warrior looked up from the Beretta he was loading and gave a cold smile as the clip snapped into place. 'Let's do it.'

Together they headed up the winding corridor of the compound to the elevator that would take them to the Order's fleet garage on street level.

As the doors closed, Dante's nostrils began to tickle with the acrid tang of smoke. He glanced at Tegan, but the other male seemed unaffected, his gem-green eyes fixed before him, characteristic in their unblinking, emotionless calm.

The elevator car began its silent climb upward. Dante felt an intense heat lapping at him from the ghost of a flame, just waiting for him to slow down enough that it could catch him. He knew what this was, of course. The death vision had been dogging him all day, but he'd managed to beat it back, refusing to give in to the sensory torture when he needed his head fully in the game tonight.

But now, as the elevator reached its destination, the precognition slammed into his head like a hammer. Dante went down on one knee, leveled by the force of the hit.

'Jesus,' Tegan said from beside him as Dante felt the warrior take his arm to keep him from sprawling on the elevator floor. 'What the hell? You all right?'

Dante couldn't answer. His sight filled with billowing black smoke shot with bright plumes of flame. Over the crackle and hiss of encroaching fire, he could hear someone talking – taunting him, it seemed – the voice low, indistinct. This was new, a further detail in the elusive nightmare he'd come to know so well.

He blinked away some of the haze, struggling to stay present. To stay conscious. He caught a glimpse of Tegan's face in front of him. Shit, he must look bad, because the warrior who was known for his ruthless lack of feeling now suddenly flinched back, pulling his hand away from Dante's arm with a hiss. Behind his pained grimace, the tips of Tegan's fangs shone white. His light brows dropped down low over his narrowed emerald eyes.

'Can't . . . breathe . . .' Dante gasped, every panting breath he took dragging more phantom smoke into his lungs. Choking him. 'Ah, God . . . dying . . .'

Tegan's eyes bored into him, flinty sharp. His gaze was unsympathetic but level with a strength Dante knew would keep him steady.

'You hang on,' Tegan demanded. 'It's a vision, it's not reality. Not yet, anyway. Now, stay in there, ride it out. Go back as far as you can, and absorb all of the detail.'

Dante let the images swamp him once more, knowing Tegan was right. He had to open his mind to the pain and fear so he could look past it to the truth.

Panting, his skin searing from the heat of the inferno surging all around him, Dante forced himself to focus on his surroundings. To place himself deeper into the moment. He stretched his mind backward from the worst of the vision, halting the action, then sending it into reverse.

The flames shrank away. The smoke reduced from massive, roiling clouds of black ash to thin gray tendrils that crept in along the ceiling. Dante could breathe now, but fear still clogged his throat with the realization that these would be his last few minutes of life.

Someone was in the room with him. A male, judging from the scent of him. Dante was lying prone on something icy cold and slick while his captor yanked his hands behind his back, then bound him at the wrists with a length of wire cord. He should have been able to snap it like twine, but it wouldn't budge. His strength was useless. The captor bound Dante's feet next, then hog-tied him on his stomach, a slab of bare metal beneath him.

Loud crashes sounded from somewhere outside the room. He heard bansheelike shrieks, smelled the coppery stench of death nearby.

And then, a low taunt sounded near his ear: 'You know, I thought killing you was going to be difficult. You've made it very easy for me.'

The voice faded into a self-amused chuckle as Dante's captor came around to where his head hung over the edge of the metal platform that held him. Denim-clad legs bent at the knee, and slowly the torso of his would-be killer came into Dante's line of sight. Rough fingers grasped him by the hair, lifting his head up to face him in the instant before the vision started to fade away, as quickly as it had come . . .

Holy hell.

'Ben Sullivan.' Dante spat the name out like ash on his tongue. Released from the clutches of the premonition, he dragged himself to a sitting position on the floor. Dante wiped the sheen of sweat from his brow as Tegan stared at him in grave acceptance. 'Son of a bitch. It's the Crimson dealer, Ben Sullivan. I don't fucking believe it. That human – he's the one who's going to kill me.'

Tegan gave a grim shake of his head. 'Not if we kill him first.'

Dante pushed himself up to his feet, planting one palm against the concrete wall next to the elevator while he tried to catch his breath. Beneath his fatigue, rage simmered, for Ben Sullivan and for former Agent Sterling Chase, who'd evidently taken it upon himself to let the bastard go.

'Let's get the hell out of here,' he growled, already stalking across the cavernous garage, flipping one of his *malebranche* blades between his fingers.

⊰ CHAPTER TWENTY-SIX ⊱

Ben's captors had let him sit forever by himself in an unlit, windowless, securely locked room. He kept waiting for the one they'd called Master to appear – the nameless, faceless individual who'd been covertly financing the development and distribution of Crimson. Time dragged, maybe a full twenty-four hours since he'd been picked up and taken here. No one had come for him yet, but they would. And in a dark corner of his mind, Ben understood that when they did, he wouldn't get out of the confrontation alive.

He got up off the floor and made his way across the bare concrete to the closed steel door on the other side of the room. His head was screaming from the beating he'd taken before he was dragged off the street to this place. His broken nose and neck wound were crusted over with dried blood, both injuries on fire with raw pain. Ben put his ear to the cold metal door and listened to movement getting louder on the other side. Heavy footsteps clopped nearer and nearer, the purposeful gaits of more than one man, punctuated by the metallic jangle of chains and weaponry.

Ben backed up, retreating as far as he could into the darkness of his holding cell. There was a snick of a key turning the lock, then the door swung open and the two huge guards who'd brought him here came inside.

'He's ready for you now,' one of the thugs growled.

Both men took Ben by the arms and wrenched him hard

before shoving him forward, out the door and into a dim hallway outside. Ben had suspected he was being held in some kind of warehouse, based on the crude quarters he'd been stowed in until now. But his captors led him up a flight of stairs and into what looked to be an opulent, nineteenth-century estate. Polished wood gleamed in elegant, low lighting. Beneath his muddied shoes, a soft Persian rug spread out in an ornate pattern of deep red, purple, and gold. Above his head in the foyer his captors pushed him through, a large crystal chandelier twinkled.

For an instant, some of Ben's alarm eased. Maybe everything would be okay, after all. He was deep into the shit lately, but this wasn't the nightmare he'd expected it to be. Not some torture chamber of horrors as he'd feared.

Ahead of him, a set of open double doors framed yet another impressive room. Ben was guided there by his handlers, who then held him securely in the middle of the large formal sitting room. The furniture, the rugs, the original oil paintings on the walls – all of it reeked of extensive wealth. Old wealth, the kind you didn't get without a few hundred years of practice.

Surrounded by all that opulence, seated like a dark king behind a massive, carved mahogany desk, was a man in an expensive black suit and dark sunglasses.

Ben's palms started to sweat the instant his eyes lit on the guy. He was immense, broad shoulders straining beneath the impeccable fall of his jacket. The pressed white shirt he wore was unbuttoned at the neck, but Ben didn't think it was a sign of casualness so much as an indication of impatience. Menace permeated the air like a thick cloud, and some of Ben's hope strangled on the spot.

He cleared his throat. 'I, uh . . . I'm glad to finally have the chance to meet with you,' he said, hating the tremor in his voice. 'We need to talk . . . about Crimson—'

'Indeed, we do.' The deep, airless reply cut Ben off with its appearance of calm. But from behind those dark glasses trained on him, fury seethed. 'It looks as though I'm not the only one you've annoyed recently, Mr. Sullivan. That's quite a nasty gash on your neck.'

'I was attacked. Son of a bitch tried to tear my throat out.'

Ben's shadowy employer grunted with obvious disinterest. 'Who would do a thing like that?'

'A vampire,' Ben said, knowing how crazy it had to sound. But what had happened to him down by the riverfront was only the tip of a very disturbing iceberg. 'That's what I need to talk to you about. Like I said when I called the other night, something's gone really wrong with Crimson. It's . . . doing things to people. Bad things. It's turning them into bloodthirsty lunatics.'

'Of course it is, Mr. Sullivan. That's precisely what it was meant to do.'

'What?' Disbelief made Ben's stomach drop in his gut. 'What are you talking about? I created Crimson. I know what it's supposed to do. It's just a mild amphetamine—'

'For humans, yes.' The dark-haired man stood up slowly, then came around the side of the enormous desk. 'For others, as you've discovered, it is something much more.'

As he spoke, he glanced toward the open doors of the room. Another pair of heavily armed guards stood at the threshold, their hair shaggy and unkempt, fierce eyes seeming to burn like embers under their heavy brows. In the dim light from the candles in the room, Ben thought he saw the gleam of fangs behind the guards' lips. He flicked a nervous glance back at his employer.

'Unfortunately, I have discovered something troubling myself, Mr. Sullivan. After your call the other night, a few of my associates visited your laboratory in Boston. They searched your computer and records, but imagine my dismay to hear that they could not find the formula for Crimson. How do you explain that?'

Ben held the sunglass-shaded gaze that pinned him from only an arm's length away. 'I never keep the true formula in the lab. I thought it would be safer kept off-site, with me.'

'You need to give it to me.' There was little inflection in the words, no movement in the powerful body that stood before him like an impassable wall. 'Now, Mr. Sullivan.'

'I don't have it. That's the God's honest truth.'

'Where is it?'

Ben's tongue froze. He needed a bargaining chip, and the formula was all he had. Besides, he wasn't about to sic these thugs on Tess by telling them he'd hidden the Crimson recipe in her clinic. He hadn't meant to leave it there for long, only until he'd sorted out his options in this mess. Too late to call back that misstep, unfortunately. Even though saving his own ass was his primary concern at the moment, putting Tess in the middle of this was out of the question.

'I can get it for you,' Ben said, 'but you'll have to let me go. Let's agree on this like gentlemen. We sever all ties right here and now and go our separate ways. Forget we know anything about each other.'

A tight smile curved his employer's mouth. 'Don't try to negotiate with me. You are beneath me . . . *human*.'

Ben swallowed hard. He wanted to believe that the guy was just some kind of demented vampire fantasist. A nut job who was heavy on cash but light on sanity. Except he'd seen what Crimson had done to the kid he'd dealt it to the other night. That horrific transformation had been real, hard as it was to accept. And the ragged, searing gash in his neck was real too.

Panic started hammering hard in his chest.

'Look, I don't know what's going on here. Frankly, I don't wanna know. I just want to get the hell out of here in one piece.'

'Excellent. Then you should have no trouble complying. Give me the formula.'

'I told you, I don't have it.'

'Then you will have to re-create it, Mr. Sullivan.' A brief nod brought the two armed guards inside. 'I've taken the liberty of bringing your lab equipment here. Everything you need is in order, including a test subject for the finished product. My associates will show you the way.'

'Wait.' Ben shot a look over his shoulder as the guards began to remove him from the room. 'You don't understand. The formula is . . . complex. I don't have it memorized. To get it right could take me several days—'

'You have no more than two hours, Mr. Sullivan.'

Bruising hands grasped Ben in an unyielding hold and pushed him back toward the descending stairwell that gaped ahead of him, as black as endless night.

Chase strapped on the last of his weapons, then checked his ammo supply one final time. He had one pistol loaded with regular rounds; another held a clip of the hollow-nose titanium specials that he'd been given by the warriors for the express purpose of killing Rogues. He sincerely hoped he wouldn't need to use those, but if he had to blast through a dozen feral vampires to reach his nephew, he damn well would.

Grabbing his dark wool pea coat from the hook near the door, he stepped into the hallway outside his private quarters in the Darkhaven. Elise was there; he nearly ran into her in his haste to be on his way.

'Sterling . . . hello. Have you been avoiding me? I'd been hoping I could talk with you.' Her lavender eyes swept him in a quick glance. She frowned, seeing the array of guns and knives that circled his hips and crisscrossed his chest. He felt her apprehension, could smell the sudden, bitter note of dread mingling with the delicate scent that was simply her own. 'So many terrible weapons. Is it very dangerous out there?'

'Don't worry about that,' he told her. 'Just keep praying for Camden to come home soon. I'll take care of the rest.'

She picked up the tail of her scarlet widow's sash and idly smoothed the silk through her fingers. 'That's actually what I wanted to talk to you about, Sterling. Some of the other women and I have been discussing what more we can do for our missing sons. There is strength in numbers, so we thought that perhaps if we banded together . . . We would like to do some daytime searches of the waterfront or the old subway tunnels. We could look in the places where our sons might have gone for shelter from the sun—'

'Absolutely not.'

Chase hadn't meant to cut her off so abruptly, but the idea of Elise leaving the sanctuary of the Darkhaven during daytime hours to venture into the worst parts of the city made his blood run cold. She would be beyond the protection of himself or any other members of the Breed so long as the sun was out, and while the Rogues would be no danger then for the very same reason, there was always the risk of running into their Minions.

'I'm sorry, but it's out of the question.'

Her eyes widened momentarily in surprise. Then she quickly glanced down, giving him a polite nod, but he could see that she bristled beneath the veneer of her propriety. As her closest kin, even by marriage, Breed law gave Chase the right to impose a daytime curfew on her – an antiquated measure that had been in existence from the origination of the Darkhavens nearly a thousand years ago. Chase had never imposed it, and while he felt like an ass for doing so now, he could not allow her to risk her life while he stood by and watched.

'Do you think my brother would approve of what you want to do?' Chase asked, knowing that Quentin never would agree to such an idea, not even in an effort to save his own son. 'You can help Camden the most by staying here, where I know you are safe.'

Elise lifted her head, those pale purple eyes flashing with the spark of a determination he'd never seen in them before.

'Camden is not the only child missing. Can you save them all, Sterling? Can the warriors of the Order save them all?' She let out a small sigh. 'Nobody saved Jonas Redmond. He's dead, did you know that? His mother senses that he's gone. More of our sons are disappearing, dying every night, yet we are supposed to do nothing but sit here and wait for bad news?'

Chase felt his jaw go rigid. 'I have to go now, Elise. You have my answer on this subject. I'm sorry.'

He brushed past her, shrugging into his coat as he headed out. He knew she followed; her white skirts rustled softly behind him with each quick step she took. But Chase kept going. He grabbed his keys out of his pocket and threw open the main door of the Darkhaven building, clicking the remote lock of his silver Lexus SUV in the driveway outside. The vehicle chirped, lights flashing in response, but Chase wouldn't be going anywhere fast.

Blocking the drive was a black Range Rover, its engine idling in the dark. The windows were tinted beyond legal opacity, but Chase didn't need to see through them to know who was inside. He could feel Dante's rage pouring through the steel and glass, rolling toward him like a frost heave.

The warrior wasn't alone. He and his companion, the stone-cold one called Tegan, got out of the vehicle and strolled around to the lawn. Their faces were deadly calm, but the menace radiating off both huge males was unmistakable.

Chase heard Elise's gasp behind him. 'Sterling—'

'Get back inside,' he told her, keeping his eyes locked on the two warriors. 'Now, Elise. Everything's all right.'

'What's going on, Sterling? Why are they here?'

'Just do as I say, damn it! Go back in the house. Everything is going to be okay.'

'Oh, I don't know about that, Harvard.' Dante prowled toward him, those wicked, arced blades at his hip glinting in the moonlight with every long stride of the warrior's legs. 'I'd say things are about as fucked up as they could be right about now. Thanks to you, that is. You get lost last night or something? Maybe you just misunderstood what I told you to do with that drug-dealing scum – that it? I told you to haul his ass in to the compound, but you thought I said let the bastard walk?'

'No. There was no misunderstanding.'

'What am I missing here, Harvard?' Dante drew one of his blades from its sheath, the steel whisking out as softly as a whisper. When he spoke, Chase saw the tips of his fangs. A bright amber gaze locked on him like twin laser beams. 'Start talking fast, because I've got no problem cutting the truth out of you right here in front of the woman.'

'Sterling!' Elise screamed. 'Leave him alone!'

Chase whipped his head to the side just in time to see her dash down the brick steps of the Darkhaven entry and onto the pavement below. She didn't get far. Tegan moved like a ghost, vampire speed no match for Elise's human limbs. The warrior captured her around the waist and held her back as she struggled to get away from him.

Fury rose in Chase like a lit match on dry tinder. His fangs ripped out of his gums, his vision going sharp as his pupils narrowed with his transformation. He roared, ready to take on both warriors simply for the offense of touching Elise.

'Let her go,' he growled. 'Damn it, she is not a part of this!'

He pushed at Dante, but the vampire didn't budge.

'At least we have your full attention now, Harvard.' Dante shoved back at him, a freight train coming at full steam. Chase's feet left the ground, his body propelled backward by the force of Dante's rage. The brick facade of the residence stopped their trajectory, slamming hard against Chase's spine.

Dante's enormous fangs came right up in Chase's face, his eyes burning into Chase's skull. 'Where is Ben Sullivan? What the fuck is really going on with you?'

Chase glanced over at Elise, hating that she had to witness

this brutal side of their world. He just wanted it over for her. He saw the tears streaming down her cheeks, the fear in her eyes as Tegan held her so coldly against all of the deadly steel and leather that girded his immense body.

Chase swore roundly. 'I had to let the human go. I had no choice.'

'Wrong answer,' Dante snarled, bringing that hellish blade up under his chin.

'The Crimson dealer would do me no good if he was locked up at the compound. I need him on the street, helping me look for someone – my nephew. I let him go so he would help me find Camden, my brother's son.'

Dante scowled, but the blade eased up a little. 'What about the others who've gone missing? All those kids Ben Sullivan has been feeding with his drug?'

'Getting Camden back is what I care about. He's been my true mission from day one.'

'Son of a bitch, you lied to us,' the warrior hissed.

Chase met the accusing amber glare. 'Would the Order have bothered to help me if I'd come around asking for you to find one missing Darkhaven youth?'

Dante cursed, low and furious. 'You'll never know, will you?'

He wondered now, having come to understand some of the warriors' code – having seen firsthand that, despite their ruthless methods and the efficiency that made them such a mysterious and deadly force among the Breed and humankind alike, they were not without honor. They were merciless killers when needed, but Chase suspected that every one of them was, at heart, a far better man than him.

Dante abruptly released him, then pivoted around to stalk back toward the waiting Rover. Across the lawn, Tegan let Elise go as well, the warrior's steady green gaze lingering on her as she anxiously stumbled away from him, rubbing at the places where he had touched her.

'Get in the truck, Harvard,' Dante said, indicating the open back door with a look that promised hell to pay if Chase didn't cooperate. 'You're going back to the compound. Maybe you can persuade Lucan that we ought to let you keep breathing.'

⫸ CHAPTER TWENTY-SEVEN ⫷

Cold sweat trickled down the back of Ben Sullivan's neck as he finished up the first sample of his new batch of Crimson. He hadn't been lying about not having the recipe committed to memory; he did his best to re-create the drug in the absurdly short time he'd been allowed. With barely a half hour to spare, he collected a dose of the reddish substance and carried it over to his test subject. The young man, dressed in filthy blue jeans and a Harvard sweatshirt, slumped against the restraints that held him prisoner in a wheeled office chair, his head down, chin resting on his chest.

As Ben neared him, the door to the makeshift basement lab opened and his dark employer strode inside, walking between the two armed guards who'd been supervising Ben's progress the whole time.

'I didn't have a chance to vacuum-filter the moisture out of the stuff,' Ben said, making excuses for the cup of pasty goo he'd produced and hoping to hell he got the recipe right, 'This kid looks like he's in rough shape. What if he can't chew it?'

There was no reply, only measuring, deadly silence.

Ben blew out a nervous breath and approached the kid. He knelt down in front of the chair. From under the fall of unkempt hair, listless eyes opened to heavy slits, then closed again. Ben peered up into the drawn, sallow face of what had probably been a good-looking kid at one time –

Ah, shit.

He knew this kid. Knew him from around the clubs – a fairly regular customer – and this was also the smiling, youthful face he'd seen in the photograph just last night. Cameron or Camden was his name? Camden, he thought, the kid Ben was supposed to help locate for the fanged psycho who'd promised to kill him if he didn't oblige. Not that that threat was any more serious than the one Ben faced now.

'Let's get on with it, Mr. Sullivan.'

Ben spooned a bit of the raw Crimson out of the cup and lifted it to the kid's mouth. The instant the substance touched his lips, Camden's tongue snaked out hungrily. He closed his mouth around the spoon and sucked it clean, seeming to revive for an instant. A junkie nuzzling up to what he hoped was his next fix, Ben realized, a pang of guilt sticking him.

Ben waited for the Crimson to take effect.

Nothing happened.

He gave Camden more, and then some more again. Still nothing. Damn it. The recipe wasn't right.

'I need more time,' Ben murmured as the kid's head lolled back down with a groan. 'I've almost got it, but I just need to try it again.'

He stood up, turned around, and was shocked to find his menacing patron standing directly in front of him. Ben hadn't heard the guy move at all, yet here he was, looming over him. Ben saw his own haggard reflection in the sheen of the man's dark glasses. He looked desperate and terrified, a cornered animal trembling before a fierce predator.

'We're getting nowhere, Mr. Sullivan. And I'm out of patience.'

'You said two hours,' Ben pointed out. 'I still have a few minutes—'

'Not negotiable.' The cruel mouth stretched into a sneer, revealing the bright tips of sharp white fangs. 'Time's up.'

'Oh, Jesus!' Ben recoiled, knocking into the chair behind him and sending it and the kid held captive on it rolling backward in a clatter of spinning wheels. He stumbled away in a graceless crawl, only to feel strong fingers bite into his shoulders, hauling him up off the floor as if he were weightless. Ben was spun around harshly and sent crashing into the far wall. Agony splintered through the back of his skull as he crumpled in a heap. Dazed, Ben felt behind his head. His fingers came away bloody.

And when he focused his bleary gaze on the others in the room, his heart went tight with dread. The two guards were staring at him, their pupils narrowed to thin slits, glowing amber irises fixed on him like floodlights.

One of them opened his mouth on a rasping hiss, baring huge fangs.

Even Camden's attention had roused from where he sat several feet away. The kid's eyes burned through the fall of his hair, his lips peeling away from long, gleaming canines.

But as terrifying as those monstrous faces were, they had nothing on the ice-cold approach of the one who was clearly calling the shots here. He strolled over to Ben at a calm pace, polished black shoes moving soundlessly on the concrete floor. He lifted his hand and Ben was rising, drifting back onto his feet as if attached to invisible strings.

'Please,' Ben gasped. 'Whatever you're thinking, don't . . . don't do it, please. I can get the Crimson formula back for you. I swear, I'll do whatever you want!'

'Yes, Mr. Sullivan. You will.'

He moved so fast Ben didn't know what hit him until he felt the hard bite of fangs in his throat. Ben struggled, smelling his own blood pouring out of the wound, hearing the wet sounds of the creature at his neck drawing deeply at his vein. The fight leaked out of Ben with every draining pull. He hung there, suspended, feeling life flow out of him, feeling consciousness dim along with his will. He was dying, all that he was flowing away from him into a pit of darkness.

*

'Come on, Harvard, or whatever your name really is,' Tess said, guiding the little terrier across the street as the pedestrian light changed.

After closing up the clinic at six o'clock, she had decided to take a walk past Ben's apartment on the South Side, one last attempt to find him on her own before she placed a missing-persons report with the police. If he was back to trafficking narcotics, he probably deserved to get arrested, but deep down she truly cared about him and wanted to see if she could talk him into getting help before things escalated that far.

Ben's neighborhood wasn't the most desirable, particularly in the dark, but Tess wasn't afraid. Many of her clients were from this general area: hardworking, good people. Ironically, if there was anyone to be wary of in this stretch of tightly clustered duplexes and three-deckers, it was probably the drug dealer living in Apartment 3-B of the building where Tess now stood.

A television blared from the unit on the first floor, casting an eerie blue wash onto the sidewalk outside. Tess tipped her head up, looking to Ben's set of windows for any indication that he might be there. The ratty white miniblinds were drawn closed over the balcony sliders and the bedroom window. The apartment was all dark, no light showing from anywhere inside, no movement.

Or . . . was there?

Although it was difficult to tell, she could have sworn she saw one of the sets of blinds sway against the window – as if someone inside had moved them or walked by them and bumped them, unaware.

Was it Ben? If he was home, he evidently didn't want anyone to know, including her. He hadn't returned any of her phone calls or e-mails, so why would she think he'd want her showing up at his place now?

And if he wasn't home? What if someone had broken in? What if it were some of his drug contacts waiting for him to return? What if someone was up there right now, turning his place upside down looking for the flash drive she had in her coat pocket?

Tess backed away from the building, an anxious crawl working its way up her spine. She held Harvard's leash in a death grip, silently shooing him from the dried-out shrubs that lined the sidewalk.

Then she saw it again – a definite shift of the blinds in Ben's unit. One of the sliders began to open on the dark third-level balcony. Someone was coming out. And this someone was enormous, definitely not Ben.

'Oh, shit,' she whispered under her breath, stooping to pick up the dog so she could bolt the hell out of there in the next second.

She started jogging up the sidewalk, braving only the quickest glance over her shoulder. The guy was at the railing of the rickety balcony, peering out into the dark. She felt the savage heat of his stare like a lance slicing through the dark. His eyes were impossibly bright . . . glowing.

'Oh, my God.'

Tess dashed out to cross the street. When she looked back at Ben's building again, the man on the balcony was climbing onto the railing, two more coming out behind him. The one in the lead swung his legs over the edge and dropped, as neatly as a cat, down onto the lawn. He started running up behind her, moving too fast. As if his speed had rendered her own to slow motion, her feet as sluggish as if they'd been mired in quicksand.

Tess hugged Harvard close to her chest and ran up onto the other sidewalk, darting between the cars parked at the curb. She glanced once more behind her, only to find that her pursuer was gone. She knew hope for a brief fraction of a second.

Because when she looked forward again, she saw that he was somehow, suddenly there, less than five paces in front of her, blocking her path. How could he have gotten there so fast? She hadn't even seen him move, hadn't heard his feet on the pavement.

He cocked his large head at her and sniffed at the air like an animal. He – or rather it, because whatever this was, it was far from human – began to chuckle low under its breath.

Tess backed up, moving woodenly, disbelieving. This wasn't happening. It couldn't be. This was some kind of sick joke. It was impossible.

'No.' She stepped back and back, shaking her head in denial.

The big man started moving then, coming toward her. Tess's heart stuttered into a panicked beat, her every instinct clanging on high alert. She pivoted on her heel and bolted –

Just as another beastly-looking man came between the cars and hemmed her in.

'Hello, pretty,' he said in a voice that was all gravel and malice.

In the pale wash of streetlight overhead, Tess's gaze locked on the guy's open mouth. His lips peeled back from his teeth in a thick hiss, revealing a huge pair of fangs.

Tess dropped the dog from her limp grasp and sent a terrified scream shooting high up into the night sky.

'Hang a left up here,' Dante said to Tegan from the passenger seat of the Range Rover. Chase sat in back like he was awaiting his execution, an anticipation that Dante was about to prolong a bit more. 'Let's swing through Southie before we head for the compound.'

Tegan gave a grim nod, then turned the vehicle at the light. 'You got a feeling the dealer might be home?'

'I don't know. Worth a look, though.'

Dante rubbed at a cold spot that had settled behind his sternum, a strange void that was squeezing his lungs, making it hard to breathe. The sensation was more visceral than physical, a hard tweaking of his instincts that put his senses on full alert. He hit the window control next to him, watching the dark glass slide open as he inhaled the cold night air.

'Everything cool?' Tegan asked, his deep voice drifting over from across the dim cockpit of the SUV. 'You heading for a repeat of what happened earlier?'

'No.' Dante gave a vague shake of his head, still staring out the open window, watching the blur of lights and traffic as the downtown buildings fell behind them and the old neighborhoods of South Boston came into view. 'No, this is . . . something different.'

The damn knot of cold in his chest was boring deeper, becoming glacial even as his palms began to sweat. His stomach clenched. Adrenaline dumped into his veins in a sudden, jolting flood.

What the hell?

It was fear running through him, he realized. Shell-shocked terror. Not his own, but someone else's.

Oh, Jesus.

'Stop the car.'

It was Tess's fear he was feeling. Her horror reaching out to him via the blood connection they shared. She was in danger out there. Mortal danger.

'Tegan, stop the fucking car!'

The warrior hit the brakes and dragged the steering wheel hard to the right, coolly skidding the Rover onto the berm. They weren't too far from Ben Sullivan's apartment; his building could be no more than half a dozen blocks' distance – twice that if they had to navigate the maze of one-way streets and traffic lights between here and there.

Dante threw open the passenger door and jumped out onto

the pavement. He dragged air into his lungs, praying he could get a tack on Tess's scent.

There it was.

He locked on to the cinnamon-sweet note braided among the thousand other mingled odors carrying on the chill night breeze. Tess's blood scent was trace, but growing stronger – too much so.

Dante's veins ran cold.

Somewhere, not far from where he stood, Tess was bleeding.

Tegan leaned across the seat, one thick forearm draped over the wheel, his shrewd gaze narrowed. 'Dante, man – what the fuck? What's going on?'

'No time,' Dante said. He pivoted back around to the car and slammed the door shut. 'I'm taking off on foot. I need you to haul ass to Ben Sullivan's place. It's off—'

'I remember the way,' Chase piped up from the backseat, meeting Dante's gaze through the Rover's open window. 'Go. We'll be right behind you.'

Dante nodded once at the grave faces staring at him, then he swung around and took off at a dead run.

He cut through yards, leaped over fences, sped down tight alleyways, firing off every cylinder of his Breed-born speed and agility. To the humans he passed, he was nothing but cold air, a brush of icy November wind on the backs of their necks as he barreled over and around them, all of his focus honed on one thing: Tess.

Halfway down a side street that would dump him onto Ben Sullivan's block, Dante saw the little terrier Tess had brought back from the brink of death with her healing touch. The dog was wandering loose on the dark sidewalk, its leash dragging limply behind it.

Hell of a bad sign, but Dante knew he was close now.

God help him, he had to be.

'Tess!' he shouted, praying she could hear him.

That he wasn't already too late.

He peeled around the corner of a three-decker, jumping over the toys and bicycles that littered the front yard. Her blood scent was stronger now, a shot of dread hammering his temples.

'Tess!'

He tracked her like the beam of a laser sight, racing in a mindless panic when he picked up the low snuffles and grunts of Rogues fighting over a prize.

Oh, Christ. No.

Across the street from the building where Ben Sullivan lived, Tess's handbag lay near the curb, the contents spilling out of it. Dante veered right, racing down a foot-worn path that cut between two houses. There was a shed at the end of the path, the door swinging idly on its hinges.

Tess was inside. Dante knew it with a dread so deep it made his step falter.

Behind him, in the split second before he could reach the shed and tear the thing down with his bare hands, a Rogue came out of the shadows and pounced. Dante twisted as he fell, withdrawing one of his blades and slicing it across the suckhead's face. The Rogue gave an un-earthly shriek, flying off him in agony as his corrupted blood system got a good taste of lethal titanium. Dante rolled out of his crouch and shot to his feet as the Rogue spasmed into swift death and decomposition.

On the street now, the black Range Rover roared up and lurched to a sharp halt. Tegan and Chase jumped out, weapons in hand. Another Rogue came out of the dark, but he took one look at Tegan's icy stare and decided to run the opposite way. The warrior sprang like a great cat, leaping into pursuit.

Chase must have seen more trouble at Ben Sullivan's apartment, because he held his pistol in ready position and started off across the street at a stealth jog.

As for Dante, he was hardly aware of the peripheral action. His boots were already chewing up earth, moving toward the shed and the terrible noises that were emanating from it. The wet, slick sounds of vampires feeding was nothing new to him, but the idea that they were harming Tess threw his rage into the nuclear zone. He stalked to the flapping shed door and yanked it loose with one hand. It sailed across the empty back lot, instantly forgotten.

Two Rogues held Tess down on the floor of the outbuilding, one sucking at her wrist, the other latched on to her throat. She lay motionless beneath them, so still that Dante's heart froze in terror as his eyes took in the scene. But he could sense that she lived. He could hear her thin pulse echoing weakly in his own veins. Another few seconds and they might have drained her.

Dante let out a bellow that shook the place, his fury boiling up and out of him like a black gale. The Rogue feeding from Tess's wrist leaped back with a hiss, her blood circling the peeled-back lips and staining the long fangs scarlet. The suckhead twisted in midair, flying up to the corner of the shed's ceiling and clinging there like a spider.

Dante tracked the flash of movement, releasing one of his *malebranche* blades and sending it airborne. The spinning wheel of titanium made lethal contact with the Rogue's neck. It dropped to the floor with a shriek, and Dante turned his hatred on the bigger one, which had moved around to challenge him to its prey.

The Rogue crouched low in front of Tess's limp body, facing off against Dante with fangs bared and eyes aglow with feral amber light. The suckhead appeared young behind the Bloodlust that had transformed it into a beast, probably one of the missing Darkhaven civilians. Didn't matter; the only good Rogue was a dead one – especially this one, which had its hands and mouth all over Tess, sucking precious life out of her.

Might have killed her already, if Dante didn't get her out of there quick.

Blood screaming into his muscles, Tess's pain and one that was wholly his own galvanizing him for the fight, Dante bared his own fangs and flew at the Rogue with a roar. He wanted to deliver brutal, hellish vengeance, tear the bastard apart piece by piece before gutting it with one of his blades. But expedience was paramount. Saving Tess was all that mattered.

Latching on to the Rogue's snapping jaw, Dante levered his arm and shoved down hard, cracking bones and severing tendons. As the suckhead screamed, Dante flipped a blade into his free hand and buried the titanium-edged steel into the vampire's chest. He shoved the corpse off him and went to Tess's side.

'Ah, God.' Kneeling down, he heard her soft, rasping breath. It was shallow, so thin. The wound on her wrist was nasty, but the one on her neck was savage. Her skin was pale as snow, cool to the touch when he brought her hand to his mouth and kissed her slack fingers. 'Tess . . . hang on, baby. I've got you now. I'm taking you out of here.'

Easing her into his arms, Dante gathered her close and carried her outside.

✥ CHAPTER TWENTY-EIGHT ✥

Chase stepped over the body of a dead human male that lay just outside the first-floor apartment door, the television blaring from inside the living room. The old man had been mauled by Rogues, at least one of which still remained in the building. Chase climbed the stairs to Ben Sullivan's apartment in utter silence, his thighs pumping, senses tuned to his surroundings. He held the Beretta in both hands up near his right shoulder, the safety off, barrel tipped up toward the ceiling. He could have the weapon leveled and firing off titanium rounds in a fraction of a second. For the Rogue moving carelessly around in the apartment at the top of the stairs, death was imminent.

Reaching the last step, Chase paused in the hallway adjacent to the open unit door. Through the crack beside the jamb, he saw that the place had been sacked. The Rogues who'd come there were looking for something – definitely not Ben Sullivan himself, unless they expected to find him hiding in one of the dozens of drawers and file boxes that had been upended inside the apartment. He saw a flash of movement from within and drew back just as a Rogue came out of the kitchen with a butcher knife and began slicing into the cushions of the recliner, tearing the thing apart.

With the toe of his boot, Chase eased the door open wide enough for him to slip through, then he cautiously entered the unit, his 9mm trained on the Rogue from behind. The vampire's frenzied search made him oblivious to the threat creeping up on him until Chase stood not two feet away, the barrel of the gun dropped level with the center of the Rogue's head.

Chase could have fired in that instant, probably should have. All of his training and logic told him to pull the trigger and release one of those custom-made titanium rounds into the back of the Rogue's skull, but instinct made him hesitate.

In a fraction of a second, his mind took a visual inventory of the vampire before him. He noted the tall, athletic build, the civilian clothes . . . the shadow of youthful innocence hidden beneath the filthy sweatshirt and jeans, the greasy, unkempt hair. He was looking at a junkie, there was no doubt about that. The Rogue smelled of sour blood and sweat – hallmarks of a vampire lost to Bloodlust.

But this addict was no stranger.

'Jesus,' Chase whispered, low under his breath. 'Camden?'

The Rogue went utterly still at the sound of Chase's voice. His shoulders came up, shaggy head began to pivot to the side, cocked at an exaggerated angle. Through bared teeth and fangs, he grunted, sniffing at the air. His gaze wasn't totally visible, but Chase could see that his nephew's eyes were bright amber, glowing from out of his sallow face.

'Cam, it's me. It's your uncle. Put down the knife, son.'

If he understood, Camden gave no indication. Nor did he let go of the huge butcher knife gripped in his hand. He started to turn around, slowly, like an animal suddenly made aware that it was cornered.

'It's all over,' Chase told him. 'You're safe now. I'm here to help you.'

Even as he said the words, Chase wondered if he truly meant them. He lowered his pistol but kept the safety off, every muscle in his arm taut, his finger hovering over the trigger. Apprehension wormed up his spine, as cold as the night breeze floating through the apartment from the open door and sliders. Chase, too, felt cornered here, uncertain of his nephew and himself.

'Camden, your mother is very worried about you. She wants you to come home. Can you do that for her, son?'

A long moment ticked off in wary silence as Chase watched his brother's only offspring pivot around to face him. Chase wasn't prepared for what he saw. He tried to keep his expression schooled, but bile rose in his throat as he took in the bloodstained, ragged appearance of the kid who not a couple of weeks ago had been joking and laughing with his friends, a golden child whose future had been so full of promise.

Chase could find no sign of that hope in the feral male looming before him now, his clothing soiled from the slaughter he'd taken part in downstairs, the knife from the kitchen gripped at the ready in his hand. His pupils were fixed and narrow, mere slivers of black in the center of his vacant amber gaze.

'Cam, please . . . let me know that you're in there somewhere.'

Chase's palms began to sweat. His right arm started coming up of its own accord, slowly raising the weapon. The Rogue grunted, legs moving into a crouch. The feral gaze flicked from side to side, calculating, deciding. Chase didn't know if the impulse running through Camden in that moment was fight or flight. He brought the 9mm higher, and higher still, his finger trembling on the trigger.

'Ah, fuck . . . this is no good. No goddamn good.'

With a bleak sigh, he arced the pistol's barrel straight up in the air and shot a round into the ceiling. The crack of gunfire echoed sharply, and Camden jolted into action, leaping across the room to escape. He ran past Chase toward the open sliders. Without so much as a backward glance, he vaulted over the balcony and dropped out of sight.

Chase sagged on his feet, an oppressive mixture of relief and regret pouring over him. He'd found his nephew, but he'd just let a Rogue go back onto the streets.

When he finally lifted his head and glanced to the open doorway of the apartment, he found Tegan standing there, watching him with a keen, knowing gaze. The warrior may not have seen him release the Rogue, but he knew. That flat, emotionless green stare seemed to know everything.

'I couldn't do it,' Chase murmured, shaking his head as he looked down at the discharged weapon. 'He's my kin, and I just . . . couldn't.'

Tegan said nothing for a long moment, measuring him in the silence. 'We have to go now,' he said evenly. 'The woman is in bad shape. Dante's waiting with her in the car.'

Chase nodded, then followed the warrior out of the building.

His pulse still throbbing with fear and rage, Dante arranged Tess in the backseat of the Rover, her head and shoulders cradled in his arms, his jacket covering her to keep her warm. He had torn off his shirt and cut it into strips, wrapping makeshift bandages around the wound at her wrist and the more severe laceration in her neck.

She lay so still against him, her weight so slight. He looked down at her face, grateful that the Rogues' attack had not gone so far as to strike her or torture her, as their diseased kind was wont to do with their prey. They hadn't raped her, and that was an enormous blessing too, given their savage, animal natures. But the Rogues had taken her blood – a great deal of it. If Dante hadn't found her when he did, they might have drained her completely.

He shuddered, cold to his bones at the thought.

Seeing her lying there, her eyelids closed in unconsciousness, her skin pale and cool, Dante knew the one sure way to help her. She needed blood to replace what she had lost. Not the medical transfusions her human sisters would require, but blood given from one of the Breed.

He had already forced one half of the blood bond on her, the night he took her blood to save himself. Could he be so callous as to shackle her with the completion of that bond while she had nothing to say about it? The only other choice was to stand by and watch her die in his arms.

Unacceptable, even if she might hate him for giving her a life that would link her to him by unbreakable chains. She deserved so much more than what he had to give her.

'Damn it, Tess. I'm sorry. It's the only way.'

He brought his wrist up to his mouth and scored a vertical gash with the razor edge of his long fangs. Blood swelled to the surface, running in a rivulet down his bare arm. He was vaguely aware of urgent footsteps approaching the SUV as he lifted Tess's head in preparation of feeding her.

The front doors opened and Tegan and Chase got in. Tegan glanced into the back, his gaze lighting on Tess's arm – on her limp right hand, which had slipped out from under the cover of Dante's jacket. The hand that bore the teardrop-and-crescent-moon mark. The warrior's eyes narrowed, then came up to Dante's in question as much as caution.

'She's a Breedmate.'

'I know what she is,' Dante told his brother-in-arms. He didn't even attempt to mask the grave concern in his voice. 'Drive, Tegan. Get us to the compound as fast as you can.'

As the warrior threw the Rover into gear and gunned it, Dante placed his wrist against Tess's slack lips and watched as his blood trickled into her mouth.

CHAPTER TWENTY-NINE

Tess thought she must be dying. She felt weightless and leaden at the same time, floating in a neverland between the pain of one world and the deep unknown of the next. The dark undertow of that further, unfamiliar place tugged at her, but she wasn't afraid. A soothing warmth enveloped her, as if strong angel's wings were folded around her, holding her aloft over the rising tide that lapped gently at her limbs.

She sank into that warm embrace. She needed that abiding, steady strength.

There were voices around her, pitched low and urgent in tone, yet the words were indistinct. Her body vibrated with the constant hum of motion beneath her, her senses gone sluggish with the occasional sway of her limbs. Was she being carried somewhere? She was too exhausted to wonder, too content to simply drift away in the protective warmth that cocooned her.

She wanted to sleep. Just melt away and sleep, forever. . . .

A droplet of something hot splashed against her lips. Like silk, it ran along the seam of her mouth in a slow trail, its enticing fragrance drifting up into her nose. Another drop fell against her lips, warm and wet and heady as wine, and her tongue drifted out to taste it.

As soon as her mouth parted open, it was flooded with liquid heat. She moaned, uncertain what she was tasting but full with the knowledge that she needed more. The first swallow roared through her like an enormous wave. There was more for her to take, a steady flow that she latched on to with her lips and tongue, drawing from the font as though she were dying of thirst. Maybe she was. All she knew was that she wanted it, needed it, and couldn't get enough.

Someone murmured her name, softly, deeply, as she drank the strange elixir. She knew the voice. She knew the scent that seemed to bloom all around her and spill into her mouth.

She knew that he was saving her, the dark angel whose arms protected her now.

Dante.

It was Dante with her in this peculiar void; she knew it with every particle of her being.

Tess was still floating, held aloft over the churning sea of the unknown. Slowly, the dark water rose up to engulf her, thick as cream, warm as a bath. Dante eased her into it, his arms holding her steady, so strong and gentle. She dissolved into the rolling tide, drinking it down, feeling it soak into her muscles, her bones, her smallest cells.

In the peace that washed over her, Tess's consciousness slipped into another world, one that came to her in shades of deep scarlet, crimson, and wine.

The drive to the compound took an eternity, even though Tegan had to have set a few land speed records navigating through Boston's busy, winding streets to the private drive leading to the Order's headquarters. As soon as the Rover came to a stop in the fleet garage, Dante threw open the back door of the vehicle and carefully brought Tess out in his arms.

She was still in and out of consciousness, still weak from blood loss and shock, but he felt some hope that she would live. She had taken only a small amount of his blood; now that she was safe at the compound, he would make sure she got as much as she needed.

Hell, he'd bleed himself out completely if that's what it would take to save her.

God, that wasn't just some bullshit noble idea; he really meant it. He was desperate that Tess survive, so much that he would die for her. The physical ties of their completed blood bond ensured that he felt protective of her, but this was something stronger than that. It went deeper than he could ever have guessed.

He loved her.

The ferocity of his emotion struck Dante as he carried Tess into the garage elevator, Tegan and Chase on his heels. Someone hit the button to descend and they began the smooth, silent ride down the three hundred-some feet of earth and steel that sheltered the Breed's compound from the rest of the world.

When the doors slid open, Lucan was standing in the corridor outside the elevator. Gideon was next to him, both warriors armed and wearing grave expressions. No doubt Lucan had been alerted to the others' urgent arrival when the Rover showed up on the compound gate's security camera.

He took one look at Dante and the savaged female in his arms and exhaled a dark curse. 'What happened?'

'Let me through,' Dante said as he moved past his brethren, careful not to jostle. Tess in the process. 'She needs to rest someplace warm. She's lost a lot of blood—'

'I can see that. Now, what the hell happened out there?'

'Rogues,' Chase put in, taking over the explanation to Lucan while Dante stepped out into the corridor, all his focus on Tess. 'A group of them were sacking the Crimson dealer's apartment. I don't know what they were looking for, but the woman must have come up on them somehow. Maybe she got in their way. She's got bite wounds on her arm and throat, from more than one attacker.'

Dante nodded at the facts, grateful for the Darkhaven

vampire's verbal assist since his own voice seemed to have dried up in his throat.

'Jesus,' Lucan said, turning a grim glance on Dante. 'This is the Breedmate you spoke of? This is Tess?'

'Yeah.' He looked down at her, so still and colorless in his arms, and felt a piercing chill bore into his chest. 'Another few seconds and I might have been too late. . . .'

'Goddamn suckheads,' Gideon hissed as he raked a hand through his hair. 'I'll go prep a room for her in the infirmary.'

'No.' Dante's reply was sharper than intended, and unyielding. He held out his scored wrist, the skin still red and wet at the place he'd fed her. 'She is mine. She stays with me.'

Gideon's eyes widened, but he said nothing more. Nor did anyone else, as Dante brushed past the group of warriors and headed with Tess down the maze of hallways to his private quarters. Once inside, he brought her into the bedroom and gently placed her on the king-size bed. He kept the lights dim, his voice soft and low, as he set about trying to make her comfortable.

With a mental command, he willed the bathroom sink on, running warm water into the basin as he carefully removed the makeshift bandages that covered Tess's wrist and neck. She had stopped bleeding, thankfully. Her wounds were raw and hideous on her flawless skin, but the worst of the injuries was past.

Seeing the ugly marks left by the Rogues who attacked her, Dante wished he had Tess's healing touch. He wanted to erase the injuries before she had a chance to see them, but he couldn't work that kind of miracle. His blood would heal her from within, replenish her body and give her a preternatural vitality she'd never known. Over time, if she fed from him regularly as his mate, her health would be ageless. In time the scars would mend too. Not soon enough for him. He wanted to tear her attackers apart all over again, torture them slowly instead of delivering the efficient death the Rogues had received.

The need for violence, for vengeance against every Rogue who could ever harm her, seethed through him like acid. Dante tamped the urge down, throwing all of his energy into tending Tess with reverent, gentle hands. He eased her out of her bloodstained jacket, peeling off the sleeves and then lifting her slack body to free her of it. The pullover sweater she wore beneath was ruined as well, the celery-colored wool soaked a garish red around the neck and the edge of the long sleeve.

He would have to cut the sweater off; no way he was going to try to pull it over her head and disturb the nasty bite wound at her throat. Retrieving one of the daggers sheathed at his hip, he slid the blade under the hem and ripped a clean line up the center of the garment. The soft wool fell away, exposing Tess's creamy torso and the peach-hued lace of her bra.

A sexual stirring roused within him, as automatic as breathing, as he looked down on the perfection of her skin, the sweetly feminine curves of her body. Seeing her always brought out his hunger, but seeing her marked by rough Rogue hands put a steadying calm in him that trumped even the strength of his base desire to possess her.

She was safe now, and that was all he needed.

Dante set the blade down on the nightstand, then removed Tess's ruined sweater and dropped it next to the jacket beside the bed. The room was warm, but her skin was still cool to the touch. Pulling the edge of the black silk comforter from the other side of his large bed, he covered her, then went into the bathroom to get a soapy washcloth and a fresh towel to clean her up. As he came back out to the bedroom, he heard a quiet rap on the open door of his quarters, too soft to belong to any of the warriors.

'Dante?' Savannah's velvety voice was even softer than her knock. She came in carrying a handful of ointments and medicines, her dark, gentle eyes filled with sympathy. Lucan's mate, Gabrielle, was with her, the auburn-haired Breedmate holding a plush robe over her arm. 'We heard what happened and thought we'd bring a few things to help make her more comfortable.'

'Thank you.'

He watched idly from the bedside as the other women approached to set down their items. His main focus was on Tess. He lifted her hand and carefully swept the edge of the warm washcloth over the crusted blood on her wrist, his strokes as light as he could manage with his large clumsy hands that were better suited to holding firearms or steel.

'Is she all right?' Gabrielle asked from behind him. 'Lucan said you put her to your vein to save her.'

Dante nodded, but he felt no pride over what he'd done. 'She'll hate me for it when she understands what it means. She doesn't know that she's a Breedmate. She doesn't know . . . what I am.'

He was stunned to feel a small hand light reassuringly on his shoulder. 'Then you should tell her, Dante. Don't put it off. Trust her enough that she will make sense of the truth, even if she is resistant to accept it at first.'

'Yes,' he said, 'I know she deserves the truth.'

He was gratified by Gabrielle's sympathetic gesture and by the soundness of her advice. She spoke from experience, after all. The female had been through her own astonishing truth with Lucan just a few months earlier. Although the pair were inseparable ever since and clearly in love, Lucan and Gabrielle's journey had been anything but smooth. None of the warriors knew the specifics, but Dante could guess that Lucan and his stony, remote nature hadn't made it easy for either of them.

Savannah stepped up next to him at the bed now. 'After you clean her wounds, put some of this ointment on them. Along with your blood in her system, the medicine will help speed the healing and lessen her scars.'

'Okay.' Dante took the jar of homemade remedy and set it down on the nightstand. 'Thank you. Both of you.'

The women gave him understanding smiles, then Savannah bent to pick up Tess's soiled jacket and sweater.

'I don't think these will be of any use to her now.' The instant her fingers closed around the clothing, her smooth features pinched. She closed her eyes, wincing. Her breath caught, then leaked out of her in a shaky sigh. 'My Lord, the poor thing. The attack on her was so . . . savage. Did you know they nearly bled her dry?'

Dante inclined his head. 'I know.'

'She was almost gone by the time that you – Well, you saved her, and that's what matters,' Savannah said, adopting a serene tone that didn't quite mask the discomfort she was feeling after reading the terrible details of Tess's attack. 'If you need anything at all, Dante, just ask. Gabrielle and I will do whatever we can to help.'

He nodded, already going back to work on Tess's wounds with the damp cloth. He heard the women leave, and the space around him went still with the weight of his thoughts. He didn't know how long he remained at Tess's side – easily hours. He cleaned her up and toweled her off, then climbed in bed next to her and stretched out against her, just watching her sleep and praying that she would open her beautiful eyes for him again soon.

A hundred thoughts went through his mind as he lay there, a hundred promises he wanted to make to her. He wanted her to be safe always, to be happy. He wanted her to live forever. With him, if she'd have him; without, if that was the only other way. He would look after her as long as he was able, and if – more likely when – the death that stalked him finally caught up to him, he would have already seen to it that there would always be a place for Tess among the Breed.

God, was he actually thinking about the future?

Planning for it?

It seemed so strange that, after spending his entire life living like there was no tomorrow, convinced that at any second there would be no tomorrow, all it took was one woman to throw all of that fatalistic thinking right over a cliff. He still believed death was around the corner – he knew it with the same clarity that his mother knew her own death and that of her mate – but one extraordinary woman had made him hope like hell that he was wrong.

Tess made him wish that he had all the time in the world, so long as he could spend every second of it with her.

She had to wake up soon. She had to get better, because he had to make things right with her. She had to know how he felt, what she meant to him – and what he'd done to her, by binding them together in blood.

How long should it take for his blood to absorb into her body and begin its rejuvenation? How much would she need? She had taken only the smallest amount in the ride to the compound, just the few scant drops he could work into her mouth and down her slack throat. Maybe she needed more.

Using the dagger next to him on the nightstand, Dante scored a fresh line on his wrist. He pressed the bleeding cut to Tess's lips, waiting to feel her respond, wanting to curse to the rafters when her mouth remained unmoving, his blood dripping down, useless, onto her chin.

'Come on, angel. Drink for me.' He stroked her cool cheek, brushed a tangle of her honey-blond hair from her forehead. 'Please live, Tess . . . drink, and live.'

A throat cleared awkwardly from the area near the bedroom doorjamb. 'I'm sorry, the uh . . . the door was open.'

Chase. Just fucking great. Dante couldn't think of anyone he'd like to see less right now. He was too entrenched in what he was doing – in what he was feeling – to deal with another interruption, particularly one coming from the Darkhaven agent.

He'd hoped the bastard was already long gone from the compound, back to where he came from – preferably with one of Lucan's size-fourteens planted all the way up his ass. Then again, maybe Lucan was saving the privilege for Dante instead.

'Get out,' he growled.

'Is she drinking at all?'

Dante scoffed, low under his breath. 'What part of "get out" did you fail to understand, Harvard? I don't need an audience right now, and I sure as hell don't need any more of your bullshit.'

He pressed his wrist to Tess's lips again, parting them with the fingers of his free hand in the hopes that she might take some of his blood by mild force. It wasn't happening. Dante's eyes stung as he stared down at her. He felt wetness streaking his cheeks. Tasted the salt of tears gathering at the corner of his mouth.

'Shit,' he muttered, wiping his face into his shoulder in a strange mix of confusion and despair.

He heard footsteps coming up near the bed. Felt the air around him stir as Chase reached out his hand. 'It might work better if you tilt her head, like th—'

'*Don't* . . . touch her.' The words came out in a voice Dante hardly recognized as his own, it was so full of venom and deadly warning. He swiveled his head around and met the agent's eyes, his vision burning and sharp, his fangs having stretched long in an instant.

The protective urge boiling through him was fierce, utterly lethal, and Chase evidently understood at once. He backed off, hands raised in front of him. 'I'm sorry. I meant no harm. I only wanted to help, Dante. And to apologize.'

'Don't bother.' He turned back to Tess, miserable with worry and craving solitude. 'I don't need anything from you, Harvard. Except your absence.'

A long silence answered, and for a moment Dante wondered

if the agent had actually slunk away as he hoped. No such luck.

'I understand how you feel, Dante.'

'Do you.'

'I think so, yes. Now I think I understand a lot of things that I didn't before.'

'Well, good for you. Fucking brilliant of you, former Agent Chase. Write it up in one of your pointless reports and maybe your buddies in the Darkhavens will pin a goddamn medal of commendation on you. Harvard finally clues in on something.'

The vampire chuckled wryly, without rancor. 'I've fucked up, I know. I've lied to you and to the others, and I've jeopardized this mission because of personal, selfish motives. It was wrong, what I did. And I want you to know – especially you, Dante – that I'm sorry.'

Dante's pulse was hammering with fury, and with fear for Tess's condition as well, but he did not lash out at Chase as impulse made him want to do. He heard the contrition in the male's voice. And he heard humility, something generally on short order with Dante himself. Until now. Until Tess.

'Why are you telling me this?'

'Honestly? Because I see how much you care about this woman. You care, and you're scared shitless about it. You're afraid you're going to lose her, and right now you'll do anything to hold on to her.'

'I'd kill for her,' Dante said quietly. 'I would die for her.'

'Yes. I know you would. Maybe you can see how easy it would be to lie, cheat, or even give up your life's purpose to help her – to do anything, risk anything, if it would mean protecting her from any more hurt.'

Frowning with new comprehension and suddenly unable to despise the agent any longer, Dante turned to look at Chase. 'You said you had no female in your life, no family or obligations beyond your brother's widow. . . .'

Chase smiled vaguely. Etched in misery and longing, the

vampire's face said it all. 'Her name is Elise. She was there tonight, when you and Tegan came to pick me up at my home.'

He should have known. He did know, on some level, Dante acknowledged now. Chase's reaction when the woman came outside had been virulent, unhinged. It was only when he saw her potentially in harm's way that he lost his usual cool. He'd looked like he'd wanted to tear Tegan's head off for touching the female, a possessiveness that went beyond simple defense of one's kin.

And by the look on Chase's face, he was alone in his affection.

'Anyway,' the agent said abruptly. 'I just . . . wanted you to know that I'm sorry for everything. I want to help you and the rest of the Order in any way I can, so if there is anything you need, you know where I am.'

'Chase,' Dante said as the male turned to leave the room. 'Apology accepted, man. And for what it's worth, I'm sorry too. I haven't been fair to you either. Despite our differences, know that I respect you. The Agency lost a good one the day they cut you loose.'

Chase's smile was crooked as he acknowledged the praise with a short nod.

Dante cleared his throat. 'And about that offer of help . . .'

'Name it.'

'Tess was walking a dog when the Rogues attacked her tonight. Ugly little mutt, not good for much more than a foot-warmer, but it's special to her. Actually, it was a gift from me, more or less. Anyway, the dog was running loose on its leash when I saw it a block or so away from Ben Sullivan's place.'

'You want me to go retrieve a wayward canine, is that where this is heading?'

'Well, you did say anything, didn't you?'

'So I did.' Chase chuckled. 'All right. I will.'

Dante dug the keys to his Porsche out of his pocket and tossed them to the other vampire. As Chase turned to be on his way again, Dante added, 'The little beast answers to the name Harvard, by the way.'

'Harvard,' Chase drawled, shaking his head and throwing a smirk in Dante's direction. 'I don't suppose that's a coincidence.'

Dante shrugged. 'Good to see that Ivy League pedigree of yours comes in handy for something.'

'Jesus Christ, warrior. You really were busting my ass since the minute I came on board, weren't you?'

'Hey, by all comparisons, I was kind. Do yourself a favor and don't look too closely at Niko's shooting targets, unless you're very secure about your manhood.'

'Assholes,' Chase muttered, but there was only humor in his tone. 'Sit tight, and I'll be back in a few with your mutt. Anything else you're gonna hit me up for now that I opened my big yap about wanting to get square with you?'

'Actually, there might be something else,' Dante replied, his thoughts going sober when he considered Tess and any kind of future that might be deserving of her. 'But we can talk about that when you get back, yeah?'

Chase nodded, catching on to the turn in mood. 'Yeah. Sure we can.'

❧ CHAPTER THIRTY ❧

When Chase strode out of Dante's living quarters into the hallway, Gideon was waiting there.

'How's it going in there?' the warrior asked.

'She's still unconscious, but I think she's in good hands. Dante is determined that she'll be all right, and once that warrior gets an idea in his head, there isn't much that's going to stand in his way.'

'True enough,' Gideon chuckled. He was holding a portable video device, which he now turned on. 'Listen, I tapped into some Rogue activity on satellite surveillance earlier tonight. More than one of the subjects appear to be Darkhaven civilians. You got a minute to take a look, maybe provide some ID for us?'

'Of course.'

Chase glanced down at the small screen of the handheld as Gideon called up the images and fast-forwarded to a specific frame. The night-vision footage, zoomed in on a decrepit building in one of the city's industrial slums, showed four individuals exiting from a back door. By the gait and size of them, Chase could tell they were vampires. But the human they were stalking had no idea.

The recorded feed played on, and Chase watched, repulsed, as the four Darkhaven youths closed in on their prey. They attacked swiftly and savagely, like the Blood-lusting predators they were. Gang-style attacks on humans were unheard of among the Breed; only vampires turned Rogue hunted and killed like this.

'Can you tighten up this frame?' he asked Gideon, not really wanting to see more of the carnage but unable to look away.

'Think you recognize any of them?'

'Yes,' Chase said, his gut convulsing as the focus closed in on Camden's disheveled, feral appearance. The second sighting of the youth in the past few hours, and irrefutable evidence that he was beyond retrieving. 'They're all from the Boston Darkhaven. I can give you their names, if you like. That one there is called Camden. He is my brother's son.'

'Fuck,' Gideon whispered. 'One of these Rogues is your nephew?'

'He started using Crimson and went missing nearly two weeks ago. He is the real reason I came to the Order for help. I wanted to locate him and bring him back before this happened.'

The other warrior's face was grave. 'You know that all of the individuals on this satellite feed are Rogues. They're addicts now, Chase. Lost causes—'

'I know. I saw Camden earlier tonight, when Dante, Tegan, and I were at Ben Sullivan's place. As soon as I looked into his eyes, I understood what he was. This only confirms it.'

Gideon was quiet for a long moment as he clicked off the device. 'Our policy on Rogues is pretty plain. It has to be. I'm sorry, Chase, but if we run across any of these individuals in our patrols, there is only one course of action.'

Chase nodded. He knew that the Order's stance when it came to dealing with Rogues was unwavering, and after riding shotgun with Dante for the past few nights, he knew it had to be that way. Camden was gone, and now it was only a matter of time before the Bloodlusting shell that was left of his nephew met a violent end, either in combat with the warriors or through his own reckless actions.

'I have to go topside and do something for Dante,' Chase

said. 'But I'll be back within the hour, and I can give you whatever info you need to help get these Rogues off the streets.'

'Thanks.' Gideon clapped him on the shoulder. 'Look, I'm sorry, man. I wish things could be different. We've all lost loved ones to this goddamn war. It never gets any easier.'

'Right. I'll catch you later,' Chase said, then he strode away, heading for the elevator that would take him to the Order's fleet garage on ground level.

As he rode up, he thought about Elise. He'd come clean to Dante and the others about Camden, but he was still keeping the truth from Elise. She needed to know. She needed to be prepared for what had happened to her son and to understand what it meant. Chase wouldn't be bringing Cam home now. No one could. The truth was going to kill Elise, but she deserved to have it.

Chase stepped off the elevator and reached into his coat pocket to withdraw his cell phone. As he walked toward Dante's coupe, he hit the speed dial for his home. Elise picked up on the second ring, her voice anxious, hopeful.

'Hello? Sterling, are you all right? Have you found him?'

Chase stopped walking, cursing inwardly. For a long second he could not speak. He didn't know how to phrase what he had to say. 'I, uh . . . Yes, Elise, Camden has been sighted tonight.'

'Oh, my God.' She let out a sob, then hesitated. 'Sterling, is he . . . Please, tell me he's alive.'

Shit. He hadn't expected to do this over the phone. He thought he'd call her and let her know that he'd be there to explain everything later on, but Elise's maternal worry knew no patience. She was desperate for answers, and Chase could not keep them from her any longer.

'Ah, hell, Elise. It's not good news.' In the heavy, utter silence that held on the other end of the line, Chase launched into the facts. 'Cam was spotted tonight, running with a group of

Rogues. I saw him myself, at the apartment of the human who's been dealing Crimson. He's in bad shape, Elise. He's . . . Christ, there's just no easy way to tell you this. He's turned, Elise. It's too late. Camden has gone Rogue.'

'No,' she said finally. 'No, I don't believe you. You're mistaken.'

'It's no mistake. God, I wish it was, but I saw him with my own eyes, and I've seen surveillance footage of him collected by the warriors as well. He and a group of other Darkhaven youths – all Rogues now – were caught on satellite, attacking a human in full public view.'

'I need to see it.'

'No, trust me, you don't—'

'Sterling, listen to me. Camden is my son. He's all I have left. If he's done these things, as you say – if he's become such an animal and you have some proof of this – I have a right to see it for myself.'

Chase drummed his fingers on the roof of the black Porsche, knowing that none of the warriors was going to appreciate him bringing a civilian into the compound.

'Sterling, are you there?'

'Yeah. I'm still here.'

'If you care the least bit for me or for your brother's memory, then please, let me see my son.'

'Okay,' he said, relenting at last and consoling him-self with the idea that if he granted her this dubious request, he would at least be present to catch Elise when she fell. 'I have some business topside, but I'll swing by the Darkhaven in about an hour to pick you up.'

'I'll be waiting.'

That incredible warmth was back, Tess mused from within the dark tide that held her. She stretched her senses toward the engulfing heat, toward the wondrous scent and taste of the liquid fire that fed her. Conscious thought seemed to dance just out of her reach, but her nerve endings clicked on like strings of tiny lights, as though her body was slowly thawing, coming alive inch by inch, cell by cell, after a long, cold sleep.

'Drink,' a deep voice beckoned her, and she did.

She drew more of the heat into her mouth, swallowing it down in greedy pulls. A strange awakening began somewhere deep inside her as she drank from the source of that powerful warmth. It started in her fingers and toes, then spread up into her limbs, an electricity that hummed through her in undulating waves.

'That's it, Tess. Take more. Just keep drinking, angel.'

She couldn't have stopped if she'd wanted to. It seemed as though each sip made her thirsty for another, every swallow only adding fuel to the fire that was building within the very core of her. She felt like an infant at its mother's breast, vulnerable and uninitiated, trusting completely, needing on the most basic level.

She was being given life; she knew this in that primitive part of her mind. She had been near death, maybe close enough to touch it, but this warmth – this dark elixir – had pulled her back.

'More,' she croaked. At least she thought she had spoken. The voice she heard sounded distant and weak. So desperate. 'More . . .'

Tess shuddered as an abrupt absence of warmth answered her demand. *No*, she thought, a dark panic rising with the loss. He was leaving her now. Her protective angel was gone, along with the font of life he'd given her. She moaned weakly, forcing her listless hands to reach out and search for him.

'Dante . . .'

'I'm right here. I'm not going anywhere.'

The chill vanished as a heavy weight settled in alongside her. Heat warmed her entire length, heat from him as he pulled her up against him. She felt strong fingers at her nape, guiding her head closer to his voice, pressing her mouth to the firm column of his neck. Warm, wet skin met her lips.

'Come here, Tess, and drink from me. Take all you need.'

Drink from him? Some fading part of her consciousness rejected the idea as nonsensical, unthinkable, but another part of her – the part that was still spinning wildly in the tide, grasping for solid ground – made her mouth seek out that which he so willingly offered.

Tess parted her lips and sucked long and hard, filling her mouth with the roaring force of Dante's gift.

Holy. Hell.

As Tess locked her mouth down over the vein he'd opened for her in his neck, Dante's entire body went as taut as a bowstring. The hungry suction of her lips, the silky caress of her tongue as she drew his blood into her mouth and swallowed it, made his cock stand up at attention, a fierce, stone-hard erection like he'd never experienced before.

He hadn't known how intense it would be to let her drink from him so intimately. This was the first time in all his existence that he'd ever given his blood to another. He had always been the taker, feeding out of necessity and often for pleasure, but never with a Breedmate.

Never with a woman who moved him the way Tess did.

And the fact that she fed from him now out of pure survival instinct, because his blood was the very thing – the only thing – her body needed in this moment, just made the act all the more erotic to him. His sex throbbed, hungry and demanding, a heavy pressure that he wanted to ignore but couldn't.

Christ, but it felt as if she were sucking on that very male part of him, each pull of her mouth ratcheting him up tighter, nearly sending him straight over the edge. With a groan, Dante fisted his hands in the silk sheets of his bed, holding on as Tess fed from him in primal need.

Her fingers started twitching where they clutched his shoulders, kneading his muscles in a mindless rhythm as she continued to draw his blood into her mouth. Dante felt her strength coming back to her with each passing minute. Her breathing grew deeper, no more the rapid, shallow compression of her lungs but a cadence of long, healthy draws.

Feeling her vitality return was the greatest aphrodisiac he had ever known. It took Herculean effort not to catch her in his arms and press her beneath him so he could slake his own thundering need.

'Keep drinking,' he told her, his mouth full with the presence of his extended fangs and a tongue gone thick with his own thirst. 'Don't stop, Tess. It's all for you. Only for you.'

She moved up closer to him now, her breasts crushing against his chest, and her hips . . . God, her hips were rubbing along his pelvis, undulating in a subtle, instinctual motion as her mouth continued to work feverishly at his neck. He rolled onto his back and held as still as he could for her, his eyes closed in exquisite torment, his pulse raging.

Restraint was not something he was accustomed to practicing, but for Tess he would endure the agony all night if necessary. He relished it, actually, as much as his desire for her shredded him in pieces. He lay back on the mattress and absorbed every nuance of her body's movement, every soft mewl and moan she made against his throat.

He might have lasted longer if Tess hadn't crawled up over him, her mouth still fastened to his vein, her hair falling loosely onto his chest. Dante's spine arced beneath her, rising up off the bed as she sucked deeper now, her slender body feeling hot to the touch, moving all over him in slow erotic waves.

She started riding him, her thighs spread across his hips, her sex grinding on his as if they were naked together and making love. Even through the nylon warm-ups he wore, he could feel Tess's intense heat. Her panties were wet from desire, the sweet scent of her arousal slamming into his brain like a hammer.

'Christ,' he gasped, reaching up to grab the headboard as her feeding rose to a frenzied crescendo.

She rocked on him, faster and harder, her blunt human teeth latching on to his neck as she sucked deeper than ever at his vein. He felt her climax swelling, breaking loose. His own was roaring up on him fast as well, his shaft surging, leaping, ready to blow. The second Tess came, Dante surrendered to his own release. The orgasm crashed into him, laying him low, wringing him out. He was lost to it, unable to stop the fierce pulsations that seemed to go on endlessly as Tess settled on top of him in a sated, heavy sleep.

After a while, Dante unclamped his hands from the headboard and brought them down gently on Tess's slack body. He wanted to be inside her, needed it like he needed air to breathe, but she was vulnerable right now and he would not use her. Now that she was out of danger, there would be other times for them to be together like this, better times.

God, there had to be.

❄ CHAPTER THIRTY-ONE ❄

Tess came awake gently, her face breaking through the surface of a warm, dark wave that floated her body toward a welcoming shore. She took a breath and felt cool, cleansing air rush into her lungs. Her eyes blinked open, once, twice, the lids feeling heavy as though she'd been asleep for days.

'Hello, angel,' said a deep, familiar voice very near her face.

Tess lifted her gaze until she saw him – Dante, looking down on her, his eyes sober but smiling. He stroked her forehead, smoothing damp strands of hair out of her face.

'How do you feel?'

'Okay.' She felt better than okay, her body resting on a soft mattress, cocooned in black silk sheets and the strong shelter of Dante's arms. 'Where are we?'

'Someplace safe. This is where I live, Tess. Nothing can harm you here.'

She registered his assurances with a pang of confusion, something shadowy and cold hovering at the edges of her consciousness. Fear. She didn't feel it now, not for him, but the feeling lingered like a mist clinging to her skin, chilling her.

She had been afraid a short while ago – deathly afraid.

Tess reached a hand up to her neck. Her fingers made contact there with a patch of inflamed, tender skin. Like a sudden flash of lightning, a memory ripped through her mind: a hideous face, with eyes as bright as lit coals, a mouth opened wide in a terrifying hiss, baring huge sharp teeth.

'I was attacked,' she murmured, the words forming even before the memory took full root. 'They came up to me on the street and they . . . attacked me. Two of them dragged me off the street and they—'

'I know,' Dante said, carefully removing her hand from her neck. 'But you're all right, Tess. It's over, and you don't have to be afraid now.'

In a blur of recollection, the night's events played in fast-forward through her mind. She relived it all, from her walk past Ben's apartment and the realization that someone other than him was inside the place, to the shocking sight of seeing the large men – if they even were men at all – leaping down from the balcony to the street below and chasing after her. She saw their terrible faces, felt the bruising strength of the hands that seized her and pulled her into the dark where the real brutality was to begin.

She could still feel the terror of that moment, when one man held her arms and the other pinned her down with the weight of his huge muscular body. She'd thought she would be raped, probably beaten as well, but her attackers' intent was only slightly less horrific.

They had bitten her.

The two savage monsters held her down like felled prey on the floor of a dark, dilapidated shed. Then they bit her at the neck and wrist and began to drink her blood.

She had been certain she was going to die there, but then something miraculous happened. Dante happened. He had killed them both, a fact Tess had not so much seen as felt. Lying on the rough plywood floor of the shed, the smell of her own blood choking her senses, she had felt Dante's presence. She had felt his rage fill the small space like a tempest of black heat.

'You . . . you were there too, Dante.' Tess sat up, her body seeming miraculously strong, no lingering aches from her ordeal.

Now that her mind was clearing, she felt energized and refreshed, like she had just awoken from a deep, rejuvenating sleep. 'You found me there. You saved me, Dante.'

His smile seemed haunted, as if he wasn't sure he agreed and didn't feel comfortable with her gratitude. But he wrapped his arms around her and pressed a tender kiss to her lips. 'You're alive, and that's all that matters.'

Tess held him close, feeling almost a part of him in some strange way. His heartbeat echoed in the cadence of her own, his body's warmth seeming to seep through her skin and bones to warm her from within. She felt connected to him now in a very visceral way. The sensation was extraordinary, so powerful it took her aback.

'Now that you're awake,' Dante murmured against her ear, 'there's someone waiting in the other room who'd like to see you.'

Before she could respond, Dante got off the big bed and walked toward the adjacent living room. From behind him, Tess couldn't help admiring the masculine prowl of his body, the sexy network of multicolored tattoos over his back and shoulders shifting gracefully with every rolling stride. He disappeared into the other room, and Tess heard a soft animal whine that she recognized at once.

'Harvard!' she exclaimed as Dante came back into the bedroom, carrying the squirming, adorable little terrier in his arms. 'You saved him too?'

Dante shook his head. 'I saw him running loose before I found you and brought you here. Once I knew you were safe, I sent someone back out to get him.'

He set the dog down on the bed, and Tess was immediately tackled by the perky furball. Harvard licked her hands and face as she hoisted him up for a hug, overjoyed to see him after thinking she'd lost him on the street outside Ben's apartment.

'Thank you,' she said, smiling through a sudden mist of tears as the happy reunion continued. 'I have to confess, I think I'm totally in love with this little beast.'

'Lucky dog,' Dante drawled. He sat down on the edge of the bed, watching as Tess's chin got a thorough, enthusiastic washing. His expression was too carefully schooled, too grave when her eyes met his. 'There are . . . things we need to talk about, Tess. I had hoped you might never really be part of it, but I keep dragging you further in. After tonight, you need to understand what happened, and why.'

Nodding in silence, she let go of Harvard and looked at Dante's bleak gaze. Part of her already knew where the conversation was going – uncharted territory, for sure, but after what she'd seen tonight, Tess knew that things she had long taken for granted as normal and real were somehow thrown off kilter.

'What were they, Dante? Those men who attacked me – they weren't normal men. Were they?'

His head shook vaguely. 'No, they weren't men. They were dangerous creatures, blood addicts. We call them Rogues.'

'Blood addicts,' she said, her stomach lurching at the very idea. She looked down at her wrist, where a bite mark glowed red, but healing, on her skin. 'My God. That's what they were doing, drinking my blood? I don't believe this. There's only one name for that kind of psychotic behavior, and it's vampire.'

Dante's piercing, unwavering stare wasn't even close to a refutation.

'Vampires don't exist,' she told him firmly. 'This is reality we're talking about, after all. They can't really exist.'

'They do, Tess. Not the way you might have been brought up to believe. Not as undead, soulless demons, but as a separate, hybrid species. The ones who attacked you tonight are the worst kind. They have no conscience, no capacity for logic or control. They kill indiscriminately and will continue to do so if they aren't brought under control soon. That's what I and the others in this compound are here for – to see to it that the Rogues are wiped out of existence before they become a pestilence unlike anything modern humankind has ever seen.'

'Oh, come on!' Tess scoffed, wanting to disbelieve but finding it hard to reject Dante's outrageous claim when he had never looked or sounded more sincere. Or more deadly rational. 'Are you telling me that you're some kind of vampire slayer?'

'I'm a warrior. This is war, Tess. Things have only gotten worse now that the Rogues have Crimson on their side.'

'Crimson? What's that?'

'The drug Ben Sullivan has been peddling around town the past few months. It increases the desire for blood, reduces inhibition. It creates these killers.'

'What about Ben? Does he know this? Is that why you went to his apartment the other night?'

Dante nodded. 'He says he was hired to make the drug by an anonymous corporation this past summer. We suspect that corporation was likely a front for the Rogues.'

'Where is Ben now?'

'I don't know, but I intend to find out.'

A coldness edged Dante's voice as he said it, and Tess couldn't help feeling a note of worry for Ben. 'The men who – the Rogues – who attacked me had been searching his apartment.'

'Yes. They might have been looking for him, but we're not sure.'

'I think I may know something about what they wanted.'

Dante fixed her with a frown. 'How so?'

'Where's my jacket?' Tess glanced around the bedroom but didn't see any of her clothes. She was wearing just a bra and panties under the sheets that draped her. 'I found something at the clinic the other day. A computer flash drive. Ben hid it in one of my exam rooms.'

'What was on it?'

'I don't know. I haven't tried to open it yet. It's in my jacket pocket—'

'Shit.' Dante leaped to his feet. 'I'll be back in a few minutes. Will you be all right here alone?'

Tess nodded, still trying to come to grips with everything that was happening, all the incredible, disturbing things she was learning about the world she thought she knew. 'Dante?'

'Yeah?'

'Thank you . . . for saving my life.'

Something dark flashed in his whiskey-colored eyes, softening his harshly handsome features. He came back to her on the bed and tunneled his fingers through the hair at her nape, tipping her face up to his. His kiss was sweet, almost reverent. 'Sit tight, angel. I'll be right back.'

Elise put her hand against the smooth wall of the corridor and tried to catch her breath. Her other hand was pressed to her stomach, her fingers splayed across the wide red sash of her widow's garb. A heaving roll of nausea weakened her legs, and for a moment she thought she might throw up where she stood. Wherever that might be.

She had fled the compound's tech lab in a state of complete revulsion, appalled by what she had been shown. Now, after running blindly down one length of hallway, then another, she really had no idea where she'd ended up. She only knew that she needed to get away.

She couldn't run far enough away from what she had just seen.

Sterling had warned her that the Order's satellite surveillance images of Camden were graphic, disturbing. Elise had been prepared, she'd thought, but seeing her son and several other Rogues engaged in the wholesale slaughter of a human being had been beyond even her worst imaginings. It was a nightmare that she knew would haunt her for the rest of her living days.

Her spine leaning against the corridor wall, Elise let herself sink slowly to the floor. She couldn't hold back the tears or the ragged sobs that grated in her throat. Guilt was at the root of her anguish, the regret that she hadn't been more careful with Camden. That she had taken for granted that he was too good at heart, too strong, for something so heinous to befall him.

Her son could not be the Bloodlusting monster she saw on that computer screen. He had to be in there somewhere, still retrievable. Still salvageable. Still Camden, her golden, cherished child.

'You all right?'

Startled by the deep male voice, Elise flinched, her teary gaze flicking upward. Gem-green eyes stared back at her from within a reckless fall of tawny hair. It was one of the two warriors who'd come to the Darkhaven for Sterling earlier that evening – the coldly imposing one who had caught Elise and held her back when she tried to rush to Sterling's defense.

'Are you hurt?' he asked when she could only look up at him from her humiliating collapse on the corridor floor.

He strode toward her, his expression flat, unreadable. He was half undressed, wearing loose jeans that sagged down indecently on his lean hips and a white shirt that was completely unbuttoned, baring his muscular chest and torso. An astonishing display of *dermaglyphs* covered him from groin to shoulder, the density and intricacy of the markings leaving no doubt whatsoever that this warrior was first-generation Breed. Which meant he was among the most aggressive and powerful of the vampire race. Gen Ones were few in number; Elise, for her many decades of living in the Darkhavens, had never even seen one before.

'I'm Tegan,' he said, and held out his hand to help her up. The contact seemed too forward to her, even though she could hardly pretend that this male's huge hands hadn't been clamped down on her shoulders and her waist just a few hours before. She'd felt the lingering heat of his touch for a long time after he'd let her go, the outline of his strong fingers seeming burned into her flesh.

She got to her feet on her own power and brushed awkwardly at her wet cheeks. 'I am Elise,' she said, giving him a polite bow of her head. 'I am Sterling's sister by marriage.'

'Are you recently widowed?' he asked, his head cocking to the side as that penetrating gaze of his drank in every inch of her.

Elise fidgeted with the long scarlet sash at her waist. 'I lost my mate five years ago.'

'You still mourn.'

'I still love him.'

'I'm sorry,' he said, his tone level, his face placid. 'And I'm sorry about your son too.'

Elise looked down, not ready to hear sympathy for Camden when she was still clinging to hope that he might return to her.

'It's not your fault. You didn't drive him to this, and you couldn't have stopped him.'

'What?' she murmured, astonished that Tegan could know anything about her guilt, her secret shame. A few Gen Ones were gifted in mind reading, but she hadn't felt him probing her thoughts, and only the weakest humans were penetrable without some notice of psychic invasion. 'How could you possibly—'

The answer came to her at once, the explanation for the strange buzzing of her senses when he'd touched her earlier that night, the lingering heat his fingers had left on her skin. He had divined her emotions in that instant. He had stripped her bare without her will.

'I'm sorry,' he said. 'It's not something I can control.'

Elise blinked away her discomfiture. She knew what it was like to be cursed with such an ability. Her own psychic skill had made her a prisoner to the Darkhavens, unable to bear the bombardment of negative human thoughts that assailed her whenever she was among their kind.

But sharing a similar affliction with this warrior didn't make her any more comfortable in his presence. And worry over Camden – the raw misery she felt when she thought about what he was doing out there, swept up in the violence of the Rogues – made her anxious to be alone.

'I should go,' she said, more to herself than to Tegan. 'I need to . . . I have to get out of here. I can't be here right now.'

'Do you want to go home?'

She shrugged, then shook her head, uncertain what she needed. 'Anywhere,' she whispered. 'I just need to go.'

Closer now, moving without even the slightest stir of the air around him, Tegan said, 'I'll take you.'

'Oh, no, I didn't mean—'

She shot a glance back down the corridor, in the direction she'd come from, thinking that she probably should try to find Sterling. A bigger part of her was thinking that she wasn't at all sure she should be in this warrior's company now, let alone considering going off with him somewhere unescorted.

'You afraid I'm going to bite you, Elise?' he asked, his lazy, sensual mouth quirking at one corner, the first indication she'd seen in him that he actually might feel any emotion at all.

'It's late,' she pointed out, casting about for a polite excuse to deny him. 'It must be getting close to dawn. I wouldn't ask you to risk exposure—'

'So I'll drive fast.' Now he smiled, a full-on grin that said he knew full well she was trying to dodge him and he wasn't about to permit it. 'Come on. Let's get the hell out of here for a while.'

God help her, but when he held his hand out to her, Elise hesitated only for a second before she took it.

⇥ CHAPTER THIRTY-TWO ⇤

D ante was gone longer than a few minutes, and the waiting made Tess anxious. She had so many questions, so much to sort out in her mind. And despite the internal, enlivened buzzing of her body, on the outside she felt strung out, antsy.

A hot shower in Dante's spacious bathroom helped wash away some of that feeling, and so did the fresh change of clothes that he had left for her in the bedroom. With Harvard watching from his curled-up position on the bed, Tess put on the tan cords and brown knit shirt, then sat down to slip on her shoes.

Scuff marks and small splatters of blood were vivid reminders of the attack she'd suffered. An attack, Dante would have her believe, perpetrated by inhuman creatures with a thirst – an addiction – to blood.

Vampires.

There had to be a more logical explanation, something grounded in fact, not folklore. Tess knew it was impossible, yet she knew what she had experienced. She knew what she had seen, when her first assailant leaped off Ben's apartment balcony on foot and dropped to the ground, as fluid as a cat. She knew what she had felt, when that man and another who joined him hauled her off the sidewalk and into the old shed. They had bitten her, like rabid animals. They had punctured her skin with huge fangs and drawn her blood into their mouths, feeding off her like something out of a horror movie.

Like the vampires Dante had proclaimed them to be.

At least she was safe now, wherever Dante had brought her. She looked around the large bedroom with its simple, understated furnishings. The furniture was masculine, with clean lines and dark finishes. The only indulgence was the bed. The king-size four-poster dominated the room, its glossy black silk sheets as soft and sleek as a raven's wing.

Tess found similar tasteful appointments in the adjacent living room. Dante's quarters felt comfortable and unfussy, like the man himself. The whole place seemed homey, but it didn't feel like a house. There were no windows on any of the walls, just expensive-looking contemporary art and framed photography. He had mentioned this place was a compound, and now Tess wondered precisely where she was.

She walked out of the living room to a tiled foyer. Curious, she opened the door and peered out onto a corridor of glossy white marble. Tess looked up the long hallway, then down the other side. It was empty, just a curving tunnel of polished stone. On the floor, inlaid into the snowy marble, was a series of symbols – interlocking geometric arcs and swirls rendered in obsidian. They were unusual and intriguing, some of them forming similar patterns to the beautiful multihued tattoos Dante sported on his torso and arms.

Tess bent down to get a closer look. She was so involved in studying the symbols that she didn't realize Harvard was near until the terrier slipped past her and started trotting off down the corridor.

'Harvard, get back here!' she called after him, but the dog kept running, disappearing around a bend in the curved hallway.

Damn it.

Tess stood up, shot a glance up and down the vacant corridor, then went after him. The pursuit led her down one long stretch of corridor, then another. Every time she got close to catching the errant terrier, he dodged capture, trotting through the endless maze of hallway as if they were playing a game.

'Harvard, you little shit, stop right now!' she whispered sharply and to no avail.

She was impatient now and uncertain if she should be traipsing around the place alone. Even though she couldn't see them, she was sure security cameras were clocking her every move from within the opaque glass orbs that were installed every few feet in the corridor ceiling.

There were no signs anywhere to indicate her location or to note where any of the labyrinthine corridors led. Wherever it was that Dante called home, it was rigged up like some high-tech government agency. Which only gave more credibility to his outrageous claims of an underworld war and the existence of dangerous creatures of the night.

Tess followed the dog around a sharp right turn that opened onto another wing of the compound. Finally, Harvard's run was thwarted. A pair of swinging doors blocked his path at the end of the hall, the small square windows at eye level cloudy with frosted glass.

Tess approached cautiously, not wanting to frighten the dog out of her reach but also unsure what might be on the other side of those doors. It was quiet here, nothing but endless white marble everywhere she looked. There was a vaguely antiseptic smell in the air. From somewhere not far, her ears picked up the faint electronic beep of medical equipment and some other rhythmic, metallic clank that she could not place.

Was this some kind of medical wing? It felt sterile enough, but there were no outward indications of patients inside, no staff rushing about. No one at all, from what she could tell.

'Come here, you little beast,' she muttered, bending down to retrieve Harvard from where he'd stalled out near the doors.

Holding him close to her chest in one arm, Tess slowly pushed open one of the doors a crack and peeked inside. Only dim light shone beyond the doors, a soothing semidarkness. There was a row of closed doors on both sides of the interior hallway.

She slipped through the swinging doors and walked a few paces inside.

Right away she found the source of the beeping: A digital panel was mounted to a wall on her left, its array of monitoring lights dark except for a handful in a grid on the lower portion of the board. It appeared to be some kind of EKG monitor, although it was nothing like any she'd seen before. And coming from the farthest room in the hallway was the repetitive clank and thunk of something heavy.

'Hello?' Tess called into the empty space. 'Is someone in here?'

The instant the words left her lips, all other sound around her ceased, including the beeps of the monitor. She glanced to the grid just in time to see the lights blink off. Like someone had disconnected them from within the far room.

A feeling of unease crept up her spine. In her arms, Harvard started to squirm and whimper. He wriggled away from her, jumping down and scrambling back up the corridor. Tess couldn't name the dread that was running through her, but she wasn't about to stand around and wonder either.

She turned back for the doors. Started walking briskly toward them, her head turned to watch for movement behind her. She felt a sudden drop in the temperature – a chill breeze on her skin, crawling up the back of her neck.

'Shit,' she whispered, more than a little unnerved.

She put her hand out to push open the door and jumped back when her palm connected with something warm and unmoving. Tess stopped short and swung her head around in shock. Her gaze latched on to a hideously scarred face and torso of an immense, muscular man.

No, not a man.

A monster, with the huge fangs and fiercely glowing amber eyes of the ones who had assaulted her in the street.

A vampire.

In a flash of vivid, horrific remembrance, Tess was bombarded with images of the earlier attack: bruising fingers digging into her arms, holding her down; sharp teeth tearing into her, the endless, fevered pulls at her veins; awful, animalistic grunts and moans as the beasts fed on her. She saw the moonlit pavement, the darkened alleyway, the ramshackle shed where she'd thought she was going to die.

And then, just as suddenly but oddly out of place, she saw the small storage room in the back of her clinic. There was a big man with dark hair huddled on the floor, bleeding. He was dying, riddled with bullets and other terrible wounds. She reached out to him –

No, that didn't belong in her memories. It hadn't actually happened . . . had it?

She didn't have a chance to try putting the pieces in place. The vampire blocking her escape stalked forward, his head cocked as he glared at her in wild fury, those enormous fangs deadly white and sharp enough to tear her to shreds.

Dante stood in Gideon and Savannah's study, waiting for a verdict on the flash drive Tess had been carrying in her coat pocket. 'You think you can get around the encryption on that thing, Gid?'

'Please.' The blond vampire slanted him an arch look. 'You jest,' he said, leaning heavily on his faded English accent. He already had the drive plugged into his computer, his fingers flying over the keyboard. 'I've hacked into the FBI, the CIA, our own IID, and just about every other hack-proof database in existence. This will be cake.'

'Yeah? Let me know what you find. I gotta go now. I left Tess waiting—'

'Not so fast,' Gideon said. 'I'm almost in. Trust me, this won't take long, maybe five minutes. Let's make it interesting. Give me two minutes, thirty seconds, tops.'

Beside him, leaning back against the antique carved mahogany desk in dark jeans and a black sweater, Savannah smiled and rolled her eyes. 'He lives to impress, you know that.'

'Be a hell of a lot easier to take if the bastard wasn't always right,' Dante drawled.

Savannah laughed. 'Welcome to my world.'

'Too bad you can't read computer files with your touch,' he told her. 'Then we wouldn't need to put up with this guy.'

'Alas,' she sighed dramatically. 'Psychometry doesn't work that way, at least not for me. I can tell you what Ben Sullivan was wearing when he handled the flash drive, describe the room he was in, his state of mind, but I can't penetrate electronic circuitry. Gideon's our best hope for that.'

Dante shrugged. 'Just our luck, eh?'

Over at the computer, Gideon hit one last series of keystrokes, then sat back in his chair, hands clasped behind his head. 'I'm in. Looks like one minute, forty-nine seconds, to be exact.'

Dante walked around to look at the screen. 'What have we got?'

'Data files. Spreadsheets. Flow charts. Pharmaceutical tables.' Gideon rolled the mouse and clicked one of the files open. 'Looks like a chemistry experiment. Anyone need a recipe for Crimson?'

'Jesus Christ. This is it?'

'I'm betting so.' Gideon scowled, clicking through more files on-screen. 'There's more than one formula stored on the drive, however. We can't know which of them is valid until we obtain the ingredients and test each one.'

Dante raked a hand through his hair and began pacing. He was curious to know more about the formulas Ben Sullivan had stored on the drive, but at the same time he was damn itchy to be back in his quarters. He could sense Tess's restlessness too, the connection they now shared through the blood bond like an unseen tether linking him to her as though they were one.

'How is she doing?' Savannah asked, obviously aware of his distraction.

'Better,' he said. 'She's awake and healing. Physically, she's fine. As for the rest, I've been trying to fill her in on everything, but I know she's confused.'

Savannah nodded. 'Who wouldn't be? I thought Gideon was a crazy fool when he first told me about all of this.'

'You still think I'm a crazy fool most of the time, love. That's part of my charm.' He bent toward her and faked a bite of her denim-clad thigh, his fingers not skipping a beat on the keys.

Playfully batting him away, Savannah stood up and came over to where Dante was trying to wear a track in the rug. 'Do you think Tess might be hungry? I've got breakfast started in the kitchen for Gabrielle and me. I can prepare a tray for Tess, if you'd like to bring it to her.'

'Yeah. Thanks, Savannah. Food would be great.'

God, he hadn't even considered that Tess would need to eat. What a stellar mate he was proving to be already. He hardly took decent care of himself and now he had a Breedmate to think about, with human wants and needs that were well outside his areas of expertise. Oddly enough, where the thought might have given him doubts in the not-so-distant past, now he found the idea almost . . . pleasant. He wanted to provide for Tess, in every way. He wanted to protect her and make her happy, spoil her like a princess.

For the first time in his long life, he felt as if he'd found true purpose. Not the honor and duty that drove him as a warrior, but something equally compelling and righteous. Something that called to everything male in him.

He felt as if this bond he'd found – this love he had for Tess – might actually be strong enough to make him forget about the death and anguish that had been stalking him. Some hopeful part of him wanted to believe that with Tess beside him, maybe he could find a way to thwart it.

Dante hadn't even begun to enjoy that slender hope before a scream ripped through him like a blade. He felt it physically, but the assault was on his senses, a fact he realized when neither Savannah nor Gideon reacted to the terrified shriek that froze Dante's heart to ice in his chest.

It tore through him again, leaving him shuddering in its wake.

'Oh, Jesus. Tess!'

'What's wrong?' Savannah paused on her way to the kitchen. 'Dante?'

'It's Tess,' he said, already training his mind on her, homing in on her location in the compound. 'She's somewhere in the compound – the infirmary, I think.'

'I'll get a visual.' At the computer, Gideon quickly brought up the display for one of the corridor's video monitors. 'I've got her, D. Ah, hell. She's run into Rio down there. He's got her cornered—'

Dante took off at a dead run before the words were out of Gideon's mouth. He didn't need to see the screen to confirm where Tess was or what was giving her such a fright. He bolted out of Savannah and Gideon's apartments, hauling ass into the heart of the compound. Knowing the layout of the place inside and out, he took the shortest route down to the medical wing, using all the preternatural speed at his command.

Dante heard Rio's voice even before he reached the set of swinging doors that led into the medical wing.

'I asked you a question, female. What the fuck do you think you're doing down here?'

'Get away from her!' Dante shouted as he entered the infirmary, hoping like hell he wasn't going to have to do battle with one of his own. 'Back off, Rio. Now.'

'Dante!' Tess cried, panting with fear. Her face was ashen, her body trembling uncontrollably from behind the massive wall of Rio's body. The warrior had her trapped against the corridor wall, animosity radiating off him in blasting pulses of heat.

'Let her go,' Dante ordered his brethren.

'Dante, be careful! He'll kill you!'

'No, he won't. It's okay, Tess.'

'This female doesn't belong here,' Rio snarled.

'I say she does. Now back off and let her go.'

Rio relaxed only a fraction and swung his head around to look at Dante. Jesus, it was hard to remember the warrior before the ambush that had left him so wrecked, both physically and emotionally. The once-handsome face of the Spaniard with the ready smile and lazy wit was now a tangle of ruddy scars; his humor had long abandoned him for the fury that might never ease.

Dante parked himself right in Rio's face, staring past the scars on the warrior's cheeks and brow into the nearly insane eyes that looked so Roguelike even Dante was taken aback for a second. 'I said, stand down,' he growled. 'The woman is with me. She is mine. Do you understand?'

Sanity flared within the bright amber depths of Rio's eyes, a lightning-quick glint of awareness, of contrition and regret. He wheeled away from Dante with a grunt, his breath still sawing in and out of his open mouth.

'Tess, it's okay now. Step away from him and come to me.'

She let out a broken gasp but didn't seem capable of moving. Dante held his hand out to her.

'Come on, angel. Everything's all right. I promise you, you're safe.'

Looking as if it took all her courage to do so, Tess sidled away from Rio and put her hand in Dante's open palm. He brought her to him and kissed her, relieved to have her near.

As Rio slunk to the corridor wall and dropped into a huddled crouch on the floor, Dante's pulse downshifted to something almost resembling normal. Tess was still upset and trembling, and while he didn't think Rio posed any danger to her – especially now that Dante had made his position clear – he had some serious damage control to handle.

'Stay here. I'm just going to help Rio get back to his bed—'

'Are you crazy? Dante, we have to get out of here. He will tear both our throats open!'

'No, he won't.' He held Tess's anxious gaze even as he moved closer to Rio's huddled form on the floor. 'He won't hurt me. He wouldn't have hurt you either. He didn't know who you were, and something very bad happened to him that's made him wary of females. Believe me, he's not a monster.'

Tess gaped at Dante as if he'd lost his mind. 'Dante, the fangs . . . those eyes! He's one of the ones who attacked me—'

'No,' Dante said. 'He only looks like them because he's angry, and he's in a lot of pain. His name is Rio. He's a Breed warrior, like me.'

'Vampire,' she gasped brokenly. 'He's a *vampire*. . . .'

Damn it, he hadn't meant for her to learn the truth like this. God help him, but he'd thought he could ease her into his world – a world that belonged to them both – once she understood the vampire race was nothing to be feared, and once she saw how she was part of it, as a Breedmate.

As the only woman he would ever want at his side.

But everything was unraveling fast, a thread of half-truths and secrets that was spiraling down around his feet as she stared at him in panic, her eyes pleading with him to make sense of an unfathomable situation.

'Yes,' Dante admitted, unwilling to lie to her. 'Rio is a vampire, Tess. Like me.'

CHAPTER THIRTY-THREE

Tess's heart took a sharp dive into her stomach. 'W-what did you say?'

Dante looked at her, those whiskey-gold eyes far too serious, his expression much too calm. 'I am one of the Breed. A vampire.'

'Oh, my God,' she moaned, her skin going tight with alarm, with revulsion.

She didn't want to believe it – he didn't look like the creatures who'd assaulted her or the one who now lay in an anguished ball on the floor of the infirmary. But Dante's tone was so level and matter-of-fact, she knew he was telling her the truth. Maybe for the first time since she'd met him, he was finally being honest with her.

'You lied to me. All this time, you've been lying to me.'

'I wanted to tell you, Tess. I've been trying to find the words to tell you—'

'That you're some kind of sick monster? That you've been using me – for what, just to get close to Ben so that you and your bloodsucking buddies could kill him?'

'We haven't killed the human, I swear to you. But that doesn't mean I won't, if it comes down to that. And, yes, at first I needed to know if you were involved in his Crimson dealing, and I thought you might be useful in getting more information on those activities. I had a mission, Tess. But I also needed your trust so that I could protect you.'

'I don't need your protection.'

'Yes, you do.'

'No,' she said, numb with a heavy kind of dread. 'What I need is to get as far away from you as I can.'

'Tess, the safest place for you now is here, with me.'

When he came toward her, holding out his hands in a gesture that begged trust, she recoiled. 'Stay away from me. I mean it, Dante. Get away!'

'I'm not going to hurt you. I promise.'

An image slammed into the front of her consciousness as he said the words. In her mind, Tess was suddenly transported to her clinic storeroom, crouching down over a badly injured man who'd somehow found his way inside after a vicious fight on the streets Halloween night. He was a stranger to her then, but not now.

It was Dante's face she saw, bloodstained and grimy, his hair dripping wet as it spiked down over his brow. His lips moved, speaking the same words she heard him speak now: *I'm not going to hurt you . . . I promise. . . .*

She had an abrupt but very distinct memory of strong hands gripping her by the arms, holding her in place. Of Dante's lips peeling back from his teeth – revealing huge white fangs that came toward her throat.

'I didn't know you,' Dante was saying now, as if he could track her thoughts with his mind. 'I was weakened and seriously wounded. I would only have taken what I needed from you and left you alone. There would have been no pain for you, no distress. I had no idea what I had done until I saw your mark—'

'You bit me . . . you . . . Oh, God, you drank my blood that night? How . . . why am I only now remembering this?'

His stark features softened somewhat, as if in remorse. 'I erased your memory. I tried to explain things to you, but the situation was too far out of hand. We struggled, and you injected me with a sedative. By the time I came to, it was almost dawn and there was no time for talking. I thought it best for you that you didn't remember. Then I saw the mark on your hand, and I knew there could be no taking back any of what I'd done to you.'

Tess didn't need to look down at her right hand to know the mark he spoke of. The small birthmark had always been curious to her, a teardrop poised over the bowl of a crescent moon. But it didn't make any more sense to her now than it ever had.

'Not many women have the mark, Tess. Only a rare few. You're a Breedmate. If one of my kind takes your blood into his body, or gives you his, a bond is forged. It is unbreakable.'

'And you . . . did this to me?'

Another memory swamped her now, a further remembrance of blood and darkness. Tess recalled waking from a shadowy dream, her mouth filled with a roaring force of energy, of life. She had been starved, and Dante fed her. From his wrist and then, later, from a vein he had opened for her in his neck.

'Oh, my God,' she whispered. 'What have you done to me?'

'I saved your life by giving you my blood. Just as you saved mine with yours.'

'You gave me no choice, either time,' she gasped. 'What am I now? Have you turned me into the same kind of monster that you are?'

'No. That's not the way it works. You will never become a vampire. But if you continue to feed from me as my mate, you can live for a very long time. As long as I will. Longer, perhaps.'

'I don't believe this. I refuse to believe this!'

Tess pivoted for the swinging doors of the infirmary and pushed against the panels. They didn't budge. She pushed again, putting all of her strength into it. Nothing. It was as though they were fused on their hinges, completely immobile.

'Let me out of here,' she told Dante, suspecting that it was his will alone that kept the doors from opening for her. 'Goddamn you, Dante. Let me go!'

As soon as the door gave the slightest bit, Tess pushed it open and bolted through at a dead run. She had no idea where she was going and didn't care, so long as it put distance between herself and Dante, the man she only thought she knew. The man she actually believed she was in love with. The monster who had betrayed her more deeply than anyone in her tormented past.

Sick with fear and angered at her own stupidity, Tess choked back the tears that stung her eyes. She ran harder, knowing that Dante was certain to catch up to her. She just had to find a way out of the place. Running up to a bank of elevators, she pressed the call button and prayed the doors would open. Seconds ticked by . . . too many for her to risk waiting.

'Tess.' Dante's deep voice startled her with its nearness. He was right behind her, close enough to touch her, even though she hadn't heard him approach.

With a cry, she ducked out of his reach and made another mad dash down one of the corridor's twisting lengths. There was an open, arched entryway up ahead of her. Maybe she could hide in the chamber, she thought, desperation making her grasp for any means of escaping the nightmare that was pursuing her now. She slipped inside the dim space – a cathedral of some sort, with carved stone walls lit only by a single red pillar candle that glowed near an unadorned altar.

There was nowhere to conceal herself in the small sanctuary, only twin rows of benches and the stone pedestal at the front of the room. On the other side was another arched doorway, opening into more darkness; it was impossible for her to discern where it might lead. It didn't matter, anyway. Dante was standing in the open doorway off the corridor, his muscular body never looking more imposing than it did as he stepped into the small cathedral and began a slow prowl toward her.

'Tess, we don't have to do this. Let's talk.' His powerful stride faltered for a second, and he scowled, bringing his hand up to his temple as if he were in pain. When he spoke again, his voice had dropped a full octave in pitch, coming out of him in a dark snarl. 'Christ, can we just . . . Let's be reasonable, try to work this out.'

Tess backed up, inching closer to the far wall of the chamber and the arched hollow carved into the stone.

'Damn it, Tess. Hear me out. I love you.'

'Don't say that. Haven't you told me enough lies already?'

'It's no lie. I wish it was, but—'

Dante took another step, and his knee suddenly gave out beneath him. He hissed as he caught himself on one of the low benches, his fingers digging into the wood so hard, Tess thought it a wonder he didn't crush it.

Something strange was happening to his features. Even with his head dropped down, she could see that his face was growing sharper, his cheeks seeming leaner, more angular, his golden skin stretched tight over the bones. He spat a curse, something she didn't recognize any more than she did the gravelly roughness of his voice.

'Tess . . . you have to trust me.'

She moved closer to the archway, leading with her hand as she sidled along the wall. And then she was standing in front of the opening, nothing but pitch blackness behind her and a thin, chill breeze at her back. She turned her head to glance into the dark –

'*Tess.*'

Dante must have sensed her movement, because when she looked back at him, he lifted his head and met her gaze. The warm color of his eyes had changed to a fierce glow, his pupils narrowing down to bare slits as she watched his transformation in stunned horror.

'Don't go,' he rasped thickly, his words tangling on the

lengthening sharpness of a spectacular set of fangs. 'I won't hurt you.'

'It's too late, Dante. You already have,' she whispered, moving farther away from him, stepping back into the arched doorway. In the darkness, she saw that a flight of stone steps climbed steeply upward, toward the source of the cool air that drifted down around her. Wherever they led, she had to go. She put her foot on the first step –

'Tess!'

She didn't look back at him. She knew she couldn't or she might not find the courage to leave him. She climbed the first few steps tentatively, then began running, taking the flight as quickly as she could.

Down below, Dante's anguished roar echoed off the stone walls of the cathedral and the darkened stairwell, straight into the marrow of her bones. Tess didn't stop. She ran faster up what seemed like hundreds of steps, until she reached a solid steel door at the top. She slapped her palms against it and pushed it open.

Blinding daylight poured over her. A cool November breeze sent dried leaves spiraling up from the grass outside. Tess let the door close behind her with a bang. Then she wrapped her arms around herself and took off, running into the crisp, bright morning.

Dante thrashed on the floor, caught in the grip of his persistent, debilitating nightmare. The death vision had come on suddenly, intensifying as he and Tess argued.

It only worsened now that she was gone. Dante heard the topside door slam closed above and knew from the brief flash of daylight that shot down the long stairwell that even if he was able to break away from the invisible chains that held him, the sun's brutal rays would prohibit him from going after her.

He sank deeper into the abyss of his premonition, where

vines of thick black smoke curled around his limbs and throat, choking off precious air. The shattered remains of a smoke alarm hung from the ceiling by its mangled wire guts, silent as the smoke collected around it.

From elsewhere came the angry crash of objects falling, as if fixtures and furniture were being overturned and thrown to the floor by a marauding army. All around him in the small white cell that held him, Dante saw upended cabinet drawers and files, their contents spilled everywhere, rifled through in haste.

In the vision, he was moving now, stepping through the debris and making his way to the closed door on the other side of the room. Oh, Jesus. He knew this place, he realized now.

He was in Tess's clinic.

But where was she?

Dante registered that he ached everywhere, his body feeling battered and tired, each step sluggish. Before he could reach the door and try to get out, it opened from the other side. A familiar face leered at him through the smoke.

'Look who's up and about,' Ben Sullivan said, coming inside and holding a length of telephone cord in his hands. 'Death by fire is such a nasty way to go. Of course, if you breathe in enough smoke, the flames will be just an afterthought.'

Dante knew he shouldn't be afraid, but terror clawed at him as his would-be executioner entered the room and took hold of him in a surprisingly strong grasp. Dante tried to fight, but his limbs didn't seem his own to command. His struggles only slowed Sullivan down. Then the human cocked his arm back and nailed Dante with a blow to the jaw.

His vision swam crazily. When he next opened his eyes, he was on his stomach, lying on a raised slab of cold polished steel while Ben Sullivan pulled his hands behind his back, then bound him at the wrists with the cable he was holding. Dante should have been able to snap his bonds loose, but they held tight. The human moved down to his feet, hog-tying him.

'You know, I thought killing you was going to be difficult,' the Crimson dealer whispered near his ear, the same words Dante had heard the last time he'd endured this glimpse of death. 'You've made it very easy for me.'

As he'd done before, Ben Sullivan went around to the front of the platform and bent down in front of Dante. He grabbed Dante by the hair and lifted his face up off the cold metal. Past Sullivan's head, Dante saw a clock on the wall above the door, the time reading 11:39. He struggled to collect more detail, knowing he would need all he could gather in order to confront this eventuality and maybe turn it around in his favor. He didn't even know if it might be possible to cheat fate, but he was damn well going to give it a shot.

'It didn't have to be like this,' Sullivan was saying now. The human leaned in close – close enough that Dante saw the vacant gaze of a Minion staring back at him. 'Just know that you brought this on yourself. Be grateful I didn't turn you over to my Master instead.'

With that, Ben Sullivan released him, letting Dante's head fall back down. As the Minion strode out of the room and locked the door, Dante opened his eyes and saw his reflection in the polished steel surface of the table on which he lay.

No, not his reflection.

Tess's.

Not his body bound on the examination table while the clinic was being consumed in smoke and flames, but hers.

Oh, mother of Christ.

It wasn't his horrific death he'd been experiencing in his nightmares all these years. It was the death of his Breedmate, the woman he loved.

≈ CHAPTER THIRTY-FOUR ≈

Tess made her way into the city from the compound's property in a state of emotional numbness. Without her purse, coat, or cell phone, she had few options – not even a key to get into her apartment. Breathless, confused, utterly exhausted from everything that was happening to her, she headed for a corner pay phone, praying it wasn't out of order. She got a dial tone, hit 0, and waited for the operator to come on.

'Collect call, please,' she panted into the receiver, then gave the operator the number of the animal clinic. The phone rang and rang. No answer.

As it went into voice mail, the operator disconnected, saying, 'I'm sorry. There's no one there to accept charges.'

'Wait,' Tess said, worry niggling at her. 'Will you try it again?'

'One moment.'

Tess waited anxiously as the phone began ringing again at the clinic. No answer.

'I'm sorry,' the operator said again, disconnecting the call.

'I don't understand,' Tess murmured, more to herself. 'Can you tell me what time it is?'

'It's ten-thirteen A.M.'

Nora wouldn't break for lunch until noon, and she never called in sick, so why wasn't she picking up the call? Something must be wrong.

'Would you like to try another number?'

'Yes, I would.'

Tess gave the operator Nora's land line, then, when that call came up empty, she gave her Nora's cell. As each call rang unanswered, Tess's heart sank deeper in her chest. Everything felt wrong to her. Very wrong.

With dread pounding through her, Tess hung up the pay phone and began walking for the nearest subway station. She didn't have the dollar-twenty-five fare it would cost to ride to the North End, but a grandmotherly woman on the street took pity on her and gave her a handful of loose change.

The trip home seemed to take forever, each stranger's face on the train seeming to stare at her as if they knew she didn't belong there among them. As if they could sense that she had been changed somehow, no longer a part of the normal world. No longer a part of their human world.

And maybe she wasn't, Tess thought, reflecting on all that Dante had told her – everything she had seen and been a part of in the past several hours. The past several days, she corrected herself, thinking back on Halloween night, when she'd truly first seen Dante.

When he'd sunk his fangs into her neck and turned her normal world upside down.

But maybe she wasn't being totally fair. Tess couldn't remember a time when she'd really felt a part of anything normal. She had always been . . . different. Her unusual ability, even more than her troubled past, had always kept her separate from other people. She'd always felt like a misfit, an outsider, unable to trust anyone with her secrets.

Until Dante.

He had opened her eyes to so much. He'd made her feel, made her desire in ways she never had before. He'd made her hope for things she'd only dreamed of. He'd made her feel safe and understood. Worse than that, he had made her feel loved.

But that had all been based on lies. Now she had the truth

– incredible as it was – and she would give just about anything to pretend it wasn't real.

Vampires and blood bonds. A mounting war between creatures who shouldn't exist outside the realm of the imagination, of nightmares.

It was all true, though.

It was real.

As real as her feelings for Dante, which only made his deception cut deeper. She loved him, and she'd never been more terrified of anything in her life. She had fallen in love with a dangerous vigilante. A vampire.

The admission weighed her down as she stepped off the subway car and made her way up to street level in her North End neighborhood. The local shops were bustling with morning patrons, the outdoor market enjoying a steady flow of regular customers. Tess passed a knot of tourists who'd stopped to browse autumn melons and squash, weathering a chill that had little to do with the crisp fall air.

The closer she got to home, the deeper her sense of dread grew. One of the tenants came out as she reached the front stoop. Although she didn't know the old man by name, he smiled at her and held open the door for her to enter. Tess went inside and climbed the flight of stairs to her unit. Before she got within ten feet of the door, she realized that it had been broken into. The jamb was chewed up near the doorknob, as if it had been jimmied open and then closed to make it appear that nothing was out of place.

Tess froze, panic dousing her. She took a backward step, ready to turn around and bolt. Her spine connected with a solid mass, someone standing right behind her. A strong arm snaked around her waist, yanking her off balance, and a length of cold, sharp steel pressed meaningfully below her jaw.

'Morning, Doc. About fucking time you showed up.'

*

'You can't be serious, Dante.'

Although all of the warriors, including Chase, were gathered in the training facility watching him gear up for battle, Gideon was the first to challenge him.

'Do I look like I'm kidding?' Dante took a pistol out of one of the gun cabinets and grabbed a handful of rounds. 'I've never been more serious in my life.'

'Jesus Christ, D. In case you hadn't noticed, it's just after ten o'clock in the morning. That means full-on daylight.'

'I know what it means.'

Gideon exhaled a low curse. 'You're going to fry, my man.'

'Not if I can help it.'

Having been around since the eighteenth century, Dante was beyond old by human standards, but as a Breed vampire, he was fairly average, his lineage being several generations distant from the Ancients and their hypersensitive alien skin. He couldn't stay topside for very long in the daytime, but he could take a small hit of UV rays and live to tell about it.

For Tess, he would be willing to walk into the core of the sun itself if he thought it might save her from the death he knew was waiting for her.

'Listen to me,' Gideon said, putting his hand on Dante's arm to get his attention. 'You may not be as vulnerable to the light as a Gen One, but you're still Breed. You spend more than thirty minutes in direct sunlight and you're toast.'

'It's not like I'm gonna be sightseeing up there,' he said, refusing to be swayed. He shrugged off his brethren's well-meaning caution and grabbed another weapon from the cabinet. 'I know what I'm doing. I have to do this.'

He had told the others about what he'd seen, the vision that was still tearing his heart in pieces. It killed him to think that he'd let Tess leave the compound without his protection, that he hadn't been able to stop her. That she might be in danger this very moment, while his vulnerable vampire genes forced him to hide belowground.

'What if the time you saw in your vision – eleven thirty-nine – is actually twenty-one minutes to midnight?' Gideon asked. 'You can't be sure the event you saw was taking place during the morning hours. You might be putting yourself at risk for nothing—'

'And if I wait and it turns out I'm wrong? I can't take that chance.' Dante shook his head. He'd tried to reach her by phone but got no answer at her apartment or the clinic. And the searing ache in his chest told him that she wasn't ignoring him purely by choice. Even without the benefit of his hellish precognition, he knew his Breedmate was in danger. 'No goddamn way am I taking a chance on waiting around here 'til dark. Would you, Gideon? If Savannah needed you – I'm talking life-and-death needed you – would you even consider taking that kind of gamble? Would you, Lucan, if it were Gabrielle out there alone?'

Neither warrior denied it. There wasn't a blood-bonded male alive who wouldn't walk through a sea of fire for the woman he loved.

Lucan came toward him and held out his hand. 'You honor her well.'

Dante clasped his leader's strong Gen One hand – his friend's hand – and shook it firmly. 'Thank you. But to be honest, I'm doing this as much for myself as I am for Tess. I need her in my life. She has become . . . everything to me.'

Lucan nodded soberly. 'Then go get her, my brother. We can celebrate your pairing when you and Tess return safely to the compound.'

Dante held Lucan's regal gaze and slowly shook his head. 'That is something I need to discuss with you. With all of you,' he said, looking to the other warriors as well. 'Assuming I survive at all, if I am able to save Tess, and if she will have me as her mate – I intend to relocate to the Darkhavens with her.'

A long silence answered, his brethren staring at him in measured quiet.

Dante cleared his throat, knowing his decision must come as a shock to the warriors he'd fought alongside for more than a century. 'She's been through enough already – even before I met her and dragged her into our world against her will. She deserves happiness. She deserves a hell of a lot more than I can ever hope to give her. I just want her to be safe now, far away from any danger.'

'You would quit the Order for her?' Niko asked, the youngest only behind Dante, and a warrior who relished his duty perhaps even more than Dante had himself.

'I would quit breathing for her, if she asked it of me,' he replied, surprising even himself with the depth of his devotion. He looked to Chase, who still owed him that second favor from last night. 'What do you think? You got any pull left in the Boston Darkhaven to help me get a spot with the Agency?'

Chase smirked, lifting his shoulder in a casual shrug. 'I might.' He strode toward the weapons cabinet and took out a SIG Sauer. 'But first things first, eh? We have to get your female back here in one piece so she can decide if she wants your sorry ass for a mate.'

'We?' Dante said, watching the former Darkhaven agent suit up with the SIG and another semiauto.

'Yeah, we. I'm going with you.'

'What the—'

'Me too,' Niko said, sauntering over and pulling out his own cache of weapons. The Russian grinned as he nodded toward Lucan, Gideon, and Tegan. 'You're not going to leave me down here with these Gen One geezers, are you?'

'No one's coming with me. I wouldn't ask it—'

'You never have to,' Niko said. 'Like it or not, D, Chase and I are all you've got on this mission. You're not doing this alone.'

Dante swore, humbled and grateful for the show of support. 'All right, then. Let's get moving.'

⇥ CHAPTER THIRTY-FIVE ⇤

With the knife biting into her neck to keep her silent, Ben forced Tess out of her building and into a waiting car on the street. He smelled bad, like soured blood and sweat and a hint of decay. His clothes were filthy and wrinkled, his normally golden hair unkempt, hanging lank and unwashed into his brow. As he shoved her into the backseat of the car, Tess caught a glimpse of his eyes. They were dull and flat, staring at her with a cold detachment that made her skin crawl.

And Ben wasn't alone.

Two other men waited in the car, both seated in the front, both sharing the same vacant glint in their eyes.

'Where is it, Tess?' Ben asked as he closed the door and shut them inside the dark vehicle. 'I left a little something at the clinic the other day, but now it's not there. What did you do with it?'

The flash drive he'd lied about concealing. Which was currently in Dante's possession. As much as she doubted Dante after all she had learned about him, what she felt for Ben now was even stronger. She met his disturbingly lifeless gaze and shook her head.

'I don't know what you're talking about.'

'Wrong answer, Doc.'

Tess wasn't at all prepared for the fist that shot out at her and connected with the side of her head. She cried out, falling hard against the seat and cradling the pain that was exploding in her face.

'Maybe you'll think more clearly at the clinic,' Ben said.

At his indication, the driver punched the gas and the car sped up the street. Tess's vision swam as they made the drive from the North End to her clinic in East Boston. Ben's van was parked around back, right next to Nora's vintage Beetle.

'Oh, God,' Tess murmured, heartsick to see her assistant's car. 'What have you done to her, Ben? Tell me you haven't hurt Nora—'

'Come along, Doc,' he said, ignoring her question as he opened the door beside him and motioned to her with the knife to get moving.

Tess climbed out as directed, followed by Ben and the two goons who accompanied him. They brought her in through the back of the clinic, through the storeroom and into the empty kennel area. Ben shoved her forward, into the clinic's lobby. The place was trashed, file cabinets tossed over and emptied onto the floor, furniture smashed, chemicals and pharmaceuticals spilled all over the floor. The destruction was total, but, it wasn't until Tess saw Nora that her breath caught on a sob.

She was lying on the floor behind the reception station, her head coming up as Tess was brought near. They had tied her hands and feet with a telephone cord and gagged her mouth with a length of gauze from the medical supplies. Nora was crying, her face ashen, her eyes puffed and red from what looked to have been hours of torment. But she was alive, and that alone kept Tess from losing it completely.

'Oh, Nora,' she said brokenly. 'I'm so sorry. I'll get you out of this, I promise.'

Beside her, Ben chuckled. 'I'm glad to hear you say that, Doc. Because little Nora's fate depends solely on you now.'

'What? What do you mean?'

'You're going to help us find that flash drive, or you're going to watch as I slit the bitch's throat in front of you.'

Behind the gag in her mouth, Nora screamed. She started struggling wildly against her bonds, all in vain. One of Ben's big companions went over and hauled her to her feet, holding Nora in a bruising grip. He dragged her closer, until no more than a couple of feet separated the women. Nora pleaded with her eyes, sheer panic making her tremble like a leaf in her captor's hard grasp.

'Let her go, Ben. Please.'

'Hand over the flash drive, and I will let her go, Tess.'

Nora moaned, the sound imploring, desperate. Tess knew real terror then, a bone-deep dread that only bore further into her as she looked into her friend's eyes and realized that Ben and these other men were deadly serious. They were going to kill Nora – probably Tess as well – if she didn't give them what they wanted. And she couldn't give it to them, because she didn't have it.

'Ben, please. Let Nora go and use me instead. I'm the one who took the flash drive, not her. She's not involved in this—'

'Tell me where you put the drive, and maybe I'll let her go, how's that, Doc? Fair enough for you?'

'I don't have it,' she murmured. 'I took it out of the examination table where you hid it, but I don't have it anymore.'

He fixed that unfeeling stare on her, a muscle ticking in his jaw. 'What did you do with it?'

'Let her go,' Tess hedged. 'Let her go, and I'll tell you whatever you want to know.'

Ben's mouth lifted at the corner. He eyed the knife he held, toying with the razor edge of the blade. Then, in a flash of motion, he pivoted around and stuck Nora in the stomach with it.

'No!' Tess screamed. 'Oh, God – no!'

Ben swung back to her, cool as could be, 'That's just a gut wound, Doc. She can survive that if she gets help soon enough, but you'd better start talking fast.'

Tess's knees buckled beneath her. Nora was bleeding badly, her eyes rolling back in her head from shock. 'Goddamn you, Ben. I hate you.'

'And I no longer care what you feel about me, Tess. All I care about is getting that flash drive back. So. Where the fuck is it?'

'I gave it to someone.'

'Who?'

'Dante.'

That caused a spark of animosity to flicker in Ben's dull gaze. 'You mean that guy – the one you're screwing? Do you have any idea what you've done? Any idea what he is?'

When she didn't reply, Ben shook his head, chuckling. 'Well, you've really fucked up, Tess. It's out of my hands now.'

With that, his arm shot out and his blade arced back toward Nora, making good on his earlier threat. Tess wailed as her friend was dropped, lifeless, to the floor. Ben and one of his companions grabbed Tess before she could reach out for Nora – before she had even a moment's hope of saving her with her touch. They carried her away from the carnage, trapping her legs and arms as she fought them in a burst of animal desperation.

Struggling was futile. In moments, Tess found herself on the floor of one of her exam rooms, then heard the metallic click of the lock as Ben shut her inside to await her fate.

Nikolai drove like a bat out of hell, speeding the Breed's black SUV through the city at a breakneck pace. The temptation to watch the sunlit streets and buildings fly past through the dark, UV-tinted windows was tempting – a sight Dante had never seen, and one he sincerely hoped he never would need to again – but he kept his head down in the passenger side of the vehicle, his thoughts trained on Tess.

He and the others were outfitted in head-to-toe black nylon protective clothing: fatigues, gloves, ski-mask head coverings, and close-fitting wraparound shades to shield their eyes. Even so, the jog from the vehicle to the back door of Tess's clinic building was intense.

With weapons at the ready, Dante wasted no time. He led the charge, planting his booted foot in the center of the storeroom door and kicking the steel panel right off its hinges. Smoke swirled from the fires that Sullivan had begun setting inside. The roiling plumes grew thicker with the sudden influx of air from outside. They wouldn't have much time to finish this.

'What the hell is going on?'

At the crack of splintering metal and raining debris from the door, a Minion came running in to see what was wrong. Niko let him know without the slightest hesitation, firing a round of metal into the guy's skull.

Now that they were inside, Dante smelled blood and death through the smoke – not the fresh kill lying at their feet and, thankfully, not Tess either. She was still alive. He sensed her fear like his own, her current state of sorrow and pain tearing into him like heated steel.

'Sweep the place and put out the fires,' he ordered Niko and Chase. 'Kill anyone who stands in your way.'

Tess tried the tightly wound cords that bound her hands and feet together behind her on the examination table. They wouldn't budge. But she couldn't stop trying them, even when her struggles only seemed to amuse her captor.

'Ben, why are you doing this? For God's sake, why did you have to kill Nora?'

Ben clucked his tongue. 'You killed her, Tess, not me. You forced my hand.'

Sorrow choked her as Ben came over to where he had trussed her up on the table.

'You know, I thought killing you was going to be difficult,' he whispered near her ear, his hot, stale breath assaulting her nostrils. 'You've made it very easy for me.'

She watched nervously as he went around to the front of the platform and bent down to her level. His fingers were rough in her hair as he lifted her face up off the slab of cold metal. His eyes were those of a dead man, a mere shell of a human being, no longer the Ben Sullivan she once knew.

'It didn't have to be like this,' he told her, his tone deceptively gentle. 'Just know that you brought this on yourself. Be grateful I didn't turn you over to my Master instead.'

He stroked her cheek, his touch revolting. When she flinched away, he held her hair tighter, forcing her to look at him. He leaned in as if to kiss her, and Tess spat in his face, fighting back by the only means he'd left her.

Tess braced herself for retaliation as he raised his free hand to strike her. 'You fucking bit—'

He didn't get a chance to finish speaking, let alone touch her. A blast of arctic air rushed in from the open doorway, the instant before the space filled with the massive form of a man clothed in solid black and wearing opaque wraparound sunglasses. Guns and blades hung from his hips and from the thick leather holsters that crisscrossed his muscular torso.

Dante.

Tess would know him anywhere, even beneath the cover of all that black. Hope flared in her, along with surprise. She could feel him reaching out to her with his mind, assuring her that he would get her out of there. That she was safe now.

And at the same time, she could feel his rage. The icy chill of it rolled off his huge body, centering on Ben. Dante lowered his head, the focus of his gaze readable even through the dark lenses that shielded his eyes. A glow emanated from behind those black shades – ember bright, and deadly.

With the flick of a glance, Ben's body was jerked up off the floor and smashed into the cabinets on the exam-room wall. He kicked and flailed, but Dante held him aloft with just the power of his will. When another black-clad warrior appeared in the doorway, Dante growled a command.

'Get her out of here, Chase. I don't want her to see this.'

Dante's companion came over and cut Tess loose, then carefully lifted her into his arms and carried her out of the clinic to an SUV that idled out back.

Once Chase had removed Tess from the room, Dante let go of his mental hold on the human. The contact severed, Sullivan dropped like dead weight to the floor. He started to scramble up, trying to grab for a knife he'd left lying on the counter. Dante sent the blade flying with a sharp mental command, embedding the steel point in the opposite wall.

He stalked farther into the room, forgoing his own weapons in order to deliver Ben Sullivan's death with his hands. He wanted vengeance now, and he meant to make the bastard suffer for what he'd intended to do to Tess. For what he had done to her in the time before Dante reached her.

'Get up,' he ordered the human. 'It ends here.'

Sullivan chuckled, coming up slowly to his feet. When Dante met his gaze, he saw the dull glint of a mind slave in the Crimson dealer's eyes. Ben Sullivan had been turned Minion. Certainly explained his recent MIA status. Killing him by any means was going to be doing him a favor.

'Where's your Master hiding out these days, Minion?'

Sullivan only glared at him.

'Did he tell you we kicked his ass last summer, that he ran off with his tail between his legs rather than face the Order mano a mano? He's a coward and a poseur, and we're gonna take him down.'

'Fuck you, vampire.'

'No, I don't think so,' Dante said, noting the twitch of muscle in the Minion's legs, the telltale movement that told him Sullivan was about to snap. 'Fuck you, you Minion piece of shit. And fuck the son of a bitch who owns you too.'

A shrill bellow came out of the Minion's mouth as he launched himself across the room at Dante. Sullivan punched and hammered at him, fists flying fast, but not so fast that Dante couldn't block them. In the scuffle, Dante's chest covering tore away, exposing his skin. With a roar, he sent a blow into the Minion's face, relishing the crack of bone and the dull smack of giving flesh that sounded on impact.

Ben Sullivan went down in a sprawl. 'There is only one true Master of the race,' he hissed up at Dante. 'Soon he will rule as king – as is his birthright!'

'Not bloody likely,' Dante replied, lifting the Minion's bulk off the floor in one hand, then sending him airborne.

Sullivan slid across the polished surface of the table where he'd held Tess and crashed into the windowed wall on the other side of the room. He righted himself at once, leaping up to his feet but weaving in front of the blinds, which swung back and forth behind him. Dante instinctively shielded his eyes from the intermittent light, bringing his arm up to block the rays.

'What's the matter? Too bright for you, vampire?' He grinned through bloodstained teeth. In his hand was a piece of broken drawer, which he held before him like a jagged club. 'How about a little lesson from *Die Hard?*'

He swung his arm back and shattered the window, knocking the blinds askew and sending glass flying all around them. Sunlight poured in, searing Dante's eyes behind his shades. He roared at the sudden agony shredding his corneas, and in that brief second of inattention, Ben Sullivan rolled out from under him, trying to escape.

Temporarily blinded, his skin heating up through his protective clothing and sizzling where the light met his exposed flesh, Dante tracked the Minion with his other senses, all of them heightened as his rage transformed him. Fangs stretched long in his mouth. Pupils narrowed on the other side of his dark lenses.

Launching up into the air, he leaped across the room in one fluid motion, pouncing on Sullivan from behind. The impact took both of them to the floor. Dante gave the Minion no chance to react. He grabbed him by his chin and brow and leaned down so that his sharp fangs brushed the bastard's ear.

'Yippeekayay, muthafucker.'

With a sharp twist, Dante snapped the Minion's neck in his hands.

He dropped the limp corpse to the floor, vaguely aware of the acrid smell in the air and the faint sizzle that buzzed in his ears like a swarm of flies. Pain washed over him as he stood up and turned away from the broken window. He heard the heavy pound of boots outside the room, but he could hardly force his eyes to focus on the dark shape that filled the space between the jambs.

'It's all clear out – holy shit.' Niko's voice trailed off, and then the warrior was at Dante's side, ushering him out of the light-washed room at an urgent clip. 'Oh, Jesus, D. How long were you exposed?'

Dante shook his head. 'Not that long. Bastard knocked out the window.'

'Yeah,' Niko said, his voice oddly grim. 'I can see that. We have to get you out of here, man. Come on.'

CHAPTER THIRTY-SIX

'Holy. Hell.'

The black-clad warrior in the front seat of the SUV with Tess – Chase, he'd been called – threw open the driver's-side door and leaped out, just as Dante and another man came running out of the clinic.

But Dante wasn't so much running as he was stumbling, his body being held up by the warrior helping him out. His head was dropped down against his chest, uncovered, and the front of his fatigues were torn open, exposing the tawny skin of his torso, which glowed a fiery red in the bright light of the morning.

Chase opened the SUV's back door and helped the other man get Dante inside. Dante's fangs were long, the sharp points glinting white with each breath he dragged in through his open mouth. His face was contorted in pain, his pupils thin black slits in the middle of bright amber irises. He was fully transformed, the vampire Tess should fear but couldn't now.

His friends worked fast, their grim silence making Tess's blood run cold. Chase shut the back door and ran around to the driver's seat. He hopped in, threw the vehicle into gear, and they were off.

'What happened to him?' she asked anxiously, unable to see blood on Dante or any other indication of injury. 'Is he wounded?'

'Exposure,' said the one she didn't know, his urgent tone tinged with a Slavic accent. 'Fucking Crimson dealer busted out a window. Dante had to take the bastard down in direct sunlight.'

'Why?' Tess asked, watching Dante shift on the backseat, feeling his agony and the concern that emanated from both of his grave companions. 'Why would he do this? Why would any of you do this?'

With small but determined movements, Dante managed to strip off one of his gloves. He reached out to her from where he lay.

'Tess . . .'

She took his hand in hers, watching his strong fingers engulf her own. The emotion that traveled through their connection reached deep inside her, a warmth – a knowledge – that stole her breath.

It was love, so profound, so fierce, it rendered her speechless.

'Tess,' he murmured, his voice little more than air. 'It was you. Not my death . . . yours.'

'What?' She squeezed his hand, tears welling in her eyes.

'The visions . . . It wasn't me, but you. I couldn't—' He broke off, inhaling sharply through obvious anguish. 'Had to stop it. Couldn't let you . . . no matter what.'

Tess's tears spilled over, running down her cheeks as she held Dante's gaze. 'Oh, God, Dante. You shouldn't have risked this. What if you had died in my place?'

His lip lifted slightly at the corner, baring the edge of one sharp, gleaming fang. 'Worth it . . . seeing you here. It was worth . . . any risk.'

Tess grasped his hand in both of hers, furious and grateful, and not a little terrified of how he looked, lying in the back of the vehicle. She held on to him and didn't let go until they had arrived at the compound. Chase parked the SUV in a cavernous hangar filled with dozens of other vehicles. They all got out, and Tess just tried to stay out of the way while Dante's companions lifted him out of the car and moved him to a bank of elevators.

Dante's condition seemed to be worsening as each minute passed. By the time they descended and the elevator doors opened, he could hardly stand up on his own. A group of three other men and two women met them in the corridor, everyone flying into swift action.

One of the women came up to Tess and put a gentle hand on her shoulder. 'I'm Gabrielle, Lucan's mate. Are you all right?'

Tess shrugged, then gave a vague nod. 'Will Dante be okay?'

'I think he'll fare better if he knows you're near.'

Gabrielle gestured for Tess to follow her down the corridor to the infirmary, the very wing where she had fled Dante in fear earlier that day. They entered the room where Dante had been brought, and Tess watched as his friends removed his weapons, then carefully stripped him out of his fatigues and boots and placed him in a hospital bed.

Tess was moved by the concern of all in the room. Dante was loved here, accepted for what he was. He had a family here, a home, a life – and yet he'd risked it all to save her. As much as she wanted to fear him, to resent him for everything that had gone between them, she couldn't. She looked at Dante, suffering in sacrifice for her, and all Tess felt was love.

'Let me,' she said softly, moving to Dante's bedside. She met the worried faces of the other people who cared for him – the warriors gathered around him, the two women whose tender gazes said they understood what she was feeling. 'Let me help him . . . please.'

Tess touched Dante's cheek, stroking his strong jaw. She concentrated on his burns, letting her fingers trail down over his bare chest, over the beautiful markings that were blistered and raw, churning with angry color. As gently as she could, Tess placed her hands on the seared flesh, using her gift to draw away the radiation, take away the pain.

'Oh, my God,' whispered one of the warriors. 'She's healing him.'

Tess heard the awestruck gasps, the words of hope that traveled among Dante's friends – his family. She felt some of their affection pouring over onto her, but as welcome as the warmth of their regard was, Tess's entire focus was on Dante. On making him well.

She leaned over him and pressed a kiss to his slack mouth, unfazed by the rasp of his fangs against her lips. She loved him wholly, just as he was, and she prayed for the chance to tell him so.

Dante was going to live. His UV burns had been severe – easily life-threatening – but his Breedmate's healing touch had ultimately proven more powerful than the death that stalked him. Like the others at the compound, Chase had been astonished at Tess's ability and at her clear devotion to Dante. She had stayed by his side every moment, caring for him as he had done for her when he'd rescued her from the Rogues' attack.

Everyone agreed they would make a good match: both of them strong as individuals; together they would be unbreakable.

With the worst of the storm past and the compound settling down into a peaceful sense of calm at the arrival of night, Chase's thoughts turned homeward too. His own journey wasn't at an end yet; the road ahead of him was murky and uncertain. Once it had all seemed so clear to him, what his future should hold, where he belonged . . . and with whom.

Now he wasn't sure about anything.

He said his good-byes to the warriors and their mates, then left, heading out of the Order's world, back to his own. The drive back into the city was quiet. The wheels of his borrowed vehicle were spinning, the road falling away behind him, but where was he going, after all?

Could he really call the Darkhaven home anymore? With his senses honed from the short time he'd spent in the company of the warriors, his body weighted down by all the metal he was carrying under his coat – the sundry blades, the Beretta 9mm that had somehow become a comforting presence against his hip – how could he ever expect to integrate back into the staid life he'd once known?

And what of Elise?

He could not go back to that tormented existence of wanting a woman he might never have. He'd have to tell her how he felt about her and let the chips fall where they may. She had to know everything. Chase didn't delude himself with the hope that she might welcome his affection. In fact, he wasn't even sure what to hope for. He only knew that the half-life he was living was over, starting now.

Chase turned onto the Darkhaven's gated drive with a sense of freedom washing through him. Things were about to change for him. While he couldn't guess at how everything might shake down from here, he felt liberated to know that he had reached a turning point in his life. He pulled up the gravel driveway and parked near the Darkhaven residence.

The house was lit up from within, Elise's bedroom and living quarters glowing with soft light. She was awake, probably anxiously waiting for him to return with word from the compound.

Chase killed the engine and opened the door of the vehicle. The instant his boots hit the ground, he got a prickling sense that he was not alone. He pocketed the keys and got out, discreetly unbuttoning his pea coat as he stood. His eyes scanned the night shadows, peering into the darkness for some sign of the enemy he knew was there. His ears were attuned to every subtle noise in his surroundings – the rustle of naked branches as the breeze soughed through them; the muffled drone of the stereo in the house, Elise's favorite soft jazz playing in the background. . . .

And then, running counterpoint to all of that, the raspy wheeze of someone breathing not far from where Chase stood.

There was a crunch of gravel behind him. Chase's fingers were already curled around the grip of the 9mm as he slowly pivoted to face the threat.

Camden.

The déjà vu that hit Chase was like a cannon blast to the gut. But his nephew looked even worse than before, if that was possible. Caked in dried blood and gore, grisly evidence of recent kills that had not slaked his thirst, Camden came away from the hedge that had concealed him and loped closer. His huge fangs dripped saliva as he sized up Chase as his next fix for the Bloodlust that had taken over his body and mind. He had been unreachable when Chase encountered him in Ben Sullivan's apartment. Now he was dangerous and unpredictable, a rabid dog left to go feral too long.

Chase looked at him sadly, full of remorse for the fact that he hadn't been able to find him – hadn't been able to save him – in time to prevent this irrevocable transformation to Rogue.

'I'm so sorry, Cam. This never should have happened to you.' Under the fall of his dark wool pea coat, Chase flipped off the Beretta's safety, slid the weapon out of the holster. 'If it could be me instead, I swear . . .'

Behind him now, up at the house, Chase heard the metallic click of the front door opening, then Elise's sudden indrawn gasp. Time slowed at once. Everything spun out, reality descending into the thickness of a sluggish dream, a nightmare that began the instant Elise stepped outside.

'Camden!' Her voice seemed oddly distant, slowed like the rest of the moment. 'Oh . . . God . . . Camden!'

Chase swiveled his head toward her. He shouted for her to stay back, but she was already running, holding her arms wide, her white widow's garb fluttering around her like delicate moth's wings as she flew toward her son. Toward her certain and violent death, if Chase allowed her to get close enough to touch the Rogue vampire that had been her beloved son.

'Elise, stay back!'

But she ignored him. She kept coming, even when her tear-filled eyes focused on Camden's fearsome, hideous appearance. She choked on a sob, but her arms stayed open to him, her feet still moving across the lawn and down to the driveway.

In his peripheral vision, Chase saw the Rogue's savage amber gaze shift attention to Elise. Fixed on her now, the Bloodlusting vampire let out a terrible snarl, lowering into a crouch. Chase pivoted around and put himself squarely between mother and son. He had the pistol drawn and level before he even realized it.

Another second ticked by.

Elise was still coming, faster now, weeping and calling Camden's name.

Chase measured the distance with his gut, knowing that there were only seconds left before this confrontation would end in tragedy. He had no choice. He had to act. He couldn't stand by and risk her life –

The blast of gunfire cracked like thunder in the night.

Elise screamed. 'No! Oh, God – nooo!'

Chase stood there, numb, his finger still squeezing the trigger down. The titanium-filled bullet had hit its target squarely in the center of the chest, dropping the Rogue to the ground. Already the sizzle of death had begun, erasing all doubt that there might have been a chance to save Camden from the Bloodlust that possessed him. The Crimson had turned him into the walking dead; now it was ended. Camden's suffering was over.

Elise's – and Chase's too – had only begun.

She raced up to him and beat her fists against him, making contact with his face, his shoulders, his chest, anywhere she could strike him. Her lavender eyes were swamped with tears, her beautiful face pale and stricken, her voice lost to the hitching sobs and wails that poured out of her throat.

Chase took the abuse in silence. What could he do? What was there to say?

He let her vent all of her hatred on him, and only when she finally stopped, pivoting around to collapse on the ground near the body of her son as the titanium quickly reduced his remains to ash, did Chase find the will to move. He stared at her hunched form trembling on the gravel driveway, his ears ringing with the mournful sounds of her grief. Then, in weary silence, he let the gun slip from his loose grasp.

He turned away from her, and from the Darkhaven sanctuary that had long been his home, and walked off into the darkness alone.

Dante jolted awake, his eyelids flying open, breath sawing out of him. He'd been trapped by a wall of fire, blinded by the flames and ash. Unable to reach Tess. He sat up, panting, the vision still raw in his mind, scraping at his heart.

Oh, God, if he'd failed . . .

If he'd lost her . . .

'Dante?'

A profound relief swamped him at the sound of her voice, at the glorious realization that Tess was right there with him, seated at his bedside. He'd woken her from a drowsy sleep; she lifted her head from her arms, her hair in disarray, her gentle eyes shadowed with fatigue.

'Dante, you're awake.' She brightened at once, coming up nearer to him and caressing his face and hair. 'I've been so worried. How do you feel?'

He thought he should feel a hell of a lot worse than he did. But he was well enough to pull Tess into his arms. Strong enough to bring her onto his lap on the bed, where he kissed her soundly.

He was alive enough to know that what he needed more than anything right now was to feel her nude body pressed against his.

'I'm sorry,' he murmured against her lips. 'Tess, I am sorry for everything I've put you through—'

'Shh, we'll have time for that later. We can sort everything out later. Right now you need to rest.'

'No,' he said, too glad to be awake – to be with her – to think about wasting any more time on sleep. 'What I need to tell you can't wait. I saw something terrible today. I saw what it would be like to lose you. That's someplace I never want to go again. I need to know that you're protected, that you are safe—'

'I'm right here. You saved me, Dante.'

He stroked the velvety skin of her cheek, so grateful that he could. 'You're the one who saved me, Tess.'

He wasn't talking about his injuries from the UV exposure, which she had healed with her amazing gift of touch. He wasn't talking about the first night he'd found her either, when her blood had fortified him when he was at his weakest. Tess had saved him in so many ways beyond any of that. This female owned him, heart and soul, and he wanted her to know that now.

'Everything makes sense when I'm with you, Tess. My life makes sense, after so many years of running scared in the dark. You are the light, the reason I live. I'm bonded to you deep, woman. For me, there will never be another.'

'We're bonded by blood now,' she said, but her faint smile wobbled on her lips. She glanced down, frowning. 'What if you hadn't bitten me that night at my clinic? Without the blood bond, would you still . . .?'

'Love you?' he finished for her, lifting her chin so that she could see the truth of it in his eyes. 'It's always been you, Tess. I just didn't know it until that night. I had been searching for you my whole life, connected to you by the vision of what happened today.'

He smoothed her mussed hair, letting one of her honey-brown waves curl around his fingers. 'You know, my mother swore by destiny. She believed in it, even though she knew her own destiny held bitter pain and loss. I never wanted to accept that belief for myself, that anything was preordained. I thought I was smarter than that, above it. But it was destiny that brought us together, Tess. I can't deny that now. God, Tess . . . have you any idea how long I've waited for you?'

'Oh, Dante,' she whispered, blinking away a stray tear. 'I wasn't prepared for any of this. I'm so afraid. . . .'

He gathered her close, sick for everything she'd been forced to endure because of him. He knew the trauma of what happened today would stay with her for a long time. So much death and destruction. He never wanted her to feel that kind of pain again. 'I need to know that you are somewhere you'll always be safe, Tess. Where I can protect you best. There are places that we can go, safe houses within the Breed. I've already talked to Chase about securing a place for us in one of the area Darkhavens.'

'No.' His heart sank as she carefully extricated herself from his embrace and sat on her knees beside him on the bed. She shook her head slowly. 'Dante, no . . .'

God help him, but he couldn't speak. He waited in agonizing silence, knowing that he fully deserved her rejection. He deserved her contempt for so many reasons, yet he'd felt certain she cared for him. He prayed she might, even just a little bit.

'Tess, if you say you don't love me—'

'I do love you,' she said at last. 'I love you with all my heart.'

'Then what is it?'

She looked at him searchingly, her aqua eyes moist but resolved. 'I'm tired of running. I'm tired of hiding. You've opened my eyes to a world I never dreamed could exist. Your world, Dante.'

He smiled at the beauty sitting next to him. 'My world is you.'

'And it's all of this too. This place, these people. The incredible legacy that you're a part of. Your world is dark and dangerous, Dante, but it's also extraordinary – like you. Like life. Don't ask me to run away from that. I want to be with you, but if I'm going to live in your world, then I want to do it here, where you belong. Where your family is.'

'My family?'

She nodded. 'The other warriors here and their mates. They love you. I saw that today. Maybe in time they might love me too.'

'Tess.' Dante pulled her close, embracing her with a full heart and a gratitude that soared into his chest like it was borne on wings. 'You would want to be with me here, like this, as the mate of a warrior?'

'As the mate of *my* warrior,' she corrected, smiling at him with love shining brightly in her eyes. 'I can't have it any other way.'

Dante swallowed on a throat gone dry. He didn't deserve her. After all they'd been through, after all his ceaseless running, his heart had finally found its home. With Tess. With his beloved.

'What do you think?' she asked him. 'Can you live with that?'

'Eternally,' Dante vowed, then pulled her back down onto the bed with him and sealed their pact with a passionate, endless kiss.

Read on for a preview of the first chapter of the next book
in the heart-stopping *Midnight Breed* series.

MIDNIGHT
AWAKENING

⊰ CHAPTER ONE ⊱

She walked among them undetected, just another afternoon rush-hour commuter trudging through the fresh February snowfall on her way to the train station. No one paid any mind at all to the petite female in the hooded oversized parka, her scarf concealing her face to just below her eyes, which watched the crowds of human pedestrians with keen interest. Too keen, she knew, but she couldn't help it.

She was anxious being out among them, and impatient to find her prey.

Her head rang with the pound of rock music blaring in through the tiny earbuds of a portable MP3 player. It wasn't hers. It had belonged to her teenage son – to Camden. Sweet Cam, who'd died just four months ago, a victim of the underworld war that Elise herself was now a part of as well. He was the reason she was here, prowling Boston's crowded streets with a dagger in her coat pocket and a titanium-edged blade strapped to her thigh.

More than ever now, Camden was the reason she lived.

His death could not go unavenged.

Elise crossed at a traffic light and moved up the road toward the station. She could see people talking as she passed them, their lips moving silently, their words – more important, their thoughts – drowned out by the aggressive lyrics, screaming guitars, and pulsing throb of bass that filled her ears and vibrated in her bones. She didn't know precisely what she was listening to, nor did it matter. All she needed was the noise, played loud enough and long enough to get her into place for the hunt.

She entered the building, just one more person in a river of moving humanity. Harsh light spilled down from fluorescent tubes in the ceiling. The odor of street filth and dampness and too many bodies assailed her nose through her scarf. Elise walked farther inside, coming to a slow pause in the center of the station. Forced to divide around her, the flowing crowd passed on either side, many bumping into her, jostling her in their haste to make the next train. More than one glared as they passed, mouthing obscenities over her abrupt halt in the middle of their path.

God, how she despised all of this contact, but it was necessary. She took a steadying breath, then reached into her pocket and turned off the music. The din of the station rushed upon her like a wave, engulfing her with the racket of voices, shuffling feet, the traffic outside, and the metallic grate and rumble of the incoming train. But these noises were nothing compared to the others that swamped her now.

Ugly thoughts, bad intentions, secret sins, open hatreds – all of it churned around her like a black tempest, human corruption seeking her out and hammering into her senses. It staggered her, as always, that first rush of ill wind nearly overwhelming her. Elise swayed on her feet. She fought the nausea that rose within her and tried her best to weather the psychic assault.

– *Such a bitch, I hope they fire her ass* –

– *Goddamn hick tourists, why don't you go back where you belong* –

– *Idiot! Outta my way, or I'll friggin' knock you flat* –

– *So what if she's my wife's sister? Not like she wasn't after me all this time* –

Elise's breath was coming faster with each second, a headache blooming in her temples. The voices in her mind blended into ceaseless, almost indistinguishable chatter, but she held on, bracing herself as the train arrived and its doors opened to let a new sea of people pour out onto the platform. They spilled around her, more voices added to the cacophony that was shredding her from the inside.

– *Panhandling losers ought to put the same effort into getting a damn job* –

– *I swear, he puts his hand on me one more time, I'ma kill the sumbitch* –

– *Run, cattle! Run back to your pens! Pathetic creatures, my Master is right, you do deserve to be enslaved* –

Elise's eyes snapped wide. Her blood turned to ice in her veins the instant the words registered in her mind. This was the one voice she waited to hear.

The one she came here to hunt.

She didn't know the name of her prey, or even what he looked like, but she knew what he was: a Minion. Like the others of his kind, he had been human once, but now he was something less than that. His humanity had been bled away by the one he called Master, a powerful vampire and the leader of the Rogues. It was because of them – the Rogues and the evil one guiding them in a growing war within the vampire race – that Elise's only son was dead.

After being widowed five years ago, Camden was all she'd had left, all that mattered in her life. With his loss, she'd found a new purpose. An unwavering resolve. It was that resolve she leaned upon now, commanding her feet to move through the thick crowd, searching for the one she'd make pay for Camden's death this time.

Her head spun with the continued bombardment of painful, ugly thoughts, but finally she managed to single out the Minion. He stalked ahead of her by several yards, his head covered by a black knit cap, his body draped in a tattered, faded green camouflage jacket. Animosity poured out of him like acid. His corruption was so total, Elise could taste it like bile in the back of her throat. And she had no choice but to stick close to him, waiting for her chance to make her move.

The Minion exited the station and headed up the sidewalk at a fast clip. Elise followed, her fingers wrapped tightly around the dagger in her pocket. Outside with fewer people, the psychic blare had lessened, but the pain of overload in the station was still present, boring into her skull like a steel spike. Elise kept her eyes trained on her quarry, picking up her speed as he ducked into a business off the street. She came up to the glass door and peered past the painted FedEx logo to see the Minion waiting in line for the counter.

'Excuse me, miss,' someone said from behind her, startling her with the sound of a true voice, and not the buzz of words that were still filling her head. 'You going inside or what, lady?'

The man behind her pushed open the door as he said it, holding it for her expectantly. She hadn't intended to go in, but now everyone was looking at her – the Minion included – and it would draw more attention to herself if she refused. Elise strode into the brightly lit business and immediately feigned interest in a display of shipping boxes in the front window.

From her periphery, she watched as the Minion waited his turn in line. He was edgy and violent-minded, his thoughts berating the customers ahead of him. Finally he approached the counter, ignoring the clerk's greeting.

'Pickup for Raines.'

The attendant typed something into a computer, then hesitated a second. 'Hang on.' He headed to a back room, only to return a moment later shaking his head. 'It hasn't arrived yet. Sorry 'bout that.'

Fury rolled off the Minion, tightening like a vise around Elise's temples. 'What do you mean, 'it hasn't arrived'?'

'Most of New York got hit with a big snowstorm last night, so a lot of today's shipments have been delayed—'

'This shit's supposed to be guaranteed,' the Minion snarled.

'Yeah, it is. You can get your money back, but you have to fill out a claim—'

'Fuck the claim, you moron! I need that package. Now!'

My Master will have my ass if I don't turn up with this delivery, and if my ass goes in a sling, I'm going to come back here and rip your goddamn lungs out.

Elise drew in her breath at the virulence of the unspoken threat. She knew the Minions lived only to serve the one who made them, but it was always a shock to hear the terrible depth of their allegiance. Nothing was sacred to their kind. Lives meant nothing, be they human or Breed. Minions were nearly as awful as the Rogues, the bloodthirsty, criminal faction of the vampire nation.

The Minion leaned over the counter, fists braced on either side of him. 'I need that package, asshole. I'm not leaving without it.'

The clerk backed away, his expression suddenly gone wary. He grabbed the phone. 'Look, man, as I've explained to you, there's nothing more I can do for you on this. You're gonna have to come back tomorrow. Right now, you need to leave before I call the police.'

Useless piece of shit, the Minion growled inwardly. *I'll come back tomorrow all right. Just you wait 'til I come back for you!*

'Is there a problem here, Joey?' An older man came out from the back, all business.

'I tried to tell him that his stuff ain't here yet on account of the storm, but he won't give it up. Like maybe I'm supposed to pull it out of my a—'

'Sir?' the manager said, cutting off his employee and pinning the Minion with a serious look. 'I'm going to ask you politely to leave now. You need to go, or the police will be called to escort you out of here.'

The Minion growled something indistinguishable but nasty. He slammed his fist down on the countertop, then whirled around and started stalking away. As he neared the door where Elise stood, he swept over a floor display, sending rolls of tape and bubble packs scattering to the floor. Although Elise stepped back, the Minion was coming too hard toward her. He glared down at her with vacant, inhuman eyes.

'Get out of my way, cow!'

She'd barely moved before he barreled past her and out the door, pushing so hard the glass panes rattled like they were going to shatter.

'Asshole,' one of the patrons still in line muttered once the Minion had gone.

Elise felt the wave of relief wash over the other customers at his departure. Part of her was relieved too, glad that no one met with harm. She wanted to wait for a while in the momentary calm in the store, but it was an indulgence she couldn't afford. The Minion was storming across the street now, and dusk was coming fast.

She only had half an hour at best before darkness fell and the Rogues came out to feed. If what she did was dangerous in the daytime, at night it was nothing short of suicide. She could slay a Minion with stealth and steel – already had, in fact, more than once – but like any other human, female or not, she stood no chance against the blood-addicted strength of the Rogues.

Girding herself for what she had to do, Elise slipped out the door and followed the Minion up the street. He was angry and walking brusquely, slamming into other pedestrians and snarling curses at them as he passed. A barrage of mental pain filled her head as more voices joined the din already clanging in her mind, but Elise kept pace with her target. She hung a few yards behind, her eyes trained on the pale green bulk of his jacket through the light flurry of fresh snow. He swung left around the corner of a building and into a narrow alley. Elise hurried now, desperate not to lose him.

Midway down the side street, he yanked open a battered steel door and disappeared. She crept up to the windowless slab of metal, palms sweating despite the chill in the air. His violent thoughts filled her head – murderous thoughts, all the grisly things he would do out of deference to his Master.

Elise reached into her pocket to withdraw her dagger. She held it close to her side, poised to strike, but concealed behind the long drape of her coat. With her free hand, she grasped the latch and pulled open the unlocked door. Snowflakes swirled ahead of her into the gloomy vestibule that reeked of mildew and old cigarette smoke. The Minion stood near a bank of mail slots, one shoulder leaning against the wall as he flipped open a cell phone like the ones they all carried – the Minions' direct line to their vampire Master.

'Shut the fucking door, bitch!' he snapped, soulless eyes glinting. His brows dropped into a scowl as Elise moved toward him with swift, deadly purpose. 'What the hell is th—'

She drove the dagger hard into his chest, knowing that the element of surprise was one of her best advantages. His anger hit her like a physical blow, pushing her backward. His corruption seeped into her mind like acid, burning her senses. Elise struggled through the psychic pain, coming back to strike him again with the blade, ignoring the sudden wet heat of his blood spilling onto her hand.

The Minion sputtered, grasping out for her as he fell against her. His wound was mortal, so much blood she nearly lost her stomach at the sight and smell of it. Elise twisted out of the Minion's heavy lean and leaped out of the way as he fell to the floor. Her breath was sawing out of her lungs, her heart racing, her head splitting in agony as the mental barrage of his rage continued in her mind.

The Minion thrashed and hissed as death overtook him. Then, finally, he stilled.

Finally, there was silence.

With trembling fingers, Elise retrieved the cell phone from where it lay at her feet and slipped it into her pocket. The slaying had drained her, the combined physical and psychic exertion almost too much to bear. Each time seemed to weigh more heavily on her, take longer for her to recover. She wondered if the day would come that she might slide so deep into the abyss that she'd not rebound at all. Probably, she guessed, but not today. And she would keep fighting so long as she had breath in her body and the pain of loss in her heart.

'For Camden,' she whispered, staring down at the dead Minion as she clicked on the MP3 player in preparation of her return home. Music blared from the tiny earbuds, muting the gift that gave her the power to hear the darkest secrets of a human's soul.

She'd heard enough for now.

Her day's sober mission complete, Elise pivoted around and fled the carnage she'd wrought.

Elise Chase prowls the street of Boston seeking retribution against the Rogue vampires who took her beloved son from her. Using her psychic gift, she stalks her prey, well aware that the power she possesses is destroying her.

In her desperation for vengeance she turns to Tegan, who slays his enemy with ice in his veins. He is perfect in his self-control – until Elise seeks his aid.

An unholy alliance is forged, one which will plunge them into a tempest of danger, desire and the darkest passions of the heart . . .

Robinson
978-1-84901-108-2
£6.99

www.constablerobinson.com

Bound by blood, addicted to danger, they'll enter the darkest
and most erotic place of all . . .

A warrior trained in bullets and blades, Renata cannot be
bested by any man – vampire or mortal. But her most powerful weapon is her extraordinary psychic ability – a gift both
rare and deadly. Now a stranger threatens her hard-won independence – a golden-haired vampire who lures her into a realm
of darkness . . . and pleasure beyond imaging . . .

Robinson
978-1-84901-109-9
£6.99

www.constablerobinson.com

As night falls, Claire Roth flees, driven from her home by a fiery threat that seems to come from hell itself. Then, out of the flames and ash, a vampire warrior emerges. He is Andreas Reichen, once Claire's lover but now a stranger consumed by vengeance. She cannot escape his savage fury – or the hunger that will plunge her into his world of eternal darkness. So a dangerous seduction begins, blurring the line between predator and prey, love and hatred . . .

Robinson
978-1-84901-105-1
£6.99

www.constablerobinson.com

To order any of the **Lara Adrian** titles simply contact The Book Service (TBS) by phone, email or by post.
Alternatively visit our website at www.constablerobinson.com.

No. of copies	Title	RRP	Total
	Kiss of Midnight	£7.99	
	Kiss of Crimson	£7.99	
	Midnight Awakening	£6.99	
	Midnight Rising	£6.99	
	Veil of Midnight	£6.99	
	Ashes of Midnight	£7.99	
	Shades of Midnight	£6.99	
		Grand total	

FREEPOST RLUL-SJGC-SGKJ, Cash Sales Direct Mail Dept.,
The Book Service, Colchester Road, Frating, Colchester, CO7 7DW

Tel: +44 (0) 1206 255 800
Fax: +44 (0) 1206 255 930
Email: sales@tbs-ltd.co.uk

UK customers: please allow £1.00 p&p for the first book, plus 50p for the second, and an additional 30p for each book thereafter, up to a maximum charge of £3.00.

Overseas customers (incl. Ireland): please allow £2.00 p&p for the first book, plus £1.00 for the second, plus 50p for each additional book.

NAME (block letters): _____

ADDRESS: _____

_____

_____ POSTCODE: _____

I enclose a cheque/PO (payable to 'TBS Direct') for the amount of £ _

I wish to pay by Switch/Credit Card

Card number: _____

Expiry date: _____ Switch issue number: _____